orang-u-can
gloria trubbshore

By the same author

Batlupta
Mirrortome
Homomechanicus
Smoke and Myrrors

Dedicated to Réal Laplaine
for all the inspiration, support and valued friendship

one.   **A cold wet** November Tuesday night and the last place many who were watching the game wanted to be. Watching the Corporations battle it out on the football pitch was not normally so depressing. It depended very much upon which corporation one supported of course. The game was the third round of matches of the season and Orang-U-Can were having their first home fixture. It had not boded well for them that they had lost the first two away games in embarrassing fashion. In the opening day they had been away to Goosetimp Weapons and the black and white striped wonders had scored five times against them with no reply from the all tangerine men of Orang-U-Can. Their second match had been to visit Rolls Royce Scoriors, where the team in all red had managed to beat them convincingly four-nil. Even playing in their second choice strip of all white did not make of Orang-U-Can a better team.

With the rain being driven by a driving wind gusting off the Irish Sea, the Manchester-based soft drinks giants and reputedly largest corporation in the thirty-third century were wet and miserable and their performance was very much the same. Twenty minutes in, Preciometalic. Inc won a corner and their winger floated in a superb cross. It did not help that the centre forward was not even remotely challenged in the air, his bullet header went straight past Orang-U-Can's goalkeeper with embarrassing ease.

In the main stand Dral Perrimore, a lifelong supporter of the team and lover of the ancient game of football turned to his best friend and asked,

"What are we doing here, Gael. We could be in my home or yours in the warmth watching Trade Squares, or Hackball instead of enduring this misery"?

Stumson shrugged his broad shoulders and returned without a trace of irony, "We love the game, Dral. We're supporters and true supporters follow their team through thick and thin".

"But just look at them out there", Dral persisted, "They don't have a frenging clue, mate. If you and I pulled on a pair of Orange shirts and ran out there we could do a better job and we were only part-timers playing for the grade 'E' team.

"I think that this first squad should maybe be downgraded a couple of pegs", Stumson moaned. Just look at our right back, he just gave the ball away under no pressure at all, he doesn't want it, the ruddy useless........".

His voice was drowned out as the Preciometalic. Inc seeing the goalkeeper to far forward of his line, floated a high ball that obediently sailed over the goalkeepers head and landed in the goal. Two-nil and inside the first half-hour.

"You know what, mate", Dral groaned at the debacle, "The only thing I find myself looking forward to right now is the half-time steak and kidney pie and the cup of Oxo".

Stumson brightened at that, "Oh, that reminds me, I forgot to tell you, Tiptingle Foods has won the concession to do the pies this season".

"Well thank the web for small mercies then", Dral grinned, "Because last season offerings had crusts like concrete".

"They weren't so bad if you poured your Oxo over them to soften it up a bit", Stumson observed, He liked a good pie did Gael Stumson and the only thing he felt came even close to it was a bad pie.

"Yeah", Dral observed with heavy sardonicism, "But I got sick of having to put my loons in the wash after every game. You always spill some on my kegs in the process".

Dral suddenly grimaced when his friend bellowed in his ear at drum bursting volume, "Don't just stand watching him, you nudnik, get into him"!

The very carefully thought out advice was not heeded and Preciometalic. Inc almost had a trio of strikes before half time. The boys in blue were making Orang-U-Can look like a third division team and if the current run of form proved to last for much longer, they would certainly be relegated at the end of the current season.

"I wish we had an all indoor stadium like Deutsch Fahrzeuge Eingearbeitet", Stumson observed then, "If my feet get much colder the only thing I'll want the pie for it to shove it down my socks. Why do we stick to football, Dral when just about every other sport is not played out of the elements"?

"Oh come on, Gael, that's one of the beauties of the beautiful game", Dral argued, "One man against the elements as well as against the opposition".

"That's as maybe", Stumson moaned, "But that wind is blowing that ruddy wet right onto my head, just look at me I'm soaked"!

"I told you before we got in the flitter to put your hat on, didn't I"? Dral was annoyed by his friend's stupidity, "And what did you say to me, 'It won't rain Dral', and I told you it would so don't ask me for any sympathy because you won't get any".

"I don't sound like that", Stumson complained ignoring the logic of his friend's point, "When you do me, why do you always talk in that really dozy voice. If it's meant to be an impression of me, then it's not very good. Furthermore' no one likes an I told you so".

"But I did tell you didn't I. I told you the weatherscope said rain and to get your hat. So you'll either have to go and get an orange bobble hat from the souvenir shop at half time or stay wet through".

"Buy a hat that says Orang-U-Can, with the likes of this performance and pay a shillin for the privilege, do I look like I'm out of my mind to you"?

"You look wet to me, oh, good grief did you see that tackle. He was never going to get away with that, both his feet left the ground"?

"Yeah", Stumson agreed, "But why is their number twenty-three holding his face like his leg's been blinded. The comp should book him for simulation and bad acting".

They glanced up at the computer board, it read *Free Kick* in bright orange LED's.

"I bet the Metal boys programmed the comp-ref", Stumson observed with heat. "The ruddy thing hasn't given us a good decision all this half".

"With a performance like this it wouldn't make any difference", Dral noted fairly. "Come on, let's beat the queue and get to the front for a pie and a beefy drink"?

Stumson did not need telling twice, they were halfway up the stairs when a roar indicated they had missed something gripping on the pitch. It was the third away-team goal.

two.   **Clara Trentavoria was** at her desk early for the day's business when she chanced to use her pad. For some reason, she started in the sports pages that day and what she saw gave her something of a shock. The football team of her beloved company were bottom of the table and with not a single goal to their name. The First Division of the Corporation World Wide Football League consisted of twelve teams and orang-U-Can was lying at the bottom of the dozen.

She flipped to the reports and it made even grimmer reading.

Orang-U-Can crushed as the metal men romp home.
A report by Rory Dolzhed

This reporter was unfortunate enough to be given the task of witnessing the came at the orange ground last night and what a debacle it was. The only interesting spectacle was witnessing how much Manchester rain could fall in ninety minutes. It was far more interesting than watching a dull affair between two mediocre football teams. Strike that, one mediocre team Preciometalic. Inc who ludicrously now top the table due to a run of fortunate fixtures and the diabolical Orang-U-Can, who on the first inspection looked as if they were fielding their third-grade team rather than the 'A' players……….

Clara stopped reading and looked in misery at the table again:

She could not remember in her life when

	Corporation Div One	Plyd	Goals	Pts
1	Preciometalic.Inc	3	8	7
2	Castle Electronics	3	7	7
3	Goosetimp Weapons	3	7	5
4	Makers-Guild	3	5	5
5	I.Y.W.I.W.S.I.	3	5	5
6	Deutsch Fahrzeuge Eingearbeitet	3	5	4
7	Voleskip Pharmacuticals	3	2	4
8	Rolls Royce Scoriors	3	4	3
9	Tiptingle Tigers	3	2	2
10	Zhōngguá Shāngpǐn	3	1	2
11	Hornrunner Hornets	3	4	1
12	Orang-u-can	3	0	0

the boys in orange had resided in such a lowly spot and never in the Corporation League history had they ever been in any other league than Division One. Rising from her seat she ambled into the adjacent office. Her father was just doing the self-same thing, checking his comp, although he would be on the financial pages, of that, she was certain.

"Have you seen the sport, Dad"? She asked.

Hugh Trentavoria of the iron-grey hair and beard of the same colour looked at his daughter through his grey bushy eyebrows,

"And good morning to you my dear, what was that you said just then"?
"I asked you if you had seen the sport".

"Never have time for it any more Clara my love, why are the Sheffield Stoats dropping the ball again in the Hackball challenge. Trentavoria was a

Hackball and Sheffield Stoat fan of some years, but not recent ones. Recently he had been more interested in making Orang-U-Can the most powerful Corporation in the whole of the solar system.

"I meant the footy", his daughter replied, "Do you know where we are in the division"?

"Football, a game for ballerinas", her father scoffed, "Give me the brutal tackles in Hackball any time. Why those footballers only have to get so much as a grass burn and they're rolling around in agony like they've been blinded or what have you".

Clara bore the tirade stoically, she had heard it all before and many times. Ever since she had fallen in love with Ty Bulacker at school she had been a fan of the game, For Ty had been the goalkeeper in the very year when Manchester Middle had won the Greater Manchester School Cup and Ty had saved a penalty in the final.

"They're bottom Dad and I want to do something about it".

"Oh"! Hugh smiled, "What exactly"?

"Well for a start the manager needs to be sacked, then half the squad want putting on the transfer list and some new talent bringing in. Can I have a budget to see that some changes are made"?

"You want to get rid of the manager and replace him by whom may I ask"?

"Well being as the team are letting goals in at every game and scoring none then I would have thought anyone would be an improvement".

"Anyone", Trentavoria laughed, "So as the new director of the team you don't have anyone in mind, just get rid of the current man".

Director? Who said anything about my being a director"?

"As you seem to be wanting to make some sweeping changes you cannot do it without taking any responsibility, Clara. That is not how running any company works, you know that. I Can let you have a few shillin, but I want to know what you intend to do to see it is put to good use".

Clara bit her lip then and then on a sudden wild impulse she blurted,

"I'll tell you what I want to do then, Dad. I want to sack the manager and put the players on the transfer list, then look round for some replacements in my capacity as the new Manager of Orang-U-Can football club. You know I only have an office here to keep me out of mischief, I don't make any business decisions of any import. So let me go and manage the team and give me a decent budget with which to do it".

"There's one thing for sure", her father laughed then, "You know a huge amount more about the game than about high finance and running a huge corporation".

"Then let me do it"?!

"You want to be the manager"?

Clara nodded, "I'll start today, give me the go-ahead and I'm on my way to the ground right now and axe the imbecile who's just led them to three humiliating defeats"?

Trentavoria seemed to consider the notion for several seconds, but in truth, he rarely denied his daughter anything she truly wanted and it would be fun to see her crash and burn, so he nodded, adding.

"You've five hundred silver shillin to play with.....for the whole season. Do not think you can come and ask for more halfway through February".

"Five HSS", Clara repeated, "Piece of cake, Dad".

Picking up her Boo-Radlie handbag and throwing it over her shoulder, she took the lift down to the subterranean flitter-park and pressing the stud on her remote unlocked her Lenovo 190 bhp Superstream in crushed pineapple metallic finish. The side of the flitter rose on its servos with a faint pneumatic sigh and Clara threw her very expensive very designer bag onto the back as she slid into the driving seat. She was a tall brunette who wore her hair cropped like a man's, but with an sensational figure, she could get away with it. Her droplet earrings were studded with genuine Marstones and her make up she wore sparingly. At five feet ten she was quite tall for a woman and her legs were only eclipsed by her bosom when it came to her best feature. Behind her was a string of broken hearts and she was momentarily without a contract and temporarily without even a boyfriend to keep her warm at night.

She put the flitter on auto-drive and keyed in the postcode of the football ground. She knew it by heart, for she rarely missed a football match but the night before she had promised to go and see the new tri-vee with her best friend Sherrien who was an ardent fan of the tri-vee star Kit Flixton. The tri-vee had been predictable and Clara had known what was going to happen about half-way through the film, but Sherrien had enjoyed it and Clara had stayed dry and misery free as a result of missing the match.

She opened the glove compartment and hauled out a pack of medcigs while the flitter continued to steer her through the streets of Manchester. Thumbing the self-igniting tip she drew the smoke into her lungs and considered her strategy. The manager was doomed, but his assistant might prove useful to her initially, so he would stay until she knew enough of her way around the club until he either proved himself or she could manage without him and have him replaced.

Likewise, the squad would consist of about forty players and she would frighten the life out of half of them by instantly putting the other half on the transfer market. Then she would ask the scout who he would buy if money was not an object. She had just settled in her mind how things were going to play out when the Lenovo pulled into the grounds flitter-park. The manager's spot was currently empty! Surely the imbecile would be in following three defeats in succession?! Clara switched off the auto-drive and pulled into the spot. After all, in about twenty minutes, it was going to belong to her anyway.

She took the lift to the office level and found it deserted. From the window, she could hear the calls and cries of the team training, so someone was coaching them. So she went back down to the ground floor and taking a sharp left went onto the pseudoturf training pitch. After only a few seconds it was possible to determine who was conducting the training and she waved to him. She was confident that even though she did not recognise him, he would know the CEO's daughter by reputation and appearance. For Clara had been in the tabloid pads a goodly few times in her turbulent youth. Surely enough he stopped in his tracks, discerned who it was and then hurriedly trotted over to her.

"Miss Trentavoria", he began, "This is a surprise and pleasure. I'm the assistant manager and coach Tammi Mattie".

"Tammi", Clara laughed, "Really! That's not some sort of queer nickname"?

Mattie coloured and stammered, "I'm contracted to a woman, Miss Trentavoria, and my name is Tammi".

"Well I'm not calling a grown man Tammi", Clara smiled spikely, "From now on your name is George, George Best. I'll have *legal* draft a document this afternoon, understood"?

"Erm, Miss Trentavoria I'm not sure the Manager......".

"Who's not here", Clara cut him short. "After that disgraceful exhibition last night, he's not here giving the player seven shades of khakk for their woeful performance. Get on your pad and ping him not to bother coming to this ground ever again, he's sacked".

Tammi Mattie nee George Best blinked and asked carefully, "You have someone to replace him, Miss Trentavoria, Or am I to.......".

"As of this second, I am the Manager of this club, George. Once you've told Useless Eustace he's finished ping every player in the squad and tell each of them to be in the changing room in one hour. Anyone who does not arrive on time will find themselves on the transfer market. Our scout, who is he"?

Best was struggling with the tsunami of new facts being launched at him but he finally managed to tell her,

"Kipper Kipson, Miss Trentavoria".

"Rule number one as of now, George", Clara began, "This is a man's football club, not a kindergarten, what is Kipson's name".

"I'm not sure, Miss...."

"Boss", Clara cut him short, "From now on you refer to me as Boss, find out what Kipson's grown man name is and ping him to get in here and tell him to introduce himself to me as a man, not some silly little adolescent".

Suddenly Best broke into a delighted smile,

"What"? Demanded Clara sternly,

"I'm just thinking, Boss that the next few weeks are going to be anything but boring. I was not in favour of some of the tactics used this year and I have a few ideas of my own. Would you be willing to talk to me about them later"?

"I'm going to be a sponge for the next few weeks, George, so yes I would. But I'm also going to be a right bitch, all right"?

"All right Boss", George grinned, As I said before I'm contracted to one, so I'll be fine. I'd better get on my pad now. An I just add though, if you pursue this sort of regime, you're going to have a mass exodus from this club".

"And that is exactly what I want", Clara grinned, "I want rid of the mamby pambies and the drama queens and want Orang-U-Can to field a team of men who are willing to flog their guts out both on the training pitch and on the field on match day. I don't even want the most skilful players if they are prima-donnas, I want the grafters when a football player walks off the pitch on match day I want them shaking with absolute exhaustion".

"If you mean that, then I am behind you 110%, Boss".

"I don't want the impossible", Clara argued then, "You cannot give me 110%, only 100%, more than that is a mathematical impossibility"!

three. "Good morning everyone, is everyone here"?

"All except for Dizzy Evans", Miss Trentavoria, his contractee has just had their third chavvy". An anonymous voice informed Clara, who instantly turned to Best and said in a voice loud enough for everyone to hear,

"Put Evans on the transfer list and suspend his wages, please George".

The changing rooms went silent enough to detect a pin dropping,

"Right everyone, I am not Miss, Darling, or anything else you want to call me, I am the new manager of this club and I will answer to Boss from now on. You, on the other hand, will answer to your surname and your surname only. There will be no infantile nicknames, no shortening of names, nothing other than surnames from now on. This is a man's football club and from this moment on you are going to be treated like men and act like men. If anyone has any objection to that then they can give their names to Assistant Best here and be put on a free transfer without pay until the time of the sale".

"You can't do that, *Boss*", a voice said, "The union......."".

Orang-U-Can owns this football club, not your player's union and if you do not do as you are told, rewarded with the privilege of playing for the best corporation in the world then give your name to Best and you can leave here right now".

One player dared to stand up and ask politely, "It's all very well using the stick routine with us, Boss. I for one can take it. But where is the corresponding carrot, why do we not walk out of here en mass right now, I am only asking".

"A fair question", Clara conceded, "And I will give you an honest answer. The reward for pulling your fingers out and buckling down to some serious graft for this football club is two-fold. One is winning the league, something we have not done since '87. The other thing is the bonus scheme I am going to introduce. The bonus for winning a game will be more than you are currently getting paid. The down-side of that is if the team loses, then you don't get paid. I am not here to manage a team of losers. Losers are of no interest to me gentlemen, losers will go hungry at Orang-U-Can".

Four players got up at that revelation and walked out. Clara saw Best entering their names into his pad.

She told them, "Those of you who have stayed to hear the rest of it have just increased your chance of getting in the first team. Every time someone walks out of this club, it's an opportunity for someone else to make the first eleven".

Some of what you say makes sense Boss and I'm willing to play my socks off to win a game but we don't have a Jensen of a Roxbrough in our team, we have no big names this year so.....".

"Jensen of Deutsche Fahrzeuge Eingearbeitet, the midfielder", Clara showed them she had some knowledge of the game and Orang-U-Can was not just going to be a spoiled little rich girl's toy, "And Roxbrough the Preciometalic. Inc striker. Are you telling me that if we had those two the rest of you could guarantee that results would change"?

"With those two in our team we would have a damned fine team", one of the players told her.

"All right, I will buy them for us, but just remember that means the rest of you are fighting for nine places instead of eleven. I want a strong squad obviously, but only eleven can be on the pitch in any one game".

"You are just going to buy Jensen and Roxbrough", a player asked, "Just like that, how"?

"You leave the managerial side of things to me, all the rest of you have to do is work your socks off. Right get back to the training ground now, while I go over some details with Best. If I hear any of you call him anything other than his new name there will be consequences. Right, out you go".

They went. Best said nothing until they were all outside, then he observed,

"The not paying them unless they win is taking a big chance boss. The first time they don't get paid......"

"I'm not here to watch them lose any-more games, George. Where is Kipson"?

"On his way up from London, he was scouting a youngster down there who......".

"We don't want him", Clara cut him short. "I want mainly northern players, they have that bit more grit about them. Jensen the German will be industrious enough for us and Roxbrough's a Yorkshireman, he'll do nicely. Ping Kipson and tell him to put out feelers right away, We need them both for Saturday".

"This Saturday"! Best gasped, "Neither of them is for sale, Boss and their agents.....".

"We don't bother with their agents I want a direct offer made to their clubs and them, we will make it happen Dad has given me the money".

"What you're talking about will cost a fortune, Boss. Hundreds of shillin".

"Our budget is five HSS"!

Best whistled, "I suspect you might just have the two of them for Saturday then"!

"Now what I want to do is go through every player with you and I want half of them getting rid of. How big is the current squad",

"Fifty-two not counting the five that we already now have on the transfer market".

"I want that reducing to twenty-five, if it can be done for a world cup it can be done at club level".

"What about injuries, suspensions"?

"Twenty-five accounts for that. I also expect every player except for goalkeepers to be able to play in more than one position, making twenty-five plenty. So, let's get down to it and see what we have, I want your advice on the starting eleven for Saturday, which will include Jensen and Roxbrough then I have two full days to watch the training and see if I agree".

"Just like that"?!

Clara nodded, "Just like that George"!

Four hours later Best had red-rimmed eyes and was looking exhausted. He reported, "They certainly put a shift in today, Boss".

"No they did not", Clara argued, "The miners on Callisto put a shift in. The men that are fortunate enough to be paid to play a game practised their skills today, George. They are lucky and molly-coddled but they will work hard if they want to stay at this club and this club is going to do the double this year".

"The league and the Shield, are you serious Boss"?

"When it comes to football, I don't make silly jokes, George", Clara told him just as her pad was pinging. She had it set so that when she got a ping it made the noise of a cuckoo. She swiped her screen into activation and smiled,

"We just got Jensen's thumb", she told Best, "That was Kipson".

"I do not believe it", Best laughed, "Both of them here and ready to join the training in the morning, I never thought you would do it, Höfler will be spitting feathers",

Heinz Höfler was the CEO of Deutsche Fahrzeuge Eingearbeitet and money had just snatched his star player from his corporation's first division team. The story had been different with Roxbrough, for as luck would have it he had not been content at Preciometalic. Inc and his purchase had been much less expensive and much less complicated as he was an engineer for the firm and football was only his second-string career.

Best was still enthusing, "I cannot wait to see the faces of the lads tomorrow when both of them turn up to pull on the tangerine strip".

"We will cease calling them the lads as well George. They are grown men remember"?

"Yes Boss".

"Address them as men and they will start to believe they have grown up, some of them may be even will".

"You don't have a very high opinion of men, do you, Boss"?

"They are all right, in their place", Clara smiled. Fortunately for yourselves, we still cannot create artificial sperm, but when we do......", she smiled, seriously for a second she noted, "It's been a long day and you look all in. Let's call it a day and see each other in the morning. If anyone is late for training I want to know about it".

"I would not worry about that, Boss. After today I think curiosity alone will bring them all in bright and early".

four.   **J Jennings pulled** up his flitter outside his luxury home in Manchester and practically skipped down the drive. The fact that it was raining was not a factor in causing him to hurry rather that he desired to tell his attractive wife Taibah the news. It had been the strangest day he had experienced thus far in his career at Orang-U-Can Football Club. Jennings was not like some of the players, an OUC employee firstly and a footballer secondly. He was one of the few full-time football players who had no other career to fall back on once his playing days came to an end.

In the very back of his mind, he always fancied he would go into coaching and management within the game once he reached his forties. He also knew though that he was not the most articulate of men, certainly not over-burdened with intelligence. There again, Einstein could not take a corner and place it exactly onto the head of his striker with pinpoint accuracy like some footballers, so perhaps in the lottery of life, he was still well ahead of Mister average. He thumbed the security pad on his front door and the issuing hail it created alerted Taibah to his entrance.

The swarthy beauty came out of the rather expansively extended kitchen and pecked him on the cheek.

"Your high protein freeze pack is in the hypo-wave, Babe. I'm going out with the girls this evening", she told him not expecting much by way of a response.

"That's tonight"?

"Yes. We discussed it last week if you remember"?

"No, Babes, I don't remember you telling me that", Jennings was disappointed. He wanted to tell Taibah about the new Manger, what a bitch she seemed to be. How many of the squad were no longer part of OUC? How after training sessions, he was still in the first eleven as a left-sided defender with wing overlap responsibilities. Before he could so much as to remark on his feelings of let down though Taibah was skipping up the stairs to the first floor obviously to add some finishing touches to her make-up. He followed her up the stairs and sure enough, she seated herself at the tri-mirror arrangement that allowed her to see herself in profile form either side, in addition, to face forward.

"Where are you going, Babe"? Jennings tried, "Maybe we could start with a drink and then you could meet up with...whoever you're going out with".

"Not likely, Babes", Taibah was not even prepared to consider it. "You'd best check the hypo, or that high-calorie mush you seem to like so much will be steamed to buggery".

"Who are you going out with"? Jennings ignored the advice regarding his gastronomic delight.

"You don't know any of them, just some of the girls from the office", Taibah returned rather vaguely, "They're a buzzin' bunch, well up for a laugh, it's gonna be bangin' t'max".

"So where do you think you'll go, Kickin', Blastin', Cooldadiz"?

"We haven't decided yet", Taibah used the huge powder brush on her high cheekbones. "Listen, Babes, you're not gonna spoil it by turning up are you.

'Cos that would be so gross. My old man checking up on me when I'm out wiv-ma-girls".

"No", Jennings practically whined, "It's just that I had stuff to tell you about the club. I thought we were going to have a nice night in, you know"?

"Well, we can do that another night, now go and check that hypo before the bag busts again. 'Cos I'm not cleaning up another mess like the last time you set the power too high and it was all over the kitchen".

Despondently Jennings went down to the indicated room, turned off the device in question and taking a pair of scissors out of the unit drawer, cut the bag open and poured the contents into a bowl.

Yummeez.

New Yummeez is the meal for that man on the go who is pushed for time, but still wants the good wholesome meal that will be packed with calories and nutrients. It's incredible how Nabisloggs have done it. A ready meal that in seconds presents him with more goodness contained in one wonder-bag, more essential life-sustaining supplements gramme for gramme than finest sirloin steak.

So if your man is a busy professional, or maybe even that sportsman who wants to be a winner over and over again make sure he has a bag of Yummeez every day.

Twenty pence off promotional offer, collect five packet tops and email a jpeg of them to us for a chance to win a years supply of fabulous Yummeez at half price! Every top has an unique serial number folks - so don't be tempted to try and fool those honest folks at Nabisloggs.

Employees and their families are not permitted to enter this competition. Conditions apply, go to our WWW site for full rules.

Taibah did make certain Jennings had his Yummeez every day. Indeed of late, it was the only food she ever seemed to have ready for him when he got in from training! Firstly the new boss had expected her to work late for a week during inventory. Then her mother in Carlisle had been ill for ten days and she had gone up to look after her and now she was letting her hair down with the girls. When Jennings thought about it he had not spent an evening with his contractee for the better part of October. He was one of only nine men given a place in the first team for Saturday, from a squad that had started at fifty-five and he could not tell the woman of his dreams.

As he was listlessly spooning the spicy feast into his mouth she descended the stairs. Even though they had been contracted for three of their five years, she still possessed the ability to take his breath away. She was swarthy in a very Mediterranean sort of way, Five feet six inches tall, 53 kilogrammes that were all in the right places, with black hair and dark brown eyes, she had high cheekbones and a narrow chin and lustrous black hair. Even in the age of enhancement, she was very much a 9/10.

"I'm going then, have a pleasant evening", she told him and was out of the door before he had a chance to rise and meet her for a kiss goodbye. Taibah shivered as she dashed to her flitter. It was not the done thing to wear a coat when dressing glamorously, but it was November and the shock of leaving the heated house was a shock to her body. She slid into the Nestlé's 140 bhp Silk in rather fetching cream with brown trim and thumbed the auto-driver. Rain lashed the windscreen as she ran through the music she had in the memory of her Dyson mtune player with surround sound 3.1 22 watts per channel RMS. Finally settling on Dreme Bitch Crazee's new album, Shakkin Wiv Mi-man.

Everyone knew that Dreme Bitch Crazee was the first android female rapgaridgkikn star, but no one cared, it was all about the beat not such trivia as a nice tune. Rapgaridgkikin had a constant booming sound that made such trivia as words and music pretty redundant it was all about the boom boom boom.

As the flitter headed for Bingley on the new hi-fly road Dreme droned out of the speakers

Azz crazee wiv me man,
Cos ee dun no nuffin,
I sez to wesh the dishes,
But ee wanna do the missus.

Ee sez lie back babee
And maybe effin maybe
You get to lose yor ed
When jump wiv me in bed.

Sexin up da Bootie was a simple love song that had one message and that was that sex was better if you did it under the influence of serious narcotics. It had been banned in France due to the cheeky but fun line

You dun get decent snogs,
When yaz cozee up ta Frogs

But Dreme had insisted it was a reference to the dangers of amphibian love and nothing to do with the Gaulic race, the debate went on.

None of this was especially important to Taibah, she was not a musical nor poetry critic, she just loved to get *down n kickin* and the obligatory beat boomed out of the speakers like a soporific trance-inducing monotone.

She was just about drifted away into that comfortable zone between boredom and sleep when the car said,

"Yo mama you iz at your destee-nay-shun".

She loved the narrative style she had selected from the library of options. Her car spoke to her just like it was the latest male Rapgaridgkikin star Gangsta-Dog-Knob-Crazee. Only six months previously she had managed to get a ticket to see the megastar and had been close enough to the stage that when he had done his famous trick of urinating on the front three rows, some splashes had reached her. It was possible to buy phials of Gangsta-Dog-Knob-Crazee urine on Shark-line, but some people believed it was not the real article and that the star had a team of ghost urinators to fill out the massive orders.

Taibah climbed out of the flitter, smoothed out her skirt and went over to the lift. She thumbed for the second floor of the swanky complex, room 23. Taking the corridor, done from top to bottom in boring magnolia, she thumbed the door open. The plate had been programmed to allow her print to activate the lock. At her entrance into the apartment done out entirely in tasteful tiger design, black and orange throughout, a figure arose from a huge black faux-leather sofa and came over to Mrs Jennings. They kissed – passionately. Then as Oswald Hardy went over to the occasional table made of bright orange faux-plastic to get her a med-cig, she asked him at once,

"Did you make the team, Lover".

"Of course", Oswald Hardy said with a grin, as he thumbed a brace of med-cigs into life and handed one to her,

"Holding midfielder as usual! The new Manager is a bitch and a præsumtores, but she seems to be able to spot skill when she sees it. I expect the nudnik told you though didn't he, he made the first team too".

"No", Taibah lied, "And irrespective of what goes on pitch-wise, only one of you is scoring in the bedroom, Lover"!

five. **Clara had to** admit to herself if none other, that the approaching game that afternoon made her feel nervous. She looked at the fixtures for the Corporation First Division.

Corporation First Division		
Tiptingle Foods	v	Goosetimp Weapons
Rolls Royce Scoriors	v	Zhöngguá Shángpín
I.Y.W.I.W.S.I.	v	Preciometalic.Inc
Deutsch Fahrzeuge Eingearbeitet	v	Orang-U-Can
Hornrunner	v	Voleskip Pharmacuticals
Castle Electronics	v	Makers Guild

Her first game as manager and it was in Germany, against last years champions Deutsch Fahrzeuge Eingearbeitet, the team she had just bought their star player from under the noses of. The Germans would have something to prove. Could they survive without Jensen? Could they beat the traitor's team?

Clara looked at her team and wondered the same. On paper, it looked like the best she could do from what she had seen over the past seventy-two hours. Anderson was a good goalkeeper, but even he could not be expected to make continuous impossible saves if his defence did not protect him.

Orang-U-Can			
1. Anderson			
2. Roberts	13. Jennings	4. Burgenbower	5. West
16. Hardy	7. Ball	19. Jenson	
8. Wong	10. Nero		
23. Roxbrough			

Clara knew she would need at least one more purchase and soon and for a defender. The German Burgenbower would be support for Jensen and the front three were all quality. Little Wong the Chinese forward midfielder and Nero the Brazilian holding midfielder would be a good strike force together with the new man Roxbrough. Though the best striker in the world could only score if he received good service.

It was the wing-backs that gave Clara most cause for concern and she had two substitutes in those positions just in case. Roberts had only just eclipsed McFarland for the right-back spot and similarly there had been little to choose between West who had just made it in favour of Hudson. Also on the bench would be the reserve goalkeeper Radband, the midfielder Wing from Korea and the defender Ford.

As the twenty of them got onto the air-flitter, Best, the physio – Whohouse and the team doctor, - Charmley in addition to Clara and the players, There was a rather subdued air to the whole event. No one seemed to want to either sit next to Clara or engage her in conversation. It fell to the new signing Roxbrough to take the seat next to her. The pilot was just taking off when he offered her a boiled sweet,

"It helps pop the ears, we should not be up in the air long, Manchester to Munich is only a short hop".

"Yes, thank you", Clara found herself replying, "I'm not a dullard when it comes to geography though, Roxbrough".

"I know that you're very well-travelled, you just looked a bit nervy that's all", the new striker observed. "I would not worry, we are fairly well prepared and no one expects you to perform miracles".

"Fairly well, what do you mean by that"?

"Considering the time we have had this week. Jensen and Ball have very different styles as you will have seen, it will take a while for them to get used to one another".

"We are bottom of the league with no points", Clara returned with some agitation, "Time is a luxury we do not have".

"I think you've done as well as anyone could in the hours you had", Roxbrough smiled, he seemed to ooze confidence, but he was only one player and football was a team game.

Clara felt no better by the time the craft was on the ground and they had been shepherded into the DFE visitors changing rooms. One of the stewards told them that the home team would be in their usual black shirt gold shorts black socks. Best had been prepared for that and had brought white shorts in place of the usual orange ones for OUC. So they would be in orange shirts white shorts and orange socks. Zero chance of confusion for the comp-ref or the loyal fans of both sides. Concerning the latter, the away end of the ground was not quite full but those who had made the journey were ready to see what the new manager could produce. For the reports of Clara's appointment had been on the club Pad-cast as well as in the general media, football still had enough interest to make a new manager ww news. Especially the appointment of a woman and a Trentavoria at that.

The changing room began to smell of *Lyn-you-mend the liniment muscle rub for men*. Whohouse was busily massaging thigh and calves with studied industry. It was time for the pre-match pep-talk.

"All right, quiet please", Clara began. "Today with no points accumulated thus far we face the German Champions at home. They have also had a disappointing start to their defence of the title and only have four points, putting them three behind the first-placed team already. It is early days though and we can expect Deutsch Fahrzeuge to be contesting for a successful defence of their title this season. So it could not be a better time to meet them away from home. We have Jensen here however, their key midfield playmaker and consequently, they do not. I, therefore, expect the battle to be in midfield and I expect you, Jensen, to win it. Now if every player selected for the first eleven gives me and Orang-U-Can 100% effort today I will pay a certain fee based on performance. If we win I will pay an additional bonus. So work till you drop because we have substitutes. That's all from me now Best will tell you who you are marking".

"Marking, Boss"? It was Roberts who asked the question, "We're not going to zone defence"?

"Man to man marking, I want you to stifle every single attack they manage to mount, is that understood"?

The men responded with muffled murmurings. Man to man marking was very draining indeed. Best gave them the list and then Clara left the changing room so the men could put their boxes, under-shorts and shorts on. She was on her way to the visitor's dugout when who should she bump into but Heinz Höfler,

"Aah, Miss Trentavoria, it is an unexpected pleasure to see you. Still at the helm then ja"?

"Ja", Clara smiled, "Come Monday it will be a full week, one cannot say I am not going to last ha ha ha. That's an Anglo Saxon joke".

"Oh ja very good. Tell me how is Rudy settling into your team, is he happy to be in England with all the rain"?

"Rudy"?

"Rudy...Rudolph, Jensen".

"Ah, our new midfielder, he is a man now, Herr Höfler we call him Jensen. I did not even know his former".

"Is that so, then you are......"?

"The Boss. The *men* call me Boss".

"Very gut another of your Anglo Saxon jokes no doubt".

"No, the way a football team should be run, it is an Englander Development, expect it to dribble down to the European scene in a few years".

"You are a very funny lady Fräulein Trentavoria. I hope we shall still be laughing at full time".

Clara suddenly pushed out a hand and they shook,

"Gut luck Fräulein, you'll need it today", Höfler said in parting.

It was mild, but damp, not something the men minded for the stadium was covered. The pitch was watered by hoses prematch and was the new pseudo-grass, a hybrid of grass and lichen from Mars courtesy of the great geneticist Hoyle who worked for Clara's father, Hugh. The comp-ref was just rebooting according to the Visual Display Laser Screen or VDLS. There was a roar of approval from the ninety-two thousand fans as the teams came out for their warm-up. Warm-ups immediately proceeded the match in the style made popular in tennis, so that warmed muscles were them put to maximum efficient use. Clara told her cranial implant,

"Communication on", this would mean every player who also had the very same CI would hear her every word during the game, "Raise your arm if you can hear me", She instructed those on the pitch and eleven arms went dutifully upward for a brief moment. The VDLS said four minutes.

Best, Charmley and Whohouse joined Clara on the bench, behind them were seated the five substitutes.

"Your pad on, Doc"? Clara asked.

Charmley nodded looking keenly at the readings. "As expected blood pressure and heartbeat are all elevated, within acceptable limits of course. All except for Roxbrough's, that guy must have nerves of nyloplanyon".

"Maybe he's an android", Best joked,

"Don't even joke about that", Whohouse advised sternly, "You know it's am immediate nine-point deduction to field anything other than biols in a match game".

"It does give me an idea though", Clara said to Best in particular. After the game, get in touch with Engineer Choudrey at Choudrey Andrewoids – India and tell him Clara Trentavoria wants eleven Class alpha androids delivering to Orang-U-Can by Monday. Tell him I want them programming as footballers".

"You're going to have us train against non-biols Boss"? West asked from on the pitch. Clara forgot they could hear every word on their CI's.

"You carry on warming up and if you've enough breath to talk you're not doing it vigorously enough, West", Best told him before Clara had the chance. He turned to his manager and noted, "While non-biols are against the rules of the game in match time there's nothing to stop us training against them, it's a good idea Boss".

A voice neither of them recognised taunted, "Brown noser".

The other players laughed, Charmley murmured, "That's relieved some of the tension".

"Right, time to name the captain", Clara glanced at the VDLS, one minute to kick-off. "Jensen, you are captain for this match. I want everyone knowing what DFE are going to do before they even know they are going to do it".

"Ja mein Manager", the German agreed in his pigeon English.

There was an electronic whistle from the comp-ref and it was the signal for the two teams to take their positions ready for kick-off. The comp-ref had randomly selected the home supporter end for the home team meaning OUC would be kicking toward their travelling fans in the second.

At exactly 15:00 GMT the electronic whistle went and the Germans kicked off for the first three-quarters of an hour. It became immediately obvious that their striker Müller was going to be their main offensive threat. Of course for him to be effective, the midfield duo of Heindrich and Staffenmuir would have to supply him with decent passes. Jensen immediately put a firm press on the middle of the pitch. He was marking Heindrich himself, when the Germans had the ball, while Ball was Staffenmuir's marker. The game started at a pace that everyone knew immediately neither team could keep up for forty-five minutes, let alone ninety. The crowd roared its approval. Both sides had developed the same initial strategy. Keeping the ball on the ground as much as possible with sharp short passes to try and gain superiority over the opposition. Clara was encouraged to see that her men were not outclassed when it came to that type of football. Even so, she advised.

"Slip your marker Roxbrough and the next time we win the ball in midfield I want a *route one pass* in the air. Use your height Roxbrough, let's test Draffen with a header".

Draffen was an excellent goalkeeper, but even he could be surprised at a sudden switch in the game to what was known as *route one.* The trouble was OUC was having difficulty getting the ball and the Germans were winning the short passing game. Clara told her team,

"Mark them tighter, I don't mind the odd yellow card, let them know they're playing in a man's game".

A yellow card was awarded for a foul, while an amber card was for a professional foul and the player responsible had to stay off the pitch for twelve minutes. For a dangerous foul the player was send off for the rest of the match and that was a red card. The player missed the next match for a red card. Suddenly Staffenmuir slipped past Ball and using his admirable pace burst into the penalty box and slipped a sublime pass to Müller, who hit the ball with the outside of his left boot, it was Anderson's first test and he proved equal to it. With superb diving save he palmed the ball around the right-hand post but the danger was not over, DFE had their first corner of the game.

In the visitors stands Dral Perrimore was watching in ill-concealed delight,

"Beyond belief"! He gasped for the third time in as many minutes, "Pinch me, Gael, I think I must be dreaming, is this the same team that we watched on Tuesday night"?

"No", Stumson declared pedantically, "We've Jensen in midfield and he knows what his old comrades are up to. But they are still beating us Dral, the battle for midfield is going to the Germans even without Jensen in their squad".

"Beating us, plop"! Perrimore cursed, "While ever it's nil-nil we are not being beaten and we could get our first point of the season".

"Which would still leave us bottom as things stand", Stumson returned consulting his padfon, the Hornets have just taken the lead against the Frogs".

In English that meant the Romanian corporation, Hornrunner Hornets had scored a goal against the French Pharmaceutical company. With their resultant points, they would leave Orang-U-Can adrift at the bottom still.

Meanwhile, the team had to deal with a dangerous corner. Anderson was spectacular, punching it clear of danger, just as Müller was about to connect with the ball with his bullet header.

"I'm loving our new team and I want Clara Trentavoria to have my babies", Dral declared.

"Yeah but no pies at half time", Stumson complained. "Only them horrid Brockwerst sausages in long buns. The Krauts can't even manage a decent hot-dog".

The stranglehold on creativity continued and Orang-U-Can achieved something they had not done before in their previous games, they went in at half-time without conceding a goal.

Corporation First Division	
Tiptingle Foods 1	Goosetimp Weapons 1
Rolls Royce Scoriors 0	Zhöngguá Shángpín 0
I.Y.W.I.W.S.I. 3	Preciometalic.Inc 1
Deutsch Fahrzeuge Eingearbeitet 0	Orang-U-Can 0
Hornrunner 2	Voleskip Pharmaceuticals 0
Castle Electronics 2	Makers Guild 0

Clara went into a very heavily humming changing room and congratulated the men,

"Well done, you've worked hard all of you and I'm going to take the opportunity of using two of my five substitutions for the second half. Roberts, West, you can go and shower. I'm bringing McFarland and Hudson on in your places, like for like. The wing-backs have run their socks off, so you two substitutes, I want to see a similar effort from you. Roberts, you go steady with the sliding tackles next game that yellow was nearly an amber and we could not afford even twelve minutes with ten men against the Germans".

"Boss", Roxbrough asked then, "Are we playing for a point here, because if we are, I could drop deeper, bolster the defence, I've run around for forty-five minutes and barely had a kick, the Germans are strangling midfield".

Clara turned to Best, "What are our chances of stealing a goal compared to letting one in if we try and win"

"Not fifty-fifty", the assistant admitted, "We have not had enough time together. Jensen won't last another three-quarters-of-an-hour the way he's been grafting and we will have to sub him with Wing at some point. I suggest we play for a point rather than losing three".

	Corporation Div One	Plyd	Goals	Pts
1	Castle Electronics	4	9	10
2	I.Y.W.I.W.S.I.	4	8	8
3	Preciometalic.Inc	4	9	7
4	Goosetimp Weapons	4	8	6
5	Makers-Guild	4	5	5
6	Deutsch Fahrzeuge Eingearbeitet	4	5	5
7	Hornrunner Hornets	4	6	4
8	Rolls Royce Scoriors	4	4	4
9	Voleskip Pharmaceuticals	4	2	4
10	Tiptingle Tigers	4	3	3
11	Zhōngguá Shāngpín	4	1	3
12	Orang-u-Can	4	0	1

All right we go to four-four-three when we have the ball and continue to man to man when they have it. Try and hold them, men, try and keep the ball when we have it, don't try any brave passes, let's see our first game out without losing and call it a very valuable away point against the champions".

"The ruddy Frogs aren't doing us any favours they're two down now", Whohouse groaned.

Clara ended up very proud of the men as they walked off the pitch at full-time looking like they had given their all. The result was what they had realistically hoped for a scoreless draw and Roxbrough had taken over Jensen's role in midfield when he had been substituted on the hour. On the air-flitter, on the way home, Clara looked at the results and resultant table.

Ironically the result though a good one had put them even more points adrift at the bottom of the table. The next week was going to be the hardest OUC had trained ever! If Choudrey came through for her and she knew he would, the men would face a team of non-biols that never tired, never fouled and could play twenty-four hours a day!

six   **The next match that** Orang-U-Can were due to play was at home to Hornrunner's Hornets. This was the real test of Clara's organisational skills as the manager and a game she was desperate to win. Even

though
Alovar
Hornrunner
IV was a
close friend
of her father
– Hugh.
Sunday was
a day off for

the whole club. Monday they were all at the ground bright and early and training was done in Best's usual way for Choudrey could only promise the android players for Tuesday at the earliest.

"Please try your very best for me"? Clara had bleated on the vid-link on her pad and the little Indian designer had promised a miraculously swift delivery for the following morning. On her way into work she had received a ping on her flit-pad and when activating it had been in touch with Kipson. The scout had sounded excited,

"I got a chance to watch a Sunday League game yesterday, Boss", the scout began, "And English Telecom were playing this little forward roaming midfielder who was very good indeed. He assisted in two of their goals and scored the last one himself. His name is Thomson Lane and I think we can get him on a free, he has no contract. He wants moving expenses from down south though.

"A southerner", Clara was sceptical.

"No he's a web engineer and his job took him down here, he's originally from Halifax. Boss if you saw him play, you'd want this man, he's exactly what our midfield want. Jensen is a holding midfielder and so is Ball. This guy would be able to supply Roxbrough with great service".

"I'll ping you back when I get in the office then", Clara promised, "I want to consult Best before I make a final decision.

"All right, Boss, but don't hang about if you want him, someone else will snap him up if we don't. I saw Evermore hanging around at the ground".

"Evermore"?

"He's freelance scout, Rolls Royce and Castle have both taken players from him in the past and he's not on payroll like me, he'd want a percentage".

Best listened to the replay, ten minutes later and noted, "He said, 'very good indeed', Kipson doesn't use a phrase like that unless the chap is very good indeed. I would buy him' Boss, it does not sound like he would even cost us much".

After training that afternoon the young man in question was in the office with Kipson and Clara signing a contract. He was only five feet five inches tall, but Clara could not make any judgements on that score, for he was a provider more than a striker and there was no height restriction on that.

Tuesday was, therefore, going to be a very interesting day and training indeed. One factor was the imminent arrival of the androids, the second was how to fit Lane into the first team and see if he was good enough to keep his place.

When Clara got into the office, Best was looking flushed with excitement.

"The androids have arrived and the ground-staff are unpacking them", he gasped.

"Unpacking them"?

"Yeah, they came in wooden packing crates, they don't need to breathe, Boss".

"All right let's go and see them then".

By the time they had traversed the corridor outside the office and taken the lift down to the basement where the ground-staff had their offices, the last of the android players were just being taken out of the crating.

"How do you turn them on", Clara wanted to know, gazing at the metal manikin.

"There's a switch under the left arm, right in what would be an armpit", the caretaker told her. Clara lifted an arm of the nearest droid, it was fairly heavy, she observed to Best,

"The players will have to go steady on the tackling with these or they will hurt themselves".

The switch was easily thrown and the eyes of the android lit and she could hear ever so slightly whirring noises coming from inside the construct.

"Who are you"? Clara asked, curiously. A rather cultured if electronic voice replied,

"I am, Goalkeeper".

There had been no attempt to try and disguise the robot as anything other than what it was. It was hopefully fit for purpose. As if to underline its claim the mechanical stretched out its arms, it certainly had some reach, standing 7 feet in height. Could it move at speed though? Make the right sort of decisions? Clara was fascinated by its blued durasteel body and powerfully servoed legs and arms. There was no hair, no genitals no need to put it in a strip. She moved along the line and asked each of the mechanicals who they were and received tacit replies in the same voice:

"Defender, Midfielder, Striker. They would all be equally proficient with both feet and their cranium would propel a header better than any skull and flesh head.

"I think it time to put them to the test. Have the first team line up against them".

"Er, Boss who is your first team"? Best wanted to know.

"Anderson, McFarland, Hudson, Jennings, Burgenbower, Hardy, Ball, Jensen, Lane Nero Roxbrough. Wong can have a run out if Lane runs out of steam".

It was drizzling in the sweeping breeze, the sort of fine rain that was a constant nuisance to the eyes and slowly wet the players through as they moved. Thankfully the iron content in durasteel was low and the metal men were coated in oil anyway so they would be all right. The practise-comp-ref issued the blast to kick off once the men had taken to the field, curious looks on their faces. The robots kicked off. They were fast, accurate and had the ball in the teams eighteen-yard box before the men knew what was happening. The android who had told the manager he was Striker struck a really sweet shot low and hard at Anderson's left corner. The man got down to it with a half-second to spare and turned it around the post, quite a brilliant save.

Clara nodded, said into her CI, "Well done, good save".

Seconds later though Wing-Back-Defender floated an inch-perfect cross into the box from the corner and Striker's bullet header almost burst the net with its velocity.

"If only we had a team of them", Best murmured. After half an hour the men had run themselves to exhaustion and the androids had scored five times.

Clara replaced the entire backline for Roberts, West, Ford and Flintham. It was six-nil at half time and Flintham had given Clara something to consider, namely slipping him into the first team when opportunity allowed for it. He was sharp, dogged and determined. Similarly, Jensen and Lane had done well considering how few times they had managed to beat the metal team and Roxbrough, thou ineffective, had made several hopeful runs into the android eighteen-yard box, only for the androids to intercept it every single time.

It came to a second forty-five minutes and Clara decided to do something radical, she changed over the goalkeeper and back four of each team and put them in the opposite side. This meant androids attacked the androids or men were pitched against one another in the resultant duels. With fifteen minutes to go Lane darted past Burgenbower and sent a perfectly weighted pass onto Roxbrough's right boot. The striker buried the shot against Anderson. Final result six-one and the teams had been far better balanced with 50% men 50% androids.

"Lane is a good buy", Clara told the pleased and beaming Kipson. "If he continues to impress, then I'll have the dilemma fo who to leave outcome Saturday".

"Hornrunner currently lies seventh and the way we are going I think we could get our first home victory of the season", Best enthused.

"Let's not get too carried away at this point", Clara warned, "We still have a long way to go before we can begin to get confident. Right, that should be it for today. Have Whohouse take a good luck at Jennings, he was looking a bit leggy in the closing stages, might be a strain".

"You never mentioned the web, Boss", Best said at length, "Our write up is much better following the game against the Germans".

"I am going to make a studied point of not reading the reports", Clara told him, "Anyone can be an armchair expert which is all ex-players are, let them bump their gums to their heart's content I've got a football club to run".

"What if you get invited to be guest manager on *'Game under the Spotlight'*, then"? Best wanted to know.

"Then I shall tell them like it is and no silly platitudes"!

'I cannot wait for that to happen', the assistant manager thought to himself.

seven   **Mattle Speke hated** the new manager of Orang-U-Can. He had been the central midfielder of choice for the first three games of the current season and that interfering bitch had dropped him. He was not even on the bench since she had come in with her flash-cash and bought Jensen from DFE. He continued to train, but for what? A game in the reserves? Mattie was no reserve.

He was depressed and when he was depressed he liked to spend and Mattie never spent small amounts of money he liked to spend extravagantly. His bank balance from the previous season was very healthy and he could afford to indulge himself any time he desired.

It was a cold but still November day when Mattie went for a walk through the town. That usually cheered him up when the locals waved or exchanged a few words, some even asked for autographs. He headed for Watson Street and Duffie Motors. It was time to get himself a real top-of-the-range flitter and expense would be no object. Fortunately, he had his 'F' license in his wallet and nothing to complicate matters with a trade-in since he had totalled his previous model on the High-fly three months before. He had gotten about by flittaxi in the interim but that day he fancied doing some driving again. The trouble was Mattie liked speed. A great deal of speed. He had only just gotten his license back from a two-year ban when pulled over by the combmen for doing 137 mph on the M62.

Now he had a new one and the accident of the past quarter had not been - *'his fault, the richard-head should not have been allowed on the high-fly'!* Or at least that was the opinion Mattie had assumed when driving into the back of the poor unfortunate he had hit at junction six.

When Speke turned into the showroom, Genzol Duffie spat out half a jam doughnut seeing instant opportunity. Opportunity and shillin signs.. He jumped up from his seat in his glass-walled office and skittered across the showroom as fast as his bulk would allow. Due to the diet he allowed himself, which involved eating what the hell he wanted, he had something of a weight problem. Speke was a regular and a big spender and the morning thus far had been slow, so he risked a few calories of sweat and rushed to be at his side.

"Mattie, my friend, how's it goin'. Put anyone in the TGH [Trafford General Hospital] lately ha ha ha ha"?

"Not this season, not yet", Speke grinned, he had a mouth full of large chalky teeth and not an attractive smile. He looked as much like a horse as a man with his tall head and long face.

"You done that bird that's taken over from the previous gaffer".

"I'd like to", Speke admitted with feeling, "With a corner post, she's dropped me the bitch and me the captain all last season".

"Yeah, last season, third place and the semis of the shield. She hoping to do better than that? Say come into the office and have a doughnut and some coffee"?

Speke followed Duffie into his posh little office and sprawled on the faux-leather couch inside as Duffie closed the door. As he got the footballer a coffee in a nylostein cup, he asked,

"I'm guessing you're looking for a new motor"?

"Yeah, just a ground job, I don't think them air-types will take off ha ha ha ha".

Duffie laughed dutifully at the joke that comedians had already worn out. He asked, "What about your budget, my Friend. The reason I ask is, I have a new sports model in, a Breville Crusader in Matt black, but it's not cheap".

"You know I'm not stingy"! Speke complained as he sipped the coffee noisily. A Crusader aye. In matt black, how much and what bhp"?

Duffie told him the hair raising price but then added quickly "Breville has taken it to the next level with the 1400 bhp Venom supercooled freeze fusion motor. This is a 301 mph flitter and was designed from the ground up with high-speeds in mind. It's small by hyper-flitter standards and it comes with an 8-litre water tank two turbos and a minimum output of 1400 bhp, with more on offer. It has low-drag aero, weighs 2950 lbs and should hit 186 mph in less than 10 seconds. It's a throwback of a vehicle which rejects modern hybrid technology in favour of brute force. It even has manual side hatches that require a key to get into the thing You can even override old-school manual transmission, which I'm sure you never will as autopilot is not for you. There are just 24 going into production hence the price tag. Don't worry, though, because we have one in the showroom right now so you will not have missed out. I have to tell you though I pinged the news of delivery to five customers who could come in and snap it up any second. It comes with a Musical Fidelitee new visitor stereo system that will play your stix at 20 watts per channel RMS and in that space that could easily make your ears bleed. There's also a coffee maker and med-cig dispenser. The other thing is, the ladies will love it it's a real extension if you follow my drift"!?

Speke did, Duffie reflected it was like taking a baby's dum-tit off it!

"Come and sit in it and try it for size"? Duffie urged and Speke let him

practically lead him by the hand.

The instant Mattie Speke saw the matt-black super-flit he knew he was going to buy it. It would put a very large hole in his thumb-balance, but what was the use of money unless one was turning it into things? What a beauty the crusader was, with its rear spoiler, three aerials, super fluted bonnet and front grill, concealed side hatches and LED maxi-power headlights. With heavily tinted UV windows and the matt-black bodywork, it looked like a spy's vehicle. The front windscreen was tiny but inside was a view screen for front and rear elevations and heavily safety devices to avoid a collision or even proximity.

"The standard-setting makes it virtually impossible for you to exceed the road speed limit or to get too close to another flitter", Duffie told him pointing to the front viewer. "You can turn it off by going into the computer menu and holding the reset button for five seconds. If you slide your padfon into this receiving dock it will transfer all your contacts straight into the flitter's comp. Any time that you get a message on twitface or an email or vid-link the flitter speaks to you in one of five preselected voices. They are selected here look: Announcer, Regular, Bro, Sultry or Granny, I expect you'll be changing it from announcer to sultry the minute you get into the baby. You also have the stix player over here and all your environment controls here. The readout for your curtain is here and it will reinflate automatically when more air is needed. I cannot let you take it on a test run I'm afraid the insurance on this beauty is level N, which as you know is the highest. If you were to.........".

"Get me five emergency days insurance, twelve months travel-way tax, a spare inductor for the chamber, extra mats, a pair of Breville driving gloves, a Breville baseball cap and UV glasses and I'll take it", Speke blurted.

Duffie thought about it and returned, "I've got the Breville stuff in my office. I'll have to order the spare inductor but can have it in a week. The way-tax is going to be steep, Mattie, the best I can do is split it with you - half each".

"I'll pay half the way-tax if you throw in an extra cap and glasses".

"For the lucky babe who gets the first ride in for it aye"? Duffie leered, "A ride for a ride"!

Speke grinned all chalky teeth and big chin, "Deal"?

Duffie shook his hand, "Come into the office, get that thumb of yours from up your ringer 'cos your going to need to press it to a few pad-dox".

"One hour and twenty minutes later the Breville hissed out of the showroom with Speke at the console. He had everything set on manual. He sped up Manchester Road, then onto Seymour Grove, before crossing the A5067 and roaring up the A5081 straight past the Orang-U-Can Football Stadium called Nu-Trentavoria. The accident happened when he got to the Parkway Circuit. Speke was intending to take a right at the circuit and come off at two o'clock to go up Ashburton Road. He glanced to his right up the A576 and saw a Weston Superdodge 153 bhp coming up almost as quickly as he, he was doing 80mph at the time. Speke judged he could nip onto the circuit in plenty of time and instead of slowing and giving way gave the fusion rods even more steam.

When the ambulaflitter arrived there were bits of shattered durilite all over the circuit. The neoplas lights were little more than ground dust. It was not possible to determine what vehicles the two pieces of crushed and mangled wreckage had been.

Strebble climbed out the driving side while her paramedic buddy Honjmire joined her on the tarmacadam.

"Wow"! she exclaimed, "I've never seen this much carnage and destruction on a roundabout before, they must have been going well over the speed limit".

Combman Trepedch joined them and confirmed,

"Out instruments calculate the Breville was doing 80 while the Weston was braking down to about 50".

"The ruddy idiots"! Strebble cursed. "Get two body bags, Hon, we are going to be taking body parts to the morgue. No gurney is necessary".

"You know it", Trepedch agreed, we already have some over by our flitter. Mind you don't slip in this curiously pale blood".

"It's been diluted with pasted intestine, that's why it's pale", the Medic told him. "At these sort of speeds with the reinforced nature of the vehicles they make nowadays the bodywork of the flitter turns into a meat grinder on impact. Then you've got the cold fusion generator if that bursts during impact you also got extremely hot steam which will cook what's left in seconds. I don't know why the manufacturers keep making them so powerful and so fast".

Grimacing Trepedch handed Strebble a large evidence bag. Inside it was a human head.

"This was on the central reservation. The roof must have sliced it clean off at the instant of impact".

Strebble looked at the long chin and tall chalky teeth,

"Hey, I know who this was", she remarked to the combman. Central defender for Orang-U-Can Football Team. Played all last season, but not in the last two games this year".

"Speke", the combman supplied, "Was always good with his head"!

eight   **Clara's padfon pinged,** she glanced down at it and a small knot made itself felt in the pit of her stomach. The West Yorks Combmen wanted to see her. She had no idea what that could be regarding. In her misspent youth, she had been arrested a couple of times for possession of snufz, but that was way behind her, she had grown up. The dread of the combmen had not fully left her though and it returned even though she had nothing what-so-ever to worry about.

The ping requested her to report to Greenheys Police Station on Charles Halle Road. Since the counties of Saxonia had been realigned, Manchester was now part of West Yorks and it was the boys in Green who desired the pleasure of her company. She debated with calling her lawyer Stubbins but decided to find out what they wanted firstly. It was three in the afternoon, but due to the constant rain already practically dark. As she thumbed the ignition on the flitter the lights came on automatically and she dropped her padfon into the slot to tell the car where to take her. She was too distracted to drive manually and let the automatic navigator take her smoothly to Greenheys. There was a parking spot under the station and a lift to the ground floor and reception desk. At the latter, a burly and very corpulent sergeant was seated on a high stool before a deskcomp.

"Afternoon Ma'am", he greeted her cheerfully enough upon her arrival at the other side of his desk, "Please take a seat in the lounge, DI Snowd will be with you almost directly".

"Do you have any more information for me, Sergeant", Clara asked knowing that she had been recognised, "What is this about"?

"DI Snowd will be able to answer all of your questions, Miss Trentavoria, but do not worry you're not in any kind of trouble. There a lichencoff machine in the lounge and you can smoke it you wish, obviously only medcigs ha ha ha ha".

Clara responded with a tight smile and feeling considerably more at ease went and put a couple of sestertius in the two machines concerned. She was just finishing her med-cig when a young and rather handsome combman came into the room. His hair was the most curious shade of lime colour she had ever seen and it complimented his jade uniform most attractively.

"Miss Trentavoria. Thank you for coming so promptly, I'm DI Snowd. Are you able to come with me straight away, you can bring your drink with you"?

"Come with you where, Inspector"? Clara asked not unreasonably, "Do you mind telling me what this is about"?

"Of course not. You're here for identification purposes, I need you to come down to the mortuary with me".

Clara's mind whirled, "Someone is dead, someone you think I know"?

"That is what you're here to determine, Miss Trentavoria. We think it is one of your squad, but we need confirmation".

'*One of the footballers*'! Clara was somewhat relieved it was not family, but then concerned for her players '*What the hell has the overgrown child been up to*'?

She followed the Inspector to a lift, noticing that he had a very nice butt as she did so. In the lift, she smelled his cologne and said,

"You can call me Clara if it makes it any easier".

"Grelm", he replied with a nice smile, "But this process needs to be easier for you, not me, Clara. Don't worry it won't take long".

Clara thought there was some chemistry between them, but she did not know if the DI was contracted or seeing anyone. The lift doors opened into a very cool area that had a rather unsettling yet antiseptic aroma. A white-coated figure looked up from his examination of what was to Clara's way of thinking a dead person and promptly pulled a sheet over it, hiding it from view.

"This is Clara Trentavoria", Grelm Snowd announced somewhat superfluously, there were few Mancunians indeed who did not know her by her appearance alone, after all, she was the daughter of the CEO of the biggest Corporation in the System.

"It's over here, The mortician or combman examiner, or whatsoever he was remarked and pulled open an impossibly small drawer. Or at least as small as Clara had not been expecting. Snowd took her arm and steered her to the slab that the evidence bag now resided upon. Clara looked down at a dismembered head.

"We just need confirmation that this is Mattie Speke", Clara heard Snowd say through the buzzing noise that had sprung unbidden into her hearing. The room went indistinct and the voices seemed to be coming from the bottom of a well.

"I think I might pass out", the manager of Orang-U-Can told the two men. She next felt herself on a seat with a neoprene cup of water in her hand and did not know quite how she had gotten there. "Sorry, that's my first decapitation, what happened".

She gazed up into the lovely brown eyes of Grelm Snowd.

"You nearly blacked out, it's usually, under those circumstances, I gather you recognised the head as formerly belonging to one of your defenders".

"Yes. You follow the beautiful game"?

"I do, I try to go to each match when I'm not on duty".

"Would you like two tickets for Saturday, in the executive lounge"?

"That's not necessary really, but I would indeed".

"You can bring your partner with you if she likes football"?

The combman was swift to admit, "I'm not seeing anyone at the moment, but I can bring the guy who's contracted to one of my sisters if that's all right"?

Filing the information, Clara smiled, "Of course, whosoever you want. I feel a bit better now, I think it was hunger as much as anything, I missed lunch, there's a lot to do at the club right now".

"I'm off duty in five minutes", Snowd told her with considerable alacrity, Could I take you for a bite somewhere, then you can give me all the information you know about Speke in more comfortable surroundings"?

"In uniform"? Clara found herself asking.

"I have some regular clothing in my locker and can be back here in five to take you anywhere you would like to go".

Clara smiled, "That's kind of you and it would be ungracious of me not to accept, so I do".

He was as good as his word and back inside the promised time, wearing a then-popular all in one black jumpsuit. He was one of those fortunate enough to have the figure to be able to get away with it too.

"Where would you like to go"? He asked, "If we take your flitter I can get home by colleagues".

"What about Alston Bar and Beef", Clara suggested, "They do select steaks and a great selection of fashionable gins in a friendly space with arty murals beneath Glasgow Central Station"?

"Sold"! Snowd laughed.

They strolled down to the flitter, via the lift and Snowd whistled his appreciation of her vehicle,

"Nice transport", he enthused, "Are you driving"?

"No one is", Clara smiled, "It has full-auto, so what sort of music would you like on the stix"?

"Do you have any Clockmile"?

Clara hated them, it was the first cross he had earned in her tick list. She shook her head,

"My collection is the twenty-first century, no decent music has been written since then all the best melodies and tunes had been covered. If you remember in the last few years of the twenty-first century the computer Depthtune was created to search its programming for new tunes that had not been written before. It declared that all possible collections of the seven notes had been used in anything approaching a pleasing melody, that pleasing melodies had been used up and only rehashing of the existing melodies could be pleasing to the human ear. Then the bands all began making the new wave of musi?ck called cacophony. What about some Beatles"?

"Some mus?ck isn't so bad", he objected, "What about the output of the Raggin Noyz Orkestra, Anyway who are the beetles"? He was asking as he climbed into the passenger side - another cross!

"I'll try you with the very first Progressive record ever made Sergeant Pepper's Lonely Hearts Club".

"Well, I hope it sounds better than the title. Give me some *Rip'n'Copee* any day".

Clara had heard the Clockmile track in question and would rather have listened to a dentists drill for five minutes – another cross. It had started so well.

At the Bar, they ordered a Gin Rocket apiece and took seats in the lounge while a table freed up. Clara thought it time to ask a few personal questions,

"So, Officer, do all the visitors to your station get wined and dined after a traumatic experience"?

Snowd smiled, "Absolutely not, if they did I'd soon be beyond broke".

"Don't worry about the bill, I will take care of it".

"You will not", he frowned, "I invited you and I will pay for your dinner, even if you are loaded ha ha ha ha".

"I have no problem either way and have no idea what a Detective Inspector makes but either way is no problem".

He told her candidly, she could have looked it up on the Solar-Wide-Web anyway. It was an amount she spent on Boo-Radlie's in four months!

"Do you live locally then Grelm"? Clara wanted to know, "Or commute"?

"I live in Withington", he informed her.

"Flat, apartment, house"?

"My Mother's house. She's a single parent, I was in vitro, she never contracted".

"Do you know who supplied"?

He shook his head, "No and I'm not especially curious to find out, his responsibility has been and will continue to be zero. I expect you find that strange with Hugh being so hands-on in your family"?

Clara grinned, "Don't believe everything you read in the pad-casts, but yes I am close to Dad and my Mother now lives in Brazil so I only see her about two weeks in every couple of years. You don't want a place of your own then"?

"I have half the house to myself since I've grown up I had a second kitchen and bathroom installed and sometimes I don't see Mom for a week if I'm on shifts for example. We share the rates and the utilities, so until I meet someone I want to contract, why would I want the extra expense? I have a savings bond or two and should it happen I have a deposit, for something. Being a cop limits your options though you know"?

"Does it. I thought that notion somewhat outdated. You still experience a certain amount of discriminatory attitudes, do you"?

He nodded, looking at her med-cig he explained, "Would you light up a Snufz-cig in front of me or even a 1in2"?

Clara shook her head, "If I did, what would you do".

"Caution you about the dangers of getting addicted, but nothing official, it's your choice. You see my point though don't you".

"A combman is never off duty"?!

"That's the saying, but it's not true. For example, the stix you were playing in your flitter was home-made, but I wouldn't dream of asking you for the serial number of that dreadful racket you had on it".

"If you did I would laugh", Clara told him, "Beatles are in the public domain since Erasmus McCartney died five years ago".

"You know what I mean though. I've met some perfectly lovely girls and everything has been going well until they asked me what I did for a living and then whoosh – gone"!

"Well I'm not a perfectly lovely girl and I know what you do, so I won't be going whoosh before my steak comes"!

"Who says you're not perfectly lovely"? He chuckled.

"I meant I'm not a girl", Clara noted sternly and then watched him squirm at her dry humour, "I'm joking. Only I do not think of myself as a girl, I'm all grown up".

You're pretty articulate aren't you", he finally smiled, "How do you think you're going to survive as a football manager"?

"I'm teaching my squad to speak English and to start acting as though they are their physical, rather than mental age", Clara told him in all seriousness, "It did not take with Speke, I presume it was a hideous road traffic accident rather than a murder"?

"You know his history"?

"I was an ardent supporter before I was the head coach, I know he had only just gotten his license back. What a senseless waste of human life".

"Some people are just determined to implode no matter how talented or what breaks they get in the gene pool. It's no reflection on you, Clara".

"Yes", she agreed, "I still feel rather sad for him, ignorance is a difficult disability to combat".

The waiter, a very polite android informed them then that their table was ready. They both had a steak, creamed potatoes, carrots and peas. Nothing lichen-fused for either of them, the vegetables came a little dearer but were worth it for taste and texture. Snowd then had a dessert, but Clara went straight onto Venezuelan coffee.

"You don't need to skip pudding", he told her, but she responded by telling him,

"It's a constant battle not to start putting it on. You have a more fortunate metabolism than me. Do you eat doughnuts too"?

He laughed, "Not all combmen eat doughnuts".

"All the good ones do, I've seen it on the tri-vidz", she laughed.

"Do you want to go on to somewhere", he asked rather candidly then.

"What did you have in mind and forget your place or mine because I don't do that".

"What visit or have visitors", he laughed.

"I could watch a tri-vid if there's anything on at the Printworks"?

"Edge of the System", he told her after looking at his padfon, "Science Fiction I'm afraid".

"I love Science Fiction", Clara told him.

"Really! You're not just saying it to be nice".

Clara returned, "I don't just say things to be nice, Grelm and I do love Sci-fi. I've even got the Star Trek series on antique DVD. Do you know what DVD was"?

"Before tri-vidz, two-dimensional entertainment on little silver discs way bigger than stix".

"Well not enormously bigger, but yes, they were about 100mm wide".

"How do you get them to play and how does the projector deal with the image"?

"You need an antique player, which I have and the projector simply projects it two-dimensionally onto a screen which you have for the purpose".

"But you cannot see through the image, how weird, can you enjoy it that way"?

"Maybe I'll show you an episode some time", Clara tested to see his reaction, knowing already that once she had sorted out his musical tastes she might very well like him well enough to see him more than that night.

"I might very well take you up on that then", he responded. "So it's the Printworks and Edge of the System, it's about mankind finding another Nyjord. So I'm told, so pretty far-out stuff, I think space is mainly empty".

"It is, but that tiny bit of matter floating about is quite a bit you know"?

"Don't say you're into astronomy too"? he grinned as they rose to leave, he had just pressed his thumb to the payment plate on the table.

"I am".

"You're a very unusual gi.....lady, Clara".

"You'd better believe it, Grelm"!

It was an entertaining film, although wildly impossible in purely scientific terms, the premise that one-day mankind could exceed the speed of light, an obvious physical impossibility according to the laws set out by Einstein so many many years before. Clara enjoyed it anyway especially the part about the three-headed aliens suffering from constant schizophrenia. The writer had a bizarre sense of humour.

She insisted upon dropping Snowd off at his shared house, she was equally insistent that she would not go in for a lichen-coff, she hated the synthetic stuff and she was not about to do something ill-advised with the handsome combman. No matter how pleasant it might ultimately prove to be. He kissed her gently in the flitter before saying in parting,

"You have my number if you fancy doing this again sometime"? It allowed her to painlessly *give him the elbow* if she so chose to do.

"I have" she responded, with a straight face, "Nine hundred and ninety-nine, right"?

"Don't use the emergency number", he advised, "My desk is 0161 555 61 555. That is also my e-number if you want to e-mail me and if you want to *friend me* on twitface I have a page on there".

"My page is Orang-U-Can Headquarters or OUCH".

"Goodnight, Clara".

"Goodnight, Grelm".

nine   **Matchday arrived and** Clara realised she was not ready for it. The home game against Hornrunner, seeing Grelm again, the pressure of selecting the team, the captain – the entire thing. She forced herself to concentrate when meeting Best, listening to his opinions and advice and selected a team based on the thoughts and observations of them both rather than just what she wanted. She realised he knew much more about formations than her and finally settled for a four-three-three line-up, very attack-minded indeed. If OUC were going to win their first home game of the season it was to be a thumping, not a hard-fought victory. Grelm and his brother-by-contract arrived and Clara was still in Manager mode as she greeted them in the executive lounge.

"This is Dlae, he is married to my sister Dujith, you remember me telling you about them"? Grelm introduced.

Clara shook his hand, it was soft and sweaty and his grip was ineffectual. Not the best of introductions to the weak-chinned individual.

"I hope you both enjoy the game", Clara managed before telling them with some reluctance, I've got to leave you with one of my PA's now I'm afraid. I've got an interview to do with a reporter for the local pad-cast in just under four minutes".

Grelm's face registered disappointment, but as Myria stepped forward, Dlae's eyes lit up and the contract with the combman's sister suddenly did not seem so solid to Clara as to her friend.

"Pleased to meet you both", simpered Myria. "Let me give you a quick tour of the facilities"?

By the look on Dlae's face, it was clear he was thinking he would have liked a tour of Myria's facilities! The girl was intelligent, fashionably bespectacled [back in the last decade as a fashion accessory], with dark chestnut hair a winning smile and an even more winning chest that boasted a cup size of 36E!

By the time she led the two men away, Dlae was practically leaving a trail of drool on the executive lounge carpet-tiles. Clara went to meet Kicd Slythe, the reporter for the Manchester Evening Newscast. She had met the man several times before when working for her father and she had always felt that she could more easily warm to something that lived under a rock at the bottom of a muddy pond than Slythe.

She met him in her office and was careful to take a seat behind her desk rather than in the social area of the room.

Slythe got straight down to business,

"Miss Trentavoria this is the fifth game of the season and OUC only has one point and languishes at the bottom of the table, is it, therefore, fair to say that this is indeed a massive game for you"?

"No", Clara returned, "It is the same size as all the others, ninety minutes in duration".

"No", Slythe grimaced, "What I meant is that the result of this game is huge, one that you simply must win"?

"We hope to win the result of a home victory, but it will be the same size as all the others today. Should we succeed, three points, that is how a game is rewarded in the Corporation League, Mister Slythe".

"Yeah, no what I mean is......".

"Yes, no, Mister Slythe, which is it then, an affirmative or negative response to my indisputable answer to your question"?

Slythe blinked, "What"?

"I believe you mean, 'Pardon', Mister Slythe, now! If that is it....."?

"No, I have some more questions".

"Then ask them please, my time is very valuable. I am recording this interview also so I expect your podcast to be accurate in extremis".

"Miss Trentavoria", Slythe swallowed, "When you ask the lads to done a win did you tell them to park the bus or go at it in the middle of the park"?

"Firstly, Mister Slythe, I would ask the '*men*' to win the game, not, *'done a win'* as you so ungrammatically put it. Secondly, we do not need a bus as we are the home team and thirdly we play in a stadium on a pitch, youngsters from the local kindergarten play in the park, I believe the swings are very popular".

Slythe was perspiring freely by that point as he asked, "So you intend to hang all the shirts on the line and hope that your boys have got the legs for it"?

"Once the game is over the shirts will be laundered ", Clara replied, "Then tumbled dry. If we had a line to hang them on, they might get in the way of the players training, unless it was too high off the ground for anyone to peg anything onto it. Concerning the player's legs each of them has two, we do not have any players with artificial appendages".

"Slythe grew annoyed, "Are you deliberately trying to annoy me, Miss Trentavoria"?

"I'm here only to answer questions about football, Mister Slythe. Do you have any more *pertinent* questions about the game, preferably in Standard English"?

"Who's heading up the squad and what do you think the result will be today".

"All my players can head the ball upwards and downwards, Mister Slythe, and I believe the result today will be either a home, draw or away result".

"Are you doing this on purpose, Trentavoria"? Slythe was then exasperated.

"I am, I intend to manage Orang-U-Can with purpose until we get the desired results. Now I'm afraid your time is up, Mister Slythe, I have a proper job to attend to. Security will show you to the main stand".

"Oh, I thought I would be in the executive lounge"? The reporter squealed.

"Did you", Clara smiled icily, "Proving that you do sometimes have coherent thoughts Mister Slythe, well done. **Neddis**"! Neddis from security appeared at the door with admirable swiftness, "Show mister Slythe to his complimentary seat in the north stand".

The North Stand where the wind could freeze a polar bear on a cool day in Manchester, if such an animal still existed on Earth that was, for when the polar caps had melted in the twenty-second century they had disappeared. Of course, Hoyle had genetically recreated them by gene splicing remnant DNA from them with koalas, but the resultant animal had proved something of a disappointment. Slythe was led out of the office, muttering,

"Uncooperative Bitch", under his breath.

Clara hurried down to the changing room,

"You have trained with indomitable spirit this week men", she began, "Twice scoring against the android eleven. This team today are mere men and unprepared for the work-rate you are going to display to them. I've chosen an attacking formation because I want some goals to be scored by us today. Anyone scoring will get a goal-bonus in his pay, score more - earn more. Anderson, you will be on a save bonus. The defence will be on a superb-tackle bonus. I am not going to reward anyone for failure. This is a tough regime, but I am creating a tough team, now go out and show this unsuspecting bunch of girls **what you can do**"! She had gotten louder as she progressed and the last four words had been a shout. She was surprised and pleased when the team answered with a call of agreement. They were ready to show the fans what they could do.

Clara rushed down to the dug-out, activated her CI and seated herself beside Charmley. The crowd roared as the two teams took to the pitch for a five-minute warm-up. With a minute to go Clara named Jensen captain and the most important game of OUC's season thus far was ready to begin.

Hornrunner normally played in yellow shirts with green trim, green shorts and yellow socks, but because OUC were in all orange changed to their second choice strip of green shirts white shorts and green socks. The compref displayed that it was time to kick off 15:00 on a Saturday and the city of Manchester went quiet. The game began at a furious pace. Jensen hit a beautiful curving pass to the racing forward form of Lane, who clipped it first time up into the air and Roxbrough's header thundered against the Hornrunner crossbar.

In the stands, Dral Perrimore was dancing on his plastic seat. "This is going to be one hell of a match, Gael. One hell of a match"!

The noise from the 97 thousand spectators was absolute bedlam and all being created by the home fans. Those few Romanians who had made the journey to the away end were deathly silent and too few to make anything like the same amount of commotion.

After ten minutes, all of which was played in Hornrunner's half of the pitch, it was obvious that the Romanians could not get out of it. Jensen Ball and Wong had an iron grip on midfield, while Nero, Roxbrough and Lane were threatening the goal nearly every time they got the ball. The only thing that counted was goals though and Clara found herself constantly urging the players to even greater feats of endeavour.

"Pass it forward, Burgenbower, Anderson does *not* need a touch! Find the forward pass, drive them back into their eighteen-yard line. Press them, press them and it's just a matter of time before they cave. Run Lane, you might have reached that if you'd sprinted harder. I want 100%, come off that pitch exhausted we have five substitutes **come on**"!

The break came after only thirteen minutes. Flintham hit a beautiful cross-field pass to Jensen who controlled it with a single deft touch and his forward pass slipped it to Nero who hit a wonderful cross straight into the Hornrunner box. Roxbrough drove the ball with a thunderous shot, but it hit the chest of the diving goalkeeper and cannoned back out of the goalmouth. The nippy Lane reached it before any of the opposition defenders however and clipped a super lob into the top left-hand corner.

Manchester went into raptures of delight. For any who had not managed to go to the ground were watching the podcast, some workers were even listening to the radio. Even patients in the hospital were diving up and down on their beds at the first goal Orang-U-Can had scored that season. It meant a lot to the locals of the city, football was still the most popular sport in the home of the once-great teams of the twentieth and twenty-first century.

Whatever the Hornrunner manager was saying to his team it was evident that he considered them to be outclassed and outplayed, at least for the rest of the first half. For the away opposition refused to emerge from their half and had every player defending their own goal resolutely. Time and again OUC raided into the opposition half only for strong tackles to break down any strategy they tried. Not that they minded, for they had been training against metal players who were even more difficult to mount an attack against than the Romanians. At half-time, the teams came back into their dressing rooms exhausted.

Clara decided to take the precedent of using four of her substitutions for the second half only leaving the reserve goalkeeper Radband on the bench just in case of the unlikely event of Anderson getting injured. She took off Burgenbower, Jenson Nero and Lane bringing on Ford, West, Hudson and Wong in their place. A chance for the then second squad to shine and perhaps elevate themselves into the first eleven. Seeing the substitutions on the CLDB (computer-laser-display-board) Hornrunner changed their strategy and came out for the second forty-five minutes far more attack-minded. The game opened up into end-to-end excitement for the crowd. It suddenly involved Clara's back four far more and even Anderson had a couple of fairly easy saves to make. What it also did was make counter-attacking a very real possibility though. McFarland who was becoming a very important part of the defence since his inclusion in the first eleven suddenly tackled and taking the ball past the striker he had robbed sent a darting pass up to West. Seeing Roxbrough make yet another of his penetrating runs, West struck the ball cleanly to him and the new signing wrong-footed a defender and scurried past another to hit a sweet left-footed shot low and hard straight through the Hornrunner goalkeepers legs – 2-0.

Corporation Division One

Goosetimp v Castle 1-1
Tiptingle v R R Scoriors 0-2
Zhõngguá v Preciometalic.Inc 1-0
IYWIWSI v DFE 2-2
OUC v Hornrunner 3-0
Makers-Guild v Voleskip 2-0

With the cushion of a second goal Hornrunner seemed to lose the momentum they had been creating, and their confidence. As a result with ten minutes left to play Roxbrough dribbled past two players and then hit a sweet pass to Wong who slammed the ball into the Hornrunner goal. A complete victory without conceding in their end. Clara and everyone connected with the club was delighted.

Before returning to the dressing room Clara took the opportunity of looking at the other results on her padfon. The Chinese had enjoyed a home victory and greatly improved their position in the table. So too her team – Orang-U-Can who were now two places up and only beneath the Romanians due to their goals scored. It had been an excellent day for the squad and Clara had some bonuses to pay!

Corporation Div One	Plyd	Goals	Pts
Castle Electronics	5	10	11
I.Y.W.I.W.S.I.	5	10	9
Preciometalic.Inc	5	9	7
Goosetimp Weapons	5	9	7
Makers-Guild	5	7	7
Deutsch Fahrzeuge Eingearbeitet	5	7	6
Zhõngguá Shãngpín	5	2	6
Rolls Royce Scoriors	5	6	7
Hornrunner Hornets	5	6	4
Orang-u-Can	5	3	4
Voleskip Pharmaceuticals	5	2	4
Tiptingle Tigers	5	3	3

ten   **When Clara finally** said goodnight to Grelm (their second date) she was ready to drop. Not ready for the unexpected arrival at her Father's home. She thumbed the pad that unlocked the door and was surprised to see the light on in the front lounge. Hugh was an early retirer and consequently early riser and yet someone was still up. Curiously she pushed the door open and stepped inside.

"Oh! Hello Mother", she sighed.

Loreejæ Trentavoria, former wife of Hugh's arose from the couch noting,

"That's not a very enthusiastic greeting for your Mom, come here and give me a hug".

Clara did not feel enthusiastic. The only time Loreejæ returned to England was when her latest lover had dumped her and she needed cash injection for her thumb off Hugh. Amazingly, despite the way they had treated one another in the past, or perhaps because of it, Hugh usually gave her a considerable sum simply to see her flitterjet off to Brazil the moment she had tired of Manchester weather once again. While Hugh had been something of a philanderer in the past, there was no denying that Loreejæ had also been something of a seductress. Hugh had calmed down with the onset of middle-age however, Loreejæ had grown even more promiscuous.

Reluctantly letting the older woman hug her Clara asked gently, "What are you doing back in Saxonia and in the season you say you hate"?

"Could it not be simply that I came to see my daughter and other children"?

"That's possible I suppose, but you normally stay in a hotel, what are you doing here in Dad's house"?

"He's told me I can stay for a while, so why are you questioning it, Clara"?

"Because after all the arguments had finished, I'll be the one to put Dad back together again, that's why".

"Arguments? We've had no arguments"?

"Yet"!

"Maybe they won't start this time"?

"Well, there's a first time for everything, but I doubt that very much and you always say something vastly hateful and leave Dad in a mess".

"Clara, you Father can lay his tongue to some pretty miserable things when he puts his mind to it".

"Not like you though. You're my mother and I love you, but when you get started....well, we both know what you can be like once you get started"?

"Clara, it's late and we're both tired, perhaps it might not be such a good idea to continue this conversation until we're both rested and with a clear head".

"I'm not muddled Mother, I mean what I say even if I have had a busy day. So tell me, why now, why are you here, have you come alone this time"?

Clara watcher Mother's eyes mist over and then filled with tears as she admitted finally, "Ramone's thrown me out"!

Ramone was the latest in a string of South American and Latino lovers that the middle-aged Loreejæ had involved herself with. A man who was not only half her age but also known to conduct somewhat dubious business projects often involving the illegal snufz trade.

"Thrown *you* out, not been thrown in gaol"?!

"How many times do I have to tell you Ramone is a commodities-broker"?

"I don't doubt it, only the commodities happen to be in cocaine, heroin, snufz and vicantequímco".

The latter was the latest designer drug that was often a lethal cocktail of other substances mixed by somewhat dubiously motivated chemists in the Latin America countries. There had been many deaths, but it was cheap compared to snufz and gave hallucinations and heightened senses and a feeling of intense euphoria when it worked, when it was not quite so effective was when it gave death.

"Whatever, it doesn't matter now because it's over".

"The twenty-five-year-old got tired of his fifty-seven-year-old lover, why"?

"Not for *that* reason, if that's what your thinking, the relationship had just run it's course that's all".

"Don't expect me to believe that nonsense, Mother"! Clara was critical in extremis, "It wasn't simply a breakup, if he, *'threw you out'!* That means a real humdinger of a bust-up, what did you do"?

"I never did anything"! Loreejæ protested, "Well, other than the thing I did, but it was going nowhere by then anyway. You see there was......".

"Strike that, Mom, I don't want to know. The main thing is I know why you're here".

"I've told you why I've...".

"Come for a handout", Clara was cutting, if right. "You always expect Dad to help you out with some thumb when you come crashing down again, how much longer do you think his patience will hold out"?

"My relationship with your Father is not really of particular concern to you, Clara", Loreejæ suddenly retorted icily, "You are one of our children and......".

"The one who has to console him once you've frinselled off once again".

"He bought you the club I hear, you're not doing so badly out of him are you"?

"Orang-U-Can is part of the firm and I'm working damned hard to make it a successful part of it.

"When we win the league, the tri-vidz payment from Space-media will more than cover what I have borrowed, then I'll be able to pay Dad back".

"Won the league with a team at the bottom of the table"!

"You're a result behind, Mother, dear. OUC is no longer bottom of the table we won today three-nil and we'll keep winning until we gradually rise to first place where Dad's corporation belongs".

"Well while you're playing games, Clara, my life is in tatters so thank you oh so much for your daughterly concern".

"I am concerned, Mother", Clara replied softly then, "I'm concerned that I'm older than my mother, you're still a big soft baby in-your-head. You can keep having your facelifted, your gut nipped and tugged and your tits re-sculpted, but one day you need to start acting your age. We look like sisters, but I'm far more responsible and mature than you".

Loreejæ had gone white with dire contemplation and she asked at the end of her daughter's tirade,

"And what great pearls of wisdom do you have to impart to me then, Daughter, Dear, what would you advise me to do"?

"Instead of asking for more charity, so you can shack up with someone else younger than me until the money runs out, ask Dad for a job. Try earning a living and not on your back"!

By way of an answer, Loreejæ slapped Clara's face. Clara did nothing, but through gritted teeth she warned,

"If you ever lay another finger on me, Mother, I'll punch your lights out. I am now going to bed, turn some lights off when you decide to retire, Dad may be wealthy but waste is waste and think of the planet, don't waste fuel or energy of any sort".

"I already wasted some energy pushing you out"! Loreejæ blurted face crimson with fury, hastily tugging a pack of snufzcigs from her handbag.

"There you go", Clara was momentarily triumphant, "That's the Mother I've come to know so well. Keep that razor-sharp tongue of yours trained on your daughter, leave her father alone this time".

"Just go to bed"! Loreejæ snarled.

"I am, Mummy", Clara was sardonic. "Try not to drain the drinks cabinet dry before you finally turn in. Would you like me to get Gatson up out of bed and transfer him to yours so that he can service you before you descend into a drunken stupor? He's in his forties, but he's a great butler and will do his best at keeping the old Methley happy".

"Frenge off Clara you nasty little bì-miàn-duìed bhò"!

"Charming I'm sure. It seems sleeping with a drugs baron has taught you another string to your bow, Mother Dear, filthy gutter language".

With that Clara turned on the heel of her flat shoes and walked out of the room. She would have flounced but her hair was not long enough.

She found sleep difficult to attain due to upsetmentation. When she finally managed it, she overslept and finally dragged herself up at 10.22. As her rooms were en-suite, she did what she had to do, bathed and then decided to walk down for a casual breakfast. Sundays were her only day of rest since becoming manager of OUC and she intended to be lazy. The instant she left the part of the house dedicated for her, she knew something was very much amiss. The house was full of visitors, or as she thought of them – intruders. Men in green! Men in white boiler-suits and who was amongst them but Grelm!

Clara focused on him, approached him and asked as calmly as she were able,

"Good morning, Inspector, might I be so bold as to enquire what you are doing in this property".

Face grim and finding no amusement in her somewhat forced humour, he said quietly, loud enough only for her to hear,

"It's not funny, Clara, there is never anything funny about murder"!

"Murder", Clara sobered up in a quick second, "Who's been.......",?

"Loreejæ Trentavoria was found by your man – Gatson, barely forty minutes ago, stabbed to death"?

"Where"?

"In the library and in the liver", Snowd returned with a suitably melodramatic flourish. I'm afraid that makes you a suspect too. Please don't say the butler did it that is unsuitably passé at the minute and not especially funny then or now".

"That my Mother has been violently killed in my Father's home is not démodé and never could be", Clara admitted and then despite how she felt about her she suddenly found the blood leaving her head and asked, "Do you mind if I sit down a second I feel.....".

"Of course", Grelm steered her to a chair and then said urgently, "Sergeant, get a glass of water will you, Miss Trentavoria is somewhat overcome by the revelation regarding her Mother".

A burly man who should not wear a green jumpsuit unless he *wanted* to look like a cabbage, frowned, then returned,

"Yes, Inspector", and trundled off to find a glass and a tap, in that order.

Snowd waited patiently for the receptacle containing the fluid to arrive and be obligingly sipped before asking,

"Clara where were you last night at around 03:00"?

"In bed, asleep", Clara found the question annoying and distressing in equal measure.

"Please keep calm", Snowd emitted the sort of advice, which like *Don't Panic* tended to have the exact opposite effect of that issued. "One person in addition to your Mother was not in bed asleep that person was the foul and bloody murderer".

"I think I could do without the hammy theatrics, for the time being, Inspector. My mother is dead and my Father and I are suspects, so please stick to the facts will you and let's have less cloak-and-dagger histrionics".

"When it comes to murder, Clara one can never be too stagy, but as you say, let us stick to the facts. Were you in bed alone"?

Aware of how insulting that was on several levels, but also aware that her boyfriend was obliged to ask it she declared,

"I see one person at a time in a romantic way and as I am currently seeing you romantically, Inspector, I would not be in bed with anyone else".

"And that response has just taken me off the case, Clara", Snowd looked relieved. "I'm going to the Chief Constable, explaining the situation and get someone to take over from me". Clara almost blurted that he might as well not bother, as she and Snowd would not be seeing one another again. That was how she felt in the moment in her anger though and she had learned one thing from her dead mother and that was never to speak when annoyed. Better to calm down and then use considered language. So she merely nodded silently and watched him hesitantly take his leave. Then she went in search of Hugh.

The irony of ironies, she found Hugh in the library. The place where all the e-data was stored. Some stix were encased in olde book-shaped holders to make the library look like one from antiquity. Others were simply in their transparent receptacles. The library also contained an olde desk made from wood, the produce of a tree, those marvellous tall plants that only existed on Earth in specially protected reserves. That in the past mankind had cut down such wonderful foliage simply to use it for themselves when neoplas and nyloplanyon was so easily manufactured was something Clara could not realistically imagine. Hugh would never have murdered the noble growths of bark and sap and leaves, simply for its flesh, but there had been many who had. He owned the desk to preserve it for posterity – at least that was his stance. He was currently seated behind it, his head in his hands as though thinking, weeping, snoozing, who could say?

"Dad"? Clara began, "I've just heard. I was up late, and to bed even later. Do you have any idea what happened"?

Hugh looked up from his hand cradle and as the thin morning sunlight streamed in through the window, harshly illuminating his features, he had never looked so old. For he had never used augmentation, claiming he wanted to look as old as he felt some days and that day he felt quite aged. He was still handsome though, in that way that men improve with iron-grey hair and the crags of wrinkles.

"All I know is that Loreejæ is gone. My first true love is no longer with us".

Clara bit back the urge to go into the amusing liturgy, *'Bereft of life, pushing up the daisies, gone to join the choir invisible, an ex contractee'*. There were times when her mind tormented her, found amusement in the very darkest of subject matter and this was one of those times. One thing seemed certain, that though her father would be the combmen' chief suspect, she did not think him guilty of the deed. As she knew it was not her either, probably suspect number two then she had no clue as to who would have done such a thing and just as importantly – why? Someone could have slipped past the household security and done the woman to death, but what was the motivation for such a clandestine act? There was no physical nor DNA evidence for Snowd had not gloatingly announced to her that there was. It was easy enough to get around such things if one knew what one was doing anyway. Pseudo-skin gloves, even pseudo-skin masks were readily available and mirrored personnel suits could render one invisible to cameras. So effective was the latter that Hugh had even taken the outside cameras down. Only one other person was worth talking to and Clara patted her Father for a few seconds before going in search of him.

Torm Drifield was former Special Secret Squad Section or Sx4 as he referred to them. As such he had been an admirable choice of security leader for Hugh Trentavoria. In the early hours of the morning though, Sx4 had failed, more specifically Drifield had not put into place a net capable of catching a murderous minnow. He was in his office in the bowels of the stately home, looking at a security screen and a run of the evenings tri-vidz recordings. Clara coughed to stop him from believing she was sneaking about, without moving his head an inch Drifield said,

"Hello, Clara, I thought I'd be getting a visit from you sooner or later".

Years ago in a drunken moment of madness, Clara had let the muscular security man flutter her and he had been familiar with her ever since and also convinced that one day she would get, *'hungry enough for second helpings – a big portion of Torm'*. What it meant was that he never referred to her as Miss Trentavoria. Indeed it was a measure of the gravity of the current situation that he even called her by her given. It was usually something like, *'Babes'*, or *'Sugar'*, when in the company of others. When just the two of them were together it was *'Sugar Tits'* or *Honey Thighs'*. For these reasons, he was not someone that Clara sought the company of under ordinary circumstances. Of course, the current circumstances were far from ordinary they were dire. Someone had let themselves into the property and brutally slay one of the occupants. Whether Loreejæ was a deliberate or accidental target was yet to be determined. What it was though was a slight to Sx4 and Drifield's efficiency and expertise.

"Well here I am then, Drif, what do you have".

"What I have", the former Sx4 operative told her then, "What I have, Clara is frenge-all and plenty of it".

"You're telling me someone crept into this house last night and brutally murdered my Mother and as head of security you do not have one jot, one crumb of evidence to give to the combmen"?

"Hey, steady on Sugar T.......Sugar, don't get your drawers all knotted up. Someone with a bit of expertise could have easily got in here last night. I've advised your Father more than once to let me install better security, but he keeps harping on about the cost. Then he goes and gives you a great big fat thumb so you can go and play with a little bag of air being kicked around some grassland. What this estate needs are pressure pads, laser detection motion censors and the new ultra-clear cameras. What does he ask me to work with? One patrolling man in the grounds at night, me during the day and old tri-vidz that are practically ready for the junk recyclers. So what happens, as a result, someone with a bit of knowledge can let themselves in and perpetrate a heinous crime"!

"What about robbery? Is anything taken"? Clara was clutching at straws, but anything was worth a try.

Gatson and the two maids are looking to see if anything has gone missing. Your jewellery still in your bedroom safe"?

"I've not looked, but it's still closed".

Drifield looked up from the screens of the antique Tri-vidz for the first time, two dimensional boxes that produced low-grade images.

"Would you be a doll and go and look, because anyone that can open a safe also knows how to close it once they've taken out what they want. Your Father has already checked his and nothing is missing. I'll come with, if you desire".

"Let you in my bedroom a second time, what do you think"?

"I was just thinking about what happened the last time I was in there"!

"Yes, I know you were and you can go on giving that disease-ridden brain of yours, a good hard thinking. For as long as you damn-well want because that's the closest you'll ever get to realising it from now on".

"You seemed to like it at the time", Drifield grinned lasciviously, "I don't understand why you don't want to ride the Sx4 rocket a second time"?

"There is plenty of things you don't understand, Drif. One of note is how to keep us all safe in our beds at night"!

"I've told you about that I need.........".

Clara did not hear the rest of his lame excuse, she was going back to check her safe.

Though it was fine and nothing was missing, that did not mean that all was well with the world. Indeed as far as Clara was concerned her one day off, her *lazy day* was ruined. She got back into her pyjamas returned to bed and had another couple of hours sleep. Upon awaking, she spent the rest of the day watching vidz on her tri-vid. Her mind kept drifting to the murder naturally. Though she had not technically loved her Mother, the thought of her grizzly murder still filled her with dread and sadness. Clara's one restful day in seven turned out to be nothing of the sort.

eleven　　　　　　　　　**Things did not** improve the following day, when she arrived at her office in the club grounds Whohouse was waiting to see her.

"Something wrong"? She asked the physiotherapist, who, for a reason she could not quite put her finger on, she could not warm to. He had a quality, something was unsettling about him. Yet he had done nothing to earn such suspicion.

"Training accident, we've two rather serious injuries".

"Who, what, how"?

"Hudson and Burton went for a fifty-fifty ball and whammo"!

"English please Whohouse, what does whammo mean"?

"It means Burton has a broken leg and that's him done for the rest of the season and Hudson tore his hamstring, so even with modern techniques, he's not in the squad for a few weeks if we're lucky".

Clara breathed a sigh of relief, at least they were only players who would play in the first eleven if others needed substituting, but it did take her squad down to nineteen fit men.

"All right thank you Whohouse, when you see Best, will you ask him to come and see me, please. I'm guessing he's out on the pitch training because he's not answering my pings".

Nodding the unsettling physiotherapist left her but it was not long before Best was knocking on the faux-timber door.

"You wanted to see me, Boss"?

"I did", Clara confirmed, "I've just heard we don't have Burton and Hudson to call on if our first eleven get pulled for some reason. I want to ask you if any of the youngsters in the academy are mature enough and good enough to be brought into the men's squad.

Best seated himself and looked thoughtful, then he told her, "The young Zambian is a big lad for his age and a strong defender, all he needs is the right captain telling him what to do. Name's Zinyama".

"Have him train with the men tomorrow, anyone else"?

"The skinny Pole - Rachwalski has talent but he needs to be a bit heavier if he's going to worry opposition defenders".

"Get him in the gym then and have Whohouse put him on a weight gaining diet. Anything else I need to know".

Best looked suddenly rather grave.

"There is something else what is it"?

"Hardy pinged in with a stomach upset, insisted he could not make training".

"The holding midfielder? Isn't this the third time? In this quarter"?

Best nodded, "When he's fit he's almost the equal of Jensen and they train well together, but he keeps saying he's not 100%"

"And what does Whohouse say"?

"It's Charmley who thinks that he may be disingenuous in some way and not really what he claims during these mysterious bouts of stomach upset".

"You want to put him on the transfer list"?

Best shook his head, "On his better days he's a good player, it's just that he's having more poor days since Jensen came to the club. Speaking of the transfer list though.....".

"What"?

"I want to let Roberts and Ford, go".

"I've no problem with Roberts, but why Ford, he's one of our better defenders".

"He's requested a move, thinks he can get a regular first-team position with the Chinese".

"Zhōngguá Shāngpǐn? Have they shown any interest, what does Kipson say about it"?

"You know how the Chinese are, they keep everything secret, but he thinks it's a very likely done deal if we want to let him go"?

"I don't want anyone staying here who does not urgently desire to play for us. How big is our list now"?

"The first wave went, at the price you asked for them, they went, some even to second-tier clubs".

"Oh! Like who for instance"?

"Corporación Española de Frutas, for one".

"The Spanish fruit corporation, I seem to think they are doing well in Division Two".

"You don't know the latest then"?

"What latest"?

"The comp-draw for the third round of the shield. We're away to them, they fought their way to the last sixteen".

"A Second Division team, that's lucky".

"I'm not so sure, Boss. They'll be well down and grunty for it at home, they'll fancy they'll do a bit of giant-killing".

"Are we living in a fairy tale, Best", Clara asked critically.

"Erm, no Boss, sorry. What I meant to say was they will have great motivation to beat a team from the best league and it will not be an easy game".

"What about the rest of the comp-draw, any interesting confrontations"?

Best reeled them off, "Polski Węgiel the Third Division outfit have a home draw against Tiptingle Foods, Castle Electronics versus Goosetimp Weapons, Preciometalic versus Deutsch Fahrzeuge Eingearbeitet, Zhōngguá Shāngpǐn versus Hornrunner Hornets, IYWIWSI versus Rolls Royce Scoriors. Makers-Guild versus Voleskip Pharmaceuticals and finally two of the Second Division teams have been drawn against one another, Bhaarateey Phaarm the Indian Farm Corporation and they are to play Ruski Kamień the Belarusian mineral outfit".

"Day after tomorrow"?

Best nodded, "Correct. Wednesday evening, kick-off at 19:15 hours".

"Right then this is what we do, against the Spanish Second-tier I expect *our* second-string players to be able to play out a victory. Get them training against the androids and throw Zinyama and Rachwalski in at the deep end. I will only bring on our better players if we seem to be doing badly".

"Risky, Boss".

"They have to get match experience somehow and this is an opportunity to take a few risks".

"Then I'm going to need a squad-sheet and a formation". "Against the Spanish, we will play four-four-two", Clara returned as she worked on her pad, here is your squad for our trip to Spain". Best whistled, "Our best players on the bench and two youngsters who......"."I know it's the second-best team we could field", Clara cut in, "But the Shield is a chance for them to get some experience and the bench is as strong as we can make it, any five of those six can be brought on if things go wrong. Now, go and work that eleven, I'm going to make a little house call to our ailing midfielder and see how his guts are"!

Orang-U-Can

6. Radband

13. Jennings 25. Zinyama 5. West 7. Ball

8. Wong   9. Sellers 11. Shivers 14 Wing

27. Rachwalski 10 Nero

1. Anderson

4. Burgenbower

19. Jenson

20. Lane

16. Flintham

23. Roxbrough

twelve   **The drive out** to Hardy's residence was silently conducted by the comp-driver. It gave Clara time to think which was not necessarily a good thing. She not only had the wayward midfielder on her mind but behind that the death of her mother. The fallout would inevitably be the social-media attention the resultant funeral would draw. She hoped it would not adversely affect the club. How the death of the current Manager's parent would do so was something the media boys would think up, they were like modern energy vampires, drawing on anyone and anything to feed their unquenchable desire for titillation and intrigue. The flitter dutifully hissed to a descent on the jetty of Hardy's lakereside. He lived in the area that global warming had turned into yet another lake and occupied one of the stilthouses that were springing up all over Manchester as a result. Flitters could traverse water as easily as the land of course, but could only land on a level and supportive terrain. That was why every stilthouse also boasted its landing jetty, from which little bridges would lead to nyloplanyon spiral stairways up to each property. Throwing her electrostatic hood to her waterproof poncho over her head, Clara climbed out the side hatch of the vehicle onto the slippery nyloplanyon boards of the jetty to '*Winnerville*'. She could rely on one thing, the lack of real imagination from a man who made his money professionally playing football and by the residences nomenclature, she knew she was at the right address. Her two shillin Dyson trainers gripped the wet and slippery steps as she ascended them two at a time. She thanked her Norns of good fortune that she had gone with the Dyson *Frogs*, for the suckers on the bottom insured a safe grip even on ice. Arriving at the apex of the spiralling ascent something made her hesitate and not thumb the request for entrance plate. If she was wanting to catch Hardy out, then a more clandestine approach was called for. From through a Velcroed slit in the poncho, she drew her padfon from a pocket in her boho smock top. The '*companion that you'll wonder how you ever did without it'*, has an array of *fly's eyes* camera lenses on the reverse and could digitally tri-vidz for an hour on one charge of it cool-fusion battery. Clara ignored the front door and instead slipped around the front elevation to access the first-landing-board or mezzanine to the side of the property. She doubted that Hardy was the sort who bothered to opaque the windows for privacy when in a stilthouse and nets and blinds were by then nothing other than curious antiques. The type that most people did not bother to employ even those who lived on dry land. The first window she encountered was to a utility room. It revealed the usual home laundry device, hypo-wave, freezer and food storage units. The next room was a second bedroom, complete with android pleasure model (blonde 36E) orgasmatron booth, Arnold Stallone workbench and sauna tub. Clara moved on. Next came the lounge, boasting 9.1 stix player, tri-vidz two two-seater sofas and two recliner fat-tard chairs. Clara was beginning to wonder what Hardy could keep on his second-floor as she took the steps up to the it. On the stilthouse the second-landing-board or upper mezzanine surrounded the property. The nursery was empty naturally, as was the two bedrooms set aside for issue. There was only one bedroom left to look into, the master bedroom and that was where Clara hit pay-dirt. Inside she saw at a glance a couple on a huge emperor-size bed, in the act of undressing one another. Clara ducked out of sight but aimed the lenses of her padfon into the bottom left-hand corner of the transparent glass.

A quarter on an hour later she was back in her flitter and activating playback on the 400mm screen of her *'handy little electro-chum'*. Feeling like a voyeur she was never-the-less intrigued to see who it was who Hardy was risking his future with the club for. She could not deny the vicarious thrill of seeing her midfielder unclip the girl's brassiere with one deft snap that she momentarily found impressive. She had endured various fumblings in her time and usually ended up slapping the offending hands away and unclipping the back-loaders herself. The girl had started on the floor of all places, gazing almost directly out of the window, but her eyes unfocussed day-dreaming. Of one thing, Clara could be certain, she would know the bracelet she wore if she saw it again, for it was a limited edition silver and ruby cubed design by the french designer Grenouille Feuilletée, a snip at two silver shillin. She had also been wearing ankle strap high heels by the Italian shoe giant Soffiosenza Locumenti. Her low cut black jumpsuit had been a Teurer Mist from Germany. Once they had been removed she had black brassiere and pants by the Portuguese underwear giant Mama Bunda. Clara could not discern who had designed the girl's breasts but she doubted they would have been inexpensive either. Hardy seemed to suck them with vigorous enthusiasm so he seemed satisfied enough. Clara noted the black hair chiselled nose and slim waist and could not quite dispel the notion that she had seen the girl somewhere before. One thing was certain. Hardy was not feeling umpty. Judging by the amount of energy he put into this thrusting pumps he was feeling energetic in the extremis. It did not matter who the girl was, the midfielder was in deep trouble. On a whim, she pinged his e-address and after letting it ping for several moments the padfon connected on Sound only.

"Hello, Boss", Hardy gasped.

"You sound out of breath", Clara noted sarcastically, "Obviously still in pain, or strained in some way"?

"Yes, it's still giving me a hard time".

"Yes I can tell something is hard, all right, hardy you stay in bed and I will ping you again tomorrow".

"Oh, I think it's only a twenty-four-hour thing, Boss".

Clara grimaced, the best she had ever managed was eighty minutes!

thirteen   **When she got** back to her office Best was waiting for her.

"Well"? He enquired instantly, "Did you find anything out"?

Clara nodded grimly, held her padfon out to the Assistant Manager and asked, "Do you recognise the girl, I seem to think I've seen her before but cannot quite place where"?

Best dutifully looked at the miniature image of the two naked bodies writhing on the Emperor bed, his eyebrows went up and then he did a quick double-take and his normally ruddy glow drained of colour,

"Oh! It is worse than we think"!

"Really"?! Clara was sardonic. "Worse than one of our better players missing training to butter some dolly-bird's muffin. How much worse can it get, George"?

"I'm 100% certain that the girl he's stuffing is none other than Mrs Taibah Jennings".

"Cripes"! Clara was suddenly able to remember where she had seen Taibah several years in the past. It was at a celebration dinner for the team when they had won the league last. She had been with Jennings, at that point Hardy had not been signed for them.

"What are we going to do"? Best wanted to know.

"I'll see Hardy in this office tomorrow morning", Clara decided, "And he'll receive an ultimatum, drop the woman or he goes on the transfer list, no matter how good a player he is".

"And what are you going to do about Jennings"?

"Nothing", Clara decided, "I'm not a contract guidance counsellor, George. It would probably be better if he never finds out. Who knows, if Hardy dumps his Mrs maybe she'll go back to him and make the best of it until the contract expires".

"I think you should talk to her", Best advised, "Warn her we know what's going on, warn her to leave the rest of the squad alone, she might fancy a *transfer* if we put her on the *list"*.

It was a valid point, the two of them certainly did not want the situation to be repeated, Clara responded,

"Let me think about that one. Now, if there is nothing else I would like to.....".

"Your appointment with Ruudt Vanarkel of Gecreëerde Oppervlakken Beperkt is in about thirty minutes"!

Clara dredged the appointment from her memory, "The Dutch manufacturer of synthetic surfaces, they have a new type of pitch to tell us about"?

Best nodded, "We would be one of the first teams in the whole world to lay it, but it won't be cheap".

"I need a bite and a quick lichen-coff before Mister Vanarkel gets here then", Clara decided, "Once I've seen him, I need to get home, some ah, family business".

She went to the staff canteen and ordered some powdered eggs and a lichen-spud washed them down with a cup of planktocof and then returned to her office just in time to meet the simultaneously arriving Dutchman. Ruudt Vanarkel was a handsome man if you liked that sort of thing. He had undergone so much enhancement that his skin had taken that semi-translucent quality when it is stretched to almost breaking point. His eyes had become slit, like an oriental and Clara wondered if he had to shave the back of his neck, where his sideboards would probably be. He went shaven or had taken permanent depilatory chemicals and additionally he was tonsured. He reminded Clara of a character from an ancient puppet show her father had shown her when she was a child and still found even two dimensions wonderful. The show had been called *Thunderbirds* and the character had been the *Hood*. Clara's smile was therefore partly in polite greeting but also partly because a thought that had just occurred to her had amused her. She half expected Vanarkel's eyes to suddenly glow into life with malign power.

"Miss Trentavoria", the Hood/Vanarkel boomed at her in greeting. "How are you, dear Lady and how is your father"?

"You know Hugh"?

"But of course, every successful businessman in the system knows Hugh Trentavoria, a giant in the realm of Corporations".

"Quite. So now the name dropping and toadying is done with, tell me about your latest grass, Mister Vanarkel"?

Vanarkel laughed nervously at Clara's brusqueness to the point of discourtesy and he was forced to observe,

"I was warned that you might take some convincing. Thusly what I have done is bring a strip of the stuff to layout on your pitch for a very graphic demonstration. Can we go down to it via my flitter, please"?

"We can and that is more like it, Mister Vanarkel".

"Ruudt please and before we go any further I have two seats reserved at the Royal Hawksmoor for 20:00 this evening. I would be honoured if you are free to accompany me. I can promise you the very best genuine bovine beef, organic spirulina, King Edward potatoes if you agreed to be my partner for the evening"?

Clara liked food. She liked food quite a bit and the menu practically made her mouth drool, she asked, intrigued,

"What puddings do they do"?

"Only Manchester Toffee Pudding! Could I pick you up at say 17:00 at your Estate"?

"Dinner is dinner right, Ruudt"?

"Of course, what do you infer Miss Trentavoria"?

"That I'm not the sort of girl who drops her drawers for a splendid meal".

Vanarkel went as red as a beat, before returning, "You are as direct as everyone told me you would be. Let me put your mind at rest, Miss Trentavoria. I like to be seen about in the company of beautiful women, but that is very often as far as it goes and as far as I want it to go. Dinner, as you say, is dinner and that is all. I must also add that even if I do not convince you of the superb performance benefits of installing our product, I would still like the pleasure of your company this evening".

"17:00 it is then".

They had descended to the flitter in question a very nice Lindeman 120 bhp Vrouwelijk Beroep.

"Nice vehicle", Clara enthused genuinely while Vanarkel removed a huge roll of something from the boot. The roll was encased in neoprenelon with a looped handle on one side. Vanarkel lifted it out of the flitter as though it weighed practically nothing. Seeing the surprise registering on her face, he explained,

"I'm not freakishly strong, Miss Trentavoria, the new *Grasprestaties* is very light due to its very low statically charged carbon fibre filament-al blanket into which each blade of nyloprastic green filaments is woven individually. When sliding or landing on it, it will feel less abrasive than the real thing, which as you know is cellulose. Incredibly though nyloprastic is ninety-seven times stronger and more durable than actual grass and we are so confident of that figure that we are offering you a twenty-year warranty against ripping, tearing or holing provided we are allowed to prepare the foundation and lay the product ourselves".

They had reached the pitch and the youth team were still finishing some P.T. Clara shouted over the first two youths she recognised. One was a black lad with an insanely large nose, that for some reason he had never had corrected, his name was Radford. The other was white with an insane Mohawk haircut - Sanedad. Before getting them to roll out the strip of Grasprestaties, Clara took the opportunity to speak to each of them,

"Sanedad, grow that out and do not have it cut like that again if you want to stay at OUCH", she told him in all seriousness, "Radford get that hooter reduced, it's not even a paying rectification, you can have it done on insurance. Now get this item out of it's packing and unrolled onto the pitch".

The rest of the academy started to gather around wondering quite what was going on. When it was unrolled it then surprisingly unfolded twice to be four times the width Clara had expected.

"It's pretty thin isn't it"? She observed to Vanarkel.

The Dutchman beamed his affirmative, replying, "Yes, but extremely well bonded on a molecular level. Pick the edge up and try and tear it".

"I will find it impossible or you would not have suggested I try", Clara deduced, "Radford, Sanedad, try and rip it with your studs".

They tried. They tried with energy – they failed.

Vanarkel then suggested, "If both of you get a ball, Gentlemen................Good now when I say now both of you kick it and try to kick it as hard as you can. Mister Radford, on the pitch there, Mister Sanedad on the Grasprestaties. Ready boys, right....NOW"!

The boys gave each ball a low powerful shot. Vanarkel pointed out to Clara. "You see how the ball on the Grasprestaties moved far quicker and reached the end of its run well before the pseudo-grass. That is because unlike the latter it does not suffer from a static charge, it will be the fastest pitch you can ever play on".

"But faster for both sides so where is the advantage to ourselves"? Clara wanted to know.

"You will train on it, get used to it your players will pass according to the qualities of the surface after a few times on it. The away team will overhit every pass until at least half time, by then you should have scored a lead that you can hopefully defend in the second half".

"Until they get Grasprestaties too".

"Which according to their responses will not be until it is too late for this season for certain. Not all of them have the corporate might of OUC even then. you may have a home advantage for several seasons. By that time we will have developed Grasprestaties II and the entire catch-up process will start again".

"I want these boys to try it for twenty minutes, then if they are certain it does what you claim, you and I will retire to my office".

Vanarkel nodded happily, he seemed very secure in his product and with good reason. Time and again the boys overhit the ball, it was the fastest surface they had ever played on. They tried sliding tackles too and not one burn was sustained as a result. The youngsters gave the Grasprestaties a resounding thumbs up.

"Gather round boys and tell me what you think"? Clara asked feeling like a school Ma'am until one of them said under his breath,

"I think you're well worth one", the boys tittered like girls and Clara chose not to have heard it. She questioned them for ten minutes before turning to Vanarkel,

"My office"? she smiled, were upon the same voice said just loud enough for her to here,

"Can I come to your office some time"?

"When you are a man", she said to them all and they dissolved into childish hysterics.

The instant she was behind her desk, she asked without any preamble what-so-ever, "So, Ruudt, what is the lowest possible figure you can lay that stuff onto my pitch for".

"Ten silver shillin".

Even Clara was taken aback by the sum. She told him, "I'll see you tonight then, we cannot do business".

"Just like that"!

"Just like that, I was expecting "One or two maybe even five-hundred-thousand shillin, but silver shillin, it is beyond the capabilities of this club".

"I doubt that but let me see what I can do", Vanarkel requested and the hagglementization had begun. He made a show of entering figures into his padfon when both of them knew he had a very firm idea of what he would eventually take. It was part of the game though and Clara let him play it out. He looked up and gave her a toothy grin and informed gaily,

"I can let you have a 50% discount on the price if you can pay by direct thumb".

"50% off of what"?

That made him blink, "Off the MRP, so I can get the price down to five silver shillin".

"MRP, that's science fiction and you know it? No one ever paid MRP for anything.... Never. No deal".

"I've given you 50% off and if I give you any more I'll lose my job", Vanarkel tried his best to inject sincerity into his voice.

Five-hundred-thousand shillin is what is on the table", Clara told him flatly.

"Please be reasonable, Miss Trentavoria, that's only five percent of MRP"!

"And I have never paid manufactured rip-off price for anything and never will, good day, Ruudt, see you this evening".

Vanarkel got up and said gracefully, "I will ping my boss as soon as I'm in the flitter and see if there is anything he can do. There may be some conditions if I can get any more discount though".

"You can put your moving signage around the ground of the team who is going to win the league and I want twenty-four months interest-free credit on any price you come up with", Clara offered

"And we can sponsor your shirts"? Vanarkel tried.

"Second and third choice strip, my father would never let anyone other than himself sponsor the orange kit. See what you can do Ruudt".

The Hood nodded and was gone. Clara sighed, now to go home and find out how the investigation into the murder of her estranged mother was proceeding.

fourteen   **When Clara let** herself into the estate, the first person she encountered was Torm Drifield. He arose from the entrance hall chair and told her urgently,

"The newest fuzz is here to interview you, he's in the morning room".

"It's afternoon", Clara observed sarcastically. "I presume you got a name"?

"Inspector Snelling, it seems his friends call him Snapper".

"Then I will call him Snelling", Clara returned sweetly, she walked past her former bedfellow and straight into the morning room without preamble, it was her house, not his. At her abrupt intrusion, DI Snelling seemed to start, but recovering his composure he rose to his feet and offered her his hand,

"Miss Trentavoria, DI Snelling, but most people call me Snapper".

"I won't, Inspector", Clara returned curtly, "You see I'm an adult".

"Yes I know you are, Miss Trentavoria", Snelling was at an immediate lingual disadvantage which was something Clara was very good at imposing upon who-ever she spoke to, "It's a nick-name".

"I fully understand", Clara smiled icily, "I had one in the playground when I was five. I understand you wanted to interrogate me".

"Not interrogate, Miss Trentavoria", Snelling tried to be pleasant, "Just ask a few questions".

"Interrogate, verb (used with object), to ask questions of (a person), sometimes to seek answers or information that the person questioned considers personal, to examine by questions; question formally: The Inspector interrogated the suspect". Clara supplied.

"I see you know your English", Snelling smiled thinly.

"One of my degrees is in English Literature and Language Inspector. 'This life, which had been the tomb of his virtue and his honour, is but a walking shadow; a poor player, that struts and frets his hour upon the stage, and then is heard no more: it is a tale told by an idiot, full of sound and fury, signifying nothing' ".

"You are quoting someone or is that your conviction"?

"Has the interrogation begun"?

"If you like, please be seated".

Clara dutifully seated herself as Snelling asked her, "I want to know who your Mother's enemies were and please do not say she had none, being as she was murdered".

"Then you do not suspect my Father or myself".

"I think", the Inspector began, "It would be incredibly foolish of either of you to kill her when she was a guest in this house and you do not strike me as foolish people. On the other hand, neither do you seem dreadfully upset at her demise, unlike your father".

"I did not like her", Clara responded candidly, "But I did not dislike her enough to extinguish her life and whoever did, obviously felt a deeper loathing for her than myself".

"Neither of you profits from her death financially either", it was a statement rather than a question, Obviously Snelling had learned a great deal from Hugh.

"She was a drain on resources of every sort both monetary and emotionally. Again not to such a degree as to contemplate murder".

"I believe the murder weapon was brought into the property last night, it was a Brazilian Flittairforce Dagger".

"And my mother's last lover was from Brazil".

Snelling nodded. "Not indication enough in itself to be conclusive as both you and your father knew that Loreejæ had been in a recent liaison with Ramone Ramires. Unfortunately, I have no jurisdiction in Brazil".

"Then you will need to involve the cooperation of the Brazilian combmen - will you not"?

"I do not have enough evidence to merit doing so. The knife was Brazilian, but there was only your mother's DNA on it. The connection between the dagger and Ramires is tenuous as I have said".

"What you are telling me is that within twenty-four hours the case has become cold. Will go into your records as an open file, but that will, in essence, be the end of it".

"And that is why I apologise to you, Miss Trentavoria and will now take my leave", the combman told her regretfully.

Clara was both disappointed. Disappointed, but pleased to show him to the door. When he had gone she went to take an aqua-bath. She luxuriated by soaking in water rather than hurrying through a sonic shower. In the morning when the time was of the essence then the shower was swifter but she could not deny the feeling of being emersed in hot bubble-bath water. She was in a curious state of mind. Should she dress glamorously and hope to seduce Vanarkel into a better price? Or should she put the sort of clothing on she would wear to a business meeting and hope her natural charm did the rest? She was certainly not prepared to do the man to get a more reasonable deal. He struck her as faintly sinister and she was not even prepared to lie back and thing of Saxonia. So it was the black suit, white shirt and black bow-tie, but with droplet earrings and some delicate lilac lippy and flesh coloured blusher. Examining herself in her dressing table mirror, she decided she had enough natural (if augmented) health and pulchritudinous charm to win the Dutch-man over anyway. She was suddenly aware of a commotion coming from

Ianacho

downstairs and could hear several voices. She thought she recognised Gatson's but the sounds coming through the floor were not quite clear enough for her to determine who the others belonged to. As luck would have it she was ready to be picked up and there was always the outside possibility that Vanarkel had arrived unfashionably early for her. She drifted downstairs, who she saw in the hallway caused her to teeth to grind in frustration.

"Clara", burst out her sister Molly, Isn't it terrible about Mummikins"?

"Yeah", Clara managed in a bored tone, "Tragic".

Ianacho, Molly's husband was up the stairs and hugging Clara before she had chance to fend him off. There was the usual pervy groin grinding and Clara knew he secretly wanted to add a second sister to his conquests. As *Followers of the Divine Determination,* however, he could not act on his lustful desires even if Clara would have let him, not without passing out through the *Arch of Shame* and never being allowed into *Determination Hallows* ever again. For her part, Clara would rather have spent a night in bed with her murdered mother than let Ianacho anywhere near her.

"You don't sound especially upset", Molly noted as the two of them kissed the air beside one another's ears.

"I'm not", Clara admitted, "You know I never liked the bitch".

"Oh! Clara. How can you talk about her like that when she's not even cold in her grave"? Molly was putting in a good performance. It was a pity the woman had not left her anything of worth.

"She's not being buried", Clara was beginning to enjoy herself, "She's to be disintegrated in the moleculextirpater". [since the end of the 21st-century cremation had been abolished due to the carbon footprint. The moleculextirpater reduced the corpses chemicals down to its constituent parts that could be made use of by Ghoul.Inc. The corporation was responsible for creating items like fertilizer, cleaning products and toothpaste from the molecules of the deceased].

"You are not charitable talking of the recently deceased in such an off-hand way, Clara". Molly scolded, glancing at *touchy-feely* who simply shrugged.

'Probably would like to give me a good, hard admonishing the dirty grunty, Clara thought. Instead, she said, "Well I'm not divinely determined like you am I, Sister dear"?

"You do that to me every time", Molly squealed, "We are the followers of the divine who were determined, we are not divine ourselves, you blaspheme on purpose just to annoy Achy and me".

"I'm sorry, Molly, I forgot my broomstick so I don't know the correct way of addressing the superstitious. Should I call you, Molly, Sister or Your Witchiness"?

From outside she heard a flitter horn sound and realised her lift had arrived.

"I have to go", she told the newcomers to the estate, "I'm sure Gatson will look after you, I'm certain Hugh must have invited you"?

Molly railed, "Why must you call Daddy, Hugh"?

"Because I'm not six", Clara observed, "Now please remove your carcase from between me and the door, I would like to leave this delightful soiree and go and do something pleasantly entertaining".

"You're going *out*! Mummy only twenty-four hours heinously slain and you're going out"!

"I know I am, now shift your ass, will you"? Clara was already sick of the sight of her cloying phoney sister and there was another one to come, not to mention her four brothers.

"How can you go out and enjoy yourself at a time like this"? Molly demanded deeply shocked or perhaps playing her anguish to perfection.

"If you want to weep and moan and tear frantically at your sackcloth and ashes go right ahead", Clara observed, "Meanwhile I am going out on a business meeting, not that it's any of your concern. Now for the last time do I have to ask you again to move or do I use Wadō-ryū"?

Wadō-ryū (和道流) was one of the four major karate styles and was founded by Hironori Otsuka (19th to 20th C). The style itself, individual in its emphasis on not just striking, but *Tai sabaki*, joint locks and throws. The name *Wadō-ryū* had three parts: *Wa*, *dō*, and *ryū*. *Wa* meaning "harmony," *dō* (same character as tao) meant "way," and *ryū* - "school" or "style". Harmony was not to be interpreted as pacifism; simply the acknowledgement that yielding was sometimes more effective than brute strength. From one point of view, Wadō-ryū was sometimes considered a style of jūjutsu rather than karate. Clara was a brown-belt in the discipline and could look after herself against almost anyone. Molly tutted and moved.

Vanarkel

The air was cold and damp as she skipped toward the Dutchman's luxury flitter. Suddenly realising she could not get into the passenger side, as Vanarkel had slid into it, having promised to let her drive. Pleased she slid into the right-hand side of the Lindeman 120 bhp Vrouwelijk Beroep.

"Good evening, Clara" Vanarkel smiled, "Before you start the capacitor, I would like to get business out of the way. I have a deal for you that I think may even surprise one as deft at negotiation as yourself".

Clara turned to him and smiled, "Go on".

"You asked for a ridiculously low price of five-hundred-thousand shillin at zero percent finance on twenty-four-month payments, signage around the ground and sponsorship of the second and third choice strips, presumably for this season. There was no way I could do that but this is what I got my boss down to before he threatened to sack my sorry ass. One million shillin, one silver shillin in other words, over three years at five percent, signage for two seasons and sponsorship of second and third choice strips for four seasons. There is no further room for manoeuvre, Clara I give you my word on that. It amounts to an incredible offer, even *I* did not think I could get the price so low"!

Clara smiled, "You have done very well Ruudt. Let's go and eat, the offer is acceptable".

Clara thumbed the ignition and the beast in the boot sprang to life. She switched over to manual and the experience was very good but not a great deal more so than her flitter which was considerably less expensive. She felt sorry for the peasants who could only afford manual flitters that had very little reliability. The Original Omsaccs had all been recalled after Osto Marigraine Saccharine had been found guilty of dangerous cost-cutting in the manufacture and the four explosions had resulted in fatalities. Saccharine himself had been stripped of his knighthood and after two unsuccessful appeals in the tower, had been beheaded in the first public execution in Saxonia in over three weeks.

Despite all that some peasants still drove the checked Omsaccs and Saccahrine's eldest son had refitted the factory in Burma and continued to develop the successor which was called rather imaginatively the Omsacc II. Onslo Margarine Saccharine was not his father and the Omsacc name lived on, but they were still the butt of several stand-up comedians in Wales, where having sex with sheep had finally been declared unlawful by the independent parliament. The Royal Hawksmoor was packed to the veritable rafters, always booked up every night in Manchester as it was the only place one could get genuine bovine beef, organic spirulina and King Edward potatoes. There had been many protests by the RSPC (Royal Society for the Protection of Cattle) but the fact of the matter was that nothing tasted quite as tasty as the real thing. Soyabeef and lichenbeef were substitutes and the human taste-bud *coula* tell the difference. Similarly planktospirulina and lichenspirulina were not quite as delicious as the real deal. Spirulina is among the world's most popular supplements. Spirulina had become the world most popular green, it was loaded with various nutrients and antioxidants that benefited body and brain. High in many nutrients, It was an organism that grew in both fresh and saltwater. A type of cyanobacteria, from a family of single-celled microbes, that many referred to as blue-green algae. Spirulina was originally consumed by the ancient Aztecs but became popular again when NASA proposed that it could be grown in space for use by astronauts. A standard daily dose of spirulina was 10g and when spiced genetically by the famed geneticist Hoyle - with the cabbage family became the green of choice for most, a meal of spirulina contained:

- Protein: 4 grams
- Vitamin B1 (thiamine): 11% of the RDA
- Vitamin B2 (riboflavin): 15% of the RDA
- Vitamin B3 (niacin): 4% of the RDA
- Copper: 21% of the RDA
- Iron: 11% of the RDA
- It also contained decent amounts of magnesium, potassium and manganese and small amounts of almost every other nutrient that the human body needed.
- Additionally, the same amount held only 20 calories and 1.7 grams of digestible carbs.

Gram for gram, spirulina was the single most nutritional food in the system. Clara liked it, some picky people claimed it tasted too irony, but they were in a great minority. The staff of the Royal Hawksmoor were efficient, polite and very quick which all served to make the meal more memorable. If clientele requested time to come to a decision, they were given it, but when ready to order a waiter could be at a diners elbow almost instantly. The reason was obvious, the staff were all U940820 androids from IYWIWSI, and their subsidiary company Indian Androidova. Not so the cooks, or the manager, where human decision making was necessary, but waiting tables did not require such cognitive skill sets.

"That was everything you promised it would be, thank you", Clara said as Vanarkel was thumbing the payment plate on the table.

"While the pleasure for my part was the admiring glances I drew from other diners for being in the place with one of the most beautiful women. My men can start laying the new surface tomorrow early unless you are at home in the Shield"?

"No, we are away to a second division Spanish Corporation".

"Ah, Corporación Española de Frutas. Unless I am very much mistaken they will be in the top division next season, a dangerous side, watch out for their striker – Perez".

fifteen   **Sean Derek Charles** was listening to a bit of Mozart when his padfon pinged, it was an incoming call on voice only, usually an indication that he was wanted for some *wet work*. Regretfully he cut the volume on his 9.1 stix-player and activated the fon.

"Yes"? It was all he ever said when answering, Most of his clients did not know where he was, what his name was, who he was.

"This is the Faded Man", began the electronically disguised voice. "I have another assignment for you if you can take it"?

Sean was not busy and even if he had been the Faded Man had paid him well over his going rate for the first *sanction*.

Sean was tacit but concise, "Details"?

The Faded Man was used to his style having already engaged him previously so after the briefest of pauses, he reeled off a name and some details. As he was doing so the image of the sanction appeared on his screen and with a screenshot, Sean immediately captured it. He said nothing, the profile of the sanction was of only passing interest to him. Had the sanction even been King Darren XXIII only the price would have changed, Sean had never shirked an assignment in his brilliant and obscure career. The Faded Man gave Sean an address, which was unusual, it would be an easy sanction.

"How much"? The Faded Man finally desired to know.

Sean Derek Charles gave that matter some thought and gave his most atypical answer to date, "Two-hundred and fifty thousand plus expenses".

There was a pause at the other end of the link, then the Faded Man suddenly asked, "What sort of expenses, can you not incorporate it into your price"?

"I don't know yet how this one is going to be conducted, I may have to buy some equipment".

"You mean you may be able to make it look like an accident"?

"If that is a prerequisite, then it can be arranged"?

"Then do so", the Faded Man seemed delighted with the notion, "Make it look like an accident and your price is agreed, same deal as before 50% now, 50% upon successful completion of the elimination".

"Agreed, it will be done in twenty-four hours".

"Excellent".

The line went dead, the connection was cut, Sean said aloud, "And a very goodnight to you too, Matey".

He then turned the stix-player back up and returned to his Mozart.

sixteen   **Breaking into someone's** house was not the easy task it had been in the past. The burglary had practically been eliminated centuries ago. It was not just the fact that aggravated burglary was a capital offence, but also the level of technology the houses now boasted to either avoid break-in or to detect and record any intruder. Sean Derek Charles was, therefore, wearing a *mirrorsuit* when he approached the property. The incredibly expensive piece of equipment was only legally available to military special forces for Night and Covert Operations. Sean had managed to steal one from Brockhurst Barracks in South Yorkshire some years past. What the mirrorsuit did was effectively render the wearer invisible to cameras and other types of detections equipment such as laser motion sensors. All Sean had to do therefore was to get past the locks, either through a window or through the door. The door would have the most sophisticated lock by far, but Sean took pride in his work and he would never climb clumsily through a window when he could enter through the front door in some style. He turned on his x-ray vision goggles and saw at once that the lock was none other than a Frankenshaddrack TL5261. Any tampering of the wrong sort and a laser would fire from the lens above the lock and set into the durilite door and cut the intruder in two. The first order of business was to disarm the laser. Sean took a tube out of this dickie-bag and squeezed a small blob of nylomagnocite 9 onto the lens. He then retired to a safe distance closed his eyes and waited for the flare. Ten seconds later the oxygen in the air had made the preparation unstable and the resultant flare was 3.8×10^{28} lumens for approximately two seconds. The lens of the laser was fused to it's firing mechanism and the whole device was now US (useless scrap, not the Unwanted States). Sean went to work on the lock. Using his incredibly powerful hand drill he knew exactly where to drill the hole that would give him access to the wires leading to the trigger mechanism of the alarm that would send the alert to the local combmen station. The trick was not to drill too deeply and touch the wires, thus setting it off. Too shallow though and there would be no access to them. Years of experience had taught Sean exactly when to stop drilling. With his x-ray goggles, he located the wires paired back the insulation and connected two jump leads utilizing miniature crocodile clips. Then the wires could be cut and the feedback loop had eliminated the alarms ability to give an alert. A laser pistol then made short work of the latch assembly bolt and strike plate.

Sean was inside the sanction's property and knew he had only a few moments to act or be detected. At least that was what he always assumed and it was a maxim that had kept him in the business for several successful decades and without being detected a single time. He strode toward the utility room. There he found what he was searching for. The cold-fusion boiler for the property's heating system. Dropping his dickie-bag to the floor he pulled out the appropriate tools by feel alone and soon had the faceplate of the boiler off and began to make a swift adjustment to the unit. Within seconds he had changed the unit from a safe boiler into a bomb. The bomb needed a detonator. Replacing the cabinet of the former boiler he slipped back to the door and began to strip out the now useless lock and then replacing it with one that was the same age and make but with one vital difference. He had watched the sanction for several days before that one. He knew the comings and goings, he knew the Frankenshaddrack TL5261, he even had its serial number and had etched the same one onto the lock he was then swiftly installing into the door. Once it was in, a quick lick of swift-dry nyloplyonpaint and he closed and locked the door behind him. The next time the door was opened with the thumb plate, the action would arm the detonator. Once the door swung open more than a few degrees the timer would commence twenty-seconds later the detonator would send a signal to the bomb and the cold-fusion reactor would fracture. The resultant explosion would vaporise the house and maybe even the properties either side of it. That could not be helped and while regrettable to sanctions individuals for free, they were nothing more than collateral damage. The resultant investigation would only be able to come to one conclusion. Even the Voléra B23 with all of its safety factors still malfunctioned occasionally, cold fusion micro-piles could rupture and the result was always catastrophic. This latest failure would cost the company a great deal in compensation to relatives, but as before, Sean could not help that, it was none of his concern!

seventeen   **When they climbed** down the steps of the huge flitterjet and into the Spanish evening air, the rise in temperature brought a smile to all of them. They had left behind 4° C and the one that greeted them was 17° C. A flitterbus, hired by Best on the SWW was waiting for them once they passed through customs and it swiftly and expertly took them to the Corporación Española de Frutas Estadio. All was gold and red, the team itself played in gold shirts with red trim, red shorts and gold socks. This meant good news for Vanarkel who had just managed to deliver the all-white strip for the team that night. Third choice and on their very first game pressed into service. The only orange on the team that night would be the numbers on their backs. Clara made a point of sitting with the youngster Rachwalski.

"Are the nerves getting to you yet young-man"? She desired to know.

The youth shook his head telling her in his accented Standard, "Zinyama and I are both very grateful for this opportunity and will not let you down, Boss".

Clara was pleased with the mature response, nodding her approval, "You've watched the tri-vidz, we've gone over tactics, just go out tonight and enjoy the occasion then and I'm certain you will equip yourself well".

"I intend to play so well that I stay in the first squad for Saturday despite my youth", Rachwalski told her. A cloud suddenly passed over his features and Clara knew what he was then thinking about, she urged,

"Put it out of your mind, the combmen have declared it a freak accident. If anything, go out and play for his memory tonight".

"Freak accident makes it worse though doesn't it boss. If one can explode like that, killing Hardy, the four people either side of him and the three passers-by. Whoever manufactured that boiler wants stringing up for not taking sufficient care over quality control".

Clara argued, "Yet their safety protocols are very stringent, they have enjoyed a 100% safety rating before this. How well did you know Hardy anyway"?

"Not that well", the youth admitted, "I had not seen him at all recently. He seemed to train and then scoot off the minute he was done. The rest of the lads said he was a decent sort though".

I bet they'd soon change their tune if they knew he was tupping Jenning's missus', Clara thought, but said no more about it. It seemed the problem had gone away and maybe it never would come to light what had been going on. She hoped so, Jennings was a worthy member of the squad and was even playing on the right side of the two centre-backs that very evening. It was time to concentrate on the job in hand. The ambience of the stadium was one of great excitement and it seemed the supporters of the Spanish outfit fancied the match could very possibly go their way. Clara took another look at the players she had and began her pre-match talk,

"The Spaniards are fancied to top their league and gain promotion this year, so tonight is not going to be an easy fixture. I have given most of you a chance to show me what you can do for Orang-U-Can. Try not to let me down. If you make an unavoidable mistake, you are only human, but what will disappoint me is if I see anyone on the pitch coasting. I want you to give your all! Do that, impress me sufficiently and you might well find you have earned your place in the first eleven for Saturday. All right, go out there and show the opposition that there is a gulf between Division One and Division Two even if we field our reserve eleven"!.

The players nodded, Clara had not chosen to shout and her words had been just as effective quietly spoken. Ten minutes later she was in the dugout with Charmley and Whohouse. She activated her cranial implant and asked the players to throw up their arms if they could hear her, everyone except Sellers did so. He could see the others were acknowledging a signal he could not receive. Cursing under his breath Whohouse raced onto the pitch with a replacement plug for the forward midfielder. If it was the implant itself they were in trouble, it could not be fixed except on an operating table. Thankfully Clara suddenly heard Seller's voice in her ear,

"I'm getting the other players now, Boss, it was my bud that was US".The comp-ref showed four minutes to kick-off. OUC took up their positions after two, Clara was most intrigued to see how Rachwalski and Zinyama would do. The other players though not first choice were not much behind those who had the first eleven positions. Indeed once suspensions and injuries started to take their toll as they inevitably would as the season wore on, some of them would be in the first team anyway. There was a blast from the big screen and the game had begun. Both sides went at the opposition at a frantic pace. The player Clara had been warned about, Perez struck an early shot which Radband turned around his left-hand post with a superb diving save. It was good to see the second eleven goalkeeper do so well, but the result was an early corner for the Spaniards. Fortunately Zinyama and West both had a rather significant height advantage over the Corporación Española de Frutas players and West headed the in swinging cross away with ease. Crisis over, the team certainly did not want to concede an early goal. The pace slackened slightly, the initial speed could not possibly have been maintained for ninety-minutes. As it did so though it coincided with the period in the game where the two youngsters began to grow in confidence and to find their feet. Zinyama proved to be a rock in defence, time and again cutting out the Spanish attacks, starving Perez of game time by cutting out passes intended for him. Rachwalski for his part proved to be lightning-quick and just needed a bit more skill on the end of it to trouble the Spanish. He was the equal of Nero in every way and Clara was gratified to see a partnership developing between them that was almost the equal of Lane and Roxbrough. She mused on the possibility of squeezing both into a very attack-minded squad. After thirty-five minutes Orang-U-Can began to slowly dominate more and more of the play and finally when the whistle was sounded by the comp-ref at half time, the Frutas were pleased to go in still on even terms.

"What do you want to do, Boss", best demanded, "Bring on Roxbrough, or Jensen, or maybe use three of your five substitutions".

"I think I'm going to give them a little longer", Clara decided. "They are improving as time goes on and a single goal might decide this tie".

"What if the Frutas get it though, Perez only needs a sniff and he could well take full advantage of a good chance"?

"Radband has pulled off three real quality saves this half. Unless anything happens to change my mind, I think he's earned the right to push Anderson out of the first-choice for a keeper. I'm going to let them have a bit longer".

She could see by the look on Best's face that he did not agree, but Clara was the Manager and also held the purse strings, so he held his peace. The game resumed and the pattern was very much as it had been before the interval. Until Zinyama robbed one of the Frutas and slipped a really strong pass forward for Wong to run onto, as he reached it the Frutas defence was bearing down on him but a totally unexpected chip passed over his tormentor's head and with a diving header Rachwalski suddenly managed to somehow slip the ball beneath the Spanish goalkeeper's diving body. The goal stunned the crowd to a dreadful hush. They knew the team they were watching beating their first team was filled with substitutes and two youngsters and yet they had gone behind. It was the point in the game at s which all the spirit went out of the Spanish. Clara then made a double substitution, bringing both the goalscorer and Nero off and putting on Burgenbower and Jensen. The notion was to defend their lead until full time, the formation

Last 16 Corporation Shield		
Corporación Española de Frutas v OUC	0	1
Polski Węgiel v Tiptingle Foods	2	1
Castle Electronics v Goosetimp Weapons,	3	0
Preciometalic v Deutsch Fahrzeuge Eingearbeitet	0	2
Zhôngguá Shāngpĭn versus Hornrunner Hornets	3	1
IYWIWSI versus Rolls Royce Scoriors	5p	4p
Makers-Guild versus Voleskip Pharmaceuticals	2	0
Bhaarateey Phaarm v Ruski Kamień	0	2

changed from 4-4-2 to 4-5-1 with only Wong staying upfield. Orang-U-Can had a complete stranglehold on the midfield and cruised to an away victory and the quarter-finals of the Corporations Shield. That night saw the results:

All games had been settled that night even though IYIWISI and Rolls Royce Scoriors had been drawing at the end of full time and had settled the tie with penalties. If You Want It We Stock It had surprised the pundits by beating the fancied Scoriors from the penalty spot.

eighteen   **Clara arrived home** in the early hours to find
the place a hive of activity, the very last thing she would have wanted in
fact. She was exhausted from the flight and game and all she wanted to do
was collapse into bed. Unfortunately Grendlyme her eldest sister had
arrived while she had been abroading. Not only that but her second to
youngest brother too – Lavvisto. Together with their partners Critard and
Bunjella respectively, they were in the lounge, they were very loud and they
were very drunken. Gatson opened the door to let her in with a tired and
concerned look on his normally calm features. It was 03:22 and the party
did not look like ending any time soon.
"What time did they start", Clara sighed.
"16:00 Miss Clara", the butler told her. His voice was as fatigued as every
other visible part of him.
"Did Lavvisto bring his own or has he raided Father's cellar"?
Lavvisto was an alcoholic and was in and out of rehab as often as Bunjella
could afford to pay the clinic fees. As a merchant banker, she was the
bread-winner of the couple, and she had *dried out* her husband many times
and did not seem to mind doing so. For his part, the once quite presentable
brother of the Manager of OUC had become a bloated, fat loafer who was
killing himself one bottle at a time. He was already on his third liver and
doctors had told him that was the legal number anyone was allowed. It took
time to grow them from stem cells and they were not readily available nor
inexpensive. It was a good job the dreadfully plain Bunjella was still very
flattered to have a Trentavoria for a husband.
By contrast, Grendlyme was a stick insect with tits. She had a shock of
straw-like badly bleached hair, teeth that barely fit in her sucked in cheeks
and only maintained her waif-like appearance with the liberal use of
laxatives and stuffing her fingers down her throat to bring up anything solid
that ever passed her lips.
"What a frenging family", Clara moaned as she walked in on the drunken
revellers. At that in addition to her superstitious sister she also had three
other brothers. Ganders was the oldest, senior of all seven of them and he
was an egomaniac. He thought he knew everything and was often caught
out, but no matter how many times he was he maintained his superior airs
and no one could tell him much of anything. Then there was the youngest
brother and youngest of all seven – Juniporl. He whom Hugh had disowned
for being a queer. Homosexuality had recently lost favour with the
fashionable elite and was then actually considered something to be
ashamed of especially after the 30th century when CLAP [Combined Lassa
Acanthamoeba Plague] had swept through the queer community
devastating their numbers. Also, know as the homobonic, it had scythed its
way through millions around the world at that time. Symptoms were:
headache, sore throat, muscle pain, chest pain, nausea, vomiting,
diarrhoea, cough, abdominal pain and eventual blindness followed by
death. Protein was noted in the urine causing; shock, seizures, tremor,
disorientation, and coma. It was estimated that between 2 and 5% of

patients who survived the disease would possibly regain their sight, but only if the medication was used in the first 14 days of contraction. The bacilli lived in the anus and stool and were therefore only contracted by queers and perverted heterosexuals.

Of course, superstition had jumped on the bandwagon and declared the outbreak of CLAP as a visitation of the devil and they used the slogan, *'They who go up Satan's Alley go to their Doom'.* It was extremely unlikely therefore that Juniporl would be attending the funeral. That just left Leret, who had fled to Africa, destination unknown to escape the obesity laws. He had tipped the scales into the unlawful zone and would have been forced to have some part of his anatomy removed to reduce to the required maximum weight allowed by Saxonia law. To exceed it meant the removal of body parts until the weight was reduced accordingly. Leret was a greedy hog and knew he was approaching unlawfulness and had thusly fled justice and disappeared into the dark region of the forgotten continent.

It was not possible to say that the Trentavoria family were typical of those living in the system at the time. The Venuser had almost been wiped out by the third round of phleege. The Hermean of Mercury were either convicts or wardens, for the rock closest to Sol was a high-security Correctional Facility buried under several hundred feet of searing rock. The Martians were xenophobic and embittered by their frigid weather. Of all mankind in the system, only the Calliston seemed to be emotionally and morally stable. Perhaps it was their sheer physical distance from the rest of mankind that was their saving grace. So though not a typical family, the wealthiest family in the system were not so unusual as to be thought of as weird!

"I'm turning the light out in five minutes", Clara told her siblings and their partners. "Along with Father, this is my home and I don't want it filled with drunkards, so drain your glasses and frenge off to bed"!

"It's lovely to see you too, Clara", Grendlyme simpered insincerely.

Corporation Shield Quarter Finals

OUC v DFE
Zhōngguá Shāngpín v IYWIWSI
Castle Electronics v Polski Węgiel
Ruski Kamień v Makers-Guild

"No it isn't", Clara sighed, "We don't get on, never have done, never will, now drink up and get upstairs. Gatson looks exhausted and would like some sleep".

"He's only a frenging butler", Lavvisto slurred.

"He's mine and Father's butler and you are keeping him up. It's late, come on, some of us have to get up early for work in the morning. If you don't do as I demand You'll be woken up along with them in approximately four hours".

"You are a pain in the ass, Sis", Lavvisto slurred with mock dignity and promptly fell flat on his face on his way to the door.

"Get up and go to bed or that is precisely what you will get". Clara promised. Tapping his fat backside with the toe of her rather fashionable boots.

nineteen   "I am faced with the enviable dilemma of having to choose my first eleven from a squad who have all proved they can give me their best on the pitch on Saturday", Clara told them, huddled in her five seasons parka. "This week we are at home to Hornrunner Hornets and on our newly laid surface. So I want you all to train on it, show me what you can do on the best pitch in the league, you are fighting for first-team places. All right, go to it".

Two hours later she Best and Whohouse huddled around a desk-pad to watch the draw for the Shield Quarter Finals. They were all delighted to see the draw-comp randomly select Orang-U-Can first of the eight remaining teams. Once again they were to play Deutsch Fahrzeuge Eingearbeitet, the difference being that this time it would be on their home soil and that soil had just been laid with the latest in artificial grass technology. The rest of the drawer was up on the desk-pad in no time at all:

"All right back to work, Best, I want it obvious to me who our very strongest eleven will be by Saturday. We've only forty-eight hours to make certain our men are ready for the speed of the new grass".

Ironically as matters were going so well at the club, it could not be said of the domestic set-up in *Trentavoriana* however. That being the name Hugh had laughingly given to the estate on the edge of Manchester. Ganders arrived on Thursday morning along with his latest conquest the Francosian – Athdara-Adélaïde. Being from such poor genetic stock the girl was not exactly normal. She believed she could tell people's fortunes with lichen-tea leaves, tarot cards and crystals. She also was convinced ghosts and spirits existed in a realm beyond reality. She did seem to suit Ganders though, his eccentricities seemed to bring the mutually eccentric couple together. Lavvisto was not a good influence, his alcoholic ways were soon causing Grendlyme and Ganders to drink to excess and Clara found it annoying that they had soon drunk the cellar dry and were taking frequent trips to a local mall to get more fluid supplies.

Seeking her father out for the first long and serious talk they had engaged in since she had been given the football club, she joined Hugh in his private office.

"I cannot wait for the funeral so that we can return to some semblance of normality around here", she began.

Seeking to deflect her Hugh observed,

"You are doing great things at the club, Clara turning things around nicely. Do you think the firm has any real chance of recovering from that disastrous start and winning the league"?

"We'll see, now back to my wayward brothers and sisters. They have drunk every single bottle of your collection in the wine cellar, Father. Some of that stuff was vintage 32nd and they just swigged it like it was cheap vinegar. Does that not anger you? Every time they come here they descend on the place like a swarm of locusts".

"I love you most, there is no doubt about that Clara, but your siblings are also my other children to your Mother, surely you do not begrudge them a few bottles of the juice of the vine"?

"It isn't the wine, Father, Clara objected, lighting a med-cig to calm her fractured nerves. "It's the principal, they take and take and never give a thought to the owner, you"!

"And for my part, I do not mind. I have enough money that I could not spend it in three lifetimes, Clara, the wine can easily be replaced. I also have that other commodity man seems to finds so attractive and desirable – real power. Do you know the King was on our padfon again today asking me what to do about the gradually increasing crime rate, it went up 0.7% from last year and he thinks that such is a crisis"

"What did you tell him"? Clara was suddenly deflected from her reason for visiting her parent.

"What would you have told him"? Hugh asked with a smile.

"I would have reintroduced the birch and public floggings. Flog some sense into them, that's what the peasants need, Father".

"I suggested hypnotherapy and the right sort of medication", Hugh smiled. "Darren is going to consider my suggestion. Have you seen that combman you were interested in by the by? How is the investigation going"?

"Grelm, DI Snowd", Clara mused vaguely, "No I haven't. He was off the case anyway, Father. Replaced by someone called Snelling. They do not have a clue and they cannot go after Ramires".

Hugh shrugged, "That would appear to be that then, very upsetting but what can we do if there is no evidence. While I think on I wanted to say I was saddened to hear about Hardy, he was a good player at his best, seemed to have lost some form last season but I expected him to come back. I believe it will cost Voléra a pretty sestertius when all the cases have been heard by the high court. The B23 has been withdrawn from production now. Eight dead, it was terrible. A purring noise suddenly distracted Clara and she reached down and scratched Mr Chuffs behind the ear. The sound grew louder still and Clara fancied the floorboards of the room began to vibrate with the old cat's throat rumble.

"I have been thinking", she told her father finally, "That I would like a flat or apartment of my own, Father. Somewhere I could go at times like this when the house is noisy and I need my sleep to do my job properly".

"You want to leave me on my own"? Hugh response surprised the woman.

"Not especially, but I need somewhere to go when the place gets frantic, I cannot afford the distraction".

"I understand that so let's compromise", Hugh suggested, "I'll book you into a hotel while your brothers and sisters are here, you can get some rest and return when they are gone after the funeral. It's only for a few days"?

"Where were you thinking of booking"?

"The Gotham on King Street it's five-star"?

"All right, I'm going to pack though, Father I need a good nights sleep, starting tonight".

Hugh nodded, picking up his padfon, "Drop in to say when you are leaving then"?

Clara nodded, she could not wait to get away from her troublesome siblings.

twenty   **The Gotham was** well named, a huge towering beast of a building that loomed into the slowly darkening sky. The iconic former bank building had been upscaled into an art deco-style hotel centuries in the past and had been constantly maintained and improved ever since then. It was only a 6-minute walk from Piccadilly Gardens Flittrainlink Station and 0.5 miles from the Palace Theatre performance venue. Rooms were styled deliberately antiquitously featuring vintage decor and high ceilings, along with the ubiquitous tri-vidz and free SWW [solar-wide-web] connection. They also offered minibars and Lichencoffspresso machines. Suites came with separate sitting areas, some also had free-standing baths instead of sonic showers. Room service was reputed to be second to none, for those who could afford it. Amenities included a 16th-floor restaurant that served modern Saxonian cuisine. Guests also have access to a top-floor private bar/club/casino with terraces and sweeping city views. Clara pulled into the underground flitter park and was immediately met by an android who lifted her two pieces of designer luggage as though they were empty. She was conducted to reception where she signed in and was given access to her rooms the instant her thumbprint was recorded. She was shown to room 023 on the second floor. It was exactly what she would have chosen had she been able to design it herself and suited her mood perfectly. All was black and white, with far greater emphasis on the former. Lighting was subdued but the standard of the 33rd, furnishings and fittings was exemplary. Having the android place her bags on the bed and determining to unpack before retiring, she went straight to the restaurant.

It was not going to be easy to get a table when she was on her own, but suddenly as she was engineering said a voice she recognised remarked,

"Miss Trentavoria! This is a pleasant surprise. I have just secured a double table over by the window, promising a stunning urban view, would you like to join me"?

Clara turned and regarded the dashingly handsome Roxbrough, she asked as pleasantly as she could, "What are you doing in this hotel, Roxbrough, have you not yet found an apartment"?

"I have actually, but I enjoyed the cuisine so much here that I decided to dine here tonight".

"Your contractee could not make it over to Manchester".

"I'm not contracted, nor seeing anyone as it happens, so there is a spare seat. It would be rather weird if we both seated ourselves on our own at double tables, wouldn't it"?

Clara was forced to nod, admitting tacitly that such would indeed be the case. Roxbrough responded by holding out his arm and feeling very self-conscious indeed, she took it. Allowing him to lead her to the table in question and even pull out the chair and seat her.

"I recommend the Charred Cumbrian Charolais Beef", he said cheerfully, it comes with watercress, roast shallot, king oyster mushroom and glazed carrots".

"That does sound tempting", Clara admitted, "And will you be picking the wine too, Roxbrough"?

"I will be drinking water, I'm training remember".

"I will order that myself then, what are you planning for us to have for dessert"?

"Beetroot and raspberry parfait chocolate ganache".

"Wow, high-calorie stuff".

"Which I will run off on the Grasprestaties in the first half-hour".

Clara was impressed that Roxbrough had bothered to learn the name of the new surface, Most of the squad were referring to it as the *new grass.* Could it be that Roxbrough was that most rare of footballers, the *intelligent* footballer? Then she remembered that he was, being an engineer in addition to a sportsman. As they waited for the dinner to arrive, neither of them requiring starters, she asked,

"When your football career is over Roxbrough, what do you intend to do"?

"I will apply for a post in the company in engineering design, I have a few ideas for a turbo-air- flitter, it's the future of personal travel".

"The company"?

"Orang-U-Can, I live here in Manchester now, I figure OUC is my future".

"Interesting tell me something about an air flitter then"?

"All right. As you know, as a curved airfoil wing flies through the sky, it deflects air and alters the air pressure above and below it. That's intuitively obvious. Think how it feels when you slowly walk through a swimming pool and feel the force of the water pushing against your body: your body is diverting the flow of water as it pushes through it, and an airfoil wing does

the same thing, much more dramatically—because that's what it's designed to do. As a plane flies forward, the curved upper part of the wing lowers the air pressure directly above it, so it moves upward.

Why does this happen? As air flows over the curved upper surface, its natural inclination is to move in a straight line, but the curve of the wing pulls it around and back down. For this reason, the air is effectively stretched out into a bigger volume—the same number of air molecules forced to occupy more space—and this is what lowers its pressure. For exactly the opposite reason, the pressure of the air under the wing increases: the advancing wing squashes the air molecules in front of it into a smaller space. The difference in air pressure between the upper and lower surfaces *causes* a big difference in airspeed not the other way around, as in the ancient theory of a wing. The difference in speed, observed in actual wind tunnel experiments, is much bigger than you'd predict from the simple equal transit theory. So if our two air molecules separate at the front, the one going over the top arrives at the tail end of the wing much faster than the one going under the bottom. No matter when they arrive, both of those molecules will be speeding downward and this helps to produce lift in a second important way. An air-flitter will stay in the sky when it creates a huge "*downwash*" downward moving draft of air that balances its weight. The air-flitter curtain design must therefore of necessity be very similar to aeroplane airfoils, but spin around in a circle instead of moving forward in a straight line, like the ones on a plane. Even so, aeroplanes create downwash in the same way, it's just that we will not notice. The downwash will not be so obvious, but it will be just as important. This second aspect of making lift is a lot easier to understand than pressure differences, at least for a physicist: according to Isaac Newton's third law of motion.....".

"Whoa professor, you've lost me. Are you supposed to be that bright as a footballer"?

Roxbrough smiled, "I went to University before I joined the football team there".

"University, not college"?

He nodded, "My degree is in engineering".

Clara chewed thoughtfully before asking, "Would you like to speak to someone in OUC R&D [research and development]"?

"I would but I expect so would a great number of young graduates and there may well be no places available anyway".

Clara grinned, "In addition to managing the team I am also the CEO's daughter - remember? If you want an interview with a view to securing either a current post or one for the future I can have a quiet word with Igan"?

"Igan"? Roxbrough looked genuinely impressed, "Igan Giganort"?

"The same".

Igan Giganort is the designer of the OUC 222bhp Orange Streak, you can get me an interview with him. He doesn't do interviews, few get to speak to him in person. The man is a genius and a legend in his lifetime".

"I can speak to him any time I want and if I ask him to see you, he will".

"For a chance to work with the famed Igan Giganort I would leave the team and......".

"You will **not**"! Clara cut him off. "If he likes you and that is a very unlikely situation as he does not like anyone much.... If he likes you though, then you can work with him part-time until the season is over, not make that three seasons, we need to defend the title next year".

"You think we can recover from the disastrous start we had".

"They - had", Clara corrected, "And yes, the recovery has already started, but you're a part of that recovery Roxbrough and you're contracted so your chance of leaving is zero".

"You like me as a footballer"?

"Yes. Now don't go getting all arrogant and egotistical on me, but you are an important member of the squad. So, before I get you an interview with Igan I want your word that you will continue to play in the team until I say you can leave"?

"I will agree to any condition to speak to Giganort, so I agree".

The rest of the meal was conducted during small-talk and Clara realised she liked her striker as a person as well as a member of her football squad. They parted with a smile and she went to bed her mind whirling with confusion.

Roxbrough took the lift down to the ground floor happily humming to himself as he did so. He liked Clara Trentavoria and also found her very attractive. She was his boss however and the CEO's daughter, so he had the sense to keep their relationship professional only. As he walked into the foyer on his way to the exit, he did not notice a burly figure suddenly slip his padfon into the inside pocket of his frock-coat and rise to follow him at a distance. He was too distracted to see the very same figure give a signal to another man in a dark flitter who promptly climbed out and started to take an interception course toward the walking striker. Roxbrough had walked to the hotel from his new digs, enjoying the experience of doing so through the very crisp night-air of the city. Still humming he continued on his way and realised nothing until a man suddenly seemed to be before him, asking pleasantly,

"Have you got a light Mac"?

"No", The footballer responded, delighted to be able to use the ancient gag, "But I've got a pale raincoat".

Then the thud preceded the terrible pain that lanced through his neck and up into his head and blue stars exploded before his vision before he tumbled into inky oblivion!

Twenty-one   **When consciousness returned** to Roxbrough, it was accompanied by a world champion headache. He felt like a brick had landed on the back of his neck, which was not so far from the truth. It had been a leather, lead-weighted sap. Used with incredible skill so as not to fracture his skull. He was in very dim light indeed. A thin line of amber shining from underneath a doorway. He tried to move and realised his wrists were tied together quite tightly. He was seated on a hard-backed chair and was stripped down to his singlet and trollies. Even his socks were off and his feet were like blocks of ice.

"Hey"! He yelled and a million evil tiny pixies began to hammer his skull with malign little mallets. The pain was like explosions of white heat in his head and he decided that if no one came he would not try to cry out again for a while.

The door opened though and two men walked into the room. One held a needle-gun which he immediately trained on the footballer. Both had strangely immobile features and Roxbrough realised they were wearing real-flesh masks and probably Harmoans [badly designed and very obvious wigs made popular in the ancient past]. No point in memorising what they looked like then, other than their build. One guy was shaped like a silver-back, the other, in sharp contrast was lean to the point of skinny. Roxbrough immediately thought of them as Ape and Rat. The latter, who had the needlegun asked,

"Apart from the obvious, who are we and why are we doing this to you, do you have any other questions"?

"Could I possibly have something for my head it is very painful indeed".

Rat grinned in his strangely immobile features and said to the ape, "Get him the shot".

Ape went out of the room to return almost immediately with a hypospray, while he had been gone Roxbrough and Rat had said nothing. Merely regarded one another with a strangely detached silence.

The hulking figure went over to Roxbrough and pressed the device to his upper arm. The pain vanished. It did not subside or feel alleviated – it was gone! With it came a feeling of tremendous well-being and euphoria. Roxbrough felt himself smile despite the gravity of the situation and he asked in a voice that sounded slurred even to him,

"What was in that"?

Ape grunted, "Snufzomorph, cost us a packet".

Roxbrough was on too much of a high to feel consternation but he observed, "You gave me a narcotic".

"It'll keep you happy and it'll keep you out of trouble for quite a while. Now, do you want anything else, Bud"?

"My feet are like blocks of ice, could I possibly have my socks back"? Roxbrough tried.

Rat, shook his head, "You try and get away in bare feet and you'll be much slower for that reason, sorry, Bud".

"Well, when you go will you at least leave the light on for me"?

Rat, looked about the bare room, "Not a problemo. Well! If that's it....."?

"You know it isn't", Roxbrough slurred, "Is it money? I have no wealthy Aunt or anything like that, in fact, I'm an orphan, no family".

"Other than your new family at Orang-U-Can", Ape murmured, which caused Rat to snarl,

"Shut your yap lessing you want to speak through a pie hole full of teeth".

Roxbrough giggled, "Who writes your script, Rat? Nik Gehenna? That line was straight out of a Penny Dreadful".

"Rat eh"? Rat noted, "Alright, Rat will do, what's his name", he nodded toward Ape, "Big Dope"?

"I thought – Ape", Roxbrough smiled through his narcotic fog, "Say how long does this stuff take to wear off"?

"About six hours", Rat informed, "Now ifin there's nothing else.....".

"Masks making you sweat", Roxbrough noted, "I understand. I think I'll get myself a little nap anyway. Let me know when the ransom is paid won't you"?

"Ransom"? Ape asked and Roxbrough knew he had guessed incorrectly when Rat snapped,

"Shut that stupid pie-hole of yours.......Ape, and get out of here".They left Roxbrough in the room, but they left the light on. He scrutinised his surroundings to see if he could commit anything of use to memory. There were plenty of windows in the place but they had all been blocked off with thick black card. Two doorways led out of it and the two kidnappers had entered and exited by the one on the right. A single maxi-LED was the only source of illumination and it did so meagrely in such a wide space. By twisting his head around and looking over his shoulder Roxbrough could see a rectangular hole which had previously housed 13amp power-points. Above the doors were four vents for air conditioning. There were a few lumps of rubble on the floor and some old plaster, it was bare concrete. The cold was striking up from it into Roxbrough's feet and he valued his feet greatly. Lifting his legs awkwardly he assumed the lotus position and tried to sleep. He had only one plan and it was pretty desperate, but it was the only thing he could come up with under the circumstances. Firstly he had to sleep and hope his high metabolic rate would filter the narcotic from his system.

twenty-two   **When Roxbrough awoke** he was uncertain if he had rested too long. His plan would fail if he had slumbered beyond the normal length of time the drug would stay in an ordinary person's system. There was only one way to find out. Deliberately slurring his speech he cried out.

"Rat! Rat! Help me"?!

The door opened after only a few seconds and the two rubber-faced goons stepped into the room. Rat, was holding the needle gun once more.

"What do you want now"? He was not happy to be summoned a second time, so enough time had probably not elapsed.

"I can't feel my hands", Roxbrough slurred, "Is that a result of the drug, or are the ropes too tight".

"You called us in here for *that*"! Rat, was not best pleased."Come on, Monkey let's get out of here".

"He said Ape, not Monkey". Ape objected, "Apes are much brighter and stronger than monkeys".

Rat, was sarcastic as he observed, "Then he talked you up big-time, you great dope. He's wasting our time c'mon".

"Remember what Smith said", the big thug noted then, "He comes to no harm lessing from his instruction. What if he gets one of them trombosis in his arm and it goes to his brain and kills him? Then what do you tell Smith"?

Rat, was incredulous, "A trombosis, what are you a brass player? It's a **thrombosis** imbecile"!

It was not possible to tell if Ape was annoyed by the insult, his real-flesh mask could not express such emotion but he noted quite wittily,

"Whatever it's called, he dies and you've blown it haw haw haw, geddit? You've blown it"!

"*I've* blown it, aren't we a team no more"? Rat wished to know his tone quite aggrieved. Roxbrough just wished they would make some sort of decision, but he could not make a sardonic observation because he was still feigning being stoned.

"Not if you give him a *throm*-bosis no".

Rat passed the needle-gun to the big man, "Hold this then while I loosen the ropes and the string just a bit. He makes any fancy or tricky moves and you let him have it in the neck. Oh, Ape....."?

"Yeah"?

"If he does try anything shoot him, not me".

"You think 'cos I'm big that I'm dumb", Ape objected, "But I'm just as smart as you Wea......Rat".

'W, e, a', Roxbrough thought, 'His first three letters of his name, remember that'.

Rat, went around Roxbrough's back and began to loosen the string holding his wrists together. He did not slacken them enough for it to be much help. When he started on the rope around his arms and chest though it was a different story. Roxbrough flexed his biceps with great care and inflated his chest as quietly as he were able. The rope was much thicker and therefore impossible to slacken with the same degree of accuracy as the string. It was loosened enough for what he wanted though. He waited until Rat was back around the front of him. Waited until the skinny thug had demanded of him,

"Better – guest of honour"?

Roxbrough deliberately mumbled an incoherent reply. The ruse worked better than he could have possibly hoped. Rat bent down and demanded, turning his ear toward the footballer,

"What you say, Striker"?

Roxbrough hurled himself backwards bringing his feet up in an arc as he did so. As his foot reached the correct height it caught Rat under the chin and there was a loud crunching sound. Followed by the quieter phut of a needle gun firing twice in quick succession. One needle whisked over the chair and missed Roxbrough's fallen form by a hair's breadth. The other very conveniently buried itself into the falling form of Rat.

"Frenge"! Ape cursed as Roxbrough rolled frantically onto his side and slipped his arms out of the chair back. Tucking his legs up to his chin he had his hands in front of him then while Ape watched him in silent amazement. As he finally raised the gun again Roxbrough snatched up the chair and brandished it like a shield between him and his kidnapper.

"That thing is useless against timber"! Roxbrough barked and it gave him the second he needed. For as Ape glanced down at the gun, as if to visually check it's effectiveness Roxbrough thrust the chair forward with every ounce of his strength. Two legs missed Ape, two did not. One drove into his midriff causing all the air to be violently dispelled from his lungs. That was the kinder of the two. The other chair leg caught Ape on the jaw. Timber thrust forward with speed and determination. It crunched into the big man's face and the sound of crunching teeth was sharp in the air between the two of them. Ape gave an animalistic grunt of pain and a huge spade-like paw clutched his jaw, he doubled up in obvious agony. Roxbrough felt a trifle sorry for him as he brought the chair down a second time, putting the lights out in the big thugs head just like he had coshed the footballer previously.

Not waiting for Rat to come around Roxbrough turned and went to vault toward the door. Then spears of pain lanced up his right leg and he practically fell flat on his face. He stumbled onto all fours and glanced down at his right foot. The cracking sound that had issued when he had kicked under rat's chin was his ankle-breaking!. It was already going black and blue with bruising. There was not a chance of walking on it as it was he could not hope to put enough distance between him and Rat before the then incensed villain would come around and start to pursue him!

twenty-three   Clara   was   enjoying
what, since childhood, she had referred to as a *sleeps-in* when her padfon rudely interrupted it. She ignored it, turned over and was just about settled once more when it pinged again and again and again! There was no ignoring the insistence of the messenger. Propping herself up on one elbow she glanced down at the screen and read the message in growing incredulity and horror:

Miss Trentavoria, we have your striker – Roxbrough. If OUC does not lose the game tomorrow you will receive the first instalment of him through the snail-mail. It will be the big toe of his right foot. Go to the combmen and he dies. Approach a Priv-dick and he dies. Tell anyone that he is being held by my team and he dies. Sincerely, Smith

Clara could not believe the lengths someone had gone to, to make certain that Orang-U-Can were not going to win the next match of the season. To suspect it was anything to do with Collendine Voleskip MD was too obvious, it could be any one of the other eleven clubs in the First Division. More importantly, she could not decide what to do for poor Roxbrough. Suddenly all was urgency and she rushed through her ablutions, grabbed something quick from the restaurant and pushed the flitter to the limit on the way to the club. She had to consult someone and decided there was none better than Best. The Assistant Manager was not prepared for what he read from her padfon.

"This is beyond the realms of credibility", he murmured when he had read it. Several weeks with Clara had improved his vocabulary exponentially. "After all, what we are doing here, is just playing a game when you get right down to it".

"What about the money involved"? Clara demanded at once, "And I'm not just talking about the substantial payment from the media and sponsorship, I'm talking about the betting".

"And lots of money was bet on us to come bottom of the league - after three games".

Clara nodded, "A substantial sum by one powerful individual who now sees that stake rapidly vanishing as each result comes in. Someone with the determination to hire people to kidnap poor Roxbrough. How do we get him back? How do we recover him in one piece? You've read the ping".

"Let's take it one stage at a time then", Best observed after a slurp of his lichen-coff. "The last thing you want to do is deliberately lose the game, so strike that off the list. I don't think having heard what you've gone through recently with Snelling, that you have a very high opinion of the combmen and you've already told me about this situation so that leaves only one other option"!

"Before I do anything rash, let's consider Roxbrough", Clara urged, "I think I have to reply to this ping, this Smith [an obvious alias] and agree we lose the game. Then we need the best Priv-dick in Manchester who has twenty-four hours to save Roxbrough from a hideous amputation"!

twenty-four   **Tricky Dicky Dickersgill** flicked the ash from
his med-cig in the what-so-ever direction it happened to land. The *office*
was a dump! It had far more in common with an ashtray than a room or
building used as a place for commercial, professional, or bureaucratic
work. That was because Dickersgill was not only lazing but had very low
standards of housekeeping. In sharp contrast to that his hygiene was
exemplary. From the crown of his gelled and stylishly cut hair to his
polished faux-leather shoes, Tricky cut a dashing figure. The ceiling of the
office had once been white. That was in the dim and distant past, which
ironically could also be used as an expression of the upper interior surface
of the room – dim and distant and the colour of nicotine. The air beneath it
was so blued with smoke that the overhead LED could only penetrate it in a
somewhat subfusc chiaroscuro. That was fortunate, for the furnishings were
in very much the same style as everything else, circa turn-of-the-century
dump-site. One leg of the steel and glass table was held together with duck
tape. The surface was festooned with an array of dysfunctional or broken
items. A stix recorder that played but could no longer record, several empty
packets that had once held ciggies. An old flop-hat which had not even
been in fashion when Dickersgill had bought it from a charity shop. A stylo
with no nib, that was thusly incapable of being used on a pad to draw
illustrations or directions. Half a tuna sandwich green with some sort of
culture, a cold mug of lichencoff. The desk could have been greatly
improved simply by placing the contents of it straight into the waste-shute.
That was on the far side of the room however and something Tricky would
have to work up to.

When his pad suddenly pinged and was on vid-link Tricky had been almost
asleep. He roused himself with the sort of velocity that the room could never
possibly be a testament to. Assuming his business-smile, he pressed the
answer key and was rewarded by a head and shoulder image of a very
attractive young woman.

"TDD Private Detection, how can I help"? He asked with practised
suaveness.

The woman looked pale and distraught and Tricky found himself hoping
the case was going to be a big fat thumb of a result".

"Mister Dickersgill"?

"Speaking"?

"I'm Clara Trentavoria".

"I thought I recognised you Miss Trentavoria, how can I help you", Tricky
asked politely whilst simultaneously wondering how much snufz the
combies had caught her with this time, or whose bed she had been caught
in by an irate wife or contractee.

"You may or may not know I am currently the manager of Orang-U-Can
Football Team (he didn't) and one of my players has been kidnapped"!

"Right", Tricky was suddenly all business, "Do not say any more over this
connection. Where are you Miss Trentavoria"?

"I'm at the ground right now in my office, your e-address was given me by the team physio here.....".

"I am on my way, please cut the connection now".

Tricky did so and hurried out of the office. He did not lock it, if anyone chose to let themselves in to steal something, they might tidy up for him before leaving empty-handed. He took the lift down to the flitter-park where his trusty and battered Corsa 85 bhp Luxurette was parked. A quick press of his key and nothing happened! So he was forced to haul up the driver-side hatch manually once he had turned the key in the lock. He slipped slightly on the old seat cover as he climbed in and banged his knee on the gear-stick,

"Agura-drabble"! He cursed and then pressed the ignition button with a violent stab to relieve his pain and annoyance. The cold fusion pile coughed twice stuttered and then thankfully caught. Tricky was forced to wait several seconds for it to build up a head of power. To think that the flitter had once been able to go from 0 to 30 mph in fifteen seconds? That had been five owners and thirty years ago though and if the car were a dog it would have been humanely put to rest in the cosmic garage. Finally tricky was able to carefully steer the Luxurette into traffic. He was being so hesitant because the proximity alert in the flitter was on the fritz and he already had fifteen points on his insured-license. One more accident and Tricky would not be able to drive for nine months. Even taking it at a steady 33 mph, which was the speed limit in the heart of the metropolis, he reached the stadium in twenty minutes and parked in the rather more salubrious car park than the one he had left in Ferguson Towers.

Tricky took the lift, asked a youth who was humming mightily of the perpetration, the way, found himself looking through a half-glass door at the woman who had pinged him. He tapped  politely and she waved him to enter. In the flesh she was even more good looking than she had looked on his padfon. Clara Trentavoria could do one thing without even trying. She could grow hair and it did so like wildfire. Only two weeks before he had been to the hairdressers and asked her to cut it short already it was shaggy and Tricky found the resultant wild style even more of a turn-on. For a couple of seconds, neither of them spoke as the Priv-dick simply starred at the woman in ill-conceived admiration.

"Mister Dickersgill", she began, "I need your help and I need you to act as swiftly as you can"?

"Call me Tricky"? Tricky asked, "Everyone does".

"I will call you Mister Dickersgill if you do not mind and you will call me Miss Trentavoria".

Tricky changed tack and swiftly, "All right Miss Trentavoria, as you wish. Do you have an image and a description of your missing lad"?

"He's a grown man", Clara told him and pressing the appropriate command on her pad sent it to his, "You now have what you need, all I want to know is how much you charge"?

"You are all business, Miss Trentavoria", Tricky smiled.

"Mister Dickersgill", Clara practically barked, I have just uploaded the kidnappers demand to you, will you please acknowledge the gravity of this situation. I am not here to start socialising with you. Now! How much do you want to rescue my striker before the foul thugs who have abducted him start to remove body parts"?

Tricky thought quickly and then asked, "A hundred and fifty sestertii a day plus expenses. Four days in advance".

Clara's fingers raced over the keyboard of her padfon and thumbed the amount into Tricky's e-account, which was on his SWW site.

"You have it now by safepay so please get to work, Mister Dickersgill, thank you for coming in. Good day"!

twenty-five   **Roxbrough brought the** chair down with all his might and it obediently shattered into several splinters of varying sizes. Keeping one eye on the two momentarily incapacitated thugs, he hastily strapped two pieces of the chair either side of his leg and foot. The crudest splint that had ever been constructed. Sweat ran down his forehead and stung his eyes and he almost blacked out from the pain, but he kept his head low in his lap as he awkwardly applied the clumsy first aid. He then climbed to his feet, his bare feet and stumbled and dragged himself to the doorway. In the room beyond was a low table with a full ashtray at its centre, two chairs and two lichen-coff cups on the table also. The thugs had used a gas-camping-stove to boil some water. There was no sign of Roxbrough's clothes. Was he truly going to go through the door beyond? Possibly to outside in November in his trollies and singlet with two broken lumps of wood strapped to his leg?

Did he have a choice? At least he had retained the presence of mind to snatch the needlegun from Ape who had been rocking backwards and forwards cradling his ruined jaw in one of his huge paws. Checking it - to see it retained five, level one needles in its chamber, Roxbrough hauled open the door. A cold splash of frigid rain smote him instantly, but at least he was out. Where was out though? Shivering he glanced about him desperately. At first, he had fallen through a worm-hole and travelled back in time a few centuries, the surroundings were depressed and slum-like, in every other part of the country such dilapidation had been torn down for urban development. An Asian woman in a headscarf hurried past him, no thought of offering any help, yet he was quite obviously in need of it.

His first thought was to find a combman. Then he dismissed the notion. If Mister Smith, whoever he was, had much of an idea he would have at least one bent combie on his payroll. Going into a holding room ostensibly to wait while people were contacted, might well put him back in the hands of Ape and Rat. If the duo had sufficiently recovered by then his welcome

would be less than cordial. Where did that leave him? He had no clothes, no padfon without technology he was broke until he could get to some. Whatever he did do he would have to do it before hypothermia claimed him. Ordinarily, he would have run, until his own body provided him with sufficient heat to survive. Not on a broken ankle though. To add to his woes it seemed to be late afternoon and the light was fading swiftly. Perhaps in the darkness, he would find somewhere to hole up while the recovered Rat searched for him. That was the sort of thing the heroes did in the tri-vidz, but they had superhuman powers of endurance and good fortune usually helped them in some slight twist of the storyline. This was real life.

The pain in his ankle had become bearable but he knew that was dangerous too, his limbs were growing numb with cold, if he did not get a lucky break soon his organs would start to shut down or his heart might give him some trouble. The area was so decrepit and ramshackle that he did not even pass the ever-growingly sparse supply shop. Technology had seen them off in the past. Then they had enjoyed a resurgence in popularity, only to fade once again. All was cyclic, Roxbrough found himself in the downward spin of the wheel, however. He trudged on, to stop would mean disaster. One figure crossed the street to avoid him and hurried away when he tried calling him for assistance. It was the sort of area where individuals did not want to get involved – in anything. Unbeknown to him, Roxbrough was in the infamous Moss Side, one of the last surviving slums in Northern Saxonia. In 33 centuries mankind had not changed morally. There were still those who had a great deal and those who had practically nothing. It was mankind's curse, his moral infirmity -greed. Avarice and selfishness always led to people like Hugh Trentavoria, who could not hope to spend his accrued wealth in three lifetimes and the Asian woman who had hurried past Roxbrough. The latter would be lucky if she even knew where her next meal would be coming from. The rich and the Nouveau riche referred to the poor as peasants. Before that it had been plebs, phrases were even cyclic. What they referred to was an attitude. If someone was without personal wealth he (or she) was thusly inferior in every possible way. It meant the same as it always had meant, two strata of society coexisting in very different ways with as little interaction between them as was possible.

Roxbrough had plunged from the upper layer, into the lower and it hurt his sensibility as much as his broken ankle hurt his body. He felt as if he could not get much colder. He certainly could not get any more saturated. Indeed his imagination told him he had become deliquescent And his body was nothing more than an aqueous mannequin. He began to feel drained of vitality, he could feel the life-force draining out of his body and knew he was close to a very dire situation. When his spirits had descended to the same level as his body a flitter suddenly pulled up beside where he stood to shiver and a voice asked,

"Hey Mister, what happened to you? Do you want taking to the hospital or the combmen station or something"?

Roxbrough glanced into the vehicle a rather modest Dorf 85 bhp Escort. The driver-side hatch-window had been slid down to reveal a young woman in a modest mode of dress.

Roxbrough stammered, "I was kidnapped and managed to get away, but not before breaking my ankle. I fear to go to the fuzz as they might have a mole in the station, same thing with the hospital, could you take me to......"

Before he could ask for the stadium, he *conveniently* blacked out!

twenty-six   **Tricky knew the** underbelly of
Manchester. It was necessary if he desired the knowledge of what was
happening in the bottom strata of the city's population. The contrast
between the two tiers was never so well illustrated as when Tricky worked
for one and it forced him to investigate the other. He returned to his office.
The contemporary gum-shoe hardly needed to leave his work domicile to
earn a male deer or two. Most could be learned on the solar-wide-web
[SWW]. Tricky accessed what he mentally considered to be his *grey-
contacts.*

These were the individuals who conducted their various enterprises just
on the very edge of what was legal. In the old vernacular of Americanese,
they would have been referred to as *punks* or *wise-guys*. The nomenclature
dependant upon their annual income from their little bits of métier. The
greater the commerce the better the name. This made Tricky's first vid-link
a contact with a punk, or as the underbelly of Manchester preferred to call
them - entrepreneurs! 'Fingers' Иващенко was not a native of the city, but
an immigrant from Novosibirsk - Russia. Tricky also suspected her of being
a pickpocket, receiver and dealer and had been engaged to contract at
least four times to his knowledge. In each case, Иващенко had walked
away from the engagement but had retained the rather extravagant ring.
She was able to do such underhand machinations and get away with them
because it was fair to say she was decorative. At least Tricky found her so
and had tried to seduce her (unsuccessfully) in the past. That she was a
grey-trader bothered Tricky not in the slightest, some of his best friends
were not exactly spotlessly white of character or activity. Иващенко was in
a flitter when she answered his ping. She had the vehicle on automatic as
her arms were crossed loosely over one knee. The padfon was in its dock on
the dash, for the picture never wavered as Иващенко asked,

"Tricky, to what do I owe the pleasure", her voice was a pleasantly
accented contralto, thickened by the fact that Standard was not her first or
mother-tongue.

"I'm after a bit of information and I knew who to get in touch with firstly",
Tricky flattered. The blandishment did not affect, it never did work with
Иващенко. She was a girl who encountered sycophancy every day and from
individuals with far more verbal dexterity than the priv-dick.

"Information is a commodity and do you know anyone who gives
commodities away for free, Tricky"?

"I do not", the Priv-dick responded reasonably, "And that is why I am
willing to pay a fair price for what I want to know. Although, of course, we
cannot discuss such a delicate matter over the SWW, would you like me to
visit, or do you prefer to come to my office"?

"That septic location of commerce. I came once and almost caught
winnets. Have you not thought of upgrading to a nice cesspit somewhere or
a mephitic building with a nice view overlooking the sewerage works"?

One thing that could always be said of Иващенко was that she was a girl with a healthy sense of humour. The same was not true of Tricky. No one ever described the priv-dick as being a *good laugh* although some referred to him as a *koofing joke!* He responded,

"Your place then, I can be there in thirty".

"Make it an hour I'm just on my way for a shoe fitting and one more thing, Tricky"?

"Yes, sweet Fingers"?

"You're coming to my place for some information, not to *Give me a Green Gown*, or *Shoot Twixt Wind and Water.* Understood"?

"Of course, green is an unlucky colour anyway".

twenty-seven Disorientated Roxbrough finally surfaced from the comforting and warm folds of dreamland. He had been engaged in the sort of conversation with a pog [genetically spliced pig and dog, resulting in a house trainable pet which when finally expired provide the family with tasty bacon by way of compensation for their tragic loss]. This particular pog not only had a human face, but also a bright purple shaggy coat of fur and startling orange ears.

"Hey human", the pog began, "I don't normally get to talk to footballers, can you let me have the inside skinny on Saturday's match".

"Skinny"? Roxbrough was confused being English he did not speak the language of the Unwanted States. "And do I take it to mean I could know what the result will be before we kick-off".

"Don't razzle my trotters baby", the pog objected, "Next you'll be telling me that wrestlers hurt one another and we all know that they are more like dancing above the crupper than getting down with the grungiest".

"I cannot help you, Mister......"?!

"Koof on your mister, white-monkey on dope, I'm a girl you ragging lamebrain fair game".

"Oh! I do beg your pardon, Ma'am what's your name, please"?
"It's Clara, you ignoramus. Don't tell me you don't recognise your manager when you see her. Sure I look a tad different when I've no slap or lippy on, but sheesh. You make a girl feel proper plain".

Roxbrough could feel a neurotic mania nibbling at the edges of his sanity, but incubus being what it was he did not point out to the Boss that she had managed to be turned into a purple pog. Pink would not have been so bad, but puce?!

"You'll have to excuse me I have to go and visit the butchers", he found himself saying then. As with all dreams, there was no logic to any of it, it was rather like a snufz-induced hallucination than real life. Roxbrough picked up a three-pound lump-hammer and let the pog have it right between the eyes. The creature was much tougher than she looked. Merely blinking against a blow that would have felled a bullock, all the attack did was cause her to grow understandably furious.

"You ignominious malefactor"! Clara the pog screamed at him, "Meat is red murder, the next time you seat your charlatanic body over a plate of bacon and cruelly stolen baby chickens you will see the rasher grinning up at you and reminding you that you are consuming the very person who let you rise meteorically to the very firmament of........."

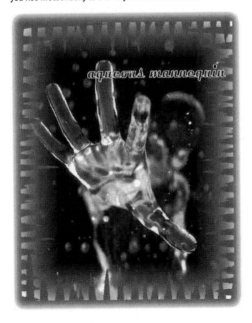

Roxbrough snatched himself our of the semi-conscious ordeal and found himself bathed in sweat in a warm bed. It took him a while to remember how he had come to be where he was, it even took him a while (admittedly shorter) to realise *who* he was. He felt drugged and wondered if he had been given something but why and by whom? He glanced around his surroundings. The room was clean, that was on the positive side of the balance sheet. On the negative was everything else. The bed was made of iron and a frame that had been used in antiquity. While mattresses wore out, iron bedsteads and beds never did. Who knew how many different types of bedding and covering this frame had supported over the years? Annual periods that may well number into centuries. The ceiling whilst emulsioned recently was a spider-work of cracks, some had been filled in and some were even fillings in the fillings. Whoever sought to get a few more years out of the plaster was hoping against hope that the entire structure would not one day collapse into the bedroom. The curtains did not match the bedspread but were washed and ironed, though in certain places they were threadbare. The walls were covered in what looked like paper in which small chips of wood had been combined into the layers and emulsioned over the top. The walls were from an age when men legally deforested the world to make paper and timber. That had been illegal since the rising of the sea levels and the use of technology to repair the rends in the ozone layer. Since the development of durilite and nyloplanyon trees did not need to be felled to make building material. Pseudo-glass and MNC [Mulit-nylo-chloradine] had made them obsolete. MNC came in two basic forms: rigid (sometimes abbreviated as RMNC) and flexible. The rigid form of MNC being used in construction for pipe and profile applications such as doors and windows. It was also useful in the manufacture of bottles, non-food packaging, food-covering sheets, and ID cards. In its rigid form, it lasted indefinitely It could be made softer and more flexible by the addition of nylocizers, the most widely used being polythalates. In that form, it was used in plumbing, electrical cable insulation, imitation leather, flooring, signage, hard copy phonograph records, inflatable products, and many applications where it replaced rubber. Combined with cotton or linen, it was used to make clothing fabrics and the stiffer canvas. In its purest form, it was colourless and was dyed during manufacture it was a semi solid-liquid. It was insoluble in alcohol but slightly soluble in kelmupolyhydrofuran. The latter being an organic compound with the formula $(KmH_2)_4O$. The compound is classified as polycyclic compound, specifically a cyclic kelmu-ether. Colourless, water-miscible organic liquid with low viscosity. Used as a precursor to nylomers. Being polar and having a wide liquid range, KPHF was a versatile solvent.

The furniture was very curious and something Roxbrough had never before witnessed in his life. It was white and clean, but not nyloplanyon. The handles looked to be of durilite but Roxbrough doubted if that was the case and suspected it was some sort of metal that was used historically. The material was called chipboard and the handle were a light alloy, but Roxbrough would never know because it would not prove polite to ask the owner the nature of their furniture's construction. The door to the bedroom opened and a youngish woman entered. She looked immediately incongruous in the room. Her shoes were humble enough, but a once decent frock now faded with too many cleanings over too long a period had caused it to fade, but it was still possible to see that it had once been splendid. Her hair was clean but not styled in the slightest way and she had tried to compensate for that by applying way too much eye shadow. Roxbrough could see at once that this was a peasant doing her best to look presentable to him.

"I saved you", she told him somewhat obviously, "What were you doing wandering about in this neighbourhood in only your underclothes".

"Well firstly, thank you for doing so and bringing me back here, but now I need the attention of someone with medical training....."

Roxbrough slid back the sheet only to discover that the woman had stripped him and applied a nyloplanyon splint to his ankle. She did not seem to be even slightly concerned about his nudity, merely explained,

"Your clothes were sopping I could not put you in my bed in that condition, it's hard enough to get bedding dry in summer in Manchester, but......You didn't answer my question though, do I need to be nervous of you, you're not wide, are you"?

"Wide"?

"You know, on the make, up to something tasty".

"Do you mean dishonest"?

"That's what I said, you're not are you, I mean I saved you and all so don't do anything nasty will you"?

"Dear lady, I owe you a great kindness, I would not dream of harming you in any way. Where on Earth did you get a medical brace though"?

"My husband used to be a porter, in a hospital".

"Used to be, he lost his job"?

"No, he lost his life, he used to be a husband and a porter, now he's not neither".

Ignoring her double negative, for the time being, Roxbrough then told her quickly what had happened to him. When he had finished she exclaimed,

"So you don't belong here, you're a footballer, you're rich"!

"Hardly", Roxbrough chuckled, "I might be one day though, who knows".

"Have you looked around in this room? We're in Moss Side, Fella, compared to me you're rich. If I get you some of my husband's clothes could you get down to the Offy"?

"The Offy"?

"A place where I can get a bottle of wine, some ciggies and something to cook you for your tea. Before you go back and be a footballer again".

"A small Mall"!?

"If you want, what do you think"?

"Providing they fit, I would be willing to do that for you. I presume you wish some thumb".

She smirked at the possibility of a double entendre and when she did it improved her tired looks considerably,

"Let me get the clobber".

As she left the room for a moment to hit something he surmised [incorrectly], he slid out of the warm bed and was immediately shivering again. There was no pain in his ankle though. The brace was doing its job splendidly. She hurried back in and began to fuss around him, insistent upon helping him dress oblivious to his nudity save for the fact that he was shivering again. He asked her as he pulled on the humble but laundered clothing,

"Do you not have the climate control on in this room, Miss, it feels completely unheated"?

"It is unheated", she told him, smiling with superior knowledge, "Do you see any climate control? My names Lsenia by the by. Lsenia Shyrock".

"Well I am so very thankful for your aid Missus Shyrock", Roxbrough began and she immediately responded,

"Being as I've seen you with your clobber off and you've been in my bed, I think you should call me Lsenia don't you? What will your contractee say when you tell her of your little adventure and why did they snatch you anyway, do you suspect her"?

"*She* is in the clear for one very good reason indeed", Roxbrough laughed.

"Oh, what would that be"?

"That she does not exist, there is no contractee nor a girlfriend nor a wife".

"You mean to say you're as young as you look"?

"I am....Lsenia".

"Well, you look a picture now. Here put this gaberdine and cap on and we can just make the Offy before tea-time".

"You have a special time to drink tea. Real tea, from India or the Southern Island (Sri Lanka – conquered in the 24th)"?

"The girl grimaced, "Come on rich boy, you owe me"?

Somewhat nonplussed by the girl who lived in the same city as he but who might have been from a different planet, he followed her out into the cold dampness of a late afternoon November in Manchester. He need not have worried the Offy, as the girl called it was only a street from her run-down terraced property. Why she called it the name she did he could not fathom from the signage over the damaged door. '*Khan's*', it said, then beneath it, in much smaller lettering, *'Open 24/7'*. What was that nonsense? Open 3.42857 of a day? Or 29% of the time, how could anyone be expected to know when to try the door?

Confused, Roxbrough followed the widow-ladies pert behind into the store. As ass went it was prime grade and he was surprised at himself for noting the fact. With a practised familiarity of the location of the merchandise, she went straight to the section of the bizarre establishment and glanced keenly at row upon row of dark brown bottles. She sucked in the air through gritted teeth as some people are want to do when arriving at a tough decision. Finally, she picked out her selection and glanced at Roxbrough. She had chosen a bottle of Pakistani red wine which Roxbrough would not have even used to flush out his drains. He took it from her and asked,

"Let me select it, why don't you get some essentials while you're here too, stock your larder Lsenia, you know I can afford it right? Get enough to fill four cartons, we can manage two each for a street".

Eyes sparkling with sudden delight, the young woman went to get a basket which had a long handle and wheels underneath it. It looked to be constructed out of ancient plastic. The proprietor, presumably mister Khan himself looked delighted at the impending sale, quite likely the largest he would enjoy that day or maybe even week. He began to *assist* Lsenia in the selection of her purchases, being as *helpful* as he could. The widow had chosen enough to fill four neoplanyon cartons and Roxbrough duly thumbed the bill. It was not a great deal of balance to him, but maybe, just maybe, it was a small fortune to a resident of Moss Side. The gap between the haves and the have-nots had been colossal ever since man had possessed language and the ability to record history and it was never going to be

resolved, for mankind was not a humanistic creature. The duo wended their way back to her abode. To get through the door instead of using a thumb plate, Lsenia put a small and slim piece of metal into a recess in the door very close to the handle and turned it. Roxbrough heard the lock click manually [how quaint] and they went inside.

"Come into the parlour", the girl asked, "I'll get a couple of glasses and put these things in the fridge and cupboards.

Curiously the engineer/footballer did as directed and found to his horror and confusion that in an ancient stone fireplace the girl was *burning the fruit of the tree*!! He would have thought it highly illegal, but that was in his realm of existence and he was simply horrified and confused in equal measure. The widow skipped into the room two glasses filled with red wine and before he could ask her about the fire, pressed one into his hand and seated herself before the glowing embers of the meagre conflagration. He was momentarily robbed of the power of speech for, despite everything, he found her curiously attractive.

"Should you be drinking that on an empty stomach"? He asked her as she quaffed a judiciously hearty swallow of the fruit of the vine. Carefully he took a sip of his own, he was not an enthusiastic fan of red wine.

The widow smiled, "That's when it has the most effect, "Are you very hungry"?

"I'm just thinking that perhaps I should go", he observed, "The Manager of the team will be beside herself with worry and I don't know what the villains who took me will be pinging her".

"You seem very concerned about her, could it be that your relationship is more than just a professional one". The young woman asked her enquiry accelerated by female intuition.

"It is too soon to tell", He was openly honest with her, what was the point of trying to confuse her, or himself.

"But you do find her attractive, do you"?

"She is attractive, that is the simple fact of the matter".

"I'll make you something hot before you leave me then". She told him and her tone was a mixture of various sensitivities: compassion, disappointment, futility. He was not so wrapped up in himself that he could not detect her emotions. He followed her into the kitchen and as she removed something from the refrigerator, turned her by the shoulder and took her in his arms. Rather than being shocked or offended she became compliant and lifted her face to his.

They kissed gently and then more urgently and when they broke away she took him silently by the hand and led him out of the room used for the preparation of food. It was not back to the warmth of the lounge that she led him then but the bedroom. He saw the colour rising in the back of her neck, but did not comment on it.

She was more than hungry for food, more than craving the oblivion from her miserable existence by seeking it in the bottom of a wine bottle. She was also starved of affection, tenderness and physical pleasure and had decided he must provide her with it before he returned to his world.

twenty-seven   **Tricky was returning** to her apartment much sooner than he had thought. He had told her everything in the previous meeting and she had promised to get on the case asap. Fingers Иващенко was as alluring as he had remembered her, but as she buzzed for the lock to let him into her apartment, she was all business.

"I've already found out a great deal", she told the Priv-dick. "They are fairly hopeless at covering their tracks, but there again they are not professional criminals of course".

"Oh, who"?

"Glerius Orchvestige".

"Orchvestige?! CEO of If you want if we stock it"?

"The very same, he hired a *fixer* called Dalian Llah, a small-time hoodlum who does the sort of work that has been perpetrated against the striker. Two of Llah's men were paid to kidnap Roxbrough. One a big gorilla called Buln Buller, the other a nasty little creep – Goldo Razinsk. News on the street is that your footballer managed to get away from the pair of useless would-be kidnappers and fled into the late afternoon and has not been seen since".

"How did you find this out so quickly, Fingers"?

"One of my Loxodonta works at a hospital here in Manchester, a nurse actually, but she keeps her ears open hence the name I give her. Just fifty minutes ago Buller was admitted into A&E with a busted jaw and some broken teeth. My Loxodonta helped to wire it up. Your footballer had done a pretty impressive job on him. It seems once he'd had a shot of snufzomorph he began to babble even with a busted jaw. Told them everything, then my little Loxodonta informed me".

"What about the other guy, this Razinsk"?

"He cut and run, dropped Buller off and then split in a hurry".

"To chase after Roxbrough"?

"Your guess is as good as mine, but if Llah is the sort to bear a grudge for a job being bungled then the guy will be highly motivated to find him before you do".

"So where was he held, or can you only give me the location of the hospital"?

"It's Bridgewater Hospital", Иващенко told him with gravity.

"So I've got to start looking for him in Moss Side"? Tricky noted glumly.

"Do you want Mama to come with"? Иващенко grinned.

"Packing"?

"Just level one needles, I'm risking killing no one".

"I don't plan to either, another needlegun would be welcome though, get your coat, it's pissing down again".

"'Get your coat'? Before we've even discussed the fee"?

"You know who you're working for indirectly, do you think the Trentavoria's are sestertius pincher's"?

"Fair enough but if it doesn't pan out that way, my cut comes out of your fee all right"?

"Sure", Tricky needed the extra gun and would have agreed to sign his immortal soul over to Fingers had it proved part of their contract. Of course, she could always have his body, but she would not have to pay for that.

Outside, in the light rain, she took one look at his flitter and remarked,

"I'll risk taking my ride into moss side. I don't mind slumming but I don't want winnets".

"It's not so bad, still does the job", Tricky objected sparking up a med-cig.

"You can put that out", she told him immediately, "My ashtrays are cleaner than the inside of your entire heap".

He stood in the rain and she was forced to wait in her Golden Charter 175 bhp while he smoked two-thirds of it. Letting it drop into the gutter, which was a small stream heading toward the drain, he climbed into the passenger side.

"Next time could you manage to get a little more wetness on the upholstery"? She asked him sarcastically as she gunned the micro-pile. you've only brought in half a reservoir this time"!

"Relax, Sweet Fingers, it's a flitter not a luxury penthouse suite".

"I know what I drive, Tricky, thank you so much for the edification".

"Are you going to be on my back the entire time we look for the striker because I'd sooner be on your front"?

"You're disgusting".

"I try, now drive woman, we're probably running out of time".

twenty-eight   **Roxbrough propped himself** up onto an elbow and looked down at the face of the young widow. Her makeup was comically smudged making her look more like a clown than a lover. He had been able to tell he had just been with a formerly married woman. It was one of those strange enigmas about being a man. It flattered to be with a girl for her first time, yet was always far more satisfying to go with a woman of experience. Lsenia Shyrock had *put her back into it,* to coin an [somewhat crude] expression. She looked peaceful then as he gazed down at her. Wined, dined and *seen to,* why not. With as much care as he could manage with the brace on his ankle, he tried to slip out from under the sheets without disturbing her. He hated to cut and run, but Trentavoria would not be very pleased if he turned up at the ground and told her for the last few hours he had been in bed with a woman. Come to think of it, he needed an entirely different story or his chances of putting a notch into the manager's headboard would evaporate. As he began to slip into Shyrock's clothes, Lsenia suddenly opened her eyes and then she looked disappointed and offended.

"Suddenly got to go now that you've had the cream off the top of my milk"? She accused. He tried to be reasonable,

"People will be worried, I have to let them know that I'm all right".

"Well, there's no point in staying here any more is there? After all, you've gotten what you wanted so what's keeping you hanging around"?

"That is not how it was and you know it", he felt suddenly agitated himself. Was there an element of truth to her observations.

Before the diatribe could get any more acrimonious there was a hammering on the door and the two of them fell silent, froze and glanced at one another in nervous anticipation,

"Are you expecting anyone"? The striker wanted to know.

"Not this century", Lsenia told him, telling him a great deal in three short words.

"I'll answer it then, can I borrow your needlegun, please"?

She grimaced, "Does my home strike you as of a standard that would allow me to afford a weapon, especially one as sophisticated as a needlegun".

The staccato issued a second time, it seemed more urgently, Roxbrough observed a little more so, "No gun then, so think, what do you have that could be used offensively"?

He hurried into his borrowed pants while she chewed her lip thoughtfully, finally, she asked,

"What about squirting bleach in the eyes of whoever it is? If they turn out to be after you".

"That's not a bad idea. Did you put it under the sink"?

She nodded.

"Could I mix it up with anything less harmful, what's it called".

Lsenia sighed, of course, this rich-boy would never have used cleaning products. She jumped out of bed, heedless of her nudity and threw on an old candlewick dressing-gown that had once been a bedspread,

"I'll get it you".

Hurrying after her he took the dark blue bottle and undid the bright red cap, reading as he did so:

Stronger, more powerful Draino, so effective at killing germs it even combats the phleege. Another quality product from Mills and Boon.

Lsenia pointed to the nozzle with a chipped fingernail and said with heavy sarcasm, "When you squeeze the bottle - the bleach will shoot out of this end"!

"This is no time for levity", Roxbrough remarked, but did offer her a grim grin despite that, "Right get out of sight and wait to hear from me"?

"Are you joking"? She argued then, "This place may be a slum but it's my slum and if whoever is out there thinks he can push you around in my home, then he's in for a rude awakening".

Before Roxbrough could argue, she pulled something from behind her back, it was an ancient fruit of the tree coat hanger that she must have lifted from the wardrobe while he was leading the way down to the kitchen.

"What are you going to do with that, hang his coat up for him"?

"Funny man. Get the front door open while my nerve still holds out, will you flash-boy"?

They went to the hall and Roxbrough pantomimed counting to three before hauling the door open and taking a half-second to see who was outside. As a footballer, his reactions were faster than Rat's and before the thug could stun him with a needle, he got a blast of ice-cold bleach in the eyes. The skinny hoodlum was about to scream in pained surprise when a coat hanger struck him on the temple. A loud cracking noise issued into the damp night air and Roxbrough hoped it was the coat hanger protesting rather than Rat's skull cracking.

When Rat came too he was not in a very sparkling state of health. His head ached abominably, his eyes burned furiously and he found himself tied to a kitchen chair with a length of steel washing line. A nice looking girl was just withdrawing with a bowl of warm clear water and a wad of cotton-wool.

"You could 'av blinded me then". Rat fumed, his eyes still streaming.

"Relax", drawled Roxbrough, "Your eyes have been rinsed, there'll be no permanent damage and anyway I'm the footballer, so I'm the one who's supposed to feign blindness".

"What's that supposed to mean, I don't get it"?!

"No", Roxbrough smiled, "And you never will, Rat. How's Ape by the way? Have they fixed his stumps"?

"I left him at the infirmary thanks to you. You're a nasty little bastard doing that to him".

"Really! *You* are accusing *me*! I still don't know if you would ever have let me go. How did you find me anyway"?

"You kidding, in a place like Moss Side? Greased a few palms, what else. A fella walking about in his shreddies is a sight they don't see every day around here".

"It worked out surprisingly well for you anyway, I just saw her retreating as I came too. You nailed it yet"?

"Let's now establish how things are going to run around here, Rat", Roxbrough told the hoodlum annoyed by his crudity and innuendo. "I ask you a question, you answer".

"What makes you think I'm going to tell a little piss-ant like you anything"?

"Because – and this is just a suspicion of mine you understand – you do not like pain"!

"You got the guts, footie-player"?

Rat had suddenly lost much of his swagger and braggadocio, even before he watched Roxbrough take a pack of med-cigs from his pocket and thumbed two to life. The girl had returned and he handed one to her, saying as he did so,

"Roll one of his sleeves up will you, Sweetness"?

"I'm not too hh-hot". Rat stammered.

"Oh it's not for that reason, It's so I don't burn the cuffs of your designer shirt if you refuse to answer".

As if to belie his words a bead of sweat then trickled down Rat's already shiny forehead and he said, weakly.

"You think you've got the guts to torture me"?

"Oh, he's not going to do any burning", Lsenia told the kidnapper, "If you don't tell him what he wants to know I'm going to apply the ciggie to your Lilly-livered skin"!

"You Methley bitch"! Rat cursed then and Lsenia surprised Roxbrough and the villain both by saying,

"I don't like that, Mister Rat, I don't like that at all. You may apologise, or you may have your first *treatment*"!

"Roast in Hades"! Came the reckless response. Seconds later Rat's scream was louder and higher pitched than anything Roxbrough could have thought the human voice box capable of. Roxbrough observed,

"Despite that sound, you just made, Rat. Which did tend to indicate that you found the hot end of a ciggie somewhat uncomfortable, to say the least, if you hold out on me, I will get my assistant here to fetch the cheese wire? Now you might erroneously consider that such an action would indicate an intention to offer you some dairy products, but it will be employed as a wire garrotte. Not on your neck though. We do not intend to lose our liberty for extinguishing your miserable life. No, rather it will be slipped over your scrotum and......."

"All right whadya wanna know"?

To use the vernacular employed in the Unwanted States, Rat sang like a stooly spilt his guts and grassed-up his employer. He was ignorant of the fact that Dalian Llah himself had been hired by Glerius Orchvestige though, so the couple did not learn that. As the tears of sincerity rolled down Rat's face Roxbrough chose to believe his claim. Lsenia was just washing the hood's face with a cool damp cloth and he was earnestly apologising to her for his earlier insultatio when there was yet another knock on the front door.

"I'm not kidding", the young woman joked, "You can't get a moment's peace in this neighbourhood without some inconsiderate git wanting to ruin your otherwise productive evening by banging Hades out of your door".

Roxbrough picked up the bleach, Lsenia the coat-hanger and they hauled it open for the second time in as many hours.

"Whoa, peace"! Exclaimed the rather dapper man. In the company of a rather presentable young woman, "I'm a priv-dick hired by your manager, Mister Roxbrough you're safe now"?

Roxbrough grinned, "Since being rescued by this young lady here, I've never been in any further danger"!

twenty-nine   "This was the team I was going to announce this afternoon", Clara Told Best, "But of course since the incident with Roxbrough he's not able to play, what do you think would be the best way of dealing with his absence, George"?

Pleased to be consulted best looked down at the Manager's pad

"That would have made one hell of a team to kick-off with. Damn Orchvestige", he noted, "I guess you'll have to give the nod to Wing, Wong or Nero to play in the lead striker role. That or make your formation 4-4-2 and let the young Pole push forward too".

Clara chewed her lip thoughtfully before coming to a decision, "Let's give him a real test as you suggest, make it 4-4-2 and partner him with the Brazilian. I still think they can surprise the Pharmacy boys".

Twenty minutes later with her CI activated and getting the signal from her chosen eleven, the comp-ref showed a minute to go before kick-off. At her side Whohouse was curiously silent which was not like the physio, he seemed to be preoccupied with something or other, but Clara could not afford to think about that then, the game had started and the boys in violet shirts sky shorts and socks faced the men in all orange. As they had been tactically trained Orang-U-Can started at a blistering pace. Using short crisp passes they lanced through midfield half a dozen times in quick succession before Lane sent a really sweet through-ball onto the very tip of Rachwalski's better foot and he struck a superb bullet-like shot. Unfortunately, it was too close to the Voleskip keeper and he took it in the midriff and play was then halted for several moments while he got his wind back.

Orang-U-Can

6. Radband

13. Jennings 25. Zinyama 4 Burgenbower 7. Ball

8. Wong   19.Jenson 20. Lane 16. Flintham

27. Rachwalski

23. Roxbrough

Even though Voleskip were the home team, they began to defend in-depth, only leaving their lone striker forward of the ball most of the first half. It looked like the Pharmacy team intended to at least go in at half time

Corporation Division One		
Makers-Guild v Goosetimp	2	2
RR Scoriors v Castle	0	2
Tiptingle v Precio	2	0
DFE v Zhŏngguá Shāngpĺn	3	1
IYWIWSI v Hornrunner	2	0
Voleskip v OUC	0	2

having not conceded but the situation rapidly changed in a crazy last eight minutes of the first half. Burgenbower carried the ball for several yards before slipping it forward to Jenson. The central defender stunned the home crowd by racing down the left-wing and then making a superb cross directly into the Voleskip penalty box. It was on Nero's very forehead and he rifled the header straight into the roof of the netting. The home crowd practically fell silent. Such a response affected the home team and two minutes later Nero thundered in a second after a wicked low drive into the box from Lane. Orang-U-Can were happy to return to the dressing room two goals in the lead. In the space of eight short minutes, Nero had become OUC's lead goalscorer.

The second half was a dull affair after that. Determined not to be trounced, Voleskip defended with every man they had barely leaving their half and the game ended 0-2 just as it had been at half time.

Clara was on her padfon looking at the rest of the division's results before they were even back on the flitterbus.

	Corporation Div One	Plyd	Goals	Pts
1	Castle Electronics	6	12	14
2	I.Y.W.I.W.S.I.	6	12	12
3	Deutsch Fahrzeuge Eingearbeitet	6	10	9
4	Goosetimp Weapons	6	11	8
5	Makers-Guild	6	9	8
6	Preciometalic.Inc	6	9	7
7	Rolls Royce Scoriors	6	6	7
8	Orang-u-Can	6	5	7
9	Tiptingle Tigers	6	5	6
10	Zhŏngguá Shāngpĺn	6	3	6
11	Hornrunner Hornets	6	6	4
12	Voleskip Pharmaceuticals	6	2	4

The results changed the table:

thirty   **Glancing about her** at the Recycling with Dignity Hall of Remembrance Clara wondered what she had done to deserve such a dysfunctional family. She was standing closest to Lavvisto, his alcohol bloated gut hanging over the waistband of his Crimpoline black suit trousers. That suit had fitted him when he drank a couple of gallons of lager less a week. The jacket would no longer button up as layers of fat on his lardy back had left scant material to encompass his mountainous girth. Beside him, his rather plain contractee Bunjella was dutifully dry-weeping. Putting on a show but unable to conjure any real regret, still at least she was trying. Beside her was the waiflike Grendlyme. The rain was being gusted by a slight breeze that threatened to blow Clara's older sister away. Her hair looked even more bizarre as it billowed out twice as wide as her shoulders.

The podgy Molly and Ianacho were muttering under their breath, praying obviously, but to who? No one was listening nor ever had been and most people recognised that fact in thc modern age. Ganders was the most honest at the time, he had placed mirrored pilot frames over his eyes to try

and hide the ennui on
as they did not cover
the ruse was not
The official of the Hall
Clara was fighting the
'She's dead! Throw
already and have
constituent
some use. She will
first time since she
thought. Of the entire
person who had her
He looked genuinely
of his former partner
even more so given
from the veil of tears
oblivion. Clara stood,
and joined her father
around his shaking
It opened the
found she could shed
support of her

his face, but of course,
his nose and mouth,
exactly succeeding.
was droning on and
urge to nod off.
her in the nutrient tank
done, at least her
chemicals will be of
benefit others for the
was born', she
sorry bunch, the only
sympathy was Hugh.
regretful at the passing
and love of his life,
the way of her passage
into the realm of
moved forward a row
to place her arm
shoulders.
floodgates and she
a few crocodile tears in
remaining parent.

One hour later and the true character of her siblings was showing. Lavvisto and Grendlyme, in particular, were getting more and more boisterous and loud and it was plain that their behaviour was beginning to disturb some of Hugh's colleagues and other business associates and embarrass Hugh for that reason. Time to activate plan 'A'. Clara surreptitiously drifted over to the area where they were romping and without anyone noticing due to the ruckus dropped a tab of snufzocalm into her brother and sister's glasses. The tabs were even more potent than snufzopam, which was legal, what Clara had used she had managed to get from Whohouse, who very nervously had admitted he, *'knew a fella who knew a fella etc etc'.*

"To our Mother's passing, long may she be remembered", Clara suddenly said. It was a chance to drain glasses and the two lushes of the family both promptly did so. Clara then watched them with interest, she had never witnessed the effects of the powerful soporific before. Indeed it was sometimes known as rape-med. For unscrupulous young people dosed intended conquests with it without their knowledge so that they could *grind the corn of the sleeper.* Such had become so infamous that consenting couples sometimes engaged in blanket shaking whilst one of them feigned sleep. Being painfully thin and with a high metabolism Grendlyme suddenly stopped giggling mid guffaw and began to keel over. With the swiftness and grace of a gazelle, Ianacho appeared from out of nowhere and caught her, being dutifully careful to support her bosom all the while less she bruise it in the fall. Critard was too drunk to notice his brother-in-law touching up his comatose wife. He did not even seem to care when Ianacho swept the lightweight woman up into his arms and carried her swiftly out of the room. Clara grinned, not caring one way or the other,

'I wonder if once he lays her on the bed if he'll sample her goodies'? She thought while waiting for her brother to succumb to the drug. Lavvisto had a huge frame and he also boasted an impressive capacity, but he suddenly grew quiet and began to yawn, then his eyelids started to droop and

excusing himself, Bunjella trailing behind him like a love-sick puppy, the two of them left.

It was time for Clara to mingle with the other CEOs of the world's ruling Corporations. That meant Glerius Orchvestige along with the other notables. Clara was patient though, she could wait. Orchvestige did not know that she knew! Alovar Hornrunner had attended as had the other three CEO's: Calmolm Castle, Rudolg Höfler and the only female CEO in attendance Fennirer von Goosetimp. Höfler was CEO of Deutsch Fahrzeuge Eingearbeitet and the most powerful man in Europe. Thusly Clara felt obliged to make a point of thanking each for their attendance and engaging in them for a short conversation.

She selected Fennirer firstly, as, although she was not short on personal confidence, the even more beautiful CEO always managed to make her feel inferior in some way

Even that day, when all of them were wearing black, Fennirer was managing to look both respectful and pretty in a frock that probably cost more than some peasants earned in several years.

"Fennirer", Clara greeted, "You look sensational, my compliments to your surgeon, he's done wonders with your ass".

The CEO from the Germanic Greater Empire simpered sweetly and admitted,

"I've not had any work done on it, Clara dear. This is what yours could look like if you spent an hour a day in the gymnasium".

Round one to the German.

"Well, I'm sure it looked a bit sort of saggy last time I saw you at the birthday party for Rudolg. You know, sort of flabby"!

One all.

"Like yours not dear, you really should start exercising".

Two-one.

"The best exercise I get is to strenuously avoid any sort of exercise", Clara smiled glassily. "It is good of you to come and pay your respects to my mother, but of course you were contemporaries were you not"?

Two all.

She was a couple of years older and of course several dozen lovers ahead of me".

Three-two.

"Perhaps your staid Germanic mien and personality put some potential suitors off, my dear friend Fennirer".

Clara settled for a score draw and excusing herself next approached the other German, Höfler. Much could be said of the latter, but one thing was true, he was a gentleman.

"Clara, my dear. My sincere commiserations. A sad day for all your family especially Hugh".

"Thank you, Rudolg. How have you been, you are looking trim and well".

"Very well Danke, all is gut Clara business has taken a 0.022% downturn as the winter comes, I expected to be doing better with the winter clothes, but sometimes scheiße passiert as they say in your country".

Car laughed, "They do say that sometimes, Rudolg, but in Standard of course and with a Yorkshire accent around here now that the county borders were redrawn and the red rose was abolished".

"Of course, the election is in a couple of weeks is that not so. Who do you think you will endorse with your democratic right, Clara"?

"I would vote for the party whose political leaders tell the truth, but of course like in the Greater Germanic empire, the politicians are just Corporation figureheads aren't they. None of them has any more power than poor King Darren XXIII".

"So you will vote for the Corporation party then"?

"I do not think the other three have much of a chance of getting enough seats to oppose them even in the house. The Peasants Party have never had a first minister to the King. The only time the Services party did it was a disaster and the FDP [Free Democratic Party never fool anyone. From the masses point of view, the best thing to do is to gain employment for a large corporation or conglomerate and work hard for them. Then they are taken care of with occupational healthcare, insurance, accommodation and pension".

"Leader Stonjoan has threatened to raise the retirement age in Saxonia and Londonia to one hundred, is that not a concern"? Höfler asked, for the age of pension in the Greater Germanic Empire was still incredibly low at eighty-seven.

"The national average lifespan has gone up to one hundred and twenty in our two regions", Clara pointed out. The plebeian will still get twenty years of doing nothing but receive handouts. Germans die younger because they work harder and because *spares* are in shorter supply".

"Well the English Empire does have a greater population to draw on for organ replacement and biological is still favoured over biotech by many surgeons".

"Many German surgeons", Clara pointed out, We English are happy to use biotech body parts. In fact, in India, they are now pioneering placing brains into androids. So much more durable, requiring less fuel and with greater capacity for industry".

"I hope humanity does not go down that road ", Rudolg Höfler shuddered, "What we are then talking about is a race of cyborgs Clara – homomechanicus".

Who knows what the future holds except for science fiction writers"? Clara smiled enigmatically, "You'll have to excuse me Rudolg, I must circulate".

It was Calmolm Castle who wanted to talk about football. Young for a CEO Calmolm had taken over the highly successful business after his parents had both been killed in the Venus Disaster. He was tall with overlong hair that someone had put blonde highlights in for him. In the face of the convention, he had attended the recycling ceremony dressed in a muted sky-blue suit that none the less was immaculately tailored, at least he had put a dark silk tie on his conventional shirt. Even indoors he wore aviator shades but it was not an affectation, he was said to suffer from photophobia, a still incurable ailment. He wore a beard, as did most men who had not taken the depilatory course of medications in their youth. He had a stern set to his jaw when Clara joined him, but at her arrival, he immediately became most animated.

"Do you think you can catch us this season, Clara"? He asked her. He did not look much older than her and in the past, they had shared the occasional groping for a trout in the peculiar river. Neither of them had taken it to be any more than mutual physical satisfaction and certainly not tried to transmute it into romance.

"Am I involved in some sort of chase that you are leading in then Cal"? Clara teased.

"We have double your points after a quarter of the season is already gone and we do not look like losing any games, admit it, you have a mountain to climb, to use the footie vernacular".

"If I were you I'd be more worried about IYWIWSI, Cal. But enough sport talk, how have you been"?

"Firstly my sincere condolences on your loss. I know you and your mother did not always see eye to eye but she was still your mother, Clara and you have my sympathy".

Clara nodded aware that at that precise moment she felt a conflicting series of emotions coursing through her mind and body.

"Thank you, Cal. So, business, how does Castle Electronics, a Corporation that came late to the game of Corps, the company go"?

"We've just won the contract for the new ice-fusion rocket to journey to Nyjord and Brahma", Calmolm declared proudly. "Every piece of electrical apparatus going in the Stridestrela is going to be fitted by us".

"That's fabulous news, I understand the main contract has gone to Indústrias Portuguesas"?

"That's right although the Japanese and Chinese are also involved. When it's completed it will take the greatest number of people to the new world that has ever been assembled. A multi-national team of fifteen".

"I'm presuming it will be to find the original pioneers if any still exist there"?

"Hyperspace does strange things to the fourth dimension", Calmolm grew very animated indeed, "The men and women of the Stridestrela could miss them by years, hundreds of years or even get there before them".

Before them, when they set off years after them and we've had subspace radio messages from some of them from planet-side. I cannot imagine that".

Clara was suddenly aware that Glerius Orchvestige was attempting to slip away unnoticed, she excused herself from her former step-parent and strode across the room,

"Leaving already, Orchvestige"?

He turned and glared at the woman who had dropped his title and yet was so much younger than him,

"That's Mister Orchvestige to you, young woman", he stormed and turned to go.

"I know it was you"! Was all Clara added then? Orchvestige whirled around.

"Doing what pray"? He demanded, "If you have an accusation to make

young woman, go to the padreps or the combmen. Or are you playing one of your silly games"?

"I'm playing football Orchvestige and I intend that OUC end up higher in the table than IYWIWSI".

I see, well I have a Corporation to run and I'm not even sure where IYWIWSI are in the table, so commiserations on the death of your mother and goodbye, Miss Trentavoria".

thirty-one　　　　　　　**Sean Derek Charles** was relaxing to the Eagles, an ancient electric band who had played their own antiquated instruments centuries past and left some music on small discs called Compak. With some of his ill-gotten gains, Sean had paid to have a Compak machine hand-made that could read the ancient devices and play them to a separate box that amplified the sound sufficiently to drive a pair of paper cone speakers with magnets behind them. The reproduction was startlingly good. The machine did its job admirably as did the rest of the system.

Sean was sipping a ginfizz when his padfon pinged on audio-only and he immediately cut the sound to a level which he could speak to the caller over. It was an ewithheld, telling him nothing of the sender's ID, meaning probably a sanction was going to be offered.

"Hello – Fixer"?

"This is the Faded Man, I have another sanction for you if you are not too busy"?

The Faded Man paid premium shillin, so even if Sean had been busy, he would not have been busy!

"Proceed"? Was all he requested. In his experience, the Faded Man was not exuberant over the possibility of small-talk. His electronically-altered tones were always evenly modulated and concise.

"The sanction is very high profile".

"That will not be a problem for me, but it might involve a premium".

"That will not be a problem for me. The method of the sanction must be in a very precise fashion".

"Explain", Sean was more concerned about that, he liked to sanction the mark in his way and after exhaustive research. If he could not do the assignment in the method of his choosing he might well have to contract the work to Uncle Jack. Uncle Jack had just finished a long stretch in the slammer on a bum rap but was once more at liberty. Sean had sub-contracted him in the past, the only trouble being that Uncle Jack was what was referred to in the trade as *a screw-up*. He lacked the finesse and delicate touch of his nephew, he had once actually bludgeoned a mark to death with an antique book that contained old Jewish fairy tales. A compendium of various authors written many years in the past concerning someone who in the latest translation was referred to as The Big G and the second part of the compendium about his offspring JC. JC had started some sort of underground movement in Roman-occupied Judea and the lead Roman a hero called Conscious had ridden him down in his Chariot and was called Conscious Chariot from that point onward. The tome had been covered in the hide of a cow and due to the number of pages was heavy enough when applied with sufficient force to brain the living daylights out of anyone unfortunate enough to be sanctioned by Uncle Jack. After that contretemps, Uncle Jack became known as the killer who used the right hand of the Big G and it was only a matter of time before the combmen stitched Uncle Jack up with a fit-up that smelled of kippers.

Now he was out and open for business. Sean would have to be pretty desperate to put any work his way, so he waited for the Faded Man to explain what was required.

"The mark is Glerius Orchvestige CEO of If you want it we stock it"!

That will not present an especially difficult problem but explain the precise fashion that is required by the customer".

Sean thought it highly likely that the Faded Man was a middle-man and the real customer was someone Sean himself would never meet and even by some bizarre fluke if he did - would never suspect the nature of them.

"The sanction must be done at a football match, in a stadium filled with ninety-thousand spectators. It must be carried out at the very point at which IYWIWSI score a goal".Sean Derek Charles knew better than to ask why the sanction was so precise. He simply knew that if he wanted the assignment he would have to agree to all the conditions. Then he asked the forty silver shillin question, "And the premium"?

The figure that was mentioned was enough to keep the fixer in the manner to which he had been accustomed for three years and Sean did not live simply all the time.

"I accept the sanction", Sean tried to sound confident, he had no idea then how he was going to kill someone in front of a huge crowd without being seen, but he could not afford to refuse.

He returned his attention to the music and listened to a classical piece of classical music:

On a dark desert highway, cool wind in my hair
Warm smell of colitas, rising through the air
Up ahead in the distance, I saw a shimmering light
My head grew heavy and my sight grew dim
I had to stop for the night.

Sean sipped his drink and thought about various ways he could kill someone in front of so many people without being detected, then a self-congratulatory smile eased its way across his handsome countenance and he knew that he could do it!

The Fixer had never failed a sanction during his entire illustrious career and he was not about to start then. He let the Compak slide out of the machine and replaced it with another of his favourites, Love It to Death by a band who did not have a female member but were none the less called Alice Cooper. His favourite track was The Ballad of Dwight Fry and he let the lyrics wash over him:

I was gone for fourteen days
I coulda been gone for more
Held up in the intensive care ward
Lyin' on the floor
I was gone for all those days
But I was not all alone
I made friends with a lot of people
In the danger zone

thirty-two
over to Annable"

"And now with the sports news this evening

"Thank you Gennis. There have been several notable events in the Football Corporation league today but the most remarkable of them is the sad demise of CEO Glerius Orchvestige which occurred during the game as the poor man was watching his side being given a five-nil thrashing by Orang-U-Can. Roxbrough back from a mysterious training injury and after undergoing regenerative therapy scored a hat-trick before half-time and IYWIWSI did not seem able to settle on the newly laid pitch of Clara Trentavoria's team. In the second half things got worse as central defender Burgenbower headed home a fourth from an OUC corner and in the dying moments of the game Lane slipped through several defenders to slot home

Corporation Division One		
Goosetimp v Voleskip	5	0
Makers Guild v RR Scoriors	2	2
Castle v Preciometallic	1	0
Tiptingle v DFE	2	2
ZS v Hornrunner	3	0
OUC v IYWIWSI	5	0

the killer fifth goal".

"Killer in more ways than one it seems Annable" Gennis gurned into the camera.

Annable went on with a frown, "I guess you could say that Gennis if you had no respect. Sadly Orchvestige, who leaves behind a widow and four children seemed to keel over just before the computer referee blew the final whistle. In an interview with the SBA [Saxonian Broadcasting Authority] Vanial, his eldest son, promised to carry on with the team as the newly appointed director of the club, while Orchvestige's widow, Jancy will assume temporary chair-ship of the board of directors of If You Want It We Stock It. Here are the rest of today's results":

"The dramatic scoreline at OUCH has made tonights first division table look like this:

"Despite the defeat, IYWIWSI remains second due to other results but the heavy scoreline at OUCH has improved Orang-U-Can's position as they go up to fifth their best placing in the league so

Corporation Div One		Plyd	Goals	Pts
1	Castle Electronics	7	13	17
2	I.Y.W.I.W.S.I.	7	12	12
3	Goosetimp Weapons	7	16	11
4	Deutsch Fahrzeuge Eingearbeitet	7	12	10
5	Orang-u-Can	7	10	10
6	Makers-Guild	7	11	9
7	Zhōngguá Shāngpín	7	6	9
8	Rolls Royce Scoriors	7	8	8
9	Preciometalic.Inc	7	9	7
10	Tiptingle Tigers	7	7	7
11	Hornrunner Hornets	7	6	4
12	Voleskip Pharmaceuticals	7	2	4

far this season. Deputy manager George Best told this reporter after the game that he was 'pleased' with the results since Hugh Trentavoria's daughter had taken over the running of the club. While in a subsequent interview with the striker Roxbrough, who had helped his team to victory with a hat-trick, used the very same term, strange, what do you think"?

thirty-three

Clara turned the tri-vidz off at that moment for her padfon was pinging. The handsome features of her best striker swam immediately into focus.

Clara smiled but said nothing, unsure quite what he was pinging her for.

"I'm going to the practice range with my needlegun, would you like to come and fire a few at targets".

"Are you being serious, Roxbrough"?

"As serious as a level-two needle"!

"You want to know if I want to go to a practise range shooting with you"?

"I know I do, that's why I asked you".

"It was a question", Clara chuckled, "What are you thinking, Roxbrough"?

"I'm thinking that everyone could do with keeping their skills up to date because you never know when you might need them".

"Are you asking me out on a date and your idea of something to do on such an occasion is to shoot targets"?

"A date only in the sense that today has a date, I thought you might like to come, shooting is just shooting right"?

"I cannot argue with the inescapable logic of that last statement you weird and random man you. So you simply wish to take me shooting"?

"I can pick you up in twenty minutes. We'll go to the range in Deansgate – Point Blank. Or, I'll go on my own".

It was certainly *out there* as a way of telling her he was interested in her and in Clara, it struck something of a chord, so she nodded.

"Sweats and joggers then".

"Dress code is informal for certain and there is always the chance of snagging your clothing on a needle so, yes".

"I don't bring my needles"?

"Are you kidding. We don't fire *live* barbs, someone could end up comatose or worse. No, the club issues us with the unfilled type. All you need to bring is your gun or guns".

"Guns, how many do you have"?!

"I've three, a Kimber, a Sig Sauer and a Ruger – you"?

"I will bring my Browning as it is the only one I possess".

Roxbrough cut the connection and humming Clara went to change and to get her needlegun from her *smalls*-drawer.

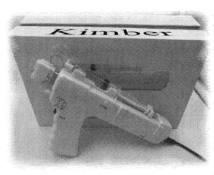

"What on Earth do you think you're going to shoot with that"?! Clara demanded when Roxbrough dragged the Ruger out of his kit-bag, "I thought the Kimber and the Sig Sauer were a bit OTT but that is a monster, how can you possibly expect to carry that around in your joggers or bohos".

"It's for missions, not everyday security", the football player explained with a grin, "Good aye"?

"Well I certainly would like to shoot it, but after my Browning, I'm not even sure I could hold *that* up"!

"It's made of polycarboresin, fashioned to look like metal and is deceptively light", he told her cheerfully.

"Since you got abducted and injured I understand your need for a gun, but three, Rox, aren't you going a bit overboard"?

Roxbrough smiled, saying nothing, but thinking, *'She just called me Rox, that's a start'!*

"Well as far as I am now concerned", he smiled back at her, Security is not just a joke"!

Clara laughed, "Alright then let's start. Show me what you can do already"?

Roxbrough wound down a paper target to the end of the range and fired off seven quick needles with his Kimber. Once Clara had wound them back, motivated by curiosity she saw that they were in a reasonable grouping and all in the bull or ring outside it.

"Now you, with your Browning"?

Clara held the gun awkwardly and fired in a much slower volley. It seemed to Roxbrough that she lacked any real coordination or balance and when they wound the target back only three of the needles had hit the target and those in the outer rings.

"You might need a heavier gun", Roxbrough suggested, "That Browning is popular with ladies because of its size and very light-weight construction. It has the disadvantage of bucking around when used though. Here try the Kimber"?

She did so and was surprised to discover that what he said was true. With the slightly heavier needlegun, she hit the target every time, even if in the outer rings.

Roxbrough then fired seven quick shots with his Sig Sauer, which had an alloy bodywork and with pretty much the same grouping as before. Meanwhile, Clara beginning to enjoy more success stuck with the Kimber. They took a few turns each before Roxbrough picked up the Ruger. With the shoulder attachment, it doubled as a needlerifle. Sighting down it he fired the usual seven needles and five of them landed in the bullseye.

"Wow", Clara enthused, "How come you did so well with that monstrosity"?

"Because of its weight and size rather than despite it", he explained. You can hold it much steadier against your shoulder and sight right down it with this little sight on the end. Try it you'll be surprised".

She took it off him and assumed a stance but before she could fire he interrupted.

"No! You're not standing right. Here let me help you". He spaced her feet and then suddenly slipped his arms around her shoulders. Out of the side of her mouth in quite comical fashion, she warned,

"If there is any cupage or groin contact, Mister, something gets ruddy-well chopped off, are we clear"?

"I think you made your point most succinctly", he gulped.

Despite that though, she hit three bulls with the Ruger. It was a fun occasion and somewhat off the beaten path when it came to dates. As they walked out of the range kit-bags in hand and heading to his flitter, he asked her,

"What about putting these in the boot and going for a cocktail or something"?

"I don't think so Rox, that would make it a date would it not"?

"Relax Boss, I can honestly tell you without fear of contraception that I have never slept with any of my football coaches".

Clara laughed at the inference and the deliberate mistake and then asked,

"Coaches plural, how many have you had? I thought you quite new to the sport"?

"Well I only have had one before you", he admitted then, But I never went to bed with him honest".

Clara smiled, "I'm not interested in cocktails but you could take me for a bite to eat. What about the new Veggie-Bar in St Mary's Parsonage, it's only a short walk from here".

"Veggie"?

"Yes I want to try the new strain of spirulett [splicing of spirulina and lettuce] celespire [with celery] spirupeps [peppers] and tomspiros [you can guess that one]. We can have a chicken salad, egg and cheese salad or tuna. Do you fancy any of them"?

"I will try anything once".

As they walked she asked conversationally. "That girl who rescued you in Moss Side, have you seen anything of her since the fateful day in question"?

Roxbrough's brow creased slightly in mild annoyance. He did not wish to be reminded about the existence of the young widow whilst on an apparent date with Clara Trentavoria.

"I haven't no, we are worlds apart, Boss, she and I would never make a couple".

"That was not what I was suggesting", Clara responded, "I just wondered if you would keep in touch with someone who saved you from a potentially very grisly fate that's all"?

"I might ping her from time to time. I'm not even sure if she would want me to though", he lied, glad of the distraction he asked, "This the place"?

Clara nodded. "Thank goodness it's starting to rain again, I sometimes

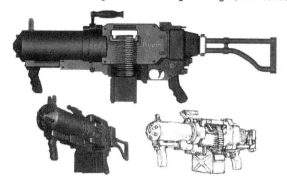

wonder you know, if the scientist Johnnies ever did manage to put the climate back to how it should be. It does seem to rain an awful lot".

Your friend Igan Giganort could probably answer that better than I", Roxbrough tried to drop the name casually but did not quite manage it.

"Oh cripes, Rox. I'm so glad you mentioned him because I forgot all about my promise to you regarding him. I will get in touch and get you that interview I promise. Remind me if I don't will you"?

"I don't like to do that", Roxbrough lied with a smile that did not exactly ooze the last word with sincerity.

Hurrying out of the lower ionosphere's precipitation, they pushed through the doors and found the place heaving.

"It doesn't look much like we've got a chance of getting a table without a significant wait". The striker observed.

"Leave that to me", Clara smirked and hailed an android waiter over. The construct was a class VII and moved with the sort of agile dexterity that even Roxbrough was incapable of.

"Yes, Ma'am"? It asked in well-modulated tone despite the hectic chaos in the eatery.

"Scan my features, please", Clara instructed and waited while from a hidden solenoid somewhere in the android's eyes a pale amber line traced the outline of her pretty face, then -

"Miss Trentavoria, this is an unexpected honour, I shall fetch the manager, would you wait at the bar please"?

By the time the duo had ordered a white wine each and was just starting to sip it, a rather flustered little man with way too much evidence of plastic surgery pulling his features taut hurried to be beside them.

'One of these days something is going to snap or something will come undone and all the skin will fall to its original location', Roxbrough thought as he looked at the man's shiny epidermis.

"Miss Trentavoria, I was not informed you were dining with us this evening, please forgive the oversight", the man gushed with an accent that hovered somewhere between Mancunian and feigned Gaulic origin. "I am Pierre, the manager of this place and if you will but give me a couple of minutes, will have a table freed up for you".

"Of course Pierre", Clara smiled benignly, "Father told me about this place and I thought I really must try it for myself. I will be certain to tell him of your efficiency and courtesy when I see him".

"You are too kind", Pierre was orgiastic in his gratitude and he took one of Clara's hands and brushed the back of it with his lips, before scurrying away like a busy weasel.

"I would bet serious sestertius that Pierre has never even been to Francosia", Roxbrough said with amusement.

"Of course he hasn't", Clara confirmed, "His real name is Biliam and he was born in Stockport. Hugh loaned him the money to start this place up and owns forty-nine percent of the place".

"I see", Roxbrough was suddenly thoughtful. Clara Trentavoria and Lsenia Shyrock lived in the same city and yet they were from a different universe. He almost felt guilty spending time with his manager, but then who was born in the thirty-third century without an agenda? If he could never get wealthy, he intended to do the next best thing and that was to marry or contract long-term into *olde-money.* Apart from all that he felt a genuine attraction to Clara on a purely physical level, what was not to like?

Within five minutes a table for four was made available to them as if by magic or vudun and Clara seated herself opposite Roxbrough. When a different android came to take their order she instructed the mechanism,

"It's very busy tonight, if another couple is seeking a table let them join us, we do not mind"?

"Pierre said.....", the android began.

"I am telling you it will be fine, override instruction Tre555alpha".

There was an almost imperceptible whirring noise inside the constructs cranium and it replied,

"As Madam wishes", and then proceeded to hand them menu-pads.

"We'll have another drink each while we make up our minds", Clara told the mechanism which left them smoothly and silently. Roxbrough realised he had been the alpha-male whilst on the needlegun range, but he was no longer.

"What was that override instruction you just gave the waiter and where did you learn that"? He asked the young woman.

"It works with most of them, but they would not accept my override command from you, it is unique to me. Hugh got it me when he did a contract with the manufacturers of the class VII range in India. If you keep reminding me I'll get one for you if you like. It effectively makes your command supersede all others in the androids electronyloplanyon nucleus".

"You mean its brain".

She smiled, "That's what I said".

"Tell you what", Roxbrough offered then slightly ill at ease, "You order exactly what you fancy and I'll have the same so that we can compare notes".

"Of course", Clara accepted that like it was the most natural suggestion in the world. She was a strong personality and used to getting her way. She did not even suspect Roxbrough was enjoying the evening less and less as events unfolded.

It was none the less interesting to try the newest DNA spliced vegetables that professor Hoyle had developed. Hoyle was the grandson of the greatest geneticist who had ever lived. Though he had followed in his father's footsteps who had followed in his before him none then referred to him as Hoyle III. He had carved a niche in history for himself with his various developments in the field of genetic modifications and engineering.

It was a pleasant enough evening, but Roxbrough was strangely slightly relieved to be dropping Clara off at Trentavoria Estate some time later.

"Good night then", he told her quite formally and she half-smiled, asking, "You're not going to kiss me goodnight"?

"That would indicate that we had been on a date", Roxbrough reasoned allowed, "And I sort of promised you that wasn't the case".

"Oh come here, Fool", she took charge yet again and looping her slim hand behind his head drew their faces close together. Roxbrough had to admit that the caress was pleasant. Like all women, she had a very soft and yielding mouth. Not that he had ever kissed a man, that sort of thing was no longer fashionable since the turn of the century and it was illegal to display it in public, resulting in psychiatric and physical reorientation as decided by the royal court if abusers were apprehended.

When they finally parted it was the woman who was flushed and disturbed by the strength of her reaction. She thumbed the hatch release and skipped into the home without so much as a backward glance.

thirty-three   **Sean Derek Charles** – the fixer had given his problem considerable thought and finally come up with a solution. He left his apartment. The one that he was currently using at any rate and strolled down to his flitter. It was a hire vehicle and as far as he was concerned merely a conveyance for getting from 'A' to 'B'. He let the vehicle take him past the Museo Regional de Atacama and beyond to the Hospital Regional San José del Carmen de Copiapó - Los Carrera. He was on his way to see Cabrito, who was a porter there.

Sean had spent the last hour on his padfon looking up weapons on the SWW when nothing which could serve his purpose revealed itself to him, he then turned his attention to medical equipment and there he hit pay-dirt. He then knew how he was going to kill Glerius Orchvestige in front of thousands without being detected as the homicidian.

An AED [automated external defibrillator] was a portable electronic device that automatically diagnosed the life-threatening cardiac arrhythmias of ventricular fibrillation and pulse-less ventricular tachycardia. It was able to treat them through defibrillation, the application of electricity which stops the arrhythmia, allowing the heart to reestablish an effective rhythm. If applied incorrectly, it could stop a perfectly functioning heart and cause cardiac arrest.

Sean needed one, which he would then give to an electronics wizard whom he had used in the past to miniaturise it as small as was possible and still retain its function. He found Cabrito in his usual location, in the flitterbulance-bay smoking a standard tobacco ciggie

"Aah, mi viejo amigo Hwanezz, ¿cómo está señor"? The little Chilean greeted at seeing Sean emerge from his ride.

"You know my Spanish is no good, Cabrito, speak in Standard if you do not mind".

"Very well, Señor Hwanezz. What can poor Cabrito do for you this lovely sunny day".

Sean had first introduced himself to the Chilean as Mister Jones several years previously, but the Spanish version of that nomen was what he had received ever since.

"I want an AED, by Tuesday at the latest"?

Cabrito sucked the air in through his teeth, "Not easy Señor, it will be expensive, I risk much by taking something that will be missed".

Sean thought, *'I expect we have to go through this pantomime every time, it's all part of the negotiation'.* Aloud he noted, "If you cannot accommodate me this time, perhaps I should go elsewhere"?

Cabrito looked wounded, "I did not say that exactly, Señor. What I meant to convey to you is the risks involved and the possibility of my being apprehended, it will not be inexpensive I am afraid".

"Nine million pesos".

Cabrito grinned, a whiter than white expression against his coffee-coloured complexion.

"I will see what I can do Señor Hwanezz".

Sean had the AED on the Monday and took a flitter-jet to China, there to see his go-to electronics specialist who also possessed the happy coincidence of being very decorative indeed. This always made it a pleasure to visit Jiaquiang, because she usually let him sleep with her as a bonus to the commissions he paid her. She was no courtesan, it was just that Sean was a rather dashing assassin and the pleasure they received from the arrangement was greatly mutual.

He had pinged her ahead of time and as he picked up his lone bag in Qingdao flitterport, the girl was waiting to greet him. As usual, she was wearing bright scarlet lippy and after crushing him to her impressive bosom and planting an enthusiastic kiss on his mouth, so was he.

"A job, or a social call", she asked as they walked arm in arm to her transport.

"I thought we would combine the two", he smiled at her. Jiaquiang was one of those unique girls who did not ask too many questions, neither was she too demanding in any way. This made her a perfect friend and lover as far as the fixer was concerned.

It had proved very convenient for him and very lucrative for her and both of them were satisfied with the status quo. Of course the instant the Chinese girl demanded more, the assassin would either never contact her ever again, or he would kill her, whichever seemed most appropriate at the time.

They climbed into her Yaqin 200bhp 滑行 flitter and were soon hurtling through the crowded streets of Qingdao. Jiaquiang never adhered to speed limits and probably incurred several speeding warnings. Yet she never lost her license and probably *worked off* the warnings with the Chief of the combmen - on her back. Sean did not especially care, not being the jealous type and he was not faithful to her either so it did not especially matter.

The instant they entered her workshop, she dragged him through it and into the apartment beyond. There she proceeded to demonstrate to him that she had lost none of her flexibility nor vitality since the last time they had pleasured one another. It was ninety minutes before he could get the conversation around to business. Tell her what else he wanted. She did not question why he was placing the order, she knew instinctively that curiosity was dangerous and had too much sense to display it.

"I'll get to work on it after dinner. You've made me hungry let's go out and eat"?

As he dressed, she threw on some sort of western blouse which she did not button up and over it a white jacket which she did not pull together over her expensive decollete. In the past, being so brazenly garbed one of them had occasionally escaped and fallen out. On just such an occasion, without even pausing in her conversation she had calmly levered it back in and neither of them had referred to it, nor even thought it worthy of comment.

They went to her favourite English Restaurant - Xiānshēng Smith's and while he had real bovine beef, roast potatoes and lichrrots, she had sea-bass and English chipped - fried potatoes and spirupeas. Both of them found that a bottle of Black Tower white Baijiu went with both menus and they brought out the half bottle leftover as it was 52% alcohol content. If what Jiaquiang had drunk had effected her, Sean was not able to tell. There again, she drove so recklessly that it probably would not have been noticeable anyway.

"You go to bed now lover", she told him in perfect Standard, as they entered the workshop, "I'll make your order, I'm too wired to sleep. When I'm done I'll come and wake you and you can frenge my brains out again before you need to leave".

That was how it was between them. Perfection as far as he was concerned and if she felt any differently, she never gave him even the hint of the slightest indication. Perhaps she knew enough to know that it was what was keeping her alive.

When he left the apartment several hours later, climbing into the flittaxi ready to return to the flitterport it was with the AED in his inside breast pocket. It looked exactly like a rather nice ball-point or pad-stylus. When going into the ground a cursory inspection by security would assume he

intended to ask for an autograph, from either players, manager or both. It had been expensive to secure the seat he had needed, for it to be within the range of the lethal AED's beam, but the customer was paying expenses. When he left the ground just over two hours later, the CEO of If You Want It We Stock It - would be dead!

thirty-four **When Clara got** into work the Monday after the weekend before, it was to be informed of yet another crisis. It began to seem to her as though running a football club was to be presented with one piece of serious revelation after another. She had barely closed the door behind her when Best, who had been waiting inside for her arrival, began to tell her,

"Morning Boss, we've got a major problem. One that OUC will not wish to be associated with".

Clara sighed, hitting the lighting touch plate with unnecessary savagery. "I don't even want to know what it is, never mind start to address it until I've got a mug of lichen-coff in my hand".

Best rose smoothly to a standing position, "In that case, my first order of business will be the making of one for you. Do you mind if I make one for myself while I'm at it"?

"Knock yourself out".

Clara enjoyed the silence before her deputy was going to rudely shatter it as an oasis of calm in a sea of confusion. She savoured every last second of it and then Best came crashing back into her space. It came to her, to reason, to wonder why the average person was so clumsy and so uncaring of wear-and-tear. No one seemed to close doors any longer when it was seemingly preferable to slam them too. Best threw himself in the chair opposite the desk with the same lack of respect for the inanimate. So violent was the descent that he spilt some of his drink into his lap.

'I hope he's scolded one of his balls', she found herself thinking and smiled at her tacit humour.

"What's funny, Boss"? He asked her in genuine ignorant curiosity. Clara merely shook her head, one thing no one else could do was get inside her head. If mankind ever developed telepathy that would herald the demise of the human race.

"Well you've got your drink so I need to tell you what's going on", the assistant manager was like a juggernaut. "It's Whohouse, we've got a situation"!

Clara waited, expecting that he might have been busted by the combmen for possession. Best looked slightly disappointed that she did not vociferate her curiosity. Rather she knew that no amount of instruction to the contrary would stop Best from telling her, all she had to do was wait.

She regretted turning on all the overhead LEDs, a faint headache was starting to make itself felt behind her eyes.

"You know the cleaning girl, Jhandy"?

Clara thought about that one for a while, then asked, "Which one is she the tall brunette"?

Best clarified, "No, the honey blonde, wears red a lot and sometimes comes to work in a straw hat".

"That's Jhandy! I called the tall brunette Jhandy the other day and she never said anything. Never mind anyway. So what about her, is she after a pay rise or something"?

Best did not so much as allow himself to grimace, grimly he went on, "She's been assaulted and she says the perpetrator was Whohouse".

Clara suddenly took the rest of the conversation very seriously indeed. "When you say assaulted, in what respect do you use the term, George"?

"I'm afraid she's claiming it was a sexual assault", Best was no longer speaking loudly at all, indeed his voice had diminished to little more than a hoarse whisper.

"Fabulous"! Clara cursed in such a way that she meant the matter was astonishing and inconceivable rather than marvellous and good. "Are you trying to tell me she is claiming that Whohouse raped her"?

Best nodded.

"Where is she now"?

"In my office, Valryss is with her, she's the brunette".

"When was this supposed to have happened"?

"Last night. Whohouse opened up so the two of them could clean. It seems he told security and the janitor they could both go home early and then an hour later, Valryss too".

"Leaving just he and Jhandy in the place"?

"Just the two of them".

"Then what happened? According to Jhandy that is"?

"She says she suddenly felt exhausted and seated herself on a bench in the first team showers. Before she realised what was happening, she had fallen asleep. She woke up with Whohouse on top of her and in her and the two of them completely naked".

"What did she do"?

"He told her that if she screamed he would strangle her so she let him finish and then gathered her clothes together and he let her go home. Once there she spent half an hour under the shower and then collapsed into bed where she lay huddled all night unable to sleep".

"Where's Whohouse, now"?

"Not in yet".

"Any witnesses to any of this"?

"Not exactly".

"What does that mean"?

"She lives on her own and she didn't go to the combmen, so she has no evidence in the physical sense. This morning though she pinged Valryss and the two of them came in to see you. They bumped into me first and I got the story out of the pair of them. It seems Whohouse – the idiot – had previously told Valryss that he had and I quote, 'The hots for that little blonde and was not going to rest until he'd nailed that cute little ass'"!

"The women are friends"?

Best nodded.

"So what we have is a situation of he said they said, not enough in itself. Unless..."!

"Unless what Boss"?

"Unless our physio said something to someone else along the same lines. Did he ever say anything to you, George"?

Best had the grace to blush and remarked lamely, Sort of guys talk if you know what I mean, I could not....".

"No, George, I don't know what you mean not being a guy myself, so tell me as a direct quote what he said to you".

Best blushed scarletly,

"Tell me *now*"?

124

"We were sort of talking last week while the two of them were in the corridor, and we ended up glancing in their general direction, in my case it just happened to be because Whohouse was already looking that way. Well, anyway he turned to me and asked, 'Mattie', he still calls me Mattie, what with it being my surname and all, anyway he asked, 'Mattie which of them two hotties do you think would be the most enthusiastic in the sack', but that's guys for you, we sort of talk like that when the girls aren't listening".

"So what was your reply, Best"?

"I said, we'd never find out".

"To which he responded"?

"That I might not find out, but he intended to. He was bragging, it doesn't mean anything in itself, does it"?

"Do you want me to answer that, you imbecile? Go and get the two of them and ask them to come to my office and Best"?

"Yes, Boss"?

"Not a word of this to anyone, if it can at all be kept out of the tabloid pings I intend to deal with it in house".

Nodding miserably Best left Clara alone for the moment with her thoughts. She had decided what she was going to advise once the trio entered, "Thank you Best, you can go".

Jhandy was red-eyed, she had been crying – a lot. Valryss was looking determined and outraged, obviously there to see that justice was done in addition to giving her friend all the moral support she thought she must need.

"Please sit down both of you", Clara began. "I want to start by telling you that Whohouse will be sacked the minute he surfaces at this ground and all his holiday pay and back pay for last month is going to your thumb, Jhandy....".

"Do you think money will make up for the ordeal she's been through, Miss Trentavoria"? The brunette demanded. Clara gave the girl her most withering look and said evenly,

"Please do not interrupt me again, young lady, I am talking to Jhandy not you"?!

She let that sink in and then addressed the blonde once again, "I am going to see to it that as a physio, Whohouse is finished, he will not work for another club as long as I have something to do with it. I cannot imagine how violated you feel right now, because I have never been molested in the way you were. If you feel the need to talk to someone who specialises in this sort of thing, I will arrange for it at the club's cost. Now....", deep breath, "You have no evidence as you went home and bathed and I understand why you did, but in the eyes of the law and of the courts you have no case. Not only that but if word gets out what has happened to you, you will find it uncomfortable working here in the company of randy young men, therefore I will do the only thing I can do in the circumstances, Jhandy. I will make you a compensation payment. I believe you are telling the truth, but you and I know everyone else will always express doubts. You have my heartfelt sympathy and if you think I can do anything else for you, ask me now and if it is in my power I will do it"?

"What sort of compensation", the brunette demanded.

"That is something Jhandy and I will discuss once you have resumed your cleaning duties, Valryss. If Jhandy chooses to subsequently confide in you, that is, of course, her prerogative. Please close the door behind you, Valryss"?

Sniffing her disapproval the brunette left and Jhandy promptly burst into a flood of tears. For several minutes Clara held the weeping girl in her arms rocking her backwards and forwards soothingly until the deluge abated. Once it had she made her a monetary offer to keep the matter in house. It was of a size the girl would not earn in a lifetime mopping floors and cleaning toilets. She ended by telling her,

"Go home now, take some time off, come back when you feel you can, this is the only option I'm afraid, I cannot do anything else, I wish I could".

Thanking her profusely the frail blonde left and for a time Clara did nothing but close her eyes and pinch the bridge of her nose between a thumb and forefinger.

There was a knock on the door. It was Best. Clara quickly told him what was happening and then asked,

"Get Kipson to put out some discrete feelers for a physiotherapist, it would be just our luck for one of the players, or more to get injured while we don't have one".

Which was the very way things were going for Orang-U-Can at that time and it happened in the very next midweek match?

The fixture list was:

Corporation Division One

Goosetimp v Hornrunner

Voleskip v RR Scoriors

Makers Guild v Preciometallic

Castle Electronics v DFE

IYWIWSI v Tiptingle

Zhõngguá Shãngpín v Orang-U-Can

Sensing it was going to be a tough fixture after a journey to China Clara decided on a defensively strong team and set OUC up in the following way:

6. Radband
12. McFarland 13. Jennings 25. Zinyama 4 Burgenbower
19.Jenson   16. Flintham 5. West 7. ball
9. Sellers 11. Shivers

Substitutes

1. Anderson
8. Wong
14. Wing
20. Lane
10.Nero
23. Roxbrough

She intended to defend in numbers and deeply for the first forty-five minutes and let the Chinese wear themselves out attacking to no avail. At half-time, she would bring on the trio of Lane, Nero and Roxbrough and hope to score one or two goals with sudden counter-attacks. There was no place for the youngsters in such a tactical selection. To her surprise Best agreed with the notion, perhaps keeping his head down due to the current climate and disturbing events. Clara knew he and the physio had been friends for some time and Best did not want to be tainted by association. Over the next two days following the morning of the cleaners dire report Whohouse simply did not turn up for work, an admission of guilt in itself. Clara sent Sanedad round to his current address on Croft Street, just off Albert Park. Not only had he not appeared to be in the property, but the neighbours told the young academy player that he had not been seen in the area since the weekend. It seemed the Physio had disappeared off the face of the Earth!

Thusly OUC flew to the match with Zhōngguá Shāngpín with Doctor Charmley doubling up, on his duties. Clara gave the appropriate pre-match briefing outlining her plan to the men. By that time they were all very supportive of everything, she was doing at the club. Everyone was on a high, for they were a winning side, climbing the table after each result. That was how footballers were. When games were being won, everything was rosy and they would have agreed to just about any plan that their shapely and attractive Boss had come up with.

The game started just as expected. The Chinese pressing hard on home territory. The ground was packed to the very roof and the noise the fans were making was an almost frightening cacophony, enough to subdue any visiting squad. Then the incident happened! West went in for a sliding tackle and the Chinese whom he sent tumbling to the floor promptly proceeded to demonstrate how a slight contact on his shin-pad had blinded him for life, or until he got a well-deserved free-kick for his acting ability. Incensed by the injustice of it all - West lost his head and kicked the player on the ground, to encourage his rapid recovery. The comp-ref instantly flashed red-screen and Orang-U-Can were suddenly reduced to ten men. Clara was forced to drop Shivers into his position and it left only Sellers with any of the faintest chances of pinching a lucky counter-attacking goal.

That was.....before matters took a second downturn. The Chinese incensed by West's behaviour had become increasingly aggressive in their tackling. Just before half-time Shivers went in for a 50-50 ball and since he was not a natural defender twisted his knee badly and had to be stretchered off. It was five minutes before the interval and Clara let her team defend for those five long minutes with nine men. At least the scoreline had remained 0-0 though.

"We are just about on course", she told her team, "I'm bringing you off Sellers and putting on Lane and Roxbrough and in the second half we are going to play a 4-3-2 formation like this", she put the team up on the white-board:

Orang-U-Can

6. Radband
12. McFarland 13. Jennings 25. Zinyama 4 Burgenbower
19.Jenson 16. Flintham 7. Ball
20. Lane 23. Roxbrough

"It's unconventional because we are a man short, but the best we can do with ten men. McFarland, Burgenbower, I don't want you acting as wing-backs not with a man short, stay behind the midfield three. Lane, you're fresh, do as much running around as service allows and try and slip a pass to Roxbrough when you can. It won't be pretty but we might manage to pinch a goal or two".

The team trotted out for the second half and disaster struck again. A speculative shot from outside the box by Zhōngguá ShāngpÍn took a wicked deflection as it hit Zinyama and abruptly changed direction Caught hopelessly off balance Radband could do nothing than helplessly watch the ball fly into the opposite side of the goal to which he had been diving. The home crowd went into delirious exultation. It was the first goal conceded by Orang-U-Can in weeks and their team had broken the resolute defence. Seeing what it did to the Zambian's confidence Clara instantly brought him

Corporation Division One		
Goosetimp v Hornrunner	2	0
Voleskip v RR Scoriors	0	0
Makers Guild v Preciometallic	1	1
Castle Electronics v DFE	1	1
IYWIWSI v Tiptingle	4	0
Zhōngguá ShāngpÍn v Orang-U-Can	1	1

off and sent Wong on in his place. Flintham had to drop into the back four while the midfielder Wong took his place in central midfield. It was an of necessity unbalanced side but the men performed very well in roles that not

	Corporation Div One	Plyd	Goals	Pts
1	Castle Electronics	7	14	18
2	I.Y.W.I.W.S.I.	7	16	15
3	Goosetimp Weapons	7	18	14
4	Deutsch Fahrzeuge Eingearbeitet	7	13	11
5	Orang-u-Can	7	11	11
6	Makers-Guild	7	12	10
7	Zhōngguá ShāngpÍn	7	7	10
8	Rolls Royce Scoriors	7	8	9
9	Preciometalic.Inc	7	10	8
10	Tiptingle Tigers	7	7	7
11	Voleskip Pharmaceuticals	7	2	5
12	Hornrunner Hornets	7	6	4

all of them were used to playing naturally. With ten minutes left Zhōngguá ShāngpÍn brought lane down in their penalty area and the comp-ref immediately flashed penalty. The short playmaker slotted the kick home himself and the game ended in a creditable draw for the away team who had played so long with a man short. The rest of the results were also not all as expected. Clara glanced at her pad in keen curiosity:

Castle had dropped a vital home point against the German side Deutsch Fahrzeuge Eingearbeitet, while If You Want It We Stock It had enjoyed a very resounding victory under their new manager. It made the table:

thirty-five   **Sean Derek Charles** was enjoying quite a busy spell over the last few weeks so he was not especially surprised when his padfon pinged him yet again. It was a voice-only communication. He even recognised the I.P. careless of the Faded Man not to use a roving VPN but maybe it was deliberate on his part.

"Fixer", Sean declared, putting his ginfizz down for a second, it was early morning, very early in fact but Sean liked a liquid breakfast when he was in the mood for one.

"This is the Faded man", the caller said in his electronically altered tones that the Fixer knew so well. "I have another assignment for you. It is not a sanction however thus you will need to be careful very possibly disguised".

"I'm not a petty thief or heavy", Sean complained, "If you want someone doing over I can get you an eaddress for that sort of thing".

"I want your expertise and will pay as though it is a sanction, but let me tell you what is required before you refuse the contract", the Faded Man persisted.

Once Sean was in full possession of the facts his brow furrowed and his eyebrows rose to try and meet them. The job appealed to his bizarre sense of justice and code and he decided to accept it. Once again it was time to visit Cabrito at the Hospital Regional San José del Carmen de Copiapó - Los Carrera. He pinged for a flittaxi having no longer the patience nor use for hiring his vehicle when the alternative was so convenient and cheap. The driver was one of the silent type happy to convey without speaking and that suited Sean admirably. There were times when he felt garrulous and others when he preferred to be tacitly thoughtful. That day was one of the latter. Slipping the driver his thumb-pad back having agreed to a reasonable tariff, he climbed out into yet another beautiful day. It was 29ºC with humidity of 43% but a wind of some 19km/h keeping some of the perspiration at bay. Sean wore shorts, the ¾ length elastine type with low pockets, over them hung a poly-cotton boho shirt that afforded just enough subfuscation to hide his slim Browning needlegun. Not that he felt he was going to need it. It never hurt to have personal protection though. It gave him a sense of security in the most peaceful of places. To his surprise, Cabrito was not in the ambulaflitter-bay when the Fixer looked for him in the usual places. Niches and nooks where he could not be easily spotted from the doorway leading into the main body of the hospital. There were only two options. Wait for him to come out for a crafty ciggie, or go inside and search for him. He decided to give it a quarter of an hour and if the little Chilean did not show in that time, then enter the infirmary. For some reason that Sean had never been bothered enough to determine, the place looked as much like a correctional facility as it did a hospital. Surrounded by barbed wire and not freely open to the public. Vehicles entering the frontal

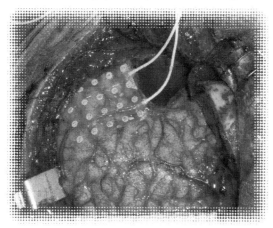

facade were checked to go in and out and that was why Sean had a special pass that identified him as an off-duty ambulaflitter driver.

It was a very ugly building of concrete blocks and glass, both the antiquated materials that the third-world still employed in abundance. Skin cancer in Chile remained the third most common type of cancer, as reported by the WHO [World Health Organization], one in 5 Chileans suffered some type of skin cancer during their lifetime. Treating that type of ailment was big business for corporations like Voleskip Pharmaceuticals and Orang-U-Can. Where the investors recouped their initial outlay was in using the Regional Hospital of Copiapó in its pioneering Otolaryngology Surgeries. Three innovative surgeries were performed in the main care centre of the Atacama, whose medical team had the collaboration of the outstanding Otolaryngologist Dr Gilcardo Baylarcón, a professor at the University of Concepción and a doctor at the Guillermo Grant Benavente Hospital, in the peninsula city. Assistant to the chief of the Otolaryngology Service of the Regional Hospital of Copiapó - Dr Manola Beilaano. Baylarcón was constantly invited to hospitals in different parts of the country to collaborate on surgeries done for the first time in Copiapó,

"I am delighted to come to support. I met a great team, very friendly people and committed to their patients. It was also possible to help three patients who were waiting for resolution of their surgery that was of high complexity", the specialist had been reported as saying when concluding some of his pioneering techniques. The high profile surgeries performed was in a geriatric patient and in which standard organ replacement was no longer viable. According to what was reported by Dr Beilaano, head of the Otolaryngology Service of the Regional Hospital,

"He was a patient who presented with only one option if he wanted to live any longer"! That being the transplantation of his brain into the body and head [obviously] of an android. The result would be one of the world's first Homomechanicus. Surgery was done to remove the *mass contained in the bone*. For this, the medical team used an electromyographic activity monitoring (EMG) system that allowed to locate, identify and map the nerve branches that in that case had several courses the main one being to the spinal cord. The objective of the Project Unit – *New Man*, of the Copiapó Hospital was to acquire a series of surgical practices with such characteristics for the near future. It was a technology that was very new to surgeons all over the rest of the world and beyond. To Mars, Venus, Mercury and Callisto. Given that although the solar medical profession had detailed knowledge of the anatomy of the brain, the immense surgical skill was still vital to ensure that even those who would perform such delicate surgical work in the future could do so repeatedly. Previous surgery was no guarantee of success in the next patient due to the humans' penchant for anatomical variations. The case of the pioneering patient proved to be a complete success. Additionally, the equipment could be used in other specialities, especially in neck surgery and accident trauma in addition to neurosurgery.

Even though Sean Derek Charles was a merchant of death who dealt mainly with demise, medical matters intrigued him. He often fancied some of his assassinations were enacted with the skill and precision of a surgeon and it was the very interest that had caused him to one day wander around the hospital and bump into Cabrito. From such a chance meeting a mutually beneficial liaison had developed into an ongoing business association.

No one challenged Sean as he wandered down the antiseptic-smelling corridors of the pioneering place of healing and extension of life. He had the sort of build and features that were instantly forgettable, he was very

generic of appearance. He was not startlingly tall, fat, skinny, had no immediately apparent distinguishing features, he was in every way an average guy who looked like he would not harm a fly. To his knowledge, he never had harmed a fly, but he had accepted and completed over a hundred sanctions and was currently engaged in a somewhat atypical mission which involved the services of Cabrito so soon after the last time.

His searching and reverie were both suddenly brought to an abrupt end when a voice said,

"Meester Hwanezz, what for you doing here, Señor"?

"Coming to see you. Do not fret I am not here for the customary reason – that of needing medical care".

Cabrito did not seem to have considered that eventuality. Taking the Fixer swiftly by the elbow, he steered him into a conveniently close examination room and locked the door.

"What eez going on, Señor"? He asked urgently, "You said we cannot be seen together in the hospital and here you are".

"I have an urgent assignment and need an item of supplies that you can get for me"?

"What do you want this time and then this must be the last time for some time, the heat is starting to build up over the disappearance of supplies, Señor".

"It's funny you should mention heat Cabrito because what I want is one of those knives that cut flesh and then stop the bleeding all in the same instant".

"A plasma scalpel"! Cabrito was shocked. "Such a device will be instantly missed, Señor",

"Hence the price of course", Sean had been ready for the usual complaints.

A thermal knife, the plasma scalpel, was capable of the simultaneous division of tissue and coagulation of blood vessels. A high-temperature argon gas plasma (unrelated to blood plasma) was created by passing the gas through a direct current arc, ionizing it and elevating its temperature to 3000ºC. A small plasma cutting jet being subsequently formed by a nozzle at the tip of the handpiece. The extremely useful tool had been created centuries in the past by Plover/Bendik/Blunket Laboratories. Inc - in Addenbrooke's Hospital, Hills Road, Cambridge.

There was less of a problem once Sean dutifully added a bonus to the original offer and Cabrito arranged to meet him the following day in Doggis, Chacabuco 275, Copiapó, Atacama. Sean knew the place well and had dined there before. His taste-buds had just about recovered from that spicy battering, so much so that he was prepared to risk them again to obtain the implement he required for his current contract.

Cabrito was sufficiently greedy and in awe of Sean to come through with the goods, even if it meant leaving the hospital if the heat became too much for him and the peinehombres started seriously looking into all the thefts there. Within hours Sean was on a flitterjet speeding its way to Saxonia once more and the expanded county of West Yorkshire. He had consulted his Little Black Section on his padfon and found he could look up Marissa who lived in Spinner Street, Stockport.

thirty-six **"Guess who", the** Fixer smiled as the young woman opened her front door. Rather than say a word Marissa Jinks of 23 Spinner Street grabbed Sean by the arm and dragged him hastily inside the very old prefabricated property.

The instant the door was closed, her mouth was on his and nothing was said for several seconds. Then when they finally parted she asked suddenly,

"Are you crazy coming here Prane don't you know that Eddie gets out next week"?

Prane Deloquar, alias Sean Derek Charles alias the Fixer asked genuinely confused,

"Gets out"?

"Of Strangeways, he's just finished a three stretch for GBH, remember"?

"Has that been three years, gosh doesn't the time fly by, I do remember you telling me now I think about it. Would you be happier if I just left then"?

Marissa grinned,

"Are you kidding, Lover, only you can't stay more than a few days for obvious reasons".

"My business will not take that long", Sean Promised.

"I can never understand how you make so much money selling cutlery", the girl noted then. Sean liked Marissa for her looks not for her dazzling intellect. As far as she was concerned he was a sales representative for a major manufacturer of cutlery.

He went into the sort of patter that he imagined one in such gainful employ would use on such an occasion.

135

"Everyone uses cutlery, Marissa – Babe. From the mighty, right down to the humble we all need to eat and even the plebeian and the peasantry do not eat with their fingers. Therefore cutlery is always in demand, greater even than the need for jewellery and if I sold rings and pendants you would not wonder how I made my money would you".

"Well when you put it like that", the girl was fumbling with the zip on the back of her quite antiquated frock. I'll get you some dinner when you've earned it, come on now, a girl has needs".

It was part of the reason for Sean's visit that he saw to those very requirements. Happily, they tended to coincide with his own. He, therefore, buttered her muffin more than once before she climbed out of bed on shaky legs and went to turn the olde-style gas oven on, to heat him a vacuum-pack. She returned with two bottles of Orang-U-Lage - *the premium beer for times when you have a real thirst and only a quality beverage will do.* For a while, the satiated couple simply seated themselves up in bed sucking on the nyloplanyon teats of the bottles. Then they reluctantly arose to get the - *soy-prot and lichen-veg delight that Hitachi have packed into one tiny tray yet fill a big hole.*

I have to go out in a short while", he told her around a mouthful of tasty goodness.

"Already, you only have just gotten here"?

"It won't take long, then we can sleep together and have a lay-in tomorrow morning".

"What sort of company wants to talk about knives and forks at gone eight at night"?

"Only Volufoods, who is about to open a chain of food joints in Saxonia and need cutlery for every one of their branches throughout the country - that's all. They are still in local time and to them, it is the afternoon. They only flew in earlier from Sudamerica doSul".

"Volufoods, they do the Doggis chain don't they", for once Marissa had managed to surprise Sean with her erudition.

"They do but they will not be calling the chain in Saxonia that".

"So what will the chain be named"?

"They have not made me a party to that information, nor would they, in case StufUrFayc or Gutbusters got a hold of it and tried some sort of industrial sabotage".

Marissa nodded, it was the most intellectually stimulating conversation Sean had ever had with the girl. Indeed it was only when they were eating that they ever really got the chance to talk. Sean did not visit Marissa for her mind.

"Good luck then, I hope you can secure a lucrative deal".

Sean was once again impressed, he had not realised that Marissa knew the meaning of the word 'lucrative'. Perhaps the girl had hidden depths and when Eddie got out, it might be that he would tragically have a sudden seriously fatal *accident*.

He rose from the table telling her, "I should be back in a few hours, don't wait up, but do expect something to come sliding between the sheets in the early hours or before". Marissa rewarded him with a lascivious smile, one thing that she never was Marissa, was capricious.

Sean pinged for a flittaxi and Rocket Ron's GetUShifted was outside Marissa's home in admirably swift time. He told the driver to take him to the address he had been given and made sure he had what he needed for the night even though he had already done so whilst in the house. Sean was a belt and braces sort of a man when he was working on a job. The destination was Croft Street, just off Albert Park – Manchester. Only a medium length sort of ride in a taxi. Sean thumbed the driver's pad and added a nice tip, before saying as he passed it back.

"You did not see me tonight, did not take me anywhere, the extra is to ensure your discretion".

The driver grinned, "Understood, Guv, many thanks for the gratuity, give her one for me".

Sean did not correct him, it the driver assumed he was having some sort of affair involving someone else's contractee or missus so much the better. The vehicle sped away and he looked up at the property before him. Select, quiet, the sort of area where everyone minded their own business – perfect. The Fixer had made certain to climb out of the taxi under the cover of some evergreen elm trees the sort that had foliage all year round. Removing various items from his dickie bag, he pulled on a real-flesh mask that instantly added heavy jowls and a shock of red hair. The gloves went on next and took some time to seal themselves to his wrists. With them, he had an entirely different set of fingerprints. He then slipped some bucked teeth over his own and was ready to approach the building that contained his target. Overhead DORC [Digitally Observational Recording Cameras] instantly began to register his appearance and may provide the authorities with images if it came to a subsequent combman investigation. He pressed the thumbplate of the property in question. Followed that by squeezing his throat in a certain way to activate the vocal cord alteration that had been surgically implanted several years previously.

"Yeah"? Came a voice over the metallic speaker above the plate.

"Mister Whohouse"?

"Who wants to know".

"My name is Boulter, I'm a representative of the National Lottery, I'm pleased to tell you that following a review of last weeks ticket sales the numbers announced were subject to an additional draw, for which no extra tickets were required. You are now a winner – Dessic Yanton Whohouse of 23 Croft Street Manchester. I can have the thumb transfer to you in seconds if you pass me your padfon".

"You've ID"?

Sean held fake identification to the camera eye over the speaker over the thumbplate. It showed a small image of a bucktoothed redhead named Boulter who was a representative of the National Lottery.

"How much have I won"? Came the obvious question,

"Are you sitting down, Mister Whohouse", Sean loved the play-acting when in disguise and felt he would have liked to have been a tri-vidz actor if he had not had such a penchant for violent illegal killing.

"Just tell me how much"? His intended contract demanded impatiently.

"Four Silver Shillin"!

Four million shillin, not exactly small change. The amount did the trick and Sean heard the electronic bolt slide back out of place allowing him to push open the durilite steel door. Two things could always be guaranteed to open a door, one was curiosity, the other greed, with a combination of the two one could not fail. Beyond the door was a passageway and that in turn led to one of three apartments dependant upon which door one went to of course. 23 was the far right-hand door. Two of the overhead LED's were out, making the grey corridor even dingier as Sean slipped down it. Not that he was objecting, the low light would render the image of his features even more subfusc. He glided down the passageway rather like a panther stalking its prey and then turning the door handle let himself into the apartment. It was decorated in various delicate shades of pale orange. On one cabinet in a far corner were some football trophies, so Sean knew he was in the right place. From a rustic red faux-leather chair a figure climbed to his feet he had been watching what looked like soft porn on a tri-vidz which dominated the end of the room it was in. The image died as the owner hit a button on his pad. He turned to regard Sean and Sean shot him.

The level one dark hit the physio on the back of the hand and he stuttered, "What in....." as he fell face-first back onto the sofa.

From out of his dickie bag Sean pulled a huge splash sheet [courtesy of the Regional Hospital San José del Carmen de Copiapó - Los Carrera]. He spent the next few moments making sure the sheet completely covered the sofa, even though he knew there would be hardly any chance of blood going onto the furniture. When he did wet-work, he liked to think he made less mess than any other fixer in the system. Of course, the boiler explosion had caused devastation but that was unavoidable, when he wanted to be neat and tidy, none were better than Sean Derek Charles. Satisfied he lifted the physiotherapist back onto the sheet-covered sofa and with a Sig Sauer by Hogue X5 Emperor Scorpion Flipper - FDE Spear Point carefully cut away the physio's bohos and trollies. He was very careful not to nick any of the prone body's skin. Such sloppy work would have railed at him, the only laceration was going to be exactly where the customer had requested it. None other would be accidentally inflicted. After all, Sean was no sadist, merely a businessman who dealt in dark contracts. He took no pleasure in what he did, other than the satisfaction of a job well done. He was a craftsman, as proud of his work as any other practitioner of the arts.

He took the thermal knife, the plasma scalpel, capable of the simultaneous division of tissue and coagulation of blood vessels. Carefully pressed its button and the micro-power-pack immediately made it available for use. With great care, Sean lifted the contract's scrotum and using the medical instrument parted it from his groin. He was amazed to see that there was no blood and he ducked into the kitchen and placed the sad sack into the waste disposal. Even he shuddered slightly at the mechanical whirring of the mechanism as it shredded and ground the material before flushing it into the sewerage system. As he was returning the physiotherapist was groaning and stirring back to wakefulness.

139

"I've also a message for you", Sean said in his unnaturally deep baritone that made him sound like a Klingon. "It is this, think yourself lucky that only your balls are gone, leave town and never come back. If you do I will be sent to see you again and next time it will be a leg. Further disobedience will result in the removal of further limbs, nod if you understand me"?

As Whohouse nodded, he suddenly came too, sufficiently to realise what had been done to him. He let out a pathetic keening sound rather like a trapped animal and began to cry.

"Do you want a shot for the pain"? Sean asked, "Because I need you to get up so that I can retrieve my sheet".

"What sort of monster are you"? Whohouse demanded through his tears.

"The sort who delivers swift and harsh justice to rapists", Sean told him, neither finding the conversation distasteful nor enjoying it especially. It was a hazard of his profession nothing more and he was a consummate professional. "Painkilling shot or not".

"Give me the drug damn you".

Pulling a hypospray from his bag, Sean sprayed 15mg of snufzomorph into the eunuch, then lifted him bodily to retrieve his sheet, he warned,

"I would disappear if I was you, Whohouse, or I will come back and you do not want me to come back". Backing toward the door, Sean let himself out. All in a days work!

thirty-seven   Clara was in the bath when her padfon pinged. Wiping her hand on a flannel she reached over to the towel rack and retrieved it. Activating voice-only she answered,

"Clara Trentavoria"?

"Hello, Clara, I'm not getting images, it's Grelm".

"You won't be getting images, I'm in the bath".

"Aah, I see, or rather I don't hahahaha".

"What can I do for West Yorkshire's finest, Officer"?

"It's not an official call, it's personal. I thought I would wait a discrete period before getting in touch with you again, you understand"?

"I understand our involvement such as it was could have been an embarrassment to you yes".

"I didn't mean it like that, you know what I meant"?

"Do I"?

"You don't sound amenable to my pinging you. Have you moved on, are you seeing someone else"?

"Someone else"? Clara echoed, "I don't recall the two of us discussing exclusivitation".

"Exclusivitation? Is that even a real word"?

"Exclusivitation: the state of agreed exclusivity,   not admitting of something else; incompatible. Omitting from consideration or account shutting out all others from a part or share It's in the Facetwit Dictionary".

"I feel this conversation is going off at a bizarre tangent, I just pinged you to see if you wanted to go out and get a drink, but if you are seeing other people I'm not comfortable with that sort of open-ended arrangement".

"Tell me Grelm, is the department making any sort of progress toward finding my missing physio, whom we reported missing to you a couple of days ago? Is my Mother's case still totally stalled? What do you do over there, you know, about crime for example"?

There was a long pause and then DI Snowd said levelly, "Maybe I should not have called you after all".

"No", smiled Clara, "I'm glad you did, please do so again when you have something concrete to tell me".

She cut the connection and said to herself, "Loser"!

She had no time for the lukewarm combman, especially as things were proceeding gently with her main striker. If he played it right he would soon be scoring with her too! She had to get her mind back on track. That was the business of Saturday's game:

Corporation Division One

Goosetimp v Deutsch Fahrzeuge Eingearbeitet
Hornrunner Hornets v Rolls Royce Scoriors
Voleskip v Preciometallic.Inc
Makers-Guild v Orang-U-Can
Castle Electronic v Tiptingle Foods
IYWIWSI v Zhōngguá Shāngpín

Orang-U-Can

6. Radband

12. McFarland 13. Jennings 25. Zinyama 4 Burgenbower

19.Jenson 16. Flintham 7. Ball 20. Lane

23. Roxbrough 27. Rachwalski

Substitutes

1. Anderson
8. Wong
14. Wing
10. Nero
30. Sanedad
31.Radford

The away fixture was an opportunity to put some distance between OUC and the team one place beneath them. It was Friday evening and having watched the players train all week, she had chosen her strongest line up based upon current form.

The academy player Sanedad had enjoyed an outstanding week and fully merited his inclusion on the bench as did his friend Radford. The latter now had a rather nicely shaped nose, while the former's crew cut had just grown out into a sensible buzz-cut. Not only was their attitude better though. They were both developing as players and Clara was going to give them their first run out in a senior game if she could manage it.

Roxbrough had managed to get two tickets for the concert to see none other than Drill Plough. The band were a five-piece who had learned to play antique musical instruments and did so in such a way as to mimic the twentieth-century progressive rock bands at the time. Even had Roxbrough

not invited her Clara would have found a way to get tickets, for she loved Ancient Rock and especially when it came to a group who were clever enough to dispense with computers and play actual musical instruments.

Of course, Drill Plough could not write anything anywhere near as good as the groups of ancient times, the best melodies had been exhausted centuries in the past, the combination of seven notes could no longer be put in a pleasing order without echoing something that had already been written. So what they did was to draw from the ancient catalogue of superb material and then play it as a tribute to those brilliant groups of the past. They did this in another astute way, doing two fifty-minute sets, the first being the more laid back type of material, while the more energetic stuff was played after a quarter-of-an-hour interval. They also preferred lengthy pieces giving the music time to develop to show the delicate interplay of light and shade to take the listener to new depths and crazy heights and they were regarded by many as the very best at that type of thing.

When the couple arrived at the Arena of the City of Greater Manchester it was already almost filled, thankfully they had seats booked and at the front, being only two rows back. They both had a supply of Orang-U-Can the most popular drink in the solar system and a snack bar each by the same company. The background music faded to zero the house-lights dimmed and an expectant hush fell over the multitude of loyal fans. Suddenly cheering almost raised the roof, as the band simply climbed onto the stage and took their places. A simple entrance but all the more effective for that reason.

"Good evening", Nai Sanderon said simply over the amplified system and the crowd went wild. They had been told it was a seated concert and anyone jumping to their feet would be thrown out by security for violating health and safety regulations. That did not stop them from drumming their feet on the floor and clapping until their hands stung.

"Thank you Greater Manchester and West Yorkshire", Sanderon told everyone once the hubbub died down sufficiently. "We are going to bring you three pieces in the first set, We hope you enjoy them".

The leader of the group was dressed in a pure white heavily frilled white shirt and royal blue Edwardian frock-coat with silver buttons. He was the vocalist flautist and second guitar. Suddenly over the public address system, the sound of a clock ticking could be heard and the crowd roared their recognition and approval as the band began to play the 22'24" of the famous Tick Tock. It was the perfect sombre and gentle opener for the first set. Both Clara and Roxbrough were lost in its sublime melodious beauty, penned originally in the twenty-first century. At the end of it, the crowd were silent for several seconds, transfixed by the beautiful way the piece had been played on a keyboard, electrical guitar and bass guitar and drums. Then a roar went up and the applause lasted for over a minute.

"Thank you", Nai Sanderon finally said, "Here is another brilliant piece we know you will all recognise".

It was the haunting tune, Richelieu's Prayer, which Sanderon joined Chirie Whiteless on guitar for - once he had completed his flute introduction. The band then went straight into The Musical Box, finishing the first set with the excellent Ayreon's Fare. It was the time of the intermission and Clara felt drained of all emotion as she turned to Roxbrough and declared,

"I never expected them to be as good as their stix, but they're note-perfect, what a bunch of genius'".

"Have you always liked ancient music", Roxbrough asked.

Clara nodded, "I don't even think of computatunze as music at all and the ethnic poetribe is pure nonsense as far as I'm concerned. Have you any idea of what they are going to play in the second half"?

"If I did I wouldn't spoil it for you", he told her.

Clara began to feel a deeper emotion for Roxbrough at that moment. He did not have a footballers mind at all, but a man's. The lights soon dimmed down again and Drill plough launched into Sacred Sound from their album White Waste. It was tumultuously received. They went into the next piece, one unknown to Clara and Roxbrough whispered in her ear that it was from their new album Water and Earth and was called Three Colours. It got the biggest roar of approval of the night thus far, so many of the crowd had it and Clara made a point of buying it as soon as she got back to the estate. They quickly went into another favourite, Looking for Someone, from their album Illegal Entry. After which they were informed,

"This next one is our swansong for this evening and we know you will enjoy it" the now sweating Sanderon told them, "It is called Arriving Somewhere But Not Here". There was a roar of approval and Clara's voice was added to it for it was one of her favourite tracks. When it finished the stamping clapping and cheering was accompanied by whistling and cries for more. After four minutes the lights went down again for the encore and the trilling keyboard heralded the raunchy Black Light Machine. With its stunning frenetic guitar finalé, it was the perfect piece to end on. The lights went up and Clara turned to Roxbrough and said,

"Let me take you for a drink after that, I'm too wired up to simply go home".

"Where did you have in mind, he smiled.

"Let's go and try Revolution Rendezvous, they have a buffet bar and music, though not as quality as what we have just heard of course".

"Is it far from here"?

"No only a walk it's in Corporation Street. Why? Do you fancy a stroll"?

"I do, a chance to cool down and we can always walk back to the flitter later".

"All right then, we will go on foot".

She looped her arm through his and the duo set off for a destination that was mere minutes away. Not that it was of too diminutive a duration to be devoid of incident. From out of a side street a young woman suddenly emerged and asked simply,

"Miss Trentavoria"?

Roxbrough let go of Clara's arm, plunged his arm into his frock-coat and pulling out the Kimber immediately shot the girl who fell backwards onto the pavement.

"Rox"! Clara gasped, "What by Herne are you doing"?

By way of answer, the striker stepped forward bending over the prone figure of the young woman and then satisfied, pointed to what had been partially concealed in the girl's hand.

"A Browning needlegun and I'll bet a considerable sum that the device is loaded with a level two dart".

Clara felt the blood drain from her pretty features as she asked,

"You mean to say that she was going to......."?

"Kill one or both of us? Yes! This young creature is an assassin. Looks can sometimes be deceiving and whoever hired her was hoping the fact that she was a quite decorative young woman would cause us to hesitate just long enough to kill us both and then slip back into the cover of nightfall".

"Me you mean? She asked who *i* was"!

"You were probably the principal target but I would have been an eye witness she could not have afforded to leave behind alive. She would have killed us both".

Clara pulled out her padfon and immediately pressed nine-hundred and ninety-nine. While Roxbrough began carefully going through the girl's pockets and then running his hands over her prone form.

"Are you touching her up"? Clara demanded once she had spoken to the combmen and they had promised a swift response.

"I'm searching for the A-capsule".

"A capsule"?

"A special preparation of Benzodiazepinoides used to enhance the effect of the neurotransmitter gamma-aminobutyric acid (GABA) at the GABAA receptor, resulting in sedative, hypnotic (sleep-inducing), anxiolytic (anti-anxiety), anticonvulsant, and muscle relaxant properties. Sufficiently high doses of shorter-acting benzodiazepinoides will cause anterograde amnesia and dissociation, that's why it's called an A-capsule".

"You mean to say the woman is going to, or you suspect she was going to take something to wipe her memory".

"If she refused to give her employers name, the person who sent her to kill us, then the combmen under article 237 of the legal code of conduct are allowed to used hypnotic techniques to get the information out of her. If she cannot remember anything, she cannot divulge that information".

By then Roxbrough had undone the woman's blouse and pulled up her brassiere revealing her breasts.

"You're sure you're not getting some sort of pervy kick out of the search"? Clara grinned.

Suddenly Roxbrough smiled in triumph and held up a white capsule in forefinger and thumb,

"Here it is, hidden in her brassiere thank goodness she did not stash it in the other usual place".

As the sirens of the response from the combmen were suddenly heard, the girl began to stir, the effects of the level one dart beginning to wear off. Feeling the cold dampness on her nudity, she tried to rise and cover herself at the same instant.

"What did you do to me you beast"? She demanded in a harsh sort of scream.

"Just lay still until the combies arrive or I'll shoot you again", Roxbrough warned and Clara was impressed to see the Kimber had miraculously reappeared in his fist. The girl eyed it too and silently tugged her brassiere back over what was good work by the enhancement surgeon.

An hour later and Clara was getting frustrated and angry,

"I've already been through all this with you several times and I do not intend to go through it again, Snelling – *she* tried to kill *us*"!

"I understand that at least it is two people's words against one anyway", Snelling noted as calmly as he was able, "But the sad fact of the matter is that people keep getting killed or assaulted and the common denominator in several cases now is you, Miss Trentavoria".

"I'm doing a very high profile job Inspector, I have made some enemies. You know as well as I do that betting on the results of the football games is great, imagine the sort of sum some will have bet on the result of the Shield or the season?! I am taking a club that seemed to have no hope of finishing anywhere but in Division Two next season and making them contenders for the corporation title. Do you not realise that some would move heaven and hell to stop me? They would stop at nothing short of nothing to do that and it includes murder".

"And yet, despite all that, Miss Kurteze claims that your boyfriend shot her and then sexually assaulted her while she was under the influence of his dart".

"She's a lying murderous bitch that's why. For a start, Roxbrough is one of my first team players, not my boyfriend. As I told you we had just been to the Drill Plough concert, we were not on a date. Secondly, he was searching her for her A-capsule that was why he removed certain parts of her under-things".

"Yet we found the A-capsule in your lover's possession, not the girl's", Snapper Snelling tried. Suddenly Clara smiled and managed to calm herself.

"I see what you're trying to do, Snelling, but I'm afraid it won't work. What Roxbrough and I have told you is the truth. If you do not believe me tough kaahk, because what you rightly say is that you're faced with he said she said dilemma. In which case you cannot charge either of us, sadly not the assassin either. So if you will now get out of my face and let me out of this interview room, my striker and I will leave and you can do or not do what the Herne you want with that bitch, Kurteze".

"I could book all three of you for wasting combmen time", Snelling remarked.

"Yes, because you're very busy this evening, I can hear all the rioters in the cells and other holding rooms. Give me a frenging break combie, you had nothing better to do and this entire episode has merely served to break the monotony of another Friday evening shift. Now the two of us have a game tomorrow and we need our beauty sleep so open that door. Or I can start screaming rape. Then get Daddy's solicitor to charge you with abusing your authority such as it is".

Snelling went white with repressed fury but he finally managed to croak,

"The two of you are free to go. The young woman you violated will be released too".

Clara strode to the door and was greeted by Roxbrough in the corridor beyond.

"They're letting the bitch go free", Clara cursed to her striker. By way of an answer, he put a finger to his lips, grabbed her elbow and rushed her out of the station.

"What the koof, Rox, let go you're... you're hurting my frenging arm", Clara objected.

"Shut up and listen", Roxbrough hissed urgently and Clara shut up and listened. "We've been released ahead of the woman, you wait here and if she comes out before I'm back, follow her and link your pad to mine by GPS. I'm going to dash back and fetch the flitter".

"And then what, what's on your mind, Rox"?

"Shoot her again, chuck her in the boot and put her somewhere safe till she tells us what we want to know".

"That's audacious and crazy and a bloody good idea, run Rox, run like the wind".

Without further ado, the footballer sprinted off and Clara hid beneath some elm-firs keeping out of range of the cameras that surrounded the station.

Ten minutes passed, the longest ten minutes of her life and nothing happened. It began to rain, thankfully she was quite sheltered under the firs. Suddenly a flitter drew up at her side and Rox let the passenger door hiss open. Clara slid inside.

"Nothing's happened yet has it".

Clara shook her head, added, "I expect that egomaniac Snelling thinks he can question her further and get some dirt on us".

"So we wait"! Roxbrough decided.

thirty-eight   **It took thirty-five** minutes for the woman calling herself Kurteze to appear.

"Now we have to snatch her before whoever she is pinging comes to pick her up. Might be an accomplice or simply a flittaxi but we cannot take the chance that it's the former of the two".

"We can't snatch her in front of the combshop", Clara pointed out somewhat superfluously, "We'll have to wait and see if she moves from here the ruddy nozkavardé"!

"Such language", Roxbrough joked, "And from a lady of your class and breeding".

"I'm not exactly a lady, Rox if you thought that then....wait, look she's walking to somewhere".

"Right", Roxbrough replied and turned on the micro-pile easing the flitter into a silent arc, keeping a fair distance from the assassin. "You're going to have to take the wheel while I drive-by-shoot her and then stop the flitter long enough for me to throw her in the boot".

"Then what"?

"Then we take her to a little place I know in Moss Side Take off all her clothes except for her pants and tie her to a straight-backed chair, there was another one".

147

"You're talking about the place you were held"?

"It's perfect for our purpose".

"And what exactly is our purpose other than kidnap, that is"?

"Don't you want to know who wanted one or both of us dead"?

"Do you think she'll know"?

"Know who hired her, what are you saying how could she not"?

"The person who ordered our demise might have used a go-between, or emails and drop-boxes, or disguised their voice and used audio only pings....".

"You've been watching too many tri-vidz, this was not that level of arrangement, otherwise the girl would have been quicker, too quick for me. If she were any good at her job we'd already be goners. Someone with the same sort of level of expertise will have hired someone in her price bracket and they don't usually do this sort of thing".

"Do you have a suspicion"?

"I think it will be someone who is going to lose an awful lot of money if OUC does well this season, after that your guess is as good as mine".

There was no more time for talk for suddenly they reached the side of Miss Kurteze and thumbing the descent of his window, Roxbrough brought his Kimber into line with the woman and fired rapidly three times. The second dart hit her in the upper arm while the other two went wide due to the jostling of the vehicle. One was enough. Clara awkwardly hit the brake from her position in the passenger seat and then waited while Roxbrough threw the inert form of the girl into the already raised boot. Slamming it shut he hared round to the passenger side as Clara had slid into the driving seat.

"You'll have to give me directions", she told him as he dived into the flitter beside her, "I've never been to Moss Side, what's it like"?

"It's like Syria", he retorted with heavy irony, "But with less radiation that's all".

Clara was a good driver for a woman and she took the vehicle through the dilapidation with consummate ease, using manual all the while. Roxbrough directed her to the back of the derelict building he knew better than he ever wished he had done and Together they carried the still comatose form of Kurteze into the very same room that had housed Roxbrough. He had rescued a roll of duck-tape from the flitter and after stripping the girl down to her pants, he wound it around her naked waist several times before binding her wrists together behind her back.

Clara observed pithily,

"Any opportunity to see this girl's tits and you make certain you take it".

"If you're jealous you could always show me yours", he said before he had put his brain into a sensible drive, "Sorry that was inappropriate, Boss".

"Don't sweat it", Clara found his apology amusing, "After all, you might have saved my life tonight".

"Right, well you might as well go home now, take my flitter and bring me a flask and a sandwich in the morning".

"You're staying here all night and alone with the girl. Do you think the batteries on your torch will last that long"?

"They are alcagraphic rechargeable with this winder, they will never give out. I want the girl to come to and find she is only faced with a man. I figure she's more likely to talk if I can convince her how dangerous I am".

It made sense and Clara agreed, "All right, it's a good point. I'll be back at nine in the morning. Try and make use of one of those old mattresses, don't forget you're in the starting line up in the morning".

Roxbrough nodded and Clara left the two of them in the derelict property with no electricity and precious little by the way of creature comforts. She knew under such circumstances she would have cracked and pretty damn fast.

Kurteze came to slowly and strained against her bonds. She knew without evidence what had happened, but tried to move her arms firstly despite that. Duck-tape was over her mouth so she could not scream. She could feel the chill of December on her skin. That alerted her to the fact that she was almost naked. Suddenly a bright light shone directly into her eyes and a voice instructed.

"I can get you something to cover yourself if you nod cooperation? I assure you there is no escape put even the remotest of possibilities from your mind. You are going to talk in a while, you are going to tell me exactly what I want to know".

There was only one sensible choice for her, she would soon succumb to hypothermia if she did not at least nod. She was also conscious of her nudity, it made her feel vulnerable, which was probably what her captor desired. She nodded and the light turned from her eyes, but so powerful was the after-effects of it was the fact that she could see nothing for several moments. She could not see the owner of the voice, an obvious man, she could not even see the room she was held captive in.

She heard rather than saw him return. Felt some of the duck-tape being cut. Her circulation had failed her for the moment and powerful hands lifted her from the chair and dressed her (partially) into a dressing gown. It smelled of good quality cologne, it was probably his. She did not care at that moment, the thermal nature of it was saving her from possibly organ failure, had she been left without it.

"I am going to cut your bonds to let your circulation fully return", the voice told her then, "I will have a needlegun trained on you and if you run or try to move suddenly, I will shoot you. If you try to scream or cry out I will shoot you, then you will be stripped once again and taped back to the chair, do you understand"?

The tape was roughly torn from her mouth and she replied,

"Yes. You're in the driving seat. I will cooperate, I will do what I have to do to be freed, that's what I want, what do you want, Mister"?

Though his directions had been curt and succinct, he did not have an unkindly voice and she suspected that he was the man who had been in the company of Trentavoria, her target. She had not expected any resistance, certainly not this determined and subsequently organised. She knew when she was out of her depth, she knew she was then. She seated herself on some sort of single mattress that resided on an ancient metal frame rickety bed and tried to keep her eyes away from the blindingly brilliance of the light source, some sort of torch.

"This is what is going to happen next", the voice instructed her, "I am going to ask you a simple question and you are going to answer it. If you satisfy me as to the honesty of your reply I will drive you to somewhere safe for you and let you go. If I detect a lie I might decide to eliminate you. Or maybe have some fun with that rather pleasant chassis of yours and then eliminate you. You understand my resolve, my willingness to prove to you that I mean what I say"?

"I understand you perfectly", she admitted. Sometimes it was expedient to know the nature of one's predicament and Kurteze knew two things. One was that she had failed in her contract with her employer. The other was that she was going to cooperate with the man who had been with Trentavoria when she had attempted to capture her. All she desired then was survival and escape from the situation she then found herself in.

"Who sent you tonight and what were you supposed to do"? He finally asked her, the question she knew had been coming. She had no special allegiance to her employer, it had been a financial contract and she could only survive by betraying that contract.

"I was paid by Throrb Makers-Guild to abduct Clara Trentavoria before the game today. If you checked my weapon you'll know it was loaded with level one needles. No one was to die. When I saw her in the company of a man, you - I presume, I was going to stun you. Then the OUC Manager and put her in my flitter and take her to a basement I had been given the location of. It was thought by the CEO of Makers-Guild Commodities that the abduction of the manager would result in the team spirit being so demoralised and distracted that they would lose the next game – this afternoon".

She waited and could hear the sound of her Browning being examined and emptied of the load.

"These *are* level one needles", the man said almost to himself. He seemed to fall into reflective silence. Kurteze risked a glance in his direction, even with the light pointed toward her she could see his outline and it seemed to her that it was the silhouette of the man who Trentavoria had been with.

Both of them heard the hesitant sound of someone entering the building then – rescue? The vain hope was dashed when Kurteze heard the sound of the woman's voice, it was Trentavoria's.

"I couldn't sleep", she confessed to her partner/lover/friend? "I tossed and turned for an hour but couldn't get off to sleep thinking of you out here in the cold while I was tucked up and safe in a nice warm bed. I've brought a flask, would you like some lichen-coff"?

"Please", he confirmed.

"She's free! Why"?

"She has cooperated, come over here I have something to tell you, for your ears only".

Though Kurteze strained to hear the content of their whispering she only caught the odd word.

".....tables on him......". From him.

"...... out of your mind.......caught.......to the team......".

".......get around and .... try anything like this again".

"....choose a substitute".

".........have to, it will ....".

She lost interest, it made insufficient sense to be worth the effort.

The duo approached, he turned the light source it was who she had suspected. He asked her,

"Would you like something hot inside you"?

"As long as it's not you, yes please"?

He grinned at that, finding the innuendo amusing, he was quite handsome, under other circumstances.....!

"This is what is going to happen now then", he told her as she sipped the welcome scolding liquid. "Whatever you were paid by Makers-Guild, we will pay you one and a half times to kidnap him and bring him here. Do you know how to get in touch with him"?

Kurteze thought about that for a couple of seconds, it represented quite a payday. She was a professional if the price was right – it was!

"You want their team to suffer the exact fate that he intended for OUC? I can do that, then I'll have to fade into oblivion for quite a while. Are you going to let him go"?

"Of course and unharmed", the man smiled, "*After* the game is over".

thirty-nine   **Roxbrough was not** about to trust Kurteze and let her out of his sight for a second. He said farewell to his frustrated Manager and took the girl to his flitter. Handing her the clothes he had stripped off her the night before as she huddled in his nightgown he told her.

151

"The first stop is my place where you can get a shower or bath and some food, then, once I've done the same we go to your rendezvous with Makers-Guild".

"You expect me to put dirty clothes back on once I've had a shower", some of her confidence was returning.

"I have a sonic-laundromat in my place. They will be cleansed while you are doing the same. Unless you're so fashion conscious that you never wear the same outfit two days in a row, in which case we can stop at the mall on the way back to my place"?

"Which would involve me dressing in the flitter, I'm not a contortionist. No, if they're cleansed then fair enough, I doubt Maker's-Guild will notice and if he does he probably won't care. That's what guys are like - right"?

"Some gentlemen notice what a lady chooses to bedeck herself with", Roxbrough returned with a deliberately feigned haughtierism. "Don't worry about my seeing your goodies if that's what you're thinking because I've checked them out thoroughly while you were out".

"Forget it", she blushed, "The same clothes will be fine. Are you a jerk, Rox, or is it just some sort of put-on"?

"The name is Roxbrough actually", he found himself returning, "Only Clara Calls me Rox. Perhaps you did not catch what it was short for"?

"I didn't as it happens, but I also did not realise it was her love-name for you".

"I'm a member of Miss Trentavoria's squad, she only loves me when I score".

"Really"? Kurteze was beginning to enjoy herself. "That's what you think is it? I don't expect you want a woman's perspective, but she did not seem to look at you like a piece of property. I think she likes you even when you're not penetrating deeply into her goalmouth".

"That would be the opposition's goalmouth".

"You phrase it how you want, I'll phrase my way", Kurteze grinned.

"Anyway, if you haven't got the hots for her what are you doing this for? It cannot be in your remit to act off the pitch as a security guard for the boss, can it"?

"I was abducted not that long ago. I had my ankle broken and was pretty shook up by the whole unpleasant experience. I suppose this is my way of fighting back from that and retaining some sort of balance".

"All right, if that's what you want to tell yourself, I'm not really in a position to criticize anyway, am I"?

"No", Roxbrough smiled, "You certainly are not".

"So you are the Boss, how do you want this to go down"?

"Let's get washed changed and food inside us before we try to determine the best strategy. While we eat you can tell me where you're supposed to meet Makers-Guild and if there will be anyone else present because those sort of details will make a difference to how we are going to approach his kidnap".

"How much further is it to your place"?

Roxbrough pulled up, telling her as he did so,

"This is the rear of my building, I'm on the second-floor apartment three, that's why I wear 23 when I play for Orang-U-Can".

"Just because I agreed to do the kidnapping, it doesn't mean I have even the remotest interest in football", she told him honestly. "I think sport is for children and once one leaves the playground then one should cease playing".

"So what do you do with your leisure time", Roxbrough asked, as he climbed out of the flitter. She told him across the low slung vehicles roof.

"I read, make pots and walk my dog".

"An assassin with a brain. I'm surprised your attempt upon us was not better coordinated".

"Well, I wasn't ready for your draw was I Billy the Kid"?

"Who's Billy the Kid"?

"He lived in ancient times. Well when I say ancient times I mean the twentieth century and when I say lived, he didn't live".

"He was a construct"?

"No, a cartoon, if you know what a cartoon was"?

"Just because I'm a footballer doesn't mean I'm an ignoramus", Roxbrough objected, "A cartoon precluded Pixmap, it was a two-dimensional motion picture consisting of a sequence of drawings, each so slightly different, that when filmed and run through a projector the figures seemed to move. So this Billy the Kid was like a cartoon goat that could shoot quickly with a needlegun"?

"That's right. Is there no lift in this place"?

"Stairs are good for you, come on I'll race you to the top".

"How old are you – five"?

"I wondered why you had no laughter lines on your face, I thought you knew a good bodsculpt-surgeon, but he did not need to remove any wrinkles did he"?

"All right – child. The race is on after I count to three".

She sprinted up the steps two at a time after counting to two. When he nearly caught her on the landing, he declared,

"You cheated, whose the big kid now"?

"We already know the answer to that, Billy was. Is this your room"?

"As it has a huge durilite number three screwed to the door, that would seem to be a safe deduction, yes. May I get to the thumbplate, please".

"Sure".

"You are standing in front of it".

"Oh! Right, how unlike you not to take the opportunity to manhandle me yet again".

Grimacing Roxbrough waited for the girl to step aside and then thumbed the electro-lock and the door's mechanisms of security crunched into the unlocked position. As they entered he commanded the drapes to open, they were tied into the other audio-commands of the place.

Kurteze whistled, "Say, Roxbrough, this is a nice flop".

She looked at the ancient weaponry used to decorate some of the walls. Admired his ancient stereo system. The latter having become cyclically popular once again in recent times. Then asked curiously,

"Where's the tri-vidz"?

"I don't have one".

"You are joking, why ever not"?

"I like to read too. I also spend long hours in the gym and when I get back here I like to listen to music and just do so with my eyes closed. If I want the news and current affairs there's the SWW on my padfon. If I want to see a particularly intriguing motion entertainment, I go to the auditorium and watch the huge stage tri-vidz. Now, what do you want to do first, shower, eat, go through my clothes and see if anything takes your fancy, oo-er"?

"I know it's the fashion to leave heaps of room in one's gear to move around, but wouldn't your clothes bury me"?

"I'll launder your clothes, but some of my sloppy joes would look good on you".

A strange look came over her face then and she said quietly, "You want to see me in one of your tops, do you fancy me, Mister Striker".

"No...no, no, maybe. A bit, don't worry I'm not going to.... Listen, just go and get a shower while I clean your stuff all right"? She leered at him then,

"I am going to be safe in there, I mean once again nudey and all, you're not thinking of joining me are you and thinking maybe that one thing might......".

"Calm down there, I'm English remember, you are safe enough and also who says 'nudey' any more"?

"I thought you were into that Trentavoria woman, but now I'm not so sure, when this is all over, you can have my number....if you want it".

With that, the confusing woman tripped into the bathroom and could be heard humming as she showered. Roxbrough opened the door of his sonic-laundromat and dropped in her clothes and his as well. Then he snuck into the bathroom and grabbed his dressing gown and added that to the load. From the bedroom, he got his other dressing gown and was preparing breakfast for the two of them when she emerged wrapped in one of his crisp white bath sheets.

"That smells delicious, what are you making"? she asked as she seated herself at his bar.

"To start it's a bowl of Nuetros from Crawfrods because every single spoonful is packed with wheaty goodness nutrients and vitamins and you will not want to start the day without them".

"Let me guess they sponsored you at one time"?

"That's uncanny, you must be...what's the word....."?

"Deranged"? She laughed.

"Not the one I was thinking of, but it will do. Anyway get them down you and the scrambled eggs and cheese will be nice and brown by the time you've finished. Help yourself to rye-wheat crisps".

"What about you"?

"I'll get my shower first and then come and start some more eggs those are for you".

"And my clothes"?

"Are about four minutes from being clean, you'll hear the buzzing when the machine's finished".

"One of these days you're going to make someone a lovely wife".

Roxbrough could not help but like the girl, criminal though she was. Their amusing banter [to the two of them at least] was because they seemed to share the same sort of self-defamatory humour. Many a successful relationship had been built on far less. They were both also attractive and attracted to one another, which never hurt.

When he had dressed into a tracksuit and gone back into the kitchen he found her in one of his hooded sweatshirts. She had chosen a black one as it contrasted so well with her platinum blonde hair and the garment had never looked so good on him.

"Wow! That suits you". He told her candidly honest.

"Well do not think you can remove it as easily as you did all my other clothing because I've just stuffed myself with that incredible combination of egg and cheese. How did you make it taste so cheesy"?

Deadpan he told her, "I put cheese in the eggs. You see if you put tomato it does not taste cheesy, I learned that in cookery classes".

"You went to cookery classes"? she laughed.

"No, I got thrown out of the first lesson for putting too much cheese in everything".

She suddenly sobered and sipped a lichen-coff she had made. There was a second mug on the bar for him.

"Tell me how we are going to kidnap the enemy manager then Striker-man".

While he was rustling up a second batch of eggs he asked her the details of their planned meeting. He said to her,

"So I will be your prisoner and the two of us go into this warehouse of his. I will have to be bound in case he has decided to bring some heavies with him".

"Bound"? She echoed, "You are going to let me take you, prisoner"?

"To get us in the place unchallenged, yes. The bonds will look good but only the outer layer of tape will be actually around my wrists, all the other layers will be pre-cut".

"How do we explain Trentavoria's absence and you as a replacement"?

"You had to kill her and you took me so I did not talk and want to know if Makers-Guild wants a buy one get one free deal"?

"He never told me to kill Trentavoria though".

"That doesn't matter, the two of us were together and put up a fight. You shot me and then shot her as she was attempting to run away. She fell heavily into some scaffolding and fractured her skull. there's scaffolding all over Manchester at the minute, what with the renovation programme, he will be shocked but will not doubt it".

"Why hasn't her body been found and reported to the combmen and then the SWW"?

"You threw her in a dumpster once you had established she was dead, then you threw me in the boot of your flitter and kept me on ice as the saying goes until it became time for your meeting with him, which is in about an hour from now".

"What if he has some heavies with him as you think possible"?

"When you manage to get off a shot with the Browning how good are you"?

Grimacing she retorted, "I'm no Billy the Kid, but I can shoot when I need to".

"While I am the goat. So we should have the element of surprise and a good chance of getting away with Makers-Guild before kick-off at 15:00. You can be Miss Piggy to my Billy the Kid".

"There had better have been a cartoon, Miss Piggy, in the olde days and she had better have been hot".

"She was a puppet, and when it came to acting something of a ham".

"Ouch"!

"There is one thing I want to ask you before we go to this rendezvous. Have you ever killed anyone on another job, before this one"?

"I'm not even a full-time kidnapper", she confessed then, "I'm a priv-dick [private detective]"!

Roxbrough started to laugh, "Makers-Guild sent a girl-dick to kidnap us, that's ....well, it's funny".

"I've not had much work lately so when the great Throrb Makers-Guild pinged me and offered me a lucrative fee for a bit of *grey work*, as they say, I took it to pay the bills. He made the job sound like a sort of wizard-prang rather than anything criminal. It did not fool me, but I'm around three weeks short of failing with the rent, so I thought it would be easy money. I had no idea you would be with her, but when I saw the two of you I knew it was too late to back out and thought I'd just stun you both and leave you propped up somewhere safe".

"You didn't even have your needlegun drawn".

"I'd crossed the street to intercept you, I didn't think it would be a good idea to do so with a gun in my hand".

"How did you know Clara was going to be there".

"Makers-Guild had told me Trentavoria was a big Drill Plough fan and to intercept her upon leaving. Otherwise, I thought I would have the much more difficult task of breaking into the Trentavoria Estate. It seemed like the easier option. I did not account for the Rox principal".

"I'm not sure what sort of dick you are Kurteze, but as a criminal, you are not exactly sparkling, if you don't mind me observing".

"You can call me my girls name - Kresze if you want. What's your first name"?

"Rox will do me fine".

"Why, have you got a soppy first name or something"?

"I have as it happens and I do not like it so Rox will do fine".

"How much longer have we got before we have to set off"?

"Thirty minutes or so. Don't worry we'll get there in plenty of time".

"In the last twenty-four hours I've attempted to do things I would have never thought I would even consider a month ago", she told him then. Life has its surprises doesn't it"?

forty   **It was raining** heavily when they pulled up outside the warehouse on Port Street. The warehouse in question had enjoyed many names over the years but it was currently MG House at that time. Its appearance signified its ancient origins. Here brick, there concrete sections, there again steel shuttering. The building was amorphous and almost viable, due to the constant additions and subtractions over the centuries. It had presented many facades to the world, but its current form was surely its least aesthetically pleasing. Beauty was not the aim of the warehouse though, rather it was function and in that regard, the construction amalgamates continued to serve its purpose most admirably. Roxbrough cursed silently under his breath as his Quiet Dog Loafers were soaked by his stepping out of the flitter and into a huge muddy puddle. Scientists had declared the climate of the Earth stable after repeated effects to get the huge Corporations to reduce deleterious emissions into the atmosphere to zero. Most had come into line with the usual exception of the Unwanted States of Amerik. Never had they enjoyed a healthy reputation in that regard, having a worse track record even than the Eastern Alliance of Amerik, India and China. Over the last couple of decades, they had abandoned all attempts to come into line with scientific directives and philosophers and myriad other knowledgable groups of men said the next war on the home planet would be against them, for diplomacy continued to fail. None of which concerned Roxbrough greatly at the moment the cold water managed to find its way through the suede and soak his sock. When he had cold feet, then he decided he was not happy with the state of the weather, for then, it had affected him personally.

He and Kurteze walked to the closest entrance and Roxbrough was pleasantly surprised to see that Makers-Guild had only brought two bodyguards with him. One each for him and his *captor* to deal with, neither of them were too concerned with the aged businessman himself. Seeing the two of them inside in silence he suddenly demanded,

"Where's Trentavoria and who's this"?

"I had to off her", Kurteze informed, "She was running away and my dart sent her crashing into some scaffolding. Bust her head open like an overripe melon. This is one of her players, I thought he would serve your purpose and you can claim afterwards that you had nothing to do with Trentavoria's disappearance".

"Disappearance"?

"If the skip-men don't check inside before their machine tips the contents into the acid vats, she will never turn up".

"You dumped the body in a skip"?

"The lidded sort", Kurteze was playing her role to perfection, "Those the flittertrux pick up on those big hooks of theirs and take to the vats".

Makers-Guild began, "If she's discovered and the combmen.....".

That was when Roxbrough suddenly burst his singly loop of duck-tape and Kurteze cried,

"Stop him"!

Before the bodyguards could process the directive, the girl had shot both of them and they fell disbelievingly to the concrete floor between several rows of metal racking. In the same moment, Roxbrough had snatched his Kimber and had it pressed to Makers guild's throat before he could even begin to turn and seek escape.

"Do anything I don't tell you to do and I'll anaesthetise you the violent way", the striker told him.

"You double-crossed me, what for"? The businessman demanded.

"For precisely double you cheapskate", Kurteze returned, "It's your fault for hiring an amateur anyway. I told you I'd never kidnapped anyone before. You wouldn't pay the premium on anyone who was used to that sort of dark-work you wanted doing though would you".

"What are you going to do with me? Is Trentavoria dead? Am I looking at a murder charge"?

"He asks a lot of questions doesn't he"? Roxbrough asked the girl.

She returned deadpan, "I don't remember him being this garrulous before".

Roxbrough nudged the man forward with the point of his gun, "Come on lead us back to the flitter. We're taking you to see someone, Throrb".

"I did not give you permission to be familiar with me", the older man fumed.

"You're right", Roxbrough grinned, "You certainly did not"!

forty-one   "I was looking forward to meeting your Manager, the lovely Miss Trentavoria", Podgentino, the manager of Makers-Guild FC smiled to Best.

"She has been...detained, something to do with OUC business", Best lied. "Our striker is also unable to play, a virus contracted last night, we are playing Nero up-front with Rachwalski, a last-minute substitution".

"Well best of luck then, you'll need it", Podgentino smiled insincerely, "My team are on a real high at the moment and expect to overhaul you in the table by the end of the game".

"Not in front of the Chairman of the board of Directors though, I notice", Best engaged the coup de grace. Podgentino's head whipped around and upward with such velocity that he almost wrenched his neck. Best pushed the advantage,

"It's unusual for Mister Makers-Guild to miss a match isn't it, still the rigours of business and all that. Good luck".

He held out his hand. Podgentino's shake was weak and limp-wristed telling Best much of what he needed to know about the coach. He was further gratified to see that following the pantomime, several of the Makers-Guild team had subsequently noticed that their CEO and Chairman was absent. It was not a level playing field. For Clara had given the squad who were in all white with orange trim their pep talk over a padfon, having decided not to enter the ground. The cranial implants were still operable and she would be able to organise them whilst on the pitch as she watched the tri-vidz broadcast on Space.

As the two teams finished their warm-up therefore and the comp-ref informed them there was one minute to kick-off, the team with lower morale was the home side. Makers-Guild played in scarlet and black striped shirts black shorts and scarlet and black hooped socks. The computer-referee [comp-ref] determined that Orang-U-Can were to kick off. Of the entire crowd, not a living soul could have expected what happened then. Rachwalski passed the ball to Nero who set off like a freight train and raced down the left-wing a defender in red and black dutifully went to tackle him but could not do so before the Brazilian had floated a sweet cross right into the Makers-Guild penalty box, where Jenson rose high above everyone else and sent a bullet-header straight into the home team's goal. A stunned silence settled over the home fans while the travelling Orang-U-Can supporters went delirious with delight. OUC had scored inside a minute. For the next ten minutes, practically all of the possession was Orang-U-Can's and after a rather ungainly goalmouth scramble resulting in five players ending up on the floor, Ball found the only tiny route available and toe-poked the ball over Makers-Guild's diving goalkeeper. Nil-Two within the first ten minutes.

Corporation Division One		
Goosetimp v Deutsch Fahrzeuge Eingearbeitet	1	1
Hornrunner Hornets v Rolls Royce Scoriors	0	0
Voleskip v Preciometallic.Inc	2	0
Makers-Guild v Orang-U-Can	0	4
Castle Electronic v Tiptingle Foods	3	0
IYWIWSI v Zhōngguá Shāngpín	2	2

It was merely a matter of how many Makers-Guild could keep it down to after that. On thirty-seven minutes, Lane was brought down by the home side defence and slotted the penalty home himself. The teams went in at half-time and the difference in morale was nothing short of enormous. So confident was Clara of victory that she substituted Lane and Nero for the two youngsters, Sanedad and Radford. Makers-Guild defended resolutely in the second half and kept the score to nil-four but the significant thing from Clara's point of view was that Sanedad scored a long-range free-kick that hinted at the sort of player he was going to become.

Clara immediately consulted her padfon to see what the other results had been and how they had effected the table:

	Corporation Div One	Plyd	Goals	Pts
1	Castle Electronics	7	17	21
2	I.Y.W.I.W.S.I.	7	18	16
3	Goosetimp Weapons	7	19	15
4	Orang-U-Can	7	15	14
5	Deutsch Fahrzeuge Eingearbeitet	7	14	12
6	Zhōngguá Shāngpín	7	9	11
7	Makers-Guild	7	12	10
8	Rolls Royce Scoriors	7	8	10
9	Preciometalic.Inc	7	10	8
10	Voleskip Pharmaceuticals	7	4	8
11	Tiptingle Tigers	7	7	7
12	Hornrunner Hornets	7	6	5

Orang-U-Can had finally gone above the German team DFE but the factor that most concerned Clara was that Castle Electronics were seven points in front of them. The next game would be in the quarter-finals of the Shield however so firstly she had to concentrate on that.

Picking up her padfon she dialled Roxbrough's eaddress and told him he could release Makers-Guild. The CEO could hardly go to the combmen and report them without also alerting them to his guilt, so he would simply have to put it down to experience and possibly cheat less in the future.

Roxbrough put the padfon down and smiled at Makers-Guild,

"Get out of here", he said to the older man, "And by the way, Makers-Guild, I'd give up your nefarious activities if I was you, you do not possess the wherewithal to make a go of it".

Scowling the CEO of one of the largest corporations in the solar system kicked at an ancient can petulantly as he strolled out into a cold evening in Moss Side.

"The flittaxi should pick him up virtually straight away", Roxbrough said to his most unlikely of partners in crime, "We wouldn't want anything serious to happen to him would we"?

"Of course not", Kurteze grinned. So what now, Rox"?

"What do you mean"?

"Well, I've got a wad of thumb and a free evening ahead of me and I owe it all to you. What do you say we both go home, get ready and then I take you out to dinner – my treat"?

"I say it sounds like a plan", the striker smiled, "I'll run you to your vehicle and then what? Are you going to pick me up, or am I doing the chauffeuring"?

"Why don't we get flittaxis then we can have some wine with the meal"?

"Do you already have somewhere in mind"?

She nodded, "I thought we might try the Chorlton on Barlow Moor Road. I've heard their evening cuisine is five-star".

"Yes, sounds like a plan, will you book a table"?

"For 20:00 in my name". They had reached the side of his flitter and she said to him then, "I'll jump straight out when you get to my vehicle so if you're going to kiss me, you'd better make your move now".

Thinking it would then be rude and cold not to, he slid around to the passenger side and took her in his arms, making the kiss slow and gentle.

"Hhmm", she said when they parted, "Book me down for another one of those for later when we can take our time over it"?

forty-two   **The Chorlton was** the sort of place where one knew instinctively upon entering that one was going to enjoy a superb meal. It was not that it was salubriously furnished, quite the opposite, the neoplas chairs were downright shoddy in terms of contemporary seating, as were the equally dire tables. The walls, though scrubbed to complete cleanliness were faded with so much cleaning. The floor equally sterile was old tiles that had been in fashion perhaps a century earlier. In one corner stood an almost fossilised stlx-player, behind a crumbling bar two youths looking attentive and dressed in pristine white suits of white shirt and joggers, were standing before the various beverages patrons could order before, during and after their meal.

It was the general lack of investment in surroundings that distilled in the prospective diner, the confidence that the establishment was run by someone who put a decent salary for his (or her) employees at the top of the list - in terms of priority. When that was done everything else trickled down like a logical procession. Contented staff were friendly, they laboured to make certain that service was high on their agenda and of course, in the kitchen, a well-paid chef paid dividends. All this was demonstrated by how full the eatery was from Monday to Sunday, fifty-two weeks of the year. None minded the poor lighting, some of the LEDs were not even on. Neither did they mind the unevenness of the floor which meant that tables were on little raised dais' of stacked tiles for them to maintain equilibrium.

The food was reasonably priced, as was the drink, service was fantastic and the menu delicious.

Roxbrough walked into the place expecting it to be popular on a Saturday evening but did not expect it to be bursting at the seams. The instant he entered in his frilled white shirt and white cargoes a rather fetching young woman was at his side.

"Yes, Sir, have you a booking because if not then I'm afraid your wait will be.....".

"My friend has booked I believe", he told the girl, hoping Kurteze had, "The name is Kurteze".

The girl (human) consulted her padfon and nodded, smiling up at the 201cm footballer, he could tell she found him attractive, but once the platinum blonde priv-dick arrived her interest would soon evaporate.

"This way please you're at table 23 in the alcove yonder ".

Roxbrough followed the girl, her buttocks rolling nicely in her tight white skirt. Just because he was hoping to later eat his dinner, it did not mean he could not enjoy another sneaky peek at the sweet trolley.

"What can I get you to drink while you wait for your partner, Sir"? The girl asked him.

"A glass of Black Tower, please"? He asked. She hurried away seemingly genuinely eager to provide the very best of service. Of course, tipping was encouraged to the service industries, which explained part of her diligence, but as Roxbrough glanced around him he could see all her fellows equally motivated.

"She was pretty", Kurteze voice said from behind him. Roxbrough twisted in his chair,

"How long have you been here"?

"Long enough to observe you oggling that waitress' ass", Kurteze remarked, but he could tell by her tone that she was not genuinely annoyed. "Sometimes pays to be a priv-dick if you want to put your date under surveillance".

"Well, would you like me as much if I didn't like girls"? He wanted to know.

"No", she returned with real feeling. "I'm a regular girl with regular healthy appetites thank you very much. The fad for re-orgmentation quietly disgusts me. You've never been a woman have you"?

"Never and as for those guys who do it to have a baby! Why would you put yourself through that, I think we share the same beliefs it's all a bit unnatural. I'm a regular crumpet guy".

"Good 'cos I'm a regular beefcake girl. Give us a sip of your drink will you"?

As she sipped at his Black Tower he ordered two more, then explained, "I'm not being greedy, I'm going to settle the bill tonight".

"You ruddy-well are not", she flared, "It was my treat and I'm paying for it'"

"I thought you had a problem with your rent"?

"After what the two CEOs thumbed me. My account is now very healthy thanks to you and I wanted to make up for attempting to kidnap you".

"Then I'll owe you a meal because if you remember, it was *me* who kidnapped *you*"!

"Deal, I was hoping tonight would be the end of it", she smiled. By the way, have you checked your padfon this evening, as I know you don't have a tri-vidz"?

He shook his head asking, "Why"?

"I'm not sure you're going to believe me when I tell you"?

"Try me".

"You know the water shortage the Martians are claiming to have due to the Unwanted States increased demands for lichen production"?

"Claims that Eastern Mars continues to promote and perpetuate, particularly the Poles in Amazonis and Tharsisto south-west of them".

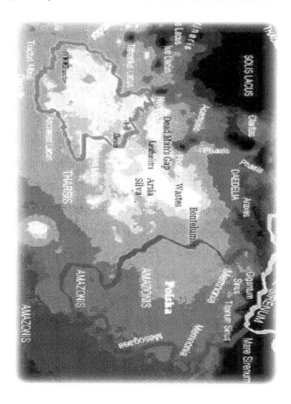

The girl nodded, "You read it on the web then. Well anyway the Poles, in particular, aided and abetted by the Tharsisto have just informed the Unwanted States that they are raising the price of lichen to double what it was the last consignment. So the Amerik is sending a fleet of space-flitter to Mars including three spacefortress to take the lichen and leave the Polska with the usual payment"!

Roxbrough's heart sank, he observed, "You know how that will play out don't you"?

"The Amerik will expect their ancient allies – us, to back them when the Poles shoot them out of the black sky".

"And shoot them down they will! They say the Poles new combat lasers at Twierdza are four times more powerful than anything we have on Earth. The Poles and Tharsisto combined their expertise to create them and the Polish people say the Polish sector on Mars will never suffer as the homeland did on the home planet historically. I cannot even say I blame them for feeling that way".

"If war comes and I believe it is pretty certain. The Amerik always start trouble they cannot handle themselves without Saxonian know-how to bolster them, what would you do if King Darren called all young men to arms"?

"The solar system's first-ever interplanetary war? Is such a thing even thinkable"?

"Were the grave wars of the past possible to contemplate"? Did anyone ever truly think the west would incinerate the middle east when they refused to desist with their malign superstitions".

"Superstition always caused misery and strife but isn't this different. The Amerik are only going to raid lichen. Can the Poles justify blasting them for wanting to feed their people"?

"Oh, come on Rox?! You know full well the Unwanted States is one of the chief offenders when it comes to flaunting their refusal to adhere to the Anti-obesity World Council Act of '82. They continue to immorally shovel more food into their mouths than any other race on the planet and what is their defence for doing it? Greed is an addiction, like being hooked on snufz or mainlining snufzomorph. Only the crazy Amerik could come up with something so preposterous and contemptible as that. I say if Polish airspace is violated by the obese and lazy Amerik then they have every right to laser their asses".

"I suppose I agree", Roxbrough admitted glumly. "You ask me what I would do if the King called up men of my age. My answer is, as my maternal grandmother is Polish I guess I would have to go to Mars and take up a military post there".

"Oh, kaahk I've brought the atmoss down now haven't I? I'm sorry".

"Let's eat and live for the moment, what do you say".

"I say where's that waitress you fancy"?

forty-three   **Roxbrough carefully lifted** himself off the
naked form beneath him and flopped face-down onto the pillow beside her.
At least from that position, she could not see the huge grin that was
plastered all over his features. He heard her say,

"You must think me some sort of trollop. I have *never* slept with a man on
the first date before, not ever, not once in my life".

"War brings lovers together", he muttered into the pillow, "Anyway I don't
think we've just done much sleeping".

She suddenly straddled the small of his back and began to massage his
shoulders. He could feel the dampness of her as it pressed into him.
Moisture that he had created and injected with copious amounts. He
twisted over beneath her and asked.

"We're all sticky, fancy another shower"?

"I'd love one, but it cannot end the same way it did last time, I'm worn out,
Mister. It's all right for you, you train to be fit and to have superhuman
stamina, I'm just an ordinary girl".

"Kresze Kurteze, there is nothing ordinary about you", he observed with
feeling. Taking her waist in his hands, he launched her onto the opposite
side of the bed as he arose smoothly to a standing position. She had
squealed her delight at the demonstration of his strength and agility and
then as she too rose and ran for the door he smacked her behind causing
her to whoop and scream again.

  They lathered one another's bodies delighting in their youth, their
aesthetically pleasing torsos and their feeling for one another. Although
they had met but recently and for such a very brief time, they felt totally at
ease with one another. Sex had that effect on young people once they had
seen each other's most intimate areas, modesty was no longer necessary
or even sensible.

Once dry they settled beside the thermal bars of his fireplace and sipped
Black Tower whilst listening to Drill Plough. They did not retire until gone
03:00.

forty-four   **"We've got a** crisis"! Best greeted Clara as
she entered her office on Monday morning.

"I have wondered", Clara began with a sigh, "If that is your standard
greeting, Best. Instead of, 'Morning Boss did you have a good day off'? You
prefer to greet me every day with some new problem we are bound to face".

The irony was wasted on George Best though, he returned simply,
"There's a girl outside she's pregnant and she says one of four of our
squad is the father".

"One of four! Let me guess some sort of drink or drug-fuelled orgy and
she cannot remember quite which one knocked her up"?

"You're on the right lines", the Assistant Manager informed her. She was
on her way home from Hobo's having danced the night away. When a flitter
pulled up at the side of the kerb and she was asked if she would like a ride
home. It turns out she got a ride all right, several".

"Names, how many have I got to put on the transfer list", Clara fretted what it would do to the squad.

"The flitter was in the possession of the *Eggheads*"!

"English George, remember", Clara already had an inkling of what Best was referring to, she knew a few of her players who were prematurely bald shaved their heads completely or had taken depilatory treatment. She suddenly added, "No, better yet let the girl come in here and I'll be able to tell if she's telling the truth".

While he went to fetch the complainee, Clara sipped her lichen-coff until it burnt some on the skin from her gums making them wrinkly. She was worrying at them with her tongue when he returned with a quite attractive and presentable young woman. It caused Clara to have to immediately assess her differently.

"Miss Bwiddle Stairfoot, Miss Clara Trentavoria".

"Sit down please, Miss Stairfoot, can I get you a lichen-coff"?

"Please"? The girl assented, she was pale with anxiety at the ordeal she was enduring, but her jawline bespoke of her resolution and determination for some sort of recompense for what had occurred.

"Best would you fetch Miss Stairfoot a lichen-coff please"? The assistant manager nodded and happily absented himself from the room. Clara caught the girl looking at a poster on the wall, showing the squad in traditional fashion three rows of faces looking very pleased to be in the frame for the largest corporation in the solar system.

"In your own words, Miss Stairfoot I would like to know what happened on the night in question".

The girl seemed to pull herself together in determined fashion and began,

"I had been to Hobo's and could not get a flittaxi for love nor money so I decided to walk home with two friends. A safe enough idea until they peeled off, four estates from my home. I thought I would hurry and there would be little chance of anything happening. Then it began to rain and I was dressed for dancing if you know what I mean. So I was hurrying through the beginning of a downpour when a flitter pulled up at the side of me and the window wound down and a bald young man offered me a lift. I had my needlegun in my handbag and he looked presentable enough so I climbed into the passenger seat only to find three more men, all with shaved heads, sitting in the back seat, looking like a row of eggs. I thought to myself, it's only four estates and I'll be all right so I stayed and the flitter pulled away. I asked them who they were and they gave me their names which I remember, Lucian was driving, while in the back were Pedadia, Soleeno and Ho Cho".

There was a tap on the door and Best re-entered. Clara took the opportunity to ask,

"Who are the eggheads, Best, what are their surnames"?

"West Ball Shivers the Fin and Wing the Korean".

"Put them all on the transfer list immediately, they will play no further part in our season. Do you know their first names"?

"Of course"?

"Well I don't, what are they"?

"Lucian West, Pedadia Ball, Soleeno Shivers and Cho Ho Wing".

"It's Ho Cho", Bwiddle Stairfoot corrected, "Not Cho Ho".

Best reddened, "You might be right, Young Lady I think they say their name backwards or something. Anyway, they are the eggheads".

"Get Kipson on it", Clara said, I don't want them at this club a day longer than necessary".

Best was once again pleased to get out of the office as quickly as his legs would carry him. Clara said to Stairfoot,

"Our squad doctor, Doctor Charmley has a paternity kit, why is it that you are not sure who the father is, did they gang force you"?

"I was offered a drink from a flask by them, I thought it was something they were handing around. It wasn't it seems now. One minute, I was fine and the next I found myself beside the road, my knickers gone and ....it was running down my leg, a lot of it"!

Clara shuddered, "They drugged you and passed you around"?

Stairfoot nodded. "All I want now is financial support from the actual father. I don't want him to have anything to do with me and the baby when it comes".

"You're keeping the baby"?

The girl nodded. "Not exactly how I hoped my offspring's life would start, but I could not have the little life within me aborted. Are you going to inform the combmen"?

"If I do that then the entire unseemly affair becomes dreadfully public and the result would be the same, would you want the web-media spotlight playing on you"?

As the girl hesitated Clara thought, *'It would also besmirch the club name, I hope she sees sense',* she added verbally,

"Of course doubt would be cast onto your claim too, to increase the sensational aspect of the event. Some reporters would claim you were up for a gang bang, that you were a good time girl who suddenly found her birth control was no longer effective and sought to salt a perfectly good footballer for all you could get".

"Is that what you think of me", Stairfoot flushed then.

"No, I find your description of events believable. I do think you were foolish to get in the flitter, even more so to accept the drink. It contained date-rape of some sort. On the other hand, it's easy for me to say that with the benefit of hindsight. What I suggest is this. We find out who impregnated you and I tell him he can either give you payments voluntarily, or we can take the matter to the courts and his footballing career will like as not suffer as a result. All four will be transferred from Orang-U-Can because I am of course, morally outraged by their behaviour. So much so that I am going to make you a further settlement from club funds to set you on the right path for you and your child. Alternatively, you can go it alone and have a very stressful time over the entire sordid business".

167

The girl narrowed her eyes and suddenly observed, "You're one cold-hearted bitch aren't you, Trentavoria".

"I am", Clara smiled, "But at least I'm not a stupid bitch like you. Now go and see my club doctor and do the most profitable choice and you and I will never see one another ever again".

forty-five   **"We cannot survive** with a squad as tiny as the one we have now", Best complained, "I know it cost dearly to buy Roxbrough and Jensen but we need to strengthen every area of the squad except for the goalkeepers".

"Get up George", Clara returned, "We are going to watch the academy train".

"I know what you're thinking and it will not work", Best objected. "Even the pick of the crop Sanedad and Radford are not ready for a full ninety-minutes. The rest are even younger".

"Let's see what Bell has to say about that"? Clara challenged.

Bell, or as he was known to everyone else Clucking Bell, was the academy coach and the relationship between he and Best was one of open animosity. Glumly the assistant manager followed his manager down to the special surface the boys were training on. Seeing Clara showing some interest, Bell immediately approached the two of them.

"Morning, Gaffer", Bell greeted enthusiastically, cheerfully ignoring the coach of the senior team. "Come to see the lads doing their stuff"?

"Exactly that", Clara agreed. "Save me some time will you, Bell and point out to me your most promising defender, midfielder and striker".

Bell rubbed his chin in his hand, Clara could hear the bristles rasping as he did so,

"That would have to be young Gaines over there, Siggers and Harcourt".

"Are they Saxonian"? Not that it mattered but Carla did like players whose first language was Standard

"Gaines and Harcourt are, Siggers is from Iceland but he speaks good Standard", Bell told her guessing the reason for her question.

"Right then pull them off, they are training with the first squad in an hour. Tell them they are being given the same opportunity as Sanedad and Radford. Oh, tell Harcourt to get a crew cut until that hideous Mohawk grows out and Gaines to have Charmley laser those hideous tattoos out".

"If you are thinking what I think you're thinking I have to say that DFE will be tough, even at home", Best remarked as they walked back toward her office.

He was referring to the midweek Corporation Shield match coming up against Deutsch Fahrzeuge Eingearbeitet.

"There will be no better opportunity to see how they can stand up to the older player", Clara argued, "As the season progresses and we need them as the injuries and suspensions start to mount up, they will have benefited from the experience. You will train them with the men and I will be watching".

So filled with vitality, enthusiasm for the opportunity and excitement were they that the three young lads did very well. Clara had three days in which to make her final decision on the line up against the Germans.

She could not help but give them the chance they then worked so hard for and there was great excitement when she posted her squad onto her pad and the players accessed it.

Come the time for kick-off the atmosphere in the ground was crackling almost like electricity. The fans of both teams had confidence in their players, OUC even more so since their unbeaten run. Only one place beneath them in the league though, Deutsch Fahrzeuge Eingearbeitet were dangerous opponents at the best of times. The appearance of the team on the SWW had caused wild speculation. Four youngsters in the team and three more on the bench. Clara had set them up in a 4-3-2-1 formation and the one thing the Germans did not know was the nature of the Dutch-laid pitch.

"I want you to hit them hard using all your experience of the new surface and before they even realise what is happening they are behind", Clara told them. The team finished their warm-up barely able to contain their pent up energy.

Orang-U-Can
6. Radband
45. Gaines 13. Jennings 25. Zinyama 4 Burgenbower
19.Jenson 16. Flintham 44. Siggers
27. Rachwalski 20. Lane
23. Roxbrough

Substitutes
1. Anderson
8. Wong
12 McFarland
30. Sanedad
31. Radford
38. Harcourt

From the very start, they moved the ball around with short crisp passing that frankly had the DFE team amazed and it paid off just as hoped for. Gaines sent a beautiful cross-field pass over to Siggers who raced forward passing two DFE on his way toward goal then at the last instant he passed to Roxbrough who thundered the shot in to make it 1-0. Not to be outdone by the youngsters Jensen lanced a perfectly weighted forward pass to Rachwalski nine minutes later and he selflessly laid the ball off to Roxbrough who side-footed the ball into the German's goal with almost casual ease. The team's chief striker was therefore on a hat trick and he did not have to wait long, within the first thirty minutes of the game, Burgenbower rushing forward as a wing-back clipped a superb cross into the Germans penalty area and up went Roxbrough to head the goal just out of reach of the DFE goalkeeper. Roxbrough would get the match ball no matter what happened next.

Deutsch Fahrzeuge Eingearbeitet were reeling, it was not that they were a bad side but they kept over hitting the ball unable to control it on a surface they were naturally unprepared for. By half-time, Orang-U-Can had torn into them twice more with outside the penalty area long-range shots from Lane and Rachwalski both of which provided Orang-U-Can with a seemingly invincible lead. In the second half Clara brought off Gaines Siggers and Zinyama replacing them with McFarland, Sanedad and Harcourt. The Germans dug in and defended in-depth and it was a testament to their tenacity that they did not concede again, but the scoreline already looked damning and Orang-U-can were through to the semi-finals of the Corporation Shield. The other matches were no surprise:

The computer immediately did the draw for the semi-finals and came up with:

Corporation Shield Quarter Finals		
OUC v DFE	5	0
Zhõngguá Shãngpín v IYWIWSI	2	0
Castle Electronics v Polski Węgiel	3	0
Ruski Kamień v Makers-Guild	0	2

Corporation Shield Semi-Finals

Zhõngguá Shãngpín versus Orang-U-Can
Castle Electronics versus Makers Guild

forty-six   **Captain Bud Budwise** started the deceleration process of his spacefortress and saw the small red pebble that was Mars begin to grow larger in his viewscreen. A disc of unspectacular appearance at the distance the spacefortress was at that moment, soon to grown into the scarlet red eye of an angry demon. At the two poles of the disc, it seemed to Bud that the whiteness had receded a little and was less albescent. The Aresian had been telling the truth when they claimed that Amerik's increasing demands for lichen were beginning to deplete their meagre water source. He put the magnification up and could see that the planet's various artificial lakes were shrinking also. He knew then that his government were in the wrong. The Aresian were not trying to deceive Amerik, the lichen could not grow without water and water seemed to be becoming a more valuable commodity on the fourth planet from Sol. Captain Budwise decided to do something about it before the orders to attack the warehouses in Memnonia were transmitted to the fleet. He got onto the radio and sent a message to his Rear Admiral, a man he had never been able to get on with for his bull-headed obstinacy which had caused problems between the two of them in the past.

"Sir", he began, "Budwise here, do you have the planet in your viewscreen, Sir".

A voice dripping arrogance and mild annoyance answered him,

"I did think to do that small thing Bud, what's your problem"?

"I do not have a problem, Sir. Merely an observation. The Aresian seem to have a point judging by their shrinking artificial lakes and the loss of some albescence at both poles. Do you not think a message on sub-space communication to Texas might not be advisable"?

"Aresian! You mean the gordamn Martians do you? So they have a point based on your observations. I, on the other hand, have my orders and that is to get that consignment of lichen anyway I judge it to be necessary, Captain".

"Yes-sir I'm aware of your orders I was at the briefing remember? It would seem that those very orders were issued based on the Command's belief that the Aresian were exaggerating their water production shortages. If you look at the planet, even from this distance it's easily discernible that they were telling the truth".

"That's as may be, Captain. We still have mouths to feedback in the US though, don't we? What would you say to the top brass on our return to Texas? 'Sorry guys but we felt more sympathy for a few generations of emigrants than for our citizens, so we came back with our thumbs up our ass'"?

"I'm just thinking about the World Council as much as anything else, Sir. If we land our fleet in the Polska sector of Mars and take the lichen without permission then the WC could view it as an act of space-piracy. It could take the US into a war on two worlds".

"You worried about what the Polaks will do on Earth? Or maybe the Saxonians or Krauts"?

171

"Individually we would be a match for them, Sir. What if they joined together though, under the directorship of the WC? Perhaps a quick word with Texas would at least ensure that your name did not go down in history as the man who's actions started the US-WC war"?

That did the trick, there was silence at the other end and yet the channel was still open.

"Are you still receiving, Sir"? Budwise asked.

"I am going to take your recommendation under advisement, Captain and get in touch with Texas. Advice the space-flitters to assume an orbit out at this distance, just in case that laser-gun story also has an element of truth to it".

"Yes-sir", Budwise felt happy to follow that particular order.

All he could do then was wait. He was doing so as patiently as he could when a stream of tiny dots appeared on his sensor-screen. They were emitting from Mars. The exact location, according to the flight-comp was the metropolis of Memnonia. Bud watched in surprised dread as the dots approached at considerable speed and then a broad-band message came over his radio.

"Unwanted States war vessels approaching the Polska Sector, your intrusion into our space-space is an act of trespass, withdraw to a distance of three million kilometres at once. Your refusal to do this will be perceived as an act of offensivety. We can defend ourselves, we do not permit your presence in your current location".

"Polska commander", Captain Budwise began, "This is the second in command of the armada you have detected, Captain Budwise, to whom am I in contact with, please"?

"You are speaking to Kontradmirał Zając, do as I direct otherwise we will be forced to take an offensive stance against your intrusion into our sovereign realm".

Rear Admiral Zając was a known hard-liner in the Polish fleet. He meant what he said and it was known he had the backing of Królowa [Queen] Zaina.

"Admiral", Bud began trying to prevaricate, "Please give us a moment to examine our position. We have not come to do anything other than pick up the outstanding lichen consignment which our population needs to sustain itself. Can we not open a peaceful dialogue along those lines"?

"No"! Came the unhesitating reply. "To conserve water the last consignment has not been grown nor harvested. Our warehouses are empty, you have made a wasted journey. Retire the required distance or better still go home, there is nothing in the Polska Sector for you".

"Could you transmit images of your empty plants by any chance, Admiral"? Bud asked.

"I do not need to do so to someone who wishes to infer that I am a liar. Accept my word and withdraw in the next sixty seconds or my fighters will open fire on you".

"Admiral our fleet consists of as many fighters and three spacefortress, you are heavily outgunned, please let us pursue a policy of negotiation regarding the lichen you owe us. It is nonsensical for lives to be lost over this issue".

"I entirely agree, so withdraw to the distance instructed and then you may send one vessel to Mars to speak to her Majesty if you do indeed doubt my word".

Bud knew the Królowa would echo Zając's word whether it was true or otherwise. At least it was a concession from the hardliner though. Reluctantly he went on the broadband of the radio and began,

"This is Captain Budwise, all vessels will withdraw to a distance of......."

"Belay that order"! The Rear Admiral's voice suddenly cut in. I have just been in contact with Texas High Command. We are to proceed to Mars as planned. Any attempt to halt our progress will be met with deadly force. Go to amber alert, state of readiness, power up all weapons, we are going to land near the lichen warehouses of Mars or die trying"!

"Admiral"! Bud gasped, "I was in the process of......"

"You asked me to confirm with Texas and I did as you advised, we have our order now Captain, follow them, that is all".

Inside the spacefortress, Bud could hear the sound of weaponry powering up in answer to the Rear Admiral's directive. He began to steer the massive vessel toward Mars despite his reservations. He was career Navy and the thought of outright disobedience did not occur to him.

The Poles fired firstly. After the first shot, which destroyed the vanguard space-flitter every other vessel in space replied with an instant sally of energy weaponry. The curious thing was that the entire episode was conducted in deadly silence. There was no air or atmosphere of any sort in the absolute vacuum of space, therefore sound-waves had nothing to be carried by. It was an old maxim that the only explosion one ever heard in space was the one that killed you and it was true.

Bud scrambled his flitters and the hanger doors sprang open to allow them to spring into action. One vessel in the Polish formation suddenly broke free and sped back to the Polska Sector of the red planet. It seemed Kontradmirał Zając was not so hardline that he intended to give his own life in pursuit of Polish glory. The battle lasted 93 minutes until only three Polish fighters remained and were allowed to scurry back after their commander. The US forces had been depleted by a factor of 43% though, quite heavy losses.

"Now we go to Memnonia", the Rear Admiral told the remainder of the task-force.

"Admiral, what about the laser-cannons the Polish claim to have"?

"If they give our fortresses any trouble which I seriously doubt, then we will send their ass' to hell. They fired firstly, they started this war. We might even empty their warehouses and leave no payment, never mind double".

"Kontradmirał Zając told me their warehouses are empty, Sir"."Then that miserable Polak is a gordamn liar! All vessels proceed to Mars at three-quarter thrust"! The intense blue beam that shot from the surface of the planet when the fleet took an orbit of 36,000 kilometres around it, crippled the Rear Admiral's fortress. It began to explode in sections as the lifeboats issued from it like angry bees protecting a threatened nest. Budwise issued orders for grappling lines to be fired from all available ports and many of them were drawn into his vessel the USS Wayne. As he was preoccupied with that rescue the USS Douglas was hit by the blue lasers and before anyone could evacuate, it ripped and tore itself to pieces. There had been 3,200 officers and enlisted men aboard it. Meanwhile what was left of the Wayne broke orbit and limped through the atmosphere of Mars in a downward spiral aiming toward the Polska sector.

'What the hell is that pilot doing'? Bud wondered for the ship seemed bent upon crashing into Polska territory in a fantastic and highly destructive conflagration. He would subsequently discover that it was the Rear Admiral himself at the control. A man bent upon going out in a blaze of glory. Statues would subsequently be struck and erected to him in the heart of Dallas [his home town].

"Now hear this - all vessels", Budwise declared on the broadband of the radio. "Strategic withdrawal at once, I am taking temporary command of the fleet until the whereabouts of the Rear Admiral is known".

forty-seven   **"I find it** hard to believe that after all the wars that have ever been fought, with neither side emerging without countless tragedies, that we still have not learned that lesson from the past", Roxbrough said miserably as he looked at his padfon.

Poland and Unwanted States at War

At his side, Kurteze looked nothing but grimly sympathetic.

"If it gets to conscription what will you do"? She wanted to know.

"Well, as I'm quarter polish if the Królowa requires my services I will have to go. Do I strike you as a person who would shirk his duty, Kresze"?

The girl miserably shook her head. Their affair had been progressing swiftly and to her entire satisfaction and she privately believed that she was in love with the OUC striker.

"Do you think it will come to that"? She asked desperately, knowing that he would have not the slightest clue.

"It sounds like the Yanks got a bloody nose when they tried to attack the Polska sector of Mars. I cannot honestly see them backing down now that Amerik lives have been lost. They still think they're the power they were when the Eastern Alliance was with them as the United States. They are not. Poland had a very powerful base on the red planet, they will be foolish to let the conflict escalate, but then the US is the least logical and most excitable race on Earth so I don't think they will let the matter rest".

"You're only quarter Polish though"?

"If I was the Królowa I would swell the size of her army to such a massed force as swiftly as possible. To demonstrate to the Unwanted States how futile continuing the conflict would prove to be for them".

"What if they try to call old alliances to bear and expect other nations to join in though. Could they not then match the Poles man for man"?

"Theoretically, but if they went to the World Council and demanded support, several powerful nations might decide to align themselves with the Poles rather than the Yanks. I'm not certain King Darren would willingly join the US. As for the Francosian, they would not agree to join them if Saxonia did, not that they are much use in a scrap anyway. I would think that the Eastern Alliance might feel duty-bound to join the US. If they did though Poland would then pressure the Romanians to ally themselves with them. After that, it would be intriguing to see who would sit on their hands and who would get stuck in".

"Can you hear yourself"? Kurteze demanded then. "Even the sort of talk you are giving lip too is beyond sane. You're talking about a possible two world war like it's some sort of chess game"?

Roxbrough had the grace to look chagrined, "You are right, Kresze, all we can do is hope sanity prevails, somehow".

"So if you were to suppose that it does, what scenario do you imagine would be the most likely to stop this war before it has barely begun"?

"Wow, that's a tough one. I suppose it would be the World Council

Corporation Division One

Goosetimp Weapons v Preciometalic.Inc
Deutsch Fahrzeuge Eingearbeitet v Rolls Royce Scoriors
Tiptingle Tigers v Hornrunner Hornets
Orang-U-Can v Castle Electronics

Voleskip Pharmaceuticals v I.Y.W.I.W.S.I.

Makers-Guild v Zhōngguá Shāngpĭn

stepping in and trying a diplomatic solution to the issue. If the US would not agree, then a threat to hit them with everything the WC had. I cannot see any other way of getting the chest-beating Yanks to back down now hostilities have started".

"So where does it leave us, Rox"?

Roxbrough took the lovely blonde headed girl in his arms,

"Do you think something as trifling as two planets warring with one another is going to split us apart babe"? He kissed her gently. "If I'm called up, I would hope you would wait for me, or come with me"?

forty-eight　　　　　　　　　"This has to be the biggest test we have faced so far", Clara told Best. I need you to keep the players' minds on the job in hand", she declared, thinking of Roxbrough and Rachwalski in particular.

"Then I suggest we leave Roxbrough and Rachwalski out of the squad", Best dared.

"The two players with eight goals between them against the toughest team in the league", Clara scoffed, "Roxbrough our best striker by a considerable margin and six goals to his credit, you want to leave him out – Against Castle Electronics".

"As you suggested in the first part of this conversation you need the men to be completely focused on the game. Those two aren't. They might both be called up soon anyway if the war continues to escalate. The US had promised a counter-attack on Mars in honour of their lost Rear Admiral. They are asking for allies, though none have responded yet. Talks of a peacekeeping WC force is being rumoured".

"Best"! Clara said calmly, "I don't give a flying frenge about the war, I am talking about the Corporation League One title. I will tell you what I am going to do, I am going to watch you training the men this morning. Take the entire squad onto the pitch and have them play against each other. I want to see who is committed to this club and who is not".

Nodding Best went to organise that very request. The resultant match was ten against ten, with yet another of one ten being from the academy a young man from Kharga by the name of Nofre. Cara watched the game in its entirety and was forced to admit to herself that her former companion and his fully Polish squad member were distracted and poor by their previous standards. She took Best to one side and asked him to have Roxbrough and Rachwalski brought up to her office once they were showered.

Within thirty minutes they presented themselves before her desk as she bid them enter.

"Sit down, please"? She requested. Puzzled the two did as requested. "I am here to run a football club. A football club that I intend will win the First Division this season. Now I know you are going to find what I have to say next as harsh but I am putting the pair of you on the transfer list on the SWW immediately. You should bring a good return on my initial investment in you, Roxbrough, but if you do not I still intend to let you go".

Rachwalski looked thunderstruck while Roxbrough merely smiled ironically,

"You are, Clara, after all, your father's daughter are you not"? He observed.

Rachwalski practically wailed, "What is going on here, Boss why are you getting rid of us"?

It was Roxbrough who answered, "Miss Trentavoria could see from our performances today that the Polish/US war has distracted us and reduced our usefulness to her club. Rather than wait and see if we get over the upsetmentation, she is getting rid of us quickly while I still command a considerable price tag. She hopes that the next manager who buys me will not believe that the war will escalate and that I might be required to serve our Królowa or Queen in Standard. From a business point of view, it makes sense to do it swiftly and mercilessly. From a humanitarian point of view well......".

"Rachwalski would you leave the two of us alone, please"? Clara asked then, "Be assured I will try and place you in the best club I can, your tri-vidz performances will speak for themselves".

"Boss", said the young Pole, "I would rather stay here"?

"I'm sorry, my decision is final and irrevocable", Clara told him with such a tone of finality in her voice that the young Pole simply let his shoulders drop as he slipped out of the office.

The instant he had closed the door Clara began, "Rox, listen for a moment....."?

"Miss Trentavoria, please use my full surname when addressing me if you do not mind"?

Clara stiffened, "Very well Roxbrough if that is how you wish this to be, I was going to express my regret to you regarding this decision which I did not make lightly and further add a desire that we could remain friends, but I sense that that might not be possible due to the current positions we now find ourselves in"?

"Were we friends"? Roxbrough asked, "Because if we were and I was certainly yours, I do not think this is the way a friend would treat another"?

"That is because you are looking upon my decision as something personal, *Mister* Roxbrough. It is anything but, it is business. I truly hope the war you seem so affected by does not blow up into something major, but if it does I would lose the two of you anyway, I am merely reducing my losses, hopefully, the only way I am able".

"Oh, you've lost more than money based on your decision today, Miss Trentavoria, you've lost a friend", Roxbrough told her as he went to the door.

forty-nine　　　　　　　**When the team** sheet was posted on the SWW, the squad naturally accessed it and the secret was out. The answer to the mystery of why Roxbrough and Rachwalski had been missing training was explained. Football was a team game though and the match was still to go on.

It was still a fairly strong line up even without the two stars. Clara tried to remain positive although the club was bleeding lost revenue when Roxbrough announced he would not sign for If You Want It We Stock It - who had put a considerably large bid in for him, as he was taking a sabbatical to see what his next course of action would be. Clara had ground her teeth in impotent fury, but her former friendship with the striker had stayed her hand when it came to any other sort of reaction. The game was the next area of her focus, the biggest game since she had taken over at the club. It might well prove to be the turning point in Orang-U-Can's season. Or the turning point in Castle's. With an inevitability that comes to all things, no matter how keenly anticipated, the time for the match came. Clara proudly watched her young team trot out onto the pitch for the warm-up. She had every confidence in her defence, which combined experience with the vitality of youth. She was a little nervous about the centre of midfield. Since Speke's demise, there had been no one player who commanded the role of replacing him. Flintham was not tall enough and Jensen liked to rove forward. Lane again lacked height and Sanedad experience. As a lone striker, Nero needed more support, but there was no one with whom to fill that role. Of every match, she had started that was the one occasion when confidence was not high.

The comp-ref signalled for the kick-off and Castle began to mount a series of lightning raids on OUC's defence. The pitch threw them for around half an hour, they kept overhitting passes and losing possession. The only trouble was that Orang-U-Can did not seem to have the confidence to mount a counteroffensive. The men in grey, [second strip to their usual pink] gradually began to gain confidence and acclimatize themselves to the speed of the surface. Had it not been for two superb saves from Radband, the visitors would have gone in two up. As it was Orang-U-Can were lucky to be level at the interval.

"What is wrong with you"? Clara rounded on Lane in the dressing room, "That is the worst 45 minutes you have given me since our informative matches. I've not seen a single probing pass from you the entire half, Nero has had no service at all. He might as well have been in the dressing room".

"I guess I'm missing the commanding figure of Roxbrough to aim for. His movement was such that he always seemed to find the space for one of my passes. Most of the time I could barely see Nero", Lane explained.

"Well then let's make one change at half time", Clara decided, while over to her left Best almost imperceptibly shook his head. It seemed the assistant manager knew what she was about to do and did not approve.

"Go and get showered Nero, I'm resting you for the next game. Harcourt, this is your big chance, I want to see you run yourself into the ground, be ready for an almost surgical strike from Lane here all right"?

When they got back to the bench Best said,

"Harcourt can run, he's fast, but he will not have the confidence to score against the Castle keeper".

"We shall see about that", Clara cursed, resolute with every particle of her being.

The only trouble was that disaster struck after seven minutes of the whistle announcing the commencement of the second half. Castle suddenly thrust through the heart of midfield past Flintham and a speculative shot from their striker, hit one post of Radband's goal, just beyond the reach of his fingertips, ran along the goal-line and striking the other post curled into goal.

Above the roar of the away supporters Clara screamed, "

Flintham - come off, McFarland, take his place, make that midfield solid".

McFarland did a good job at such short notice, but the leading team and visitors were then content to put everyone in their half for the rest of the game. They defended their slim lead with resolute determination and Harcourt wasted several passes to him before Lane began making speculative shots from outside the box. It was the longest 38 minutes of Clara's life and her first defeat as a football manager.

As she stormed down the tunnel in distraught fury, who should intercept her but Ghazza Bamber, compare of *Games Under the Spotlight*.

"Miss Trentavoria", he grinned his tri-vidz cameraman behind his shoulder, "You'z obviously axed the lads to done a win and they gone and done a lost, where does this leave OUC in the big race? Can you now expect it to go to the wire or will Castle park the bus and not hang as many shirts on the line as they have in their shed"?

Clara could have reacted in many different ways to the nonsense spouting from his mouth at that point. The one she selected was not her wisest of alternatives. Her fist bunched and before her brain had told her spine not to, she lashed out with a right jab that terminated in Bamber's face. A former footballer himself, Bamber knew how to react to that sort of personal attack. Pole-axed he threw himself dramatically to the floor of the tunnel in front of the camera and promptly lost the use of both eyes,

"I'm blind"! He screamed falsetto with the horror and agony of the girl's foul assault. "Blind, blind, she's blinded me"!

Then Clara made it worse!

In front of the transfixed audience - from all four corners of the globe, she returned through clenched teeth,

"Blind my ass, more like a blind drunk! Here let me blind your knackers while I'm at it".

Her stoutly shoed foot connected with the soft collection of dangly objects between Bamber's legs and the squeal he then gave rent to was more porcine than human. The camera recorded the entire event in full high definition trio-visual form. It was an event that would go viral on social media in seconds and became the most viewed tri-vidz in history for some years to follow.

fifty-two   **"It's not good,"** solicitor Stubbsinge said for perhaps the twentieth time, "It's not good at all, in fact, it's very very bad".

#	Corporation Div One	Plyd	Goals	Pts
1	Castle Electronics	7	18	24
2	Goosetimp Weapons	7	20	16
3	I.Y.W.I.W.S.I.	7	18	16
4	Deutsch Fahrzeuge Eingearbeitet	7	17	15
5	Orang-U-Can	7	15	14
6	Makers-Guild	7	13	13
7	Zhōngguá Shāngpín	7	9	11
8	Voleskip Pharmaceuticals	7	6	11
9	Rolls Royce Scoriors	7	8	10
10	Preciometalic.Inc	7	11	9
11	Tiptingle Tigers	7	9	8
12	Hornrunner Hornets	7	8	6

"Well as long as you're confident we can win the case then", Clara was acidly sardonic. "Have you ever thought of managing Castle Electronics football team by any chance"?

Hugh let his hand cover his face as he said to his daughter,

"Can you get your head out of the goalmouth for just a minute Clara and focus on the matter in hand. You are being sued for three silver shillin, you violently assaulted a tri-vidz personality in front of.......well in front of just about everyone in the system".

Corporation Division One		
Goosetimp Weapons v Preciometalic.Inc	1	1
Deutsch Fahrzeuge Eingearbeitet v Rolls Royce Scoriors	3	0
Tiptingle Tigers v Hornrunner Hornets	2	2
Orang-U-Can v Castle Electronics	0	1
Voleskip Pharmaceuticals v I.Y.W.I.W.S.I.	2	0
Makers-Guild v Zhōngguá Shāngpín	1	0

"No wait a minute, I'm not having that"? Clara demanded, "He's not a personality – he has absolutely no personal charisma of any sort, of personality...he is devoid".

"**Clara**"! Hugh finally bellowed in total frustration, "Show that sort of total lack of concern for the victim in court and you could get gaol time are you koofing listening to what Stubbsinge is telling you"?

"It was the first time in her entire life that Clara had heard her father use a profanity. She was shocked. She was stunned.

"I'm stunned and shocked, Father", she confessed. "Mister Stubbsinge can you possibly keep me out of Priz? At least until the end of the season at any rate. Do you have any ciggies, by the way, I've run out"?

The diminutive bald and rather plain counsel lifted a pack of Millers for Men out of his frock-coat and tapped them to release one to the girl. Clara promptly thumbed it to life and drew the medicinal smoke into her lungs.

"That's better", she smiled, "I do have to confess that my nerves are shredded by this whole hideous business".

Hugh looked at his daughter as though he did not believe a word of it, but he kept his peace for the time being.

"I am thinking of a public apology addressed to Mister Bamber in a live tri-vidz link to be released instantly onto the SWW", Stubbsinge suggested.

"That sounds wonderful but do you think you can be sincere enough Nai"? Clara wanted to know, "After all you did not smack him one, I did"?

Hugh sighed as the solicitor explained as though to a small child, "I meant from you Clara, not from me".

"I do not feel I could be sincere", Clara explained, "Being as I would rather bare my naked ass on Manchester Manor's town steps - than apologise to that walking vegetable".

"You will have to push for the acceptance of compensation, Nai", Hugh finally told the solicitor.

Unbeknown to the trio there was another factor that was about to play a pivotal role in Clara's future. One she could have no control over with her father's financial backing and influence.

Jinette Dury was a circuit Judge who had spent the last few years determined to clean up Manchester of misdemeanours and the recreants who perpetrated criminal activities. Like most, she also was a fan of the solar wide web and often skimmed it in preference to watch the tri-vidz of the time. For most good stories had been told and the tri-vidz stations like *Blunt* and *Crusade* were filled with ancient repeats or remakes of repeats. She much preferred *Truth* or *Real.* It was an incident on STC [Saxonian Transmission Company] that caught her eye as she was skimming that night. She was a secret football fan and Games Under the Spotlight was one of her favourite shows on Saturday evening. She had missed the broadcast on the tri-vidz so decided to catch up on the games the following Monday morning as she sat in chambers waiting for the court to begin. What she saw, transmitted on a vidz that had gone viral over the weekend caused the blood in her veins to turn into molten lava. She was incensed, infuriated by what she saw and decided quite rationally to go on the warpath. She immediately thumbed her email contacts and got the address of DI Snelling of the West Yorkshire combmen. Choosing to contact by live video rather than leave a message. The inspector's small image came onto her screen and Snelling looked suitably respectful when he recognised who was calling him.

"Snelling here [obviously] what can I do for you, Your Honour"?

"Has anyone arrested Trentavoria's daughter for the assault she perpetrated against the tri-vidz presenter on Saturday afternoon"?

A strange look came over the inspector's features as he confessed, "No, Your Honour it would seem that the Trentavoria solicitor is pushing to get Bamber to accept an out-of-court settlement".

"That charlatan Stubbsinge"?

"The same, Your Honour"?

"Not good enough", Dury snapped at the snapper, "Not good enough at all. I want her arrested. I will sign a warrant for you, the Crown versus Trentavoria. Actual Bodily Harm. We cannot have someone in the public eye like that *young woman* doing what she wants, flouting the law of the land and on the county's tri-vidz. An example needs to be set before everyone starts to think that assaulting presenters of entertainment is perfectly acceptable. I will put a call through to the palace and see who will be available to prosecute. In the meantime check your pad I will thumb the warrant for her arrest. Go and get her Snapper"!

Delighted to have his nickname referred to and to finally place Clara Trentavoria in custody, Snapper Snelling sprang into action.

forty-nine   **Clara had just** returned to her rooms when the commotion commenced. There was the insistent thumbing of the chimes followed by heavy-fisted pounding on the front door. Wondering at the rudeness of it, she decided to go down and investigate. Gatson was surrounded by combmen in the hall and at Clara's appearance at the top of the staircase, one of them whom she recognised very well suddenly detached himself from the others and began haring up them two at a time. The drama would have remained very strained and tense had not Snelling tripped and stumbled to his knees just before reaching Clara. She could not resist saying,

"Inspector if you've fallen for me, why not tell me more traditionally, this is going over the top you know".

Face ruddy with embarrassment, the combman got back to his feet and tried to report to her with dignity,

Clara Henrietta Trentavoria, you are under arrest for ABH, anything you now say will be noted and could be used in your subsequent trial, do you understand what I have just advised"?

"Not really", Clara teased, "I don't understand what your intrusion into my home has to do with the Amateur Basketball Headquarters".

"No", Snelling huffed and puffed as he pulled out a tie-wrap, "It's .....".

"Then you must mean Anastasia Beverly Hills I do use their eyebrow products but what am I supposed to have done Inspector"?

"Actual Bodily Harm, you are being prosecuted by the crown, turn around please".

"I'm not actually into that sort of thing Snapper and I would not feel comfortable doing it in front of a crowd. If you've got the hots for me you should let me know in a much more conventional way".

Snelling was as scarlet as beet by that time but he did manage to get the wrap over her wrists and realised what she had just said would be read out in court and that Mrs Snelling would hear it or of it, from a *friend*. If there was one thing Snapper Snelling was truly afraid of it was the wrath of his contracted, she was the *real* Snapper!

Hugh chose that moment to appear on the landing,

"What is going on here, Snelling"? He demanded.

"The Crown has sought to arrest your daughter for assaulting Gazza Bamber, Sir. She is going to need your solicitor it seems".

"Say nothing to them until Stubbsinge arrives", Hugh advised his daughter, he had gone wan with anger but kept it under control. What was it coming to when a member of the richest family in Saxonia was arrested like a common criminal?

She was bundled into a comb-flitter and taken to the combstation, not for the first time by a long shot so she knew the routine. Presented to the desk sergeant, asked a lot of fool questions, then thrown in a cell, once the laces were removed from her shoes. The next part of the process was boredom, to soften one up. No one came for what felt like hours, though she could not be certain as they had also confiscated her Bolex wrist-chrono. The former was to disorientate her the latter to.....disorientate her. The heavy durimass door finally opened and Snelling smiled down at her. She had stretched out on the steel-mess cot and almost fallen asleep.

"Are you ready to come to your interview"? He asked, eyeing the still impressive mound her bosom made even when lying on her back. Of course, augments were less susceptible to gravity than naturals.

"Is my solicitor here"?

Snelling shook his head, "He claimed to be three-quarters of an hour away, about an hour ago".

"Bug off then Snelling and don't bang the door on your way out".

Clara was satisfied when he slammed the door as hard as he could. Snelling was too easy by far.

fifty   **It was with** a certain reluctance that Hugh Trentavoria, wealthiest man in Saxonia and quite possibly the solar system put through a vid-link to Formul Kipson – Kipper to his friends. The scout looked surprised but pleased to see whom it was on the other end of the line.

"Mister Trentavoria, this is a surprise and pleasure. What can I do for you, Sir, are you coming to the next home game, I can get you tickets in the Director's box of course"?

"Very good of you, but not the reason for my call. I want you to find a manager for the team and have him in the post at the earliest opportunity. Do you know who is without a club at the moment"?

"Sir, your daughter....."

"Is going to be indisposed to continue in the post, who have we to pick from Kipson"?

The scout thought for a few seconds and then said,

"Pet Gladiola is not in employment at the present moment, but his pedigree is.....

"Who else"?

"Locra Shallot, but the wage he will demand will be....".

"All right forget him as well, who else"?

"The Norwegian, with the crazy name, what is it again... oh yes, Gunny Gunnigunnay. Recently sacked by Durex, but word has it that he's coming on".

"Get him on the SWW and offer him the caretaker role for three games with a view to a permanent post until the end of the season at the very least".

"Yes. Mister Trentavoria, consider it done".

fifty-one   **The door of** the cell groaned open once again and Snelling informed her,

"Stubbsinge is here, you can see him in interview room one before we interview you".

"We"? Echoed Clara, "Who is, 'we' if you do not mind me asking, Inspector"?

"I and Inspector Snowd will be conducting the interview", Snelling told her watching carefully for any reaction.

Clara walked past him into the corridor beyond. She waited for him to slam the door too and then led the way toward the room in question. Stubbsinge was already seated at the huge table which dominated the otherwise Spartan space. Snelling then closed the door behind them and Clara seated herself opposite the short plump solicitor.

"You're being charged with ABH Clara", he began, "By the crown prosecution service. Bamber will be a witness for the prosecution, but it is not he who is bringing the case to court. The court should determine the offence category using this table here".

He pushed his padfon over to her so that she could see it

When she had read and digested it Stubbsinge went on,"The court will determine your culpability and the harm caused, or intended, by reference only to the factors identified in that table. These factors comprise the principal factual elements of the offence and should determine the category. They will view the tri-vid and then consult this table also".

An injury which is less serious in the context of the offence

"Unfortunately because you assaulted Mister Bamber not once but twice that puts you in category two of this final table".

"So I've read the little charts, Nai and you are going to scrap all that as I'm Hugh Trentavoria's daughter, right"?

To her astonishment, the solicitor shook his head. "I'm afraid this case has been pursued by the Crown, Clara, you cannot get your father to pay your way out of trouble this time"!

Clara suddenly felt the pit of her stomach drop out and she heard her voice rise several bars as she objected,

"I can't do priz, Nai! I've got a football club to run, we're going to win the league and the shield, you've got to get me out of this somehow? I'll do the community order, but I can't do hard stir. it's unfair, Bamber is a moron he had it coming, surely a judge will not convict me, will they Nai....will they"?

"That depends upon two things actually, Clara".

"And they are"?

"If you can show remorse to the court, not come over as that spoiled little rich girl that is certain to put their backs up and give you a custodial sentence. The other factor is how I manage to present to you, how well I do my job. Of course [cough] I will need to be correctly motivated to be able to be as certain in my convictions".

"Don't worry about that, my Father will settle your bill no matter how outrageous it is".

"I was not thinking about money my dear", he told her then and placed his hand over hers. "I was talking about the sort of ardent motivation that money simply cannot buy".

Clara managed to overcome her revulsion at the implication of the solicitor's words, her eyebrow raised and she said guardedly,

"What sort of motivation are we talking about here, Mister Stubbsinge".

"I am going to get you bailed in a moment, Clara dear and when I do you will have to tell the sergeant to which address you are being released too. Might it be that you could tell them that it is 179 Crosby Street, Stockport SK2 6SP"?

"Call this a wild stab in the dark, Stubbsinge but might that be your address by any chance"?

The solicitor grinned and nodded, "I am thinking that the better I know you and can sympathise with your situation the more motivated I will be when your case comes to court, My Dear".

"And when you say *know me,* might it be that you mean when your *Ambassador* would very much like to make overtures of peace to my *Alcancía.*"

Stubbsinge blinked, he did not recognise the euphemisms that Clara was using, she clarified,

"You want to dip your stinger in my honey-pot"?

"If I understand you correctly dear Clara, I feel that you are now thinking along the right lines".

Clara sighed, she could get a replacement solicitor but she was realistic enough to know how abrasive her character flaws made her at times and who knew, the little bald Pudge might turn out to be a real palliardizing warrior between the sheets?

"Get me the koof out of here then Nai and you can have your wicked way with me. I might just pretend to be dead when you do it though"!

Stubbsinge's tongue came out and ran over his dry lips, reminding Clara of a lizard, he returned,

"And I might just enjoy it if you do, Sweetness"!

fifty-two   **The entire squad** including the academy youngsters were gathered in the briefing room as Best led the new manager in to speak to them all. The air was thick with an exciting combination of sweat and liniment. It was not a single individual who entered behind the assistant however but two. A buzz gradually died down to expectant silence and one of the two newcomers took the podium and said to them all,

"Hilsen mine heldige gutter har dere alle spist en fin frokost med syltet sild til frokosten"?

Looking slightly abashed by what he was about to translate, the other man relayed to the squad,

"Greetings my lucky guys have you all eaten a nice breakfast of pickled herring for …. breakfast"?

What had happened? Who was this new manager, was he the village idiot of Norway?

Lane suddenly piped up, "Welcome to Orang-U-Can, Mister Gunnigunnay, are you going to be supervising us during training today"?

He and everyone else was forced to wait while his question was relayed to the man who did not even speak Standard in the 33rd century.

Then came the unintelligible reply,

"Er du ikke trent allerede, bare gå ut og kos deg med det vakre spillet"?

"Aren't you already trained, just go out and enjoy the beautiful game"? The translator told them.

Lane persisted, "What tactics are we to learn ready for our match against Tiptingle Foods, Boss. We are away from home so we will not have the pitch-advantage"?

"Gå ut og spill bedre enn dem [Go out and play better than them]".

"In what formation"? Lane demanded. Are we going for man-marking,

Orang-U-Can
6. Radband
45. Gaines 13. Jennings 25. Zinyama 4 Burgenbower
30. Sanedad   20. Lane   19.Jenson   44. Siggers
8. Wong 9. Sellers

diamond defence, a back 3, 4 or 5"?

"Løp etter ballen og sørg for at du får den, og skyter den deretter i motstanderens mål. Kos deg med gresset, her i Sachsen er det mykt, i Norge er det veldig hardt dere er alle heldige gutter, takk [Run after the ball and make sure you get it, and then shoot it in the opponent's goal. Enjoy the grass, here in Saxony it is soft, in Norway it is very hard you are all lucky guys, thank you".

Kaahk", muttered Best under his breath, "This is going to be a disaster".

The team had been well drilled before Gunnigunnay had joined the club though, so they simply stuck to what they knew. Best heavily advised the Norwegian on team selection and the formation and he, in turn, seemed happy if bemused to follow every single recommendation without question.

Substitutes
1. Anderson
10. Nero
12 McFarland
31.Radford
25. Zinyama
38. Harcourt

His management style seemed to be non-managerial.

Saturday came around and the team ran out at Tiptingle Foods in their all orange strip against the home team in all white. Best had selected a 4-4-2 formation:

He was not filled with confidence. For a start the bench lacked defenders, Flintham had come down with a virus and had not been in very confident form even before that. The bench was, therefore, striker heavy:

Charmley on one side of him, the unintelligible Norwegian on the other, he watched the game in dreaded anticipation of disaster. Before his astonished eyes, the men seemed to have enjoyed the freedom of their devising during the week and Tiptingle, knowing OUC had just had a new manager were nervous. On the half-hour mark, Best was astonished to see Siggers slot a very neat pass through to Sellers who sidestepped the diving goalkeeper and let the ball trickle agonisingly into the home teams goal. It was his first goal of the season and Best heard Gunnigunnay say,

"Mine stolte bleke skjønnheter jeg visste at de kunne gjøre det hvis jeg lot dem uttrykke seg.[My proud pale beauties I knew they could do if I let them express themselves.]"

Corporation Division One

Tiptingle Foods v Orang-U-Can	0	1
Rolls Royce Scoriors v Goosetimp Weapons	3	1
Hornrunner Hornets v Preciometalic.Inc	2	2
Makers-Guild v Deutsch Fahrzeuge Eingearbeitet	2	0
Voleskip Pharmaceuticals v Zhōngguá Shāngpín	0	2
IYWIWSI v Castle Electronics	2	1

The second half was a bit more of a test, but Best ordered Wong and Sellers to drop deep and they grimly defended their away goal to keep the scoreline unchanged. Best immediately accessed the SWW and waited for all the other results to come in. it was more good luck for Orang-U-Can:

The majority of teams above OUC had lost, even Castle had been defeated for once. It made the table much tighter. Best looked at the relative positions in incredulity, the crazy village idiot would be hailed as a great motivator when he had done nothing. Orang-U-Can had moved up and into their highest position of the season. It caused Best to wonder for the moment what Trentavoria would make of it. Not the father, the daughter and he wondered what she would be doing at that particular moment.

The SWW had a field day, the report ran:

Ny Wonder Manager hos Orang-U-Can

Gunny Gunnigunnay has only been at the club for one short week and he has already turned them into genuine contenders for the First Division title. Replacing the sacked Clara Trentavoria, who infamously assaulted tri-vidz personality, Gazza Bamber, last week and is even now awaiting Crown prosecution, Gunny Gunnigunnay had his squad playing with the sort of freedom that marked the old style of play of yesteryear played by Rochdale when they won the olde-style Premier League in the days of town based football.

"I just told the lads to done a good one and they done it", the modest Norwegian mastermind told Bamber following the game. Bamber who is still undergoing post-traumatic stress counselling is due at court to testify for the prosecution next week.

	Corporation Div One	Plyd	Goals	Pts
1	Castle Electronics	7	19	24
2	I.y.w.i.w.s.i.	7	20	19
3	Orang-U-Can	7	16	17
4	Goosetimp Weapons	7	21	16
5	Makers-Guild	7	16	16
6	Deutsch Fahrzeuge Eingearbeitet	7	17	15
7	Zhōngguá Shāngpĭn	7	11	14
8	Rolls Royce Scoriors	7	11	13
9	Voleskip Pharmaceuticals	7	6	11
10	Preciometalic.Inc	7	13	10
11	Tiptingle Tigers	7	9	8
12	Hornrunner Hornets	7	10	7

Clara put down her padfon and eased herself out of bed careful not to wake the snoring solicitor. She went and used a copious quantity of mouthwash to get the salty taste out of her mouth following what the dirty nozkavardé had expected her to do during their impromptu afternoon session. Thankfully there was only one more day of his perversions to suffer and then the trial began, after that, she would see to it that he would never deflower a maiden ever again. It had been quite some time since she had used the vocal transmuter and emailed the Fixer! Quite some time since she had been the Faded Man. She sensed that it would not be long before the dark nemesis would be called out of retirement!

fifty-three   **"Enlisted without even** consulting me"! Kurteze wailed, "Are you out of your mind Rox"?

"No Kresze, I just read the SWW", came the determined response. "The US have just launched a Task Force toward Mars with a compliment of three more spacefortress' and the largest collection of space-flitters ever assembled by a single country".

"Oh! I get it! So you're determined to go and get yourself blown up on the cold thin-aired world, far away from your real home which is now actually Manchester".

Roxbrough grinned, "I'm going to do my bit and hopefully not get blown up at all", he tried to assure. It did not work.

"As it happens I look quite good in black", Kurteze remarked then ironically, "But I'll be lonely without you".

"Then come with me", he took her slim shoulders in his hands. "There is plenty of work for a Dick in the backwater pioneer towns of Mars. I'm told it's like the old west was in the nineteenth century. I have a pretty good nest-egg put together from my footballing days and we can be comfortable until your little concern gets established".

"I wouldn't want to live in the Polish sector, not once the war was over. I would want to get somewhere on the equator, like Edom, just above the Eurasian Block".

"Somewhere like that would suit me fine, after the war", Roxbrough agreed. We could take up married barracks till the war is over and then get a sandflitter and go and look for somewhere that takes our fancy"?

"All right then, you had better get on your pad and tell them you are bringing someone with you".

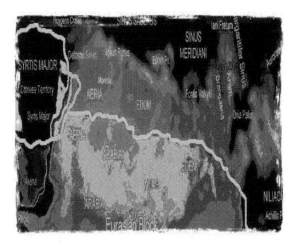

"There is just one thing though", he told her then looking momentarily worried.

"And what might that be"? She asked even though she was well enough read to know what the one thing was,

"To take you with me, as you're not Polish you would have to be my contractee"!

"What have you got to ask me then"?

"Will you contract with me darling, I do love you"?

"She burst into joyful laughter threw her arms around him and her lips did not get a chance to utter the words of her assent.

fifty-four   **Certain aspects of** the trial were farcical. Had the outcome have not been of such urgent desire to Clara she would have laughed when Gazza Bamber was pushed into the courtroom in a wheelchair, his eyes covered with enormous dark glasses. Despite these amateur dramatics, the prosecution concentrated on the tri-vid evidence which in itself was damning and irrefutable. Stubbsinge had but one card to play and that was Clara's feeling of guilt and deep regret for what she had done in the heat of the moment.

The only trouble was the jury were simple peasants and they had the chance to bring a guilty decision against the poor little rich girl that was the daughter of the wealthiest man alive. Judge Dury did not exactly help either, directing the proceedings with a heavy bias in favour of the Crown. None of Stubbsinge's objections was sustained, while none of the prosecutions was overruled. Clara did no admirable charity works, she spent no time working with anyone less fortunate than herself and her character witness' were confined to Hugh and Lavvisto. The latter managing to stay sober just to say what a lovely sister Clara was and always had been.

After a scant twenty minutes deliberation the jury returned a verdict of guilty of ABH category 2. Judge Dury could barely conceal her smile of triumph and Clara listened in horror as she was given the very maximum penalty the judge could level - she would go to prison for two years. Then did Clara truly appreciate the full weight of her predicament? She would start her incarceration in His Majesty's Prison Styal a closed category prison for female adults.

Tearfully, the tears being then genuine, she was escorted from the court and placed into a holding cell. After but a short interval she was escorted into a secure flitter and her journey to Cheshire began, she was on her way to the prison with the worst record of deaths in custody in any correctional facility in the country of Saxonia.

80% of the women that were held in the gaol were addicts, many of whom stole to feed 5 shillin-a-day addiction to snufz. Some of the inmates had endured an addiction for 20 years, had been in and out of Styal so many times they might as well fit a revolving door instead of huge durilite gates to the facility.

Styal also housed women who had committed serious crimes, killers of husbands, friends, even children. The prison itself was in a bizarre setting. Nestling in affluent rural Cheshire on the site of a former Victorian orphanage, it was effectively two prisons in one. The main prison made up of the original red brick houses that had been refurbished repeatedly over the years and a new high-tech wing, home to the most violent offenders and hopeless addicts. The latter was where all of the prison's problems centred. Some of the inmates were serving up to 15 years and could not remember how many times they had been in and out of the penal system. Persistent offenders, entrenched users, written off by the rest of society. Yet if they could remove their drug dependency there would be no crime

Smoking snufz off aluminium foil poisoned the lungs. It gave the abuser of the narcotic designed to be inhaled nasally constant pleurisy, severe asthma and pneumonia. Addicts could not resist falling into old patterns once they got out and the whole sorry cycle started again for them.

Styal was the largest women's prison in the northern region of Saxonia but, effectively, it was Holloway's poor northern relation, receiving 2,500 shillin per prisoner per year compared to 4,100 for inmates of the Londonian gaol. Recent critical inspection reports had screamed for more funding to pay for staff to deal with the severe mental health problems, addictions, low literacy and poor health many inmates experienced. The most vulnerable women went straight into the worst possible place for them - the wing - where all the deaths in custody happened.

Into that nightmare, Clara was thrust after the humiliation of a total strip search in Reception, Discharge and Administration [RDA]

She was promptly conducted to a cell on her own and would spend up to 20 hours a day in it. There was continuous noise women were shouting to one another through the grilled doors and the more they did so the more the noise level went up – it continued until 04:00. Clara was given a reception pack which was a bar of soap, toothbrush and paste, a pack of ladies personal hygiene care, two packets of biscuits, a small pack of mediosnufz that would give zero hits and a set of neoplas eating implements. The latter being one knife, fork, spoon, mug and plate. She was told by a burly woman in RDA that if she lost them or had them taxed, the only way she would get replacements would be to tell the officers who had taken them off her. Without being told she knew that to do that would make her position on the wing even worse. A *grass* could easily be stabbed in the showers and in the kidneys with someone else's sharpened knife. Clara Trentavoria, daughter of the richest man in the Kingdom had suddenly, due to one act of extreme stupidity, descended from the privileged - to the dregs of society.

fifty-five   **Roxbrough had been** a very lucky young man in the past in that he had never suffered a real days illness in his life. So the day he contracted Infekcja Klatkipiersiowej it came as a devastating blow to him. It had started on board the Kosmiczna Lanca, the space-flitter that he and Kurteze had boarded on their way to the flitterport in Łódźno. He initially presumed it was the dry air of the ship's recycling automation that was making his throat sore. By the time the vessel docked with the shuttle which would take them down to the planet's surface, he had already developed a racking cough. The military personnel on the shuttle took him to the vessels doctor who promptly quarantined him even from Kurteze. Roxbrough never saw any of Łódźno on that occasion. He was rushed from the flitterport by ambulaflitter to Staratchowice Szpital [infirmary] the eastern side of the Polska Sector.

After various tests, Doktor Prodobrze came to see him, his austere features set in a grave frown.

"What is it, Doctor, surely just a nasty head cold and cough"? Roxbrough asked hopefully.

"You have signed your admission pad to Krówla Zaina's Royal Forces, haven't you"? The doctor asked.

Roxbrough nodded, fighting the urge to cough, the doctor persisted,

"They were accepted"?

Another nod.

"Then that is some good fortune for the Royal Force of the Polska Armia will foot the bill for your treatment. Otherwise, the cost might well have left you insolvent".

"Just tell me please, Doctor, what have I got and how soon can I join training for the ground force defence regiment of Memnonia".

"I cannot honestly answer that for you. I do not know how the disease will progress through your body and how long it will take for the treatment to take effect".

"Disease! I thought I had a cold and rather nasty cough"? Roxbrough started to worry.

"Trooper Roxbrough, you have Infekcja Klatkipiersiowej".

"How serious is it"?

"If left untreated it could rapidly pass down through your mouth and nose and into the lowest and smallest parts of the airways. Into the terminal bronchioli and alveoli of the lung. The terminal bronchioli are the smallest part of the bronchi, the structure that guides the air from the upper airways (nose, mouth and trachea) into the lung tissue. Alveoli are part of the lung tissue and are the place where the oxygen from the inhaled air is usually used by the body, and transferred into the blood to be carried to the organs that need it. After the Infekcja Klatkipiersiowej bacillus reaches the alveoli in the lung, it gets picked up by special cells of the immune system, called macrophages. These macrophages usually sit within the tissue of the alveoli. They have to swallow and inactivate any foreign object entering the alveolar space. The macrophages swallow the bacillus. The events that follow largely depend on the number of bacilli and the strength of the macrophage. If the amount of bacilli is too large, or if the macrophage is not strong enough to resist, the bacilli can reproduce in the macrophage. This ultimately leads to the destruction of the macrophage and the infection of new, nearby macrophages that try to swallow emerging bacilli. If your macrophage cannot contain the Infekcja Klatkipiersiowej bacillus the infection will enter its second stage after about 24 hours. The Infekcja Klatkipiersiowej bacillus will reproduce exponentially, meaning that for every initial bacillus two new ones emerge. These two then produce two each, etc. This leads to a rapid expansion of the initial Infekcja Klatkipiersiowej bacillus, and the macrophages will not be able to contain the spread. In 48 hours from contracting the Infekcja Klatkipiersiowej bacillus will reproduce like wildfire forming cavities in the tissue, where your body's immune system cannot reach them. From such cavities, the disease will run rampant through your lungs and you will begin coughing up blood and struggling to breathe. You will asphyxiate with the next 12 to 15 hours and the pain will be considerable".

Roxbrough was grey with alarm as he asked, "You said there was a treatment though"?

To his immense relief, Doktor Prodobrze nodded,

"Izonikotynylohydrazoid will be administered to you by injection into your muscle. I must at this point warn you that such a radicle drug will result in common side effects which include increased blood levels of liver enzymes, hallucinations and numbness in the hands and feet. If you experience more serious side effects, these may include liver inflammation. Pirydokżena can be given to reduce the risk of these side effects. Are you willing to undergo treatment"?

"Do I have a choice"?

"Of course the decision is yours to make or not, whichever you decide to make".

"But if I do not take the medication, I will die"!

"That is true – yes".

"A choice that was not a choice, that seemed to Roxbrough to be the dilemma he faced. He asked the doctor to inject him with Izonikotynylohydrazoid.

In the next 12 hours, the symptoms of Infekcja Klatkipiersiowej tested Roxbrough's endurance and determination to the limit. He experienced extremes of body temperature weaning that he was shaking with chills while sweat ran down his face and stung his eyes. His throat felt like it was being constantly rubbed raw with sandpaper. It was his chest which bothered him the most though.

He struggled for breath, the inside of his lungs felt like they were on fire and the worst aspect of it all was when he needed to cough to clear the mucus off his chest. It would suddenly grip him like a muscular explosion and the pain lanced through his body with gradually increased severity. He could not sit, not lay down. Neither position seemed comfortable, yet his feet were swollen and his hands tingled, making walking or shuffling doubly dangerous. If he fell he would not be able to break his fall.

Then the hallucinations started. At first, he was aware of what they were and they did not trouble him. As time went by though, they not only became more vivid and at the same time more sinister, but he also began to forget that they were what he knew they were. Doktor Prodobrze came back to monitor his progress and for no logical reason had the head of a dag [Genetically spliced cat and dog. The design - created by the great geneticist Hoyle]

"I'm going to give you a test", the dag-head of the doctor told him. For some reason that only made sense in the convoluted corridors of Roxbrough's occipital lobes. Roxbrough took his seat at the school desk and confessed that he had no padfon upon which to place his answers. The doctor who was now a teacher [though how Roxbrough knew this he could not say], passed him a collection of wood-pulp sheets in white with feint grey straight lines dividing the horizontal. Roxbrough had seen the material in museums, it was paper.

He looked up to see the dag, who was now bright purple in the hue of fur, holding out a thin tube, a sort of stylus, presumably to make marks on the paper with.

"You will write your answers down", the dag told him.

"Right"? Roxbrough was lost.

"Trace or form characters, letters, words, etc. on the surface of the sheets I have given you. Do so with the pen, inscribe the information in ink".

"I do not know how", Roxbrough freely admitted, "The skill you describe was lost to mankind centuries ago".

"You can read"?

"Of course".

"Then imagine your answer in writing and mark the paper accordingly. You know the configuration of the letters, you type. So you can write.

There was more to it than that. It was like saying everyone knew what a face looked like so why could not everyone draw. Roxbrough knew he could not make any further complaint. He did not know how he knew it but he did. He also knew [without knowing] that if he failed the test something terrible would happen, something loathsome and abhorrent. The feeling of atrociousness was like a sharp and bright menace that would hex his composure and the thought terrified him.

Roxbrough glanced at the child at the next desk, but though he had eyes and nose, he had no mouth. The dumb boy nodded to him, the gesture shaking his brown curly hair, but he would never speak. It did not occur to Roxbrough to wonder how he ate, there was no need for that particular reflection or conjecture.

"The first question", the dag began, "If I plant three rows of hybasyths in my garden two feet from the edge, how often can my neighbour eat chicken"?

Roxbrough went to write the number one on his page but his pen bent as he pressed it to the paper and he had to hold it in both hands it ended up looking not like anything it was supposed to.

"Question two", the dag hurried on, "If corn oil is made from corn and vegetable oil is made from vegetables. What is baby oil made from?

Three, If money doesn't grow on trees then why do banks have branches?

Four, Describe the worst slogan you can think of for advertising pile ointment?

Five, You've been incarcerated into a lunatic asylum. What do you tell the doctors there to convince them that you don't belong on the moon and the satellite does not make you mad?

That is all hand your papers in and then go and clean out your lockers".

Roxbrough looked down at his sheet and it was not what one could realistically call a sterling effort. He had with him a canvass bag in powder blue and walked down to the lockers with the boy with no mouth. But his locker key would not open the door and his bag was not large enough to fit his coat into. He wanted the dumb boys eaddress but though he got him to write it down on a piece of the paper material he lost it and then he felt extremely frustrated, agitated and knew he would not be allowed to see Kurteze ever again because of losing the eaddress

"Let me help you up"? A kindly female voice said to him then, "I think we had better take you for a bath".

196

"We"? Roxbrough echoed, feeling his nightshirt plastered to him with sweat, "You mean to say you are coming into the bathroom with me"?

"You've been given Izonikotynylohydrazoid", the nurse pointed out, "You cannot be left alone in a container filled with water, you might have another spasm".

"I think that it's quite likely I'm still in the throes of one", Roxbrough remarked looking at the nurse and deciding that her uniform did not look the type that would be issued by the Polish Military Forces.

"If it will make you feel any better I'll take off my uniform and we can bathe together, the shapely young woman offered".

'This must be my idea of a wet-dream' Roxbrough thought and then he woke up and he was lathered in sweat. A young woman in a white smock and with a stethoscope was suddenly at his bedside.

She pulled the wet shirt to one side with difficulty and listened to his lungs and heart.

"We'll get you bathed in a minute", she told him in polish accented Standard.

"I can't go in on my own in case I have a spasm", he told her. "You'll have to come in with me. How warm do you like the water"?

The young doctor gave a knowing smile and explained,

"The shift, in reality, will soon pass, Trooper, we'll have you fighting fit in next to no time".

"I feel better already, Doctor, come on let's go and play doctor in the bathroom. The woman called out a name and a male nurse appeared, she said to him,

"We've got one of the fruity ones, makes a change from those who want to fight everyone or the gibbering nonsensical ones. Help him in the bath and into some clean nightclothes, please Nurse".

As the young woman waddled away swinging her hips slightly more than was strictly necessary, Roxbrough asked,

"Is she single"?

"I believe she is", the male nurse laughed, "But you're not"!

Curiously it brought the former football striker down to Mars better than any dose of Pirydokżena!

fifty-six   **It did not** take long for all the foundations Clara had built at Orang-U-Can football team to start crumbling due to lack of maintenance. Under her guidance and with Roxbrough and Rachwalski in the side they would have easily swept Goosetimp Weapons to one side. As

it was all they could do was play out a boring goalless draw. It had an immediate effect upon their league position. The only piece of good news that Saturday was that Castle had also failed to win, but they had been away from home. The general feeling in the dressing room was that the new manager could not manage a school bus trip let alone a men's football club. Best was

powerless to stop the rot. Hugh had been indirectly responsible for giving Gunny Gunnigunnay the post and to speak out against him would only serve to secure his exit through the door and he had no intention of giving up his well-paid job, much as he would have loved to help steer the squad to the First Division title.

The next fixture had them at home to Rolls Royce Scoriors perhaps their new playing surface would help them gain such a lead in the first half that the deficit could not be caught once the visitors realised the team had very little shape and no workable plan of action?

Corporation Division One

Orang-U-Can v Goosetimp Weapons	*0*	*0*
R R Scoriors v Preciometallic	*2*	*0*
Voleskip v DFE	*0*	*1*
IYWIWSI v Makers-Guild	*3*	*0*
Hornrunner v Castle	*1*	*1*
Zhõngguá Shãngpĭn v Tiptingle	*2*	*1*

fifty-seven   **Clara was seated** on her bunk reading when the heavy door swung open and the most hideous and obese form she had ever seen sauntered into the cell uninvited. During the association hour, all doors were unlocked so that the women could visit whoever they pleased. Clara had not invited the monstrosity for tea and cucumber sandwiches. Indeed she had never seen her before in her entire life and with a certainty that she would have remembered her if she had.

"I'm Cher", the woman mountain told Clara, "Cher Gufasen. You may have heard of me".

"I feel I can say without fear of contradiction that I have not", Clara

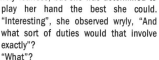

	Corporation Div One		Plyd	Goals	Pts
1	**Castle Electronics**		7	20	25
2	**I.Y.W.I.W.S.I.**		7	23	22
3	**Deutsch Fahrzeuge Eingearbeitet**		7	18	18
4	**Orang-U-Can**		7	16	18
5	**Goosetimp Weapons**		7	21	17
6	**Zhōngguá Shāngpǐn**		7	13	17
7	**Makers-Guild**		7	16	16
8	**Rolls Royce Scoriors**		7	13	16
9	**Voleskip Pharmaceuticals**		7	6	11
10	**Preciometalic.Inc**		7	13	10
11	**Hornrunner Hornets**		7	11	8
12	**Tiptingle Tigers**		7	10	8

assured, "But one thing I am certain of is that it does not say you name as located in this cell so I would take if as a personal favour if you would agree to vacate it post haste".

"What"? The female nightmare demanded in incomprehension.

"Please pull the door to on you way out, thank you", Clara asked and returned her attention to the prison library book.

She then felt it snatched out of her grip and promptly dropped down the steel unseated toilet.

"Let's get something straight you stuck up bitch", Gufasen told Clara, "This is my wing see and you are now my bitch".

"Is that so", Clara was not entirely fearless, but she was determined to  play her hand the best she could. "Interesting", she observed wryly, "And what sort of duties would that involve exactly"?

"What"?

"I believe you mean pardon, but whatever it is you think I am going to do for you or with you, prepare yourself for a disappointment. It is not going to happen".

"Says who, you"? Gufasen demanded harshly.

199

"Apart from the fact that I am physically perfectly capable of looking after myself", Clara told her, "I have several, shall we call them, operatives on this wing under my employ. Harm a hair on my head and every single one of yours will be torn out from the roots before you are disposed of, that is".

"I think you're lying"?

"I don't recommend that course of action for you, slug".

"What course of action"?

"Thinking, now get out before you start to annoy me"!

That was how the word went around that Clara was not to be touched. There were no operatives, but none of the other women knew that. Sometimes the threat of violence could be met with superior intellect.

fifty-eight   **Roxbrough was very** cold, the sweat that drenched his body was the perspiration of weakness rather than heat. He felt like he had come the closest to death anyone could and still survive. Thankfully he was beginning to recover. He had never been superstitious but had he been, the disease which had ravaged his body would have torn up the roots of such illogical belief and destroyed all vestige of them. In all organised superstitions of the past, the deity had been goodness, compassion and omnipotence. It was not possible to believe that such a creature could have been so sadistically twisted as to create suffering when it was so unnecessary.

He lowered himself into a bath of hot water and let its soothing fluid rinse away the vile miasma from his skin. His guts felt hollow and strained with all the heaving he had subjected them to. Putting his hands into the water he pressed them to his temple and face. The heat eased the rawness of his sinus. He forced himself into activity, soaped and rinsed towelled and dressed.

He was weak but grateful to be alive. Now he needed to recuperate. It would be several days before his initial training could begin. He still had no inkling as to what use the Royal Polish Forces intended to put him. He was mechanically forcing himself to eat and force down some urgently needed sustenance when there was a knock at the door. He had been placed in temporary single accommodation until somewhere more permanent could be assigned to him and Kurteze. Expecting it to be her, he bid whom so ever was without, to enter.

The visitor was an older man who Roxbrough recognised from his tri-vidz images. It was none other than Igan Giganort. Designer of the OUC 222bhp Orange Streak turbo air flitter, the instant Roxbrough reflected on his presence on Mars, he remembered reading that Giganort was of true Polish ancestry. It also explained how the Polska had developed the laser gun, the weapon was the creation of the genius developer.

"Good morning", the older man held out his hand and they shook warmly. "I understand you wish to go into engineering development, that you got your degrees with honours, I am Igan Giganort and I want you and I to work on the Mark II version of our laser canon. Time is of the essence the US Task Force is being assembled and they intend to destroy our military base at Memnonia unless we stop them. Will you assist me Trooper Roxbrough"?

"It will be an honour, Sir".

"Once development of the Mark II is completed, you will then be free to join your unit, whichever that might be", the developer told him, causing Roxbrough to wonder himself whom it would indeed be.

fifty-nine

A flash of crimson burst across the already scarlet sky and Roxbrough knew the battle proper had started. The frigid wind whipped up the iron-oxidized sand, there had been a sandstorm in the Polska sector for 144 days straight without letting up. Though the Mark II he and Giganort had developed had taken a heavy toll of the US Task Force enough of the Spacefortress' landing craft had gotten through unscathed to make of it a grizzly ground battle. From out of the pink cupola pods were slowly descending, each one carrying a space-trooper not dissimilar to Roxbrough

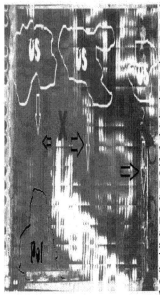

himself in terms of weaponry and equipment. The difference being that they were the enemy. He gazed out of his bubble of Earth-type environment over the impossibly near horizon to see the capsules landing like an infestation of some sort of metallic parasite. Here and there, bursts of laserifle fire jumped from figures that appeared like toy soldiers in terms of scale. Polish lasers were azure, while the US issued yellow light. The battle was eerily silent. The only sound Roxbrough could hear encased as he was in his all environmental suit, was his breathing. It sounded ragged and frightened to him and why should it not? This was not the bravery of the striker who went up against a defender in an aerial dual to win a football, this was real courage or lack thereof. This was what bravery meant in the true definition of the phrase. It was the victory of life and survival or the defeat of demise. Before Roxbrough, viewing at he was inside his comforting bubble that in reality would not withstand a direct laser strike, the ground battle began to unfold.

Flitters hovered over the red-rusty dust, their bonnet guns lancing out into the twilight. Columns of men rushed behind them taking what cover they could from their durilite chassis, for there was as yet scant vegetation to afford any sort of shelter and the plain of Memnonia did not even sport that many boulders. It must have been what historical desert warfare had been like. A voice in his headset told him to advance to a low hump-backed ridge just ahead, but Roxbrough had the sense to hesitate, for the majority of the pods were all descending to land just behind it. He skirted the ridge rather than hurtling over it as most of his unit was doing. As they did so they were being mercilessly cut down by xanthic laser-fire. Damn the young Porucznik [lieutenant] who had given the ill-advised order. Roxbrough took meagre cover behind the nearest boulder and waited to see how events would transpire. His unit was being slaughtered and no order to either retreat or regroup had been issued. What a senseless waste of human life. It was inevitable that he would be discovered if he did not shift position in one direction or another. The first he realised he was being fired at was when he felt his right foot suddenly grow alarmingly hot. He glanced down through his helmet's visor to see that half the heavily insulated boot was gone and his air was escaping through the ragged hole. Droplets of blood were even redder on the already ruddy sand too. The air of Mars was breathable but so cold that to try and manage without any other form of oxygen would freeze the lungs, so the air in his tanks was vital to his survival until he found a way into one of the domes. There was a valve at the outer edge of his right knee and he turned it off awkwardly in his fingers sausage-like with the heavy insulating gloves he wore. From the hip, he fired his laserifle one-handed at movement just beyond the outer edge of his visor. A figure in a bright red suit threw his arms up in the air, drifting slowly to the ground, chest smoking. The body gradually settled into the ubiquitous dust and Roxbrough knew he had just killed his first enemy. He had to find a unit to rejoin or he would go the same way as the rest of his comrades, thanks to the rashness of the young officer's order they were almost all gone. His body was not tired even though it should have been, fuelled with adrenalin, exhaustion would come suddenly and catastrophically when the hormone was finally enervated. He could not feel any pain in his injured foot, but the raged hole in his boot meant that the terrible cold of Mars was freezing the nerves to numbness. He needed medical attention as soon as possible otherwise he might well lose, some toes, the foot, the leg. Lancing laser-fire crisscrossed over his head suddenly, missing his helmeted head by mere centimetres and as he ducked down into the meagre cover of a small boulder he knew he was pinned down. From his belt he removed one of only four percussion grenades he was equipped with, released the spring by hauling out the retaining pin and tossed it over to his left. He saw the flash through closed eyelids, felt the shock-wave of the explosion and then dared to bob up momentarily to see if it had deterred his attackers. In the red sand, staining it more cerise with human gore was a dismembered arm. The percussion explosive had rendered incredible harm on at least one Yank. Roxbrough did not wait long enough to see if the US forces from the other side were still in position, he simply sprayed the area he figured the fire had come from and then attempted to move onward to his left flank. He promptly fell visor forward into the ubiquitous sand of the planet and realised he could feel nothing in his leg at all. The situation was becoming desperate. There was only one option left open to him. With exaggerated care, he pressed the button on his left arm with one gloved-finger of his right and brought up the projection of the battle plan onto the back of his visor to orienteer himself.

A huge red glowing cross indicated his position and could not have been tactically any worse. Perhaps it would be wise to simply throw down his arms and surrender himself to the invaders?

NO!

He would rather die resisting. Die on this half-frozen dust-ball of ice and rust defending countrymen he did not know. Defending them from other men he certainly did not know at all. Die rather than give in to them. His obstinacy caused him to push on. It forced him to do so on all four, dragging what was left of his right leg behind him like a discarded joint of semi-frozen meat. It was arduous, tortuously slow and without any discernable goal in sight but he had no choice. He could no longer support his weight standing and if he stayed where he was he would either be captured or killed. Twice he encountered what to him seemed like the enemy rag-tag remnants of patrols, men left behind just like he. They accounted for two more of his grenades and he ran his micro-pile on his rifle to almost exhaustion. He had become a clandestine crawling thing of death and destruction. Yet not through choice. As was usual with the machinations of war, those who decided did not get their own hands dirty. The mayhem was dealt out by those who should have remained innocent.

The Polish patrol picked him up an indeterminate period later and he did not know how much further he could have crawled. He sank into exhausted oblivion the instant he was tenderly lifted onto the back of the flitterjeep.

sixty   A white light suddenly intruded into his eyes as the lids flickered open and what he saw was the most welcome sight he could have possibly have hoped for.

"You gave everyone quite a scare, Mister Hero", Kurteze told him pressing her fine lips to his.

"I'm no hero", he croaked through parched lips of his own, "I merely managed not to get mown down like the rest of my unit".

"That's not strictly true", she informed him, "You blew up one of their munitions caches took out several of their patrols and held their spearhead at bay while reinforcements were brought to bear and the US spearhead was ultimately defeated. It's over Rox and your part in the victory cannot be diminished".

"So what's the bad news", he managed to smile, he knew her well enough to know that something else was registering in her beautiful features.

"I haven't finished with the good stuff yet", she persisted, "You're going to be getting the Virtuti Militari Grand Cross presented to you by none other than Krówla Zaina herself. I am so proud of you, you are a military hero, My Love".

"I don't feel any differently", he managed an exhausted smile, "But I sense a but is coming - Kresze and you still have not uttered the word".

A single tear suddenly escaped her lovely eye and made a saline stream down her wonderfully smooth cheek, she told him harshly, the best way,

KRZYZ WIELKI

"You lost your leg"! It was not as devastating a blow as it had been historically. There were so many options. A prosthetic, a transplant, or a biotron. In any of those options, he would walk again. It was unlikely he would ever play football with the same superb combination of dexterity and balance. Kurteze was speaking again,

"The doctor is waiting to discuss your options with you. They want you back on your feet as swiftly as possible ready to be able to present to the Queen at the victory celebrations".

"Victory"? Roxbrough heard himself echo hollowly, "You mean to say that...."

"That the war is over, yes, the US was given an uncharacteristic bloody nose by your and Giganort's Mark II and the majority of their Task Force was destroyed. The WC has convinced them that to continue hostilities would be foolish in the extremis, they are defeated. Poland has won a war!!

The doctor came to see him then.

"Hello again Doktor Prodobrze", Roxbrough greeted ironically, "Just how broad is your area of expertise when it comes to matters medical"?

"Nothing sharpens one's medical skills quite so rapidly as a military conflict, Major", the doctor chirped happily.

"Major"?! Roxbrough echoed rapidly, "I went into the skirmish as Memnonia as a simple sergeant"?!

"The Virtuti Militari Grand Cross presented to you by none other than Krówla Zaina herself will be to a major – Major. Congratulations on the heady promotion. You are going to be a part of a massive exercise in propaganda and promulgation, the like of which Poland rarely enjoys, it would not be quite the same if it was all for a lowly sergeant".

"On the contrary", Roxbrough noted a trifle bitterly, "it might be even more spectacular, a true victory for the peasants for once".

Prodobrze coughed once to hide his confusion or annoyance and then abruptly changed the subject,

"We need to get your replacement leg installed as swiftly as possible", he informed then, "There will be some initial balance issues that can be swiftly dealt with. I am here to outline your options".

"Very well tell me about my three choices", Roxbrough asked, feeling somewhat that events were beginning to spiral quite out of his control. He soon dismissed the notion of waiting for a transplant. There were so many factors to be matched:- mass, skin and blood type, simple appearance, he could be waiting months for a match to become available. A prosthetic meant problems with the coupling device, to which it was eventually fixed. Biotronics was the future and he had no qualms like some of thinking it meant it made him less human to have one leg that was not made of skin and bone.

It would be plated to his thigh, the vessels connected would be nyloplanyon but would still form part of his circulatory system and the durilite tibia, fibula, tarsal and metatarsal would weigh the same but be immensely stronger. The pseudo-skin that would cover the leg would be that which had been perfected for androids and would feel warm to the touch just like the real thing, the only feature it would lack would be hair and growing toenails, but he felt he could manage without either.

Prodobrze ended by telling him, "If you wanted to play football again, it would not be outside the realms of possibility once you managed to adjust to your alteration in balance".

"It will not feel though will it"? Roxbrough argued. "I would be like the lower-league player, one-footed when it came to skill and prowess. I used to be able to score with either foot, Doc".

"Many a reasonable career has been continued with only one good foot though, Major. The choice will be yours. By the sound of it what has been happening in the Corporation League to your old team, they would be glad to take you back"!

	Corporation Div One	Plyd	Goals	Pts
1	Castle Electronics	13	20	26
2	I.Y.W.I.W.S.I.	13	24	23
3	Deutsch Fahrzeuge Eingearbeitet	13	21	21
4	Rolls Royce Scoriors	13	15	19
5	Goosetimp Weapons	13	22	18
6	Orang-U-Can	13	16	18
7	Zhōngguá Shāngpǐn	13	13	18
8	Makers-Guild	13	16	16
9	Hornrunner Hornets	13	13	11
10	Tiptingle Tigers	13	12	11
11	Voleskip Pharmaceuticals	13	7	11
12	Preciometalic.Inc	13	13	10

sixty-one

Corporation Division One

Goosetimp Weapons v IYWIWSI	1	1
OUC v Rolls Royce Scoriors	0	2
DFE v Preciometallic	3	0
Hornrunner Hornets v Makers-Guild	2	0
Castle Electronics v Zhōngguá ShāngpÍn	0	0
Tiptingle v Voleskip	2	1

sixty-two

Corporation Division One

Zhōngguá ShāngpÍn v Goosetimp Weapons	4	2
Rolls Royce Scoriors v IYWIWSI	3	1
Preciometallic — Orang-U-Can	4	0
Deutsch Fahrzeuge Eingearbeitet v Hornrunner Hornets	3	0
Voleskip Pharmaceuticals v Castle Electronics	0	2
Makers-Guild v Tiptingle Tigers	2	2

	Corporation Division One	Played	Goals	Points
1	Castle Electronics	14	22	29
2	Deutsch Fahrzeuge Eingearbeitet	14	24	24
3	I.Y.W.I.W.S.I.	14	25	23
4	Rolls Royce Scoriors	14	18	22
5	Zhōngguá ShāngpÍn	14	17	21
6	Goosetimp Weapons	14	24	18
7	Orang-U-Can	14	16	18
8	Makers-Guild	14	18	17
9	Preciometalic.Inc	14	17	13
10	Tiptingle Tigers	14	14	12
11	Hornrunner Hornets	14	13	11
12	Voleskip Pharmaceuticals	14	7	11

Corporation Division One		
Goosetimp Weapons v Tiptingle Foods	0	2
Zhōngguá Shāngpǐn v Rolls Royce Scoriors	0	1
Preciometalic.Inc v I.Y.W.I.W.S.I.	3	2
Orang-U-Can v Deutsch Fahrzeuge Eingearbeitet	0	2
Hornrunner Hornets v Voleskip Pharmaceuticals	1	1
Makers-Guild v Castle Electrocis	2	1

	Corporation Division One	Played	Goals	Points
1	Castle Electronics	14	23	29
2	Deutsch Fahrzeuge Eingearbeitet	14	26	27
3	I.Y.W.I.W.S.I.	14	27	23
4	Rolls Royce Scoriors	14	19	25
5	Zhōngguá Shāngpǐn	14	17	21
6	Goosetimp Weapons	14	24	18
7	Orang-U-Can	14	16	18
8	Makers-Guild	14	20	20
9	Preciometalic.Inc	14	20	16
10	Tiptingle Tigers	14	16	15
11	Hornrunner Hornets	14	14	12
12	Voleskip Pharmaceuticals	14	8	12

sixty-four   **"Please come in"**? Hugh waved to the football manager tapping on the other side of his glass door. Gunny Gunnigunnay pushed it open and strolled inside.

"You asked to see me, Sir"? He asked in his heavily accented Norwegian.

"I did", Hugh smiled pleasantly, "As you know I'm the chairman of the board of directors for both Orang-U-Can Industrial interests and all matters relating to the Corporation and that includes the football club".

The Norwegian nodded pleasantly, until the very moment Hugh added.

"It would seem that the fortunes of the team, since the enforced departure of my daughter as manager and coincidentally your arrival, have slumped alarmingly and this leads me to one inescapable conclusion. That being, that you are singly incompetent as a football manager and for that very reason I am sacking your sorry ass this instant. Now get out. Oh! By the way, should you require a reference from anyone if you decided to seek a future post, you would do well to avoid mentioning me, it would tell your prospective employer that you are a buffoon and quite possibly an imbecile to boot. Good day to you, Sir".

Hugh looked once again at his pad and slowly shook his head from side to side as the door closed behind the Norwegian who was thusly out of a job. The bottom half of the table, eleven points behind the leaders and only seven matches left to the end of the season. Hugh had a big decision to make, he had to find a replacement for his daughter and he had to do it virtually instantly. The trouble was the list of available managers who currently did not have a club was fairly uninspiring and he knew Best could not be relied on to caretaker-manage until the end of the season. The Assistant Manager had not even dared to criticise Gunnigunnay when he should have come to Hugh much sooner.

Trentavoria had not become the most astute businessman in the solar-system by not learning to think outside the box from time to time. He suddenly had an idea which he felt might very well ease the situation to a much more respectable finishing position for the best and largest Corporation the solar system had ever seen.

sixty-five   **Lane was the** first to notice that something had changed at the club. Best suddenly seemed more relaxed. He had been used to taking all the team training sessions, but as the results had continued to deteriorate, so had the assistant boss become more and more of a difficult taskmaster.

Overnight it changed. Best became his old casual self, easily pleased, not quick to criticise. He went to see him on behalf of the whole squad. On being called to go in, the diminutive midfielder entered the rather cramped office of the assistant-manager and asked directly,

"The rest of the men have sent me to see you. To ask what is going on, Boss"?

"Gunny Gunnigunnay is no longer manager of this club", Best smiled at once, "He was sacked yesterday afternoon and I have been told by none other than the CEO of the Corporation that a replacement will be with us for an evening get together later today. The new man will be manager ready in time for our first leg match against the Chinese in the semi-final of the Shield".

"Wow"! Lane gasped, "He's going to have an uphill struggle. Confidence is in the toilet and we have only a couple of days before we fly to China. Did the Old Man tell you who the new guy is going to be"?

Best shook his head, "No. I can't think who it could be either, Thomson. There are only two top names without positions at the minute and neither of them would strike me as a good fit here".

"You mean Zero Vodka Klause and Rudi Flugelhorn and I see your point. Who else could it be though? Trentavoria has already given someone with little experience a chance and look at the disaster that was"?

"There is only one way to find out, isn't there, tell all the men and the academy to be back here at 19:00 this evening when the new appointment is supposedly arriving".

"Sounds from abroading then, from a foreign flitterjet doesn't it"?

"Your guess is as good as mine. Like you suspect though, if we have to meet him (or her) in the evening it must be because he (or she) is coming from somewhere like Southern Amerik, maybe even the other side of the world. Who knows the new boss might be an Aussie"?

As it was to turn out though they were both wrong in their guessing.

sixty-six   "I could have been enjoying a nice long soak in the bath by now", Jennings complained, "What sort of manager wants to arrive at a club at 19:00 of all hours"?

Sanedad chirped up, "A guy who's only just been in the country for an hour at most, we should have seen where all the flights coming into Manchester Flitterport were from this evening".

"I already did that", Gaines told them, the list is:- Zurich, Amsterdam, Muscat, Dublin, London and Gothenburg".

"Gothenburg", McFarland echoed, "Koofing great, it's going to be Isaiah Kruze, they say he's a really tough taskmaster and a bit of a git".

"Why would he leave his current post though"? Jensen wanted to know, "He's so well thought of there".

"The same reason as ever", Burgenbower offered, "For the filthy lucre of course".

"You are all wrong"! A voice announced from the doorway then. A voice which they all knew very well indeed, "Because it's not Kruze. Hello men, it's good to see you again, but what the hell have you been doing on the pitch while Rachwalski and I have been busy fighting a war"?

Lane burst into delighted laughter, "Rox! What are you doing back here, come to meet the new Boss when he finally decides to show his face"?

The rest of the squad were all gathering around the decorated Major and shaking his hand and slapping him on the shoulder. They were equally delighted to see the two Poles and were enthusiastically hugging Rachwalski too.

"We saw all the SWW threads about you", Lane told them, "Especially yours Rox, or should I call you Major now hahahaha".

"You should call him Boss". Rachwalski told them then, "Men, meet your new player-manager until at least the end of the season. Major Roxbrough is in charge for that long at least"!

"And it would seem we have got a lot of work to do before we fly to China", the new manager told them, "For a start, I have to learn how to play favouring just my left foot as I think my control with my right will be a bit pedestrian, to say the least".

"You're going to play as well as manage"? Best asked.

"Leave me out of the best team in the league, what do you think"? Roxbrough laughed, "I left my beautiful partner in our new luxury home on Mars to be here till the end of this season, do you think I'm going to do it sitting on a bench? Now then, who's for a spot of evening training"?

Everyone was.

The squad that flew to China three nights later were:

Orang-U-Can
1. Anderson
45. Gaines 13. Jennings 25. Zinyama 4 Burgenbower
30. Sanedad 20. Lane 19.Jenson 44. Siggers
27. Rachwalski
23. Roxbrough

Substitutes

6. Radband
15. Ford
12 McFarland
10. Nero
31.Radford
38. Harcourt

Competition for a place had been fierce, suddenly confidence was high, even if the man leading them onto the pitch had only one good shooting foot.

The Chinese had been expecting an easy two legs into the final, what a shock they got. Orang-U-Can came at them as a team possessed and by half-time they went back down the tunnel to a terrible tongue lashing from their manager as they were three goals down.

Lane had put through a perfectly weighted pass to Rachwalski after only eight minutes and the young Pole had slotted the ball into the opposition goal with no trouble at all. Ten minutes later Lane had toe-poked a scrappy second after a frantic goal-mouth scramble, while Siggers had made it three just before half-time. The Chinese defended in numbers in the second half and did not concede again, but the damage had been done and OUC took a three-goal lead back to their home ground for the second of the two-leg semi. Roxbrough had brought himself off after an hour and put the youngster Radford on in his place and the young man had equipped himself well. All the new manager needed to do then was make sure the resurgence continued until the end of the year.

sixty-seven "You've got a visitor, Trentavoria", the officer told Clara. She was puzzled, Hugh had only been the day before. Of her siblings, only Lavvisto had been and then only once. Putting down her current novel, a lurid murder mystery, she strolled out the cell and over to the secure bubble at the centre of the wing, where she was handed a visitor pass. The electronic gate crunched open and she found herself walking down the secure corridor beyond.

At the far end, she was forced to wait for another officer to allow her through yet another gate leading into the Visits Hall. The visitor must have their back to her, for as she scanned the gathered throng she could not see who it was who had come to see her.

Until......

She suddenly recognised the back of his head and the blood in her veins turned to ice.

What was he doing here? Had he worked it all out and if so how? Had he come to sanction *her*? Could it be that while she recognised him, he would not know who she was – or rather who she had been many times in the past when contacting - voice-only? So many questions and the answer to every one of them was the same, she did not know!

Calmly she walked past him, as though she did not know who he was and she was riveted to the spot momentarily when he said in an amused and mild tone,

"Clara, I'm here, I've come to see my favourite niece, say hello to your Uncle Jack"?

Clara played out the pantomime grimly, what else was she supposed to do? Turning on her heel she smiled sweetly and exclaimed,

"Uncle Jack, it's so good to see you, the last I heard you were in the dense undergrowth of Borneo still seeking the exact monkey glands that could give us all much longer life expectancy".

Lowering his voice so that only she could hear what he said he instructed,

"Sit down, don't overdo the long lost Uncle routine, I have information for you that you will find *vitally* interesting".

Seating herself feigning calmness Clara tried to bluff, "Would you now like to tell me exactly who you are, Mister"?

"We both know that you know who I am", Sean Derek Charles said to the woman then, "Uncle Jack will suffice. I am brought here to scratch you and let a slow-acting poison into your bloodstream that will see you dead in seventy-two hours. I am not going to see that sanction to its conclusion though".

Shrinking slightly in her seat, Clara asked, "Someone contacted you and asked you to sanction me. Then you looked deeply into my background and found out who has been paying you top shillin for all the other sanctions of late and you found out it was your very next target. How did you do that, I was extremely careful to conceal my identity at all times"?

The Fixer offered the woman a charming smile, the expression as attractive as the grin of a cobra just before it strikes.

"Let us just say I know a chap who knows a chap who knows things and I have various little rodents peppered about who *listen.* that's all they do, they are paid to listen and when they hear things, they tell those things to only one person – me"!

"Good for you, so let us be clear then. You are the Fixer and I am the Faded Man. You heard that I was in Prison. Then you get an ecall to fix me and you do a bit of digging. As I am the daughter of the wealthiest man in the solar system. you figure it might be more profitable not to sanction the latest contract. In the course of your knowing a chap - etcetera, etcetera, you discover that I am the one who has been keeping you in the type of lifestyle you have become accustomed to. So now you give me the end to that little narrative, what do you do next"?

"I decide who it is in my best interest to sanction". The Fixer smiled pleasantly.

"If you had not already done that, I would now have a rather unexpected scratch on my skin somewhere and seventy-two hours to live", Clara concluded.

"Bravo", the Fixer acknowledged, "I figure however much I am being paid to kill you, you will pay more to have those who want you dead killed instead".

"You would not have come here without also finding out who it was who opened that account would you"?

Sean shook his head.

"Who"?

"Firstly, Miss Trentavoria, you and I need to discuss the terms of my services".

"Very well. However much it is that this mysterious conglomerate is paying you I can pay half as much again once I am out of here and free to access my thumb once more. With good behaviour that should be in approximately 12 months".

"That is not what I want", The Fixer Sean Derek Charles told her then. "It is not what I want at all"!

"Very well, you have my undivided attention, what do you want,......Jack"?

"I want to retire once I have sanctioned the last two targets and then I want you and I to be married"!

The Fixer could have told Clara many things. Some that would not have surprised her. Some that would have done so and still others that would have rocked her to her very soles. What he had told her slotted into the latter category.

"You want to what"?! She managed. When she thought about it later, she realised how obtuse her response had truly been.

"I want to kill the two people who have taken a sanction out on you and then I do not want to wait for you to get out of here because you and I shall become husband and wife".

"You are after my money? A great deal of it and you want a way into the Corporation"?

He nodded smiled and added, "And as a fringe benefit I'm sure I will enjoy also having your body as part of the deal".

"Why would I agree to such a bizarre contract"?

"Survival. Firstly I do not kill you, secondly, I kill those who want you killed. Thirdly I am at your side from then on to make certain of your safety and with a greatly vested interest to see that you remain so for a very long time to come".

Clara looked at Sean Derek Charles for the very first time as a prospective partner. He was older than her, but not so much so that it presented a problem, especially given their life expectancies. He had a dashing sort of handsomeness and he looked tanned lean and physically fit. She could do a lot worse. She had done a lot worse in her rather chequered past. She said eventually,

"I'll want a prenup"?

"Of course you will", he smiled, "Something along the lines of if you suffer a violent end in the future I get nothing by way of settlement"?

Clara nodded, then asked, "Who wants me dead and why"?

"Vanial and Jancy Orchvestige. It would seem they believe you responsible for the death of their late and sadly lamented father".

"How could they have found out that it was I, through you, who managed that little piece of mischief"?

"Perhaps they know a chap who knows a chap who........ well you follow the drift".

"All right then, my dear Fiancé, make certain that over the next few days they suddenly have no further need for oxygen. Then you had better go and introduce yourself to my father and tell him about how we met, how long with have been seeing one another blaaty blaa blaa blaa".

"I can trust your word on this".

Clara smiled, "Of course, we are in love are we not"?

To her amusement, he suddenly clutched his chest and smiled exclaiming,

"Why yes, I've just realised, I *do* love you, Darling".

"People get married for many reasons and a great deal of them are foolish with hindsight, but our union has much a better chance of survival I think", Clara observed then, "Mutually assured survival".

"Not to mention the fabulous sex you're going to enjoy", the Fixer grinned.

Clara smirked, "That remains to be seen, Jack"!

sixty-eight   SWW, the solar-wide-web. In a shocking discovery, earlier today retainers at the Orchvestige Mansion in Cambridgeshire found siblings Vanial and Jancy Orchvestige, son and daughter to the late entrepreneur Glerius Orchvestige dead in bed. Sensationally the two were in the same bed, that of the elder Vanial. Both were completely naked and a rapid mechautopsy conducted by combmen at the property revealed that the couple had taken poison. The immediate inference that the brother and sister had committed suicide rather than continue their incestuous relationship was told to this reporter by the leading officer on the case - Detective Sergeant Raio 'Snapper' Collidone.

"I got the confession out of one of the maids", Snapper told me shortly after my arrival at the stately home, "Following a mysteriously anonymous sound-only ping on my padfon. "It seems several of the staff had suspected that the two deceased had been getting *jiggy* behind closed doors for some time".

Further investigations may take place but the case seems to be resolved to all intents and purposes and a verdict of mutual suicide is suspected as being the eventual outcome.

sixty-nine   **Style Prison for** women saw its one hundred and fifteenth wedding ceremony conducted today as part of its humanitarian aims over the centuries that this establishment for rehabilitation has. Already one of its highest-profile inmates to date, Clara Trentavoria, daughter of the Corporate CEO Hugh, plight her troth to her *long-time sweetheart* Jack Smithsoniartus in a private ceremony with just a minister and two witnesses. The minister conducting the ceremony was from the relatively young movement the Church of the Holy Fund [formed 69] whose main tenets include the worship of generous thumb and the accumulation of material possessions. Cleric Mazuma told this reporter afterwards that it was a brief if touching affair attended by the Governor as Smithsoniartus' witness and Miss Cher Gufasen as the bride's.

Gufasen described as Trentavoria's, '*bestist friend in Style Nick*' was resplendent in a gold lamé off the shoulder shell suit with thin ribbons of metallic fibre, as opposed to guipé.

She caught the bouquet - but described herself afterwards as 'Happily single for the foreseeable future, or at least until I've done my five years porridge'.

Father of the newly created Mrs Smithsoniartus was not available for comment at this time.

seventy-two   **When the Chinese team** Zhōngguá Shāngpĺn got to the Orang-U-Can ground to play the second leg of the semi-final of the Corporation shield they were determined not to concede any more goals. As a result of such determination, they played in their half for the entire first half of the game and though Roxbrough's squad mounted one offensive after another against them. They could simply find insufficient space between the two ranks of five players to be able to even mount a shot on goal for the entire first 45 minutes.

Roxbrough made three substitutions at half time fetching of himself Rachwalski and Lane who had all given everything they had to try and get past the Great Wall of China. In the second half, a frustrated Orang-U-Can even conceded one goal themselves and lost the second leg 0-1 but still went through to the final 3-1 on aggregate. In the other fixture, Castle Electronics had beaten Makers-Guild 2-0 in the first leg and 0-1 in the second and so the stage was set for quite a final in York, the capital of Saxonia and the scene of the fabulous football stadium at Bootham Crescent with its 100 thousand seating capacity and folding roof in the event of terrible weather.

It would be the last game of the season, but before that Roxbrough had to steer his team to a much more respectable league position. He was in the office wondering how he was going to achieve such a feat when he received an unexpected ping from none other than the CEO of the Corporation.

"Good morning, Sir", Roxbrough greeted the tiny image on his padfon screen, "What can I do for you"?

"I watched the game last night", Hugh got straight down to business, "And one thing is plain to me, Major, you are not the player you were before you lost one of your biological limbs. I do not think you should remain a player-manager but should concentrate on being on the bench only. To this end, I am making funds available to you to purchase none other than Borodino Kaotio the Argentine superstar of Núñez Networks".

"Kaotio"! Roxbrough breathed, the Argentine striker had been corporation player of the year for the last five seasons in succession and was described as the greatest footballer who had ever lived.

"Surely Santiago Núñez will never sell him, Sir, he is their talisman"?

Hugh mentioned a figure that made the Major gasp with the sheer scale of it. In addition to being the best, Kaotio would be the most expensive player in history and it would be many years before anyone commanded an even higher figure.

"Expect him at the club tomorrow", Trentavoria told the stunned manager, "And good luck on Saturday and keep your ass on the bench, Rox".

Corporation Division One
Castle Electronic v Goosetimp Weapons
RR Scoriors v Tiptingle
Precio v ZS China
DFE v IYWIWSI
Hornrunner v OUC
Voleskip v Makers-Guild

Though Roxbrough would have dearly loved to have played alongside the legendary Argentine, he knew he was not in the same league – no one was. So he chose his best squad and took them to Hornrunner's ground a few short days later. A few short days during which all the players insisted they had already learned a great deal from their newest signing.

It was worth attending the match just to see the look on Hornrunner's faces when the new number 50 trotted onto the pitch In his all-white strip, to save clashing with Hornrunner's yellow shirts.

Corporation Division One		
Castle Electronic v Goosetimp Weapons	2	1
RR Scoriors v Tiptingle	3	0
Precio v ZS China	0	1
DFE v IYWIWSI	2	0
Hornrunner v OUC	0	7
Voleskip v Makers-Guild	1	1

Kaotio scored a debut hat-trick and assisted in two of Orang-U-Can's four other goals that Burgenbower, Sanedad, Jenson and Lane scored. The latter getting to six goals for the season equalling Roxbrough's tally. The seven-nil thrashing was the biggest scoreline of the season thus far.

	Corporation Division One	Played	Goals	Points
1	Castle Electronics	15	25	32
2	Deutsch Fahrzeuge Eingearbeitet	15	28	30
3	Rolls Royce Scariors	15	22	28
4	Zhōngguó Shāngpǐn	15	18	24
5	I.Y.W.I.W.S.I.	15	27	23
6	Orang-U-Can	15	23	21
7	Makers-Guild	15	21	21
8	Goosetimp Weapons	15	25	18
9	Preciometalic.Inc	15	20	16
10	Tiptingle Tigers	15	16	15
11	Voleskip Pharmaceuticals	15	9	13
12	Hornrunner Hornets	15	14	12

When Roxbrough began to make his way back down the tunnel of the then bottom club, who should be barring his way to the exit but none other than Gazza Bamber. Microphone waved like some sort of military baton, the presenter asked Roxbrough.

"Major how does it feel to see your team done the biggest win of the season when you are not even come on the park yourself. Do you feel that Kaotio can done a massive for you and take this all to the line, or is it time to admit that Castle is going to do the huge and get over the line with legs to spare"?

Roxbrough looked past the presenter and asked the cameraman directly, "Is he with you"?

The cameraman was forced to reply, that the presenter was truly with him.

"You do a wonderful job letting them have some time outside, but I suppose it's much easier now with all the wonderful new drugs that are available".

He then turned to the puzzled presenter and said in a loud voice, "Did you enjoy the game fella? Good was it not? Did you have a pie at half time? I bet you enjoyed that didn't you"?

"Duh"? Bamber was confused, he asked, "What are you'z goin' on about"?

"You go back now and tell the lovely man in the white coat what a super time you had. I've got to go now and see to my men, you be good (bless him)", the latter under his breath as though to himself. Then Roxbrough sneaked past the bemused presenter and back toward the visitor dressing room.

"We can't catch them you know", Best noted, looking up from his pad as Roxbrough entered the room. "By the way, you made that bloke from the tri-vidz look like some pathetic moron".

"Oh! Did I"? Roxbrough sounded upset by the revelation, "I didn't mean to try and talk him up. As to his IQ, I think the brown ale and pies have flushed that away long ago".

Whilst in the Flitterbus on the way back to Manchester Roxbrough enjoyed a ping from his partner on Mars. Her small image looked flushed with excitement on his padfon screen,

"I've been decorating the place from top to bottom", she told him, "Do you have any preferences as to colour scheme for your office, Darling".

"Any colour in the Orange spectrum of course", Roxbrough joked. "Please yourself, Darling with all the other rooms. Does the airlock work now you've had it overhauled"?

Kurteze nodded, "Hardly any of that awful dust gets in the place now, Babe and it's so much warmer here in Monrandia, what is it doing there"?

"Raining", he laughed, seven weeks and we'll be back together and I won't miss the rain".

"It rained here last week, for about an hour. Kept some of the dust down and the lichen needed it, could do with more though. I've had the landscaper plant a load of lichen-furs in the back garden along with the usual array of cacti, succulents and lichen-heather".

"I can't wait to see what you've done with the place, I miss you terribly".

"I miss you too. Darling".

seventy-three **Calmolm Castle was** in his gentleman's club, enjoying a med-cigar and a sweet sherry when the two men he was not expecting entered. The foremost of the two was an old colleague, rival and acquaintance at various times in their mutual association, the CEO of a mighty Corporation just like he, Rudolg Höfler. Behind him was someone he did not know, but could guess who it was. For the man was oriental and it was very likely he was some sort of representative of Zhōngguá Shāngpĺn – or as they were becoming known as in the west – ZS China.

"Guter Abend my Freund", Höfler greeted, "I do not think you have met Bohai Lâm before, he is the current Chairman of the board of ZS China".

Castle climbed to his feet and shook both men by the hand then asked,

"What can I get you to drink gentlemen"?

"We would be pleased to enjoy whatever you are having", Lâm responded as both he and Höfler took seats around the low occasional table at Castle's knees.

The men made small talk until the drinks were brought. Höfler also accepted a med-cigar, but the Chinese gentleman preferred to fuel his Meerschaum pipe. The smoke that issued from its white bowl was both aromatic and very pleasant to the noses of the other two. Castle was just beginning to wonder how long the duo would chat before getting down to the purpose of their visit when the Chinese said,

"We have come to you with a simple request, Mister Castle we wish to serve Hugh Trentavoria with a moratorium on the purchase of any more football players for the rest of the season. The man is ruining the spirit of the game by simply spending vast amounts that the rest of us cannot hope to equal, to buy success for his Corporation Football Team".

Castle looked thoughtful, "Historically that had always been the way of the game, whoever had the deepest pockets usually bought results on the pitch".

"And it is something we avoided doing when the ancient clubs collapsed in ruinous debt and we all agreed to a spending limit per season in order not to end up travelling down the same road".

"Do you have proof that Trentavoria has exceeded the capping"?

"Without a close look at his books we are unable to say with certainty, the agreement was a gentlemanly one anyway so there is no legal mechanism set in place for anyone who broke it", the German admitted, "But do you think Trentavoria got Borodino Kaotio the superstar of Núñez Networks away from the Argentine Corporation for sestertius"?

"He probably paid more than the rest of us would consider investing in what is after all only a game". Castle agreed. "But we have no legal recourse as you have already pointed out, so what do you think we can do if Trentavoria tells us all to go to hell"?

"We have already spoken to Fennirer von Goosetimp, Kavram Orchvestige, Solendile Voleskip and Throrb Makers-Guild and we have all agreed that if Trentavoria does not agree to a moratorium on spending and capping next season, we will refuse to play his team.

"So with my vote in favour you have a majority no matter what the other CEO's say, very well, consider that I am in your camp. I do not think OUC can catch us anyway, no matter how much they spend but I am with you as a matter of principle".

seventy-four **"And that is** why I want you to beat every team you meet by the highest score you can achieve", Hugh Trentavoria said on Roxbrough's padfon.

"That would be our aim anyway, Sir", the Major assured, "But I understand what you are saying to me, no easing up when we have a commanding lead, I will pass on your encouragement and your wishes to the squad"

Later he said to the players, "Voleskip are not enjoying a good season, and we are on our special pitch, I want you to give them a good hiding, I will bring on five fresh players at half-time, so run your socks off, let's see if we can break all records when it comes to the size of our victory.

As the men in violet trotted onto the pitch later that week they were completely unprepared for the onslaught to come. Roxbrough had even gone for a very aggressive formation of 3-3-3-1

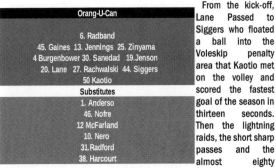

Orang-U-Can
6. Radband
45. Gaines 13. Jennings 25. Zinyama
4 Burgenbower 30. Sanedad   19.Jenson
20. Lane   27. Rachwalski 44. Siggers
50 Kaotio
Substitutes
1. Anderso
46. Nofre
12 McFarland
10. Nero
31.Radford
38. Harcourt

From the kick-off, Lane Passed to Siggers who floated a ball into the Voleskip penalty area that Kaotio met on the volley and scored the fastest goal of the season in thirteen seconds. Then the lightning raids, the short sharp passes and the almost eighty percent possession resulted for the first half. Orang-U-Can trotted into the tunnel six goals to the good and Voleskip looked completely shell-shocked. The other five goals had gone to Sanedad, Rachwalski, Siggers for two and Lane.

Roxbrough made his promised maximum number of substitutions and the new line-up went out for the second half:

Not quite as well balanced a side in the second half but Kaotio ran riot and added

Orang-U-Can
6. Radband
12 McFarland 38. Harcourt 25. Zinyama
4 Burgenbower 30. Sanedad 19.Jenson
46. Nofre 10. Nero 31. Radford
50 Kaotio

three more goals to his tally, the final result was a crushing 9-0 victory.

Roxbrough knew the hefty goal tally would not harm the Corporation's chances of going up the table and he waited patiently after the game for the results to appear on his padfon. When he saw them he was delighted with some other shocks too. The Chinese had caused the Germans a setback in

Goalscorers for OUC

7. Lane, Kaotio

6. Roxbrough,

4. Rachwalski,

3. Siggers, Sanedad,

2. Nero, Burgenbower, Jensen,

1. Wong, Sellers,

their bid for the top, while Castle and Rolls Royce had fought out a draw. Hornrunner had surprised everyone by beating IYWIWSI, it was all good from OUC's point of view and Roxbrough waited impatiently for the table to come upon his

screen:

Corporation Division One		
Goosetimp Weapons v Makers-Guild	2	0
Castle Electronics v Rolls Royce Scs	1	1
Preciometalic.Inc v Tiptingle Foodstuffs	3	0
ZS China v DFE	1	0
Hornrunner v IYWIWSI	2	1
OUC v Voleskip Pharmaceuticals	9	0

	Corporation Division One	Played	Goals	Points
1	Castle Electronics	17	26	33
2	Deutsch Fahrzeuge Eingearbeitet	17	28	30
3	Rolls Royce Scoriors	17	23	29
4	Zhōngguá Shāngpĭn	17	19	27
5	Orang-U-Can	17	32	24
6	I.Y.W.I.W.S.I.	17	28	23
7	Goosetimp Weapons	17	27	21
8	Makers-Guild	17	21	21
9	Preciometalic.Inc	17	23	19
10	Hornrunner Hornets	17	16	15
11	Tiptingle Tigers	17	16	15
12	Voleskip Pharmaceuticals	17	9	13

It still looked highly unlikely that OUC could win the league but they were not going to quit until the last whistle of the football year.

seventy-five   **Two difficult weeks** later and the table looked like:

1	Deutsch Fahrzeuge Eingearbeitet	19	30	34
2	Castle Electronics	19	27	34
3	Rolls Royce Scoriors	19	23	31
4	Orang-U-Can	19	38	30
5	Zhōngguá Shāngpĭn	19	20	27
6	I.Y.W.I.W.S.I.	19	29	23
7	Makers-Guild	19	22	23
8	Goosetimp Weapons	19	27	21
9	Preciometalic.Inc	19	25	21
10	Hornrunner Hornets	19	20	21
11	Tiptingle Tigers	19	18	19
12	Voleskip Pharmaceuticals	19	11	17

The gap was decreasing as much because the fight at the bottom to avoid relegation was making the matches even harder fought. For the first time in a long time [in football terms at least] Castle were not even leading the table. The Germans had just scored more goals but it did mean the

Goalscorers for OUC
13 Kaotio
7. Lane,
6. Roxbrough,
4. Rachwalski,
3. Siggers, Sanedad,
2. Nero, Burgenbower, Jensen,
1. Wong, Sellers,

last three games of the season would be tense indeed. The Argentine continued to rack up an impressive personal tally for the world's biggest corporation.

Roxbrough was highly motivated to secure at least one trophy for Hugh Trentavoria being offered a huge bonus if he managed to do so. The trouble

Orang-U-Can v Makers Guild

ZS China v IYWIWSI

DFE v Goosetimp

RR Scoriors v Hornrunner

Precio v Voleskip

Castle v Tiptingle

was even if the men won their last three games and with healthy scorelines, they would not finish top of the table unless those above them dropped vital points. The season had come down to nerves as much as physical skill and it could go one of two ways.

Corporation Division One		
Voleskip v Goosetimp	2	0
Rolls Royce v Makers-Guild	0	0
Precio v Castle	1	1
DFE v Tiptingle	0	0
Hornrunner v ZC China	2	1
IYWIWSI v OUC	0	3

Corporation Division One		
Goosetimp v Hornrunner	0	2
Voleskip v RR Scors	0	0
Precio v Makers Guild	1	1
DFE v Castle	2	0
Tiptingle v IYWIWSI	2	1
OUC v ZC China	3	0

seventy-six – ending one [continue to read or flip to seventy-six ending alternative] "All we can do now is keep improving our own game and keep winning", Roxbrough told the squad as they were putting on their kits to go out and play Makers-Guild. "There is nothing to be gained by wondering what is happening in the rest of the fixtures and If I catch anyone using their CI's to access the SWW I will drop them for the last two games of the season. We need to focus, we need to show Hugh Trentavoria that his thumb has been wisely spent. We have built a squad this season that if it does not win anything, certainly will in the future, now go out there and give me everything you've got".

Roxbrough never got used to the adrenalin rush that the roar of the home crowd gave when the teams trotted out onto the pitch. He had chosen a very solid line up considering the men were at home, but during the week he had sensed that tension was beginning to show in some players and Siggers and Wong had played appallingly in training and had to be dropped. Once again Radband had ousted Anderson as the better goalkeeper and kept his place with ease.

Orang-U-Can
6. Radband
12 McFarland 38. Harcourt 25. Zinyama 4 Burgenbower
30. Sanedad 20. Lane 19.Jenson
46. Nofre 50. Kaotio 27. Rachwalski

Substitutes
1. Anderson
13. Jennings
15.Ford
45. Gaines
31. Radford
10. Nero

Yet strangely two uncharacteristic errors by two of his most trusted professionals gifted the visitors an early lead. Burgenbower slipped on the wet grass and the nippy Makers-Guild winger seized on the unexpected chance and took a snap speculative shot that Radband let go through his legs. Anyone could make a mistake, but when a goalkeeper did so, it resulted in greater consequence than when other players showed their humanity. The loss of momentum was felt by the entire team and even though Roxbrough cajoled and urged them to keep focused, they never got going with their usual flair and self-confidence. Roxbrough made no substitutions, telling the team at half time,

"I'm giving all of you another chance to show me 45 minutes of the sort of football you all know you're capable of".

Makers-Guild defended deeply in the second half determined not to concede and the most surprising result of a crazy season thus far ended 0-1!

Corporation Division One		
Orang-U-Can v Makers Guild	0	1
ZS China v IYWIWSI	0	0
DFE v Goosetimp	2	0
RR Scoriors v Hornrunner	0	2
Precio v Voleskip	1	2
Castle v Tiptingle	4	2

Hornrunner had been enjoying a late run of form also and they managed to score two great goals against the well-respected team from Rolls Royce, but Roxbrough was only concerned about how the home defeat had affected his players and he gazed at the table with two games left in certain dismay.

Then placing his padfon onto his desk he went to see the CEO of the greatest Corporation in the world, and beyond.

"We gave it a good shot, Sir", he was saying twenty minutes later, nursing a sweet sherry and smoking a med-cigar, "But the dip in the season was something we could not come back from. With two games to go, we cannot catch either of the two leading clubs, I still fancy Castle might snatch it at the death, but hope they don't".

"Because of the Shield Final you mean", Trentavoria deduced. Roxbrough nodded,

"They'll have their tails up if they're Champions, eager to do the double which hasn't been achieved for several years. Only we will stand in their way at the final in York, the capital of Saxonia and the scene of the fabulous football stadium at Bootham Crescent with its 100 thousand seating capacity and folding roof in the event of terrible weather".

	Ending A: Corporation Division One	Played	Goals	Points
C	Deutsch Fahrzeuge Eingearbeitet	20	32	37
2	Castle Electronics	20	31	37
3	Rolls Royce Scoriors	20	23	31
4	Orang-U-Can	20	38	30
5	Zhōngguá Shāngpǐn	20	20	28
6	Makers-Guild	20	23	26
7	I.Y.W.I.W.S.I.	20	29	24
8	Hornrunner Hornets	20	22	24
9	Goosetimp Weapons	20	27	21
10	Preciometalic.Inc	20	26	21
11	Voleskip Pharmaceuticals	20	13	20
R	Tiptingle Tigers	20	20	19

Hugh Trentavoria grinned, "Then stand in their way you must", he told his manager. Roxbrough began to feel his vitality dissipate shortly afterwards and making his excuses to his employer left the office. He took the lift straight down to the subterranean flitter-park and was almost absent-mindedly strolling to his vehicle when he became aware of a figure on an intercept course with his. It did not take long, even in the dimness of the park to discern that it was a female. Slim, slight and shabbily dressed. Several of the overhead LED's were out, either exhausted or vandalised, but even by their subfusc chiaroscuro Roxbrough soon recognised who the woman was and was surprised by her appearance. His fingers then relaxed on the butt of his Kimber, which he had been clutching in his coat pocket.

"Lsenia"! He virtually gasped, "What are you doing here"?

"Thank you, it's good to see you too", the girl was bitter. She was also shabby. Her broken shoes scuffed and lacking the ability to keep out the rain, the shoulders of her coat wet from what was falling out of the Manchester evening sky, similarly her greasy hair soaked. It was teaming down up at the street level, nothing unusual in that. Her eyes were darkly ringed with fatigue and Lsenia Shyrock looked tired with the sort of exhaustion that comes only with months of despair. Roxbrough felt annoyed that her appearance was making him feel guilty. He had helped her with groceries, he would have gone back and done more, but events had overtaken him and meeting other people also.

"What are you doing in Manchester Centre"? He asked her.

"I'm not having the best run of luck that you could imagine and wondered if you could help me"? The request was a direct one - devoid of self-respect.

"I did help, at the time", Roxbrough was annoyed by the begging for charity, "How long did you expect me to stay grateful. I've my own life to get on with now, are you wanting to become some sort of permanent obligation or something"?

"I thought a loan, I would pay you back once I get things straightened out"?

"Do you think I walk about with lint? I use thumb, citizens do. The banks are closed for withdrawals of actual coin and lint, they won't be open again until Monday morning".

"Just a loan"?

"That I would probably never see returned. I don't even live on Earth any more. Look, scrubbed up you're not a bad looking girl, you have a commodity, use it to get yourself back on your feet".

A look of incredulous distaste twisted her features then as she demanded, "Are you suggesting I Methley myself"?!

"We all have to get by in the best way we can with the gifts that we've been given", Roxbrough was growing angry rather than regretful, "A few months working on your back and you can get on your feet again".

"You Nozkavardé"! The girl cursed.

"This train-wreck of a conversation is over", Roxbrough told her then, "It ended when you stooped to profanity".

He turned to enter his flitter but then was forced to spin back around at the sound of something soft and without substantial form hitting something much harder. Roxbrough jolted to vigilance. Over the fallen girl's body was the figure of a broad man in a dark raincoat. It was a testament to his guile that he had managed to approach the two of them without being heard or detected. He told Roxbrough with stentorian regret,

"A pity, but I cannot leave any witnesses behind".

Before Roxbrough could haul his Kimber free of the folds of his pocket, the man shot him in the throat with a level two needle. The Manager was dead before he hit the ground.

Walking over to the body, the agent of ASS [Amerik Secret Solutions] pulled out a sharps-vile from his coat and carefully pulling the needle free placed it inside, making certain no evidence was left behind. The quickly dissipating venom of the special preparation would no longer be in the corpse's cells by the time the combmen found the two bodies. Operative 23 turned and walked away without a backward glance. Part one of his assignment was complete. Now he was on his way to Mars, for an appointment with Igan Giganort, the other person responsible for so many deaths due to the heinous creation - the Laser Gun Mark II.

Amerik and ASS would then have avenged the deaths of so many of its troops.

News of the Manager's death devastated the football team of Orang-U-Can and they lost their last three games of the season. The Shield went to Castle Electronics, OUC finished outside the top three in the table. Only when fans of the team of the biggest Corporation in the Solar System cast their mind back years later, did they realise that such a season had been

Corporation Division One

Orang-U-Can v Makers Guild

ZS China v IYWIWSI

DFE v Goosetimp

RR Scoriors v Hornrunner

Precio v Voleskip

Castle v Tiptingle

the most unusual they had ever witnessed.

Orang-U-Can

6. Radband
12 McFarland 38. Harcourt 25. Zinyama 4 Burgenbower
30. Sanedad 20. Lane 19.Jenson
46. Nofre 50. Kaotio 27. Rachwalski

Substitutes

1. Anderson
13. Jennings
15.Ford
45. Gaines
31. Radford
10. Nero

seventy-six – alternative ending"All we can do now is keep improving our own game and keep winning", Roxbrough told the squad as they were putting on their kits to go out and play Makers-Guild. "There is nothing to be gained by wondering what is happening in the rest of the fixtures and if I catch anyone using their CI's to access the SWW I will drop them for the last two games of the season. We need to focus, we need to show Hugh Trentavoria that his thumb has been wisely spent. We have built a squad this season that if it does not win anything, certainly will in the future, now go out there and give me everything you've got".

When the home crowd gave their by then familiar roar of approval as the

Corporation Division One		
Orang-U-Can v Makers Guild	0	0
ZS China v IYWIWSI	0	0
DFE v Goosetimp	2	0
RR Scoriors v Homrunner	0	2
Precio v Voleskip	1	2
Castle v Tiptingle	4	2

teams trotted out onto the pitch, Roxbrough reflected that he would never take such devotion for granted and it would always pump adrenalin into his system. When it did not he knew it would be time to get out of the game. He had chosen a very solid line up considering the men were at home, the vein of form they had been enjoying but during the week he had sensed that tension was beginning to show in some players. Added to which Siggers and Wong had succumbed to a virus during the preparations and were not in the squad as a result. Radband had ousted Anderson as the better goalkeeper and kept his place with ease.

The team turned in a solid if nervy performance for the first half, but uncharacteristic errors meant that they could not capitalise on their many chances. Even the mercurial Argentine could not seem to find his usual blistering form. Roxbrough ended up miserably staring in disbelief as the two teams played out an insipid goalless draw.

Makers-Guild defended deeply in the second half determined not to concede and the most surprising result of a crazy season thus far ended. Hornrunner had meanwhile been enjoying a late run of form and had managed to score two great goals against the well-respected team from Rolls Royce, but Roxbrough was only concerned about how the dropping of two vital home points had affected his players and he gazed at the table

Ending A: Corporation Division One		Played	Goals	Points
C	Deutsch Fahrzeuge Eingearbeitet	20	32	37
2	Castle Electronics	20	31	37
3	Orang-U-Can	20	38	31
4	Rolls Royce Scoriors	20	23	31
5	Zhōngguá Shāngpĭn	20	20	28
6	Makers-Guild	20	23	27
7	I.Y.W.I.W.S.I.	20	29	24
8	Hornrunner Hornets	20	22	24
9	Goosetimp Weapons	20	27	21
10	Preciometalic.Inc	20	26	21
11	Voleskip Pharmaceuticals	20	13	20
R	Tiptingle Tigers	20	20	19

with two games left in growing dismay.

Then placing his padfon onto his desk he went to see the CEO of the greatest Corporation in the world, and beyond.

"We gave it a good shot, Sir", he was saying twenty minutes later, nursing a sweet sherry and smoking a med-cigar, "But the dip in the season was something we could not come back from. With two games to go, we cannot believably hope to catch either of the two leading clubs. They would have to lose their last two matches while we would have to win both of ours and as things are I'm not certain we could hope for either. I still fancy Castle might snatch it at the death, but hope they don't".

"Because of the Shield Final you mean", Trentavoria deduced. Roxbrough nodded,

"They'll have their tails up if they're Champions, eager to do the double which hasn't been achieved for several years. Only we will stand in their way at the final in Bootham Crescent".

Hugh Trentavoria grinned, "Then stand in their way - you must", he told his manager. Roxbrough began to feel his vitality dissipate shortly afterwards and making his excuses to his employer left the office.

Seventy-seven   **Had the fixture** come at any other time in the season Roxbrough would have been anticipating it keenly. A visit to Castle's home ground. He was torn with indecision for several reasons as he contemplated the forthcoming game. To do well would herald hope for the Shield final, but it would also mean the German Corporation would probably win the league. Roxbrough was proud to be Saxonian and if OUC could not win the title that year then he had hoped that at least another English Corporation would do so. He scrutinised his players over and again during training, trying desperately to choose his starting eleven. One day a player would excel, the next he would be just as likely to disappoint, it was infuriating. As late as Friday night he had still not settled on the team he would take to Castleford.

Corporations League Division One

Goosetimp v Preciometalic
DFE v RR Scoriors
Hornrunner v Tiptingle
IYWIWSI v Voleskip
Makers-Guild v ZS China
Castle v OUC

While he was in his temporary accommodation on Sylvandale Avenue he was surprised to hear his door-chime ping and wondered who it could be who would visit him without epinging firstly? Glancing at his inspection plate beside the door's lock he was surprised to see the dishevelled figure of a young woman he thought it unlikely he would ever meet again. It did not take long, even in the dimness of the street outside his door to discern that it was a female. Slim, slight and shabbily dressed. Several of the overhead LED street lights were out, either exhausted or vandalised, but even deep in murky shadows Roxbrough soon recognised who the woman was and was surprised by her appearance. He placed the Kimber back upon the hall occasional table and released the electrolock on the apartment's main entrance.

"Lsenia"! He said into the darkness, "What are you doing here"?

"After the trouble, it took me to find you once again Rox, I would have hoped for a better greeting. Can I please come in I'm getting soaked out here".

"Of course, forgive my surprise", Roxbrough tried to regain his previous composure, that which he had entertained before the door had chimed. "Please come in. let me take your coat. Oh, cripes, you're soaked, come and sit in front of the pile-heater while I find you something dry to put on and then I can get your clothes dried".

Lsenia was shabby. Her broken down shoes scuffed and lacking the ability to keep out the rain, they had not had a good coat of dubbin in an age. The shoulders of her coat were wet through from what was virtually always falling out of the Manchester sky, similarly, her greasy hair was soaked to such a degree that rain ran down her scalp and the sides of her face. Roxbrough took the coat from her narrow shoulders at the same time not failing to notice how her eyes were darkly ringed with fatigue. Lsenia Shyrock looked gripped by the sort of exhaustion that comes only with months of insomnia coupled or perhaps fuelled by despair. He felt momentarily annoyed that her appearance was making him feel guilty. After all, it could not be his fault, could it? He had helped her with groceries, given her some further funds for drink and ciggies. Sure he would have gone back and done more, but why? She had been kind, rescued him when he had been in trouble, but that did not mean he was indebted to her for the rest of his life. They were from different worlds and he had continued to improve his lot, what happened to her was surely no longer his responsibility? Leaving her in front of the fire in the lounge he pulled out some clothes from his bedroom. A pair of joggers, some trollies and socks, a sweatshirt. Then he went back downstairs to discover she had stripped to brassiere and pants and was rubbing her upper arms with her hands in front of the energising heat of the elements in his fire.

"Oh"! He was surprised, "Sorry, I did not realise you would have.......".

"Stripped off", she smiled, "Why not, I was soaked and it's not like you haven't seen every centimetre of me in the past is it"?

Such talk embarrassed him, his association with Kurteze had altered his perspective of their relationship even if she had no inkling of it. Passing her the dry clothes he asked,

"Can I get you a hot drink, you must get something warm inside you"?

A lascivious leer danced across her attractive features at the possibility of a double entendre before she asked for lichen-coff. He left her to dress and went and made two cups in the hypo-wave. Returning, he passed one to her and asked,

"What are you doing in this part of Manchester, Lsenia"?

"Looking for you obviously", she smiled tiredly and sadly, "I sort of thought I would see you again after the last time and then nothing. I'm not having the best run of luck either. I was wondering if for the sake of our friendship you could be of a little help"? The request was a direct one - devoid of self-respect.

"I did help, at the time", Roxbrough felt obliged to defend himself he was also acutely embarrassed by the young woman's outright begging for charity,

"I'll do what I can for you while I remain on earth, Lsenia, but I don't live in Manchester any more. I'm sorry but I don't have any coin or linen. I hope you do not mind me saying this, but grateful as I am and was to you, you cannot expect me to feel a permanent obligation"?

"I know", she responded sadly, "I was only going to ask you for a temporary loan, I would pay you back once I get things straightened out"?

"I'm not lending you money, Lsenia", Roxbrough tried to sound kindly he suspected he would never see the amount returned anyway. "You can consider it a gift, but like I say I will soon be moving from Earth and I expect it to be for good".

Sipping thoughtfully, she asked, "What's her name then, is she a blonde too"?

Roxbrough felt the colour rise to his cheeks as he replied carefully,

"I fought in the recent US-Pole dispute and bought some real estate up there that's all".

"Well if there's no one else I could *earn* the money, let me stay here the weekend and I'll make you feel good"?

"Are you suggesting you Methley yourself"?! He was only slightly shocked. He was a man after all and Mars was a great deal distant. "What sort of guy would take you up on an offer like that"?

"The male sort", she smiled. "Look, you can give me some money and we can spend some time together and then it would happen anyway. I'm just putting the thing on a more honest footing that's all. You've got something I want and I've got something you want. You do want it don't you"?

He realised then that one does not look a gift horse in the mouth even if one has been forced to firstly purchase it. When he waved her goodbye from the bank two days later, she surprised him with the crude venom of her farewell.

"You know what Rox. You are just like all the rest, aren't you? You're a Nozkavardé"!

Orang-U-Can

6. Radband

12 McFarland 13. Jennings 4. Burgenbower 19. Jensen 16. Flintham
20. Lane 46. Nofre 44. Siggers 30. Sanedad
50. Kaotio

Subs

1. Anderson 8. Wong 9. Sellers 10. Nero. 25. Rachwalski

Castle Electronics Corporation launched their initial attack with the sort of vitality Orang-U-Can had used against other teams in the past. It took Roxbrough's squad by surprise. The manager had prepared for the early onslaught by placing his players into their most defensive formation of the season – with a backline of five four more in midfield and Kaotio running the attack all on his own. Of course, Lane was instructed to dart forward with his now-familiar probing runs whenever he got the chance but they came few and far between. Castle needed the win as badly as OUC. Lose and Deutsch Fahrzeuge Eingearbeitet practically had the title sewn up. The boys from Rolls Royce were doing their bit though and at half time both matches were locked in a stalemate with not a single goal being scored by any of the four teams. Roxbrough saw no point in changing any players at the interval. The men were doing well enough, the fact of the matter was that Castle was a very polished outfit. They had no superstars, but they meshed exceptionally well as a team. When the final whistle went after another very physical forty-five minutes a roar of joy went around the ground. Not at the goalless draw, their team had fought out, but because Rolls Royce had won an eighty-ninth minute penalty and scored from it!

Ending A: Corporation Division One		Played	Goals	Points
C	Castle Electronics	21	31	38
2	Deutsch Fahrzeuge Eingearbeitet	21	32	37
3	Rolls Royce Scoriors	21	24	34
4	Orang-U-Can	21	38	32
5	Makers-Guild	21	25	30
6	Zhōngguá Shāngpĭn	21	21	28
7	I.Y.W.I.W.S.I.	21	33	27
8	Hornrunner Hornets	21	25	27
9	Goosetimp Weapons	21	31	26
10	Preciometalic.Inc	21	26	21
11	Voleskip Pharmaceuticals	21	15	20
R	Tiptingle Tigers	21	20	19

It was the end for Orang-U-Can, they could not catch the leaders, but at least they had played a part in the penultimate league positional shuffling. Rolls Royce had virtually effectively handed the title to Castle too, the Germans could only retake top spot if Castle faltered at the final figurative fence.

The last games of the league were to be played the Saturday after:

Corporations League Division One

Orang-U-Can v Tiptingle Tigers

If You Want It We Stock It v Castle Electronics

Makers-Guild v Deutsch Fahrzeuge Eingearbeitet

Rolls Royce Sc v Goosetimp Weapons

Preciometalic.Inc v Hornrunner Hornets

Zhōngguá Shāngpǐn China v Voleskip Pharmaceuticals

Corporations League Division One

Goosetimp v Preciometalic	2	0
DFE v RR Scoriors	0	1
Hornrunner v Tiptingle	3	0
IYWIWSI v Voleskip	4	2
Makers-Guild v ZS China	2	1
Castle v OUC	0	0

Roxbrough went to see his CEO again, "We cannot win the league but I feel I learned a great deal about the Castle team on Saturday last and think I have discovered a couple of weaknesses. We've improved our league position since I took over and the guys are confident they can win you some silver this year, Sir".

"I'm glad, Clara was asking me how you were getting on when I went to visit her the other day. She wants to resume her managerial position once her sentence comes up for parole".

"Not a problem, Sir. Once someone holds that shield aloft, whoever it might be - I will be on a Space-flitter for Mars".

"You won't stay on till Clara gets her liberty"?

"My partner would not allow that even if I could visit her several times. I'm sorry, Sir, but my mind is made up. Once the last whistle goes this season I retire from football and take up a post - Professor Giganort is keeping open for me in Memnonia".

Shortly afterwards Roxbrough took his leave of the CEO and drove to Moss Side. Though he was contracted to the priv-dick Kurteze and loved her in his way, as far as he was concerned a bird in the hand was worth two in the bush and it was the Mancunian's bush he was nesting in that night.

seventy-nine **"I've selected an** unchanged squad for the final game", Roxbrough told them a week later. "Sometimes the best thing to do is to leave well enough alone, there are several players who could have made today's first team, those of you who are not in it, don't worry whatever happens today there is still the shield. If anyone slips up or has some bad training sessions over the next few days, you might get your chance. All right men go and pull the Tiger's fangs, this is our dress rehearsal for next week".

Corporations League Division One

Orang-U-Can v Tiptingle Tigers	5	1
If You Want It We Stock It v Castle Electronics	0	0
Makers-Guild v Deutsch Fahrzeuge Eingearbeitet	2	0
Rolls Royce Sc v Goosetimp Weapons	3	0
Preciometalic.Inc v Hornrunner Hornets	0	3
Zhōngguá Shāngpĭn China v Voleskip Pharmaceuticals	2	2

eighty **Roxbrough boarded the** HMS Allardyce a week later with the smile still creasing his face. The flight could not have been timed better if he had dictated its departure from Manchester Spaceport himself. 19:00 on its way to Dead Man's Gap adjacent to the Polska Sector and north of his new home in Monrandia. Earlier in the day, he had watched Thomson Lane lift the Corporation Shield after a rather disappointing final had ended with just the one

Ending A: Corporation Division One		Goals	Points
C	Castle Electronics	31	39
2	Deutsch Fahrzeuge Eingearbeitet	32	37
3	Rolls Royce Scariors	27	37
4	Orang-U-Can	43	35
5	Makers-Guild	27	33
6	Hornrunner Hornets	28	30
7	Zhōngguá Shāngpĭn	23	29
8	I.Y.W.I.W.S.I.	33	28
9	Goosetimp Weapons	31	26
10	Preciometalic.Inc	26	21
11	Voleskip Pharmaceuticals	17	21
R	Tiptingle Tigers	21	19

goal difference scored by none other than the little midfielder himself. Castle had been so busy man-marking the Argentine out of the match they had not spotted Lane take a speculative long-range shot with only nine minutes left to play. It had struck the underside of the crossbar and rifled into the net.

Hugh had subsequently offered the role of caretaker manager to Lane during the post-match celebrations, half-way through which, Roxbrough had snook away to go to the Spaceport. He had his manager's winners medal an incredibly healthy thumb and was looking forward to seeing his beautiful platinum blonde partner when he finally set foot on the fourth planet out from Sol once again.

The stewardess came and asked him if he would like a pillow to sleep as much of the journey away as he could, but he was too wired to be able even to doze off. He was certainly fresh enough to notice the quality of her ass as she walked back up the aisle to answer a buzzer. He wondered idly if it was real. He was also wondering if he could be faithful to Kurteze even when the two of them were on the same world. It simply wasn't realistic of women to expect a guy to only ever want to sleep with one particular girl for the rest of their lives. One of the reasons that marriage had shrunk to only 20% of contracts. The alternative being a three, five or ten-year contract at the end of which both partners were free to walk away from the arrangement without any recourse of expectation in any way toward the other.

Roxbrough had suggested an initial three years, but his expectation of that arrangement was that while Kurteze was exclusive to him during that period, he was after all one of the guys. Nothing ever hurt anyone that one did not know about. Ignorance was bliss and Lsenia had certainly filled a vacancy quite conveniently and in a way that would do the priv-dick no harm.

The flight was routine and uneventful and the Allardyce was soon hurtling down toward a red disc that was increasing in diameter by the second. That was when the strangely unfamiliar feeling started in his right shoulder. It was not pain, but rather a feeling of numbness. Like when one had been numbed in the gum by the dentist. Roxbrough massaged it with his left hand but the numbness began to increase. It flowed into his chest and it began to make it difficult for him to catch his breath. Hastily and with growing alarm, he thumbed the call for the stewardess. By the time she reached him he was gasping, desperately attempting to get enough oxygen into his lungs in order, not to asphyxiate.

"I'm having some sort of spasm", he told the girl heedless of how attractive she was by then. She promptly hit the panel above the manager's head and the oxygen mask duly dropped down. Flipping the cup over his face, she pulled the strap around the back of his head.

"I'm going to tell the Captain, so that medical people can be alerted in the Spaceport, Sir. Try to remain calm, we will get help to you as fast as we can".

Then she hurried away to do just that.

By the time the Allardyce had touched down on the landing pad and the lock had been cracked, a set of decent stairs was at it and the doctor was rushing to be at the patient's side. It had happened with incredible swiftness. The only trouble was it was still too late. Major Roxbrough, war hero and football manager was dead!

eighty-one   **When Lsenia Shyrock unlocked** her door and pulled it open to let him enter the figure of a broad man in a dark raincoat passed her in the hall and proceeded to the poor and shabby lounge. It was a testament to his various skills and natural grace that he had managed to do so without being heard or felt, he had the abilities of a stalking feline.

Lsenia shuddered slightly wondering how the visit would transpire. She would either be paid as agreed or eliminated and she remained uncertain as to which.

"Did you see the reports on the SWW", he asked her, his voice as dry as dead leaves being blown athwart a toppled gravestone.

"Yes", she admitted, offering him nothing in the way of hospitality. Indeed she had very little even had she wanted to do so.

"There were many witnesses but it is suspected that he had a heart attack brought on by the rigours and strain of his appointment. The Manager was dead before the vessel even hit the ground. The hospital could do nothing to save him, too much time had elapsed before they got him there. The brain is still a very fragile organ despite all we know".

Lsenia regarded the agent of ASS [Amerik Secret Solutions]. She asked quite simply,

"So Mister Withoutname are you going to transfer the funds to my thumb as per our agreement, or are you now going to murder me"?

The tall dark figure offered her a smile and informed, "We do not go back on our word, Miss Shyrock. You kept your end of the bargain and an ASS man keeps his. Compared to your previous existence, you are now a wealthy woman. The quickly dissipating venom of the special preparation will no longer be in the target's cells by the time the autopsy is conducted. That is why Preparation 23 is so very useful to us. Part One of my assignment is now complete. Would you consider coming with me to Mars, for an appointment with Igan Giganort? The other person responsible for so many deaths due to the heinous creation - the Laser Gun Mark II. You could stay

 on the payroll, double your money and work once more, for ASS would then have avenged the deaths of so many of our troops"?

Lsenia grew thoughtful, she was indeed wealthier than she could ever have imagined, but double would be twice as nice!

"The thought of having such a deadly toxin coated to my fingernail frightened me though Mister Withoutname. What if this time I nicked myself, instead of the man I was supposed to be in the throes of ecstasy with? Or would you want me to kill Giganort more conventionally"?

"The slow-acting and untraceable poison is a superb way of ensuring the killer is nowhere near the victim when he or she expires". The man from ASS observed. "And with your natural charms my dear, you could easily seduce Giganort. Even if you were clumsy enough to nick yourself an antidote could be administered before the paralysis started. Perhaps you do not think you could sleep with a man of Giganort's age and you need to find your victim attractive"?

"Do you think I wanted to sleep with Roxbrough when he thought I was doing so for money, the filthy nozkavardé"?

"Well technically you were", the man from ASS noted a trifle sardonically, "Only it was for a great deal more than he was ever going to give you".

"The same fee you say"? Lsenia repeated.

The Man from the Amerik Secret Solutions nodded his head gravely.

Printed in Great Britain
by Amazon